FATED SIGHT

SKYE MALONE

FATED SIGHT
Book One of the Shifters of Ragnarok Series
by Skye Malone

Copyright 2021 - Skye Malone

Published by Wildflower Isle
P.O. Box 129, Savoy, IL 61874
www.wildflowerisle.com

ISBN-13: 978-1-940617-80-0

Library of Congress Control Number: 2021903158

Cover design by Karri Klawiter
www.artbykarri.com

Find out about all new releases:
Join Skye's mailing list at skyemalone.com/mailinglist!

TITLES BY SKYE MALONE

ADULT PARANORMAL ROMANCE
The Shifters of Ragnarok Series
The Demon Guardians Series

YOUNG ADULT PARANORMAL ROMANCE
The Awakened Fate Series

YOUNG ADULT URBAN FANTASY
The Kindling Trilogy

AUTHOR'S NOTE

A number of the words in this series are taken from actual Norse mythology, albeit with some slightly altered spellings. The ulfhednar, seidr, the fylgja, and the draugar are just a few.

While this series is a work of fiction, and as such, I have taken artistic liberties with all of these concepts, I highly recommend reading more about them from nonfiction sources. Their history is fascinating.

1

HAYDEN

THE FIRES WERE GONE, BUT THEY'D LONG SINCE KILLED THE *world.*

A frigid breeze stirred the smoke around her, the billowing clouds swathing the destruction and choking the sky. The sun had vanished. Possibly the moon as well. The day was silent, stripped of even a bird's distant call. Only the cold remained.

And the pain.

Grief gripped her, stealing the cry that would have been a scream if only she could breathe. On charred rubble rendered anonymous by flame, her feet scratched when she turned, and her mouth moved with silent shock as a tiny scrap of color appeared near her shoe. Impossible, incongruous, a photograph had survived. The picture of herself and her parents smiled up at her in colors too bright for this desolate place. Shaking, she reached down.

The photo crumbled to ash when her fingers touched it.

Her lips pressed together, her eyes burning with tears as horror swelled inside to fill her lungs, her chest, her stomach...

"I knew." Her voice was a rasp. "I—"

"I'm sorry."

The low apology came from behind her, rich like molasses but devoid of emotion. Desolate, like she felt. If she turned, his eyes would be silver, his hair black as night. She's seen him a thousand times, dreamt this moment a thousand more, and in every one, it was always the same.

Ashes fell from her fingers. In the distance, a growl carried on the wind.

She looked up. This, too, she remembered. The horizon was moving. Coming. Bearing monsters with rotted teeth and decaying hands, ready to tear her flesh from her bones. Their howls drew closer, wild and inhuman, riding like a promise of death on the smoky wind. Sounds of panic rose around her, strangled cries filled with pain from all the horrors they'd already —

A bell clanged, jerking Hayden back to consciousness. Scents oriented her as she blinked, her heart pounding from the nightmare. Flowers filled the air, hundreds of them, undercut by the chemical stink of Styrofoam and cellophane, the hoary smell of industrial carpet, and the oily tang of cash. Work, then. The door was still open as well. The stench of the roadside construction crew's equipment was stronger than normal on the crisp breeze.

"Better not let the boss catch you napping on the clock."

She glanced toward the entrance. One hand on the wooden doorframe, her best friend, Lindy, watched her, a decidedly mischievous grin on the young woman's face. In her other arm, she cradled a cardboard tray of three large to-go cups.

Hayden inhaled a quick breath that could be mistaken

for a sniffle due to the unseasonably cold weather, and ignored the gritty sting of machinery exhaust still clinging to the air. Hot chocolate with chili pepper, vanilla, and extra cinnamon.

A smile pulled at her lips.

"Before you ask," Lindy announced, letting the door swing shut behind her with another clang of the shop bell. The exhaust stench faded beneath the scent of flowers. "Yes, one of these is for you. I figured you'd need something after that final. And good thing I came when I did."

"Johanna would forgive me." Hayden stretched, trying to rid herself of the old nightmare. She'd had it so many times, it wasn't that difficult to ignore.

Some people dreamed of showing up to class naked. She dreamt about the end of the world. Never mind that waking up screaming and sobbing had ruined more than one sleepover as a child—a fact she'd been teased about by kids and questioned endlessly about by adults who thought her parents were mistreating her. It wasn't a big deal anymore.

As long as no one learned about it.

"Uh-huh," Lindy replied skeptically.

"But..." Hayden reached out to claim the cardboard drink holder when her friend came near. "Thanks all the same."

"*One* of them," Lindy emphasized, shrugging off her coat now that her hands were free. Her eggshell-white sweater looked thick, in keeping with the cold weather outside, and a long copper necklace hung from her neck, while a leather wristband with decorative trimming matched the jewelry.

Hayden's grin widened at Lindy's admonishment. Hot chocolate with all the spicy trimmings was her favorite, a heavenly mix of sweet and heat that dulled her over-whelming sense of smell for as long as it took to finish the drink. Smell was only one of her heightened senses, but often, it was the most frustrating. Music could dampen her sharp hearing, and the need to shift only came about once a month, but smells...

Gym class had been a nightmare, growing up. Hell, between the perfume, body spray, rampant pheromones, and bullies ready to pounce on the hyper-sensitive "weirdo," so had most of school. Grocery stores were a migraine-fest of bizarre aromas and human body odor, offices left her reeling and feeling trapped, and pet shops made her want to sink her teeth into anything that moved. If not for Johanna's Flower Shop—where damn near every-thing was buried under the smell of a hundred blossoms and bouquets—she'd probably be unemployed.

Just one of the perils of being a lone werewolf in a world full of humans who could never know her secret.

Lindy extracted a cup for herself and leaned against the front counter. Idly, she picked up a stray piece of green cellophane, the scrap left over from wrapping a customer's purchase. "So...how'd it go?" she asked. "The studying binge pay off?"

"Passed...I think."

"Well, congratulations, new graduate."

"*Possibly* new."

Lindy gave her a wry look. "Oh, come on."

Hayden managed a smile. She'd pulled yet another all-nighter last night, trying to get ready for her economics final, and the grades wouldn't be in for a few days. She felt pretty sure about the majority of her answers, and her grades had been fairly good in the class to begin with, but until she got that final score...

She shoved the thought aside. It'd be fine.

"So what about you?" she asked, refocusing.

Lindy beamed. "Harvard, here I come."

Hayden lifted her cup, tapping it against her friend's. "Congrats."

"You have to come visit. Loads, okay? I'm going to miss you like crazy."

"You're going to get so sick of me, you'll start begging me to stay away."

Lindy laughed. "Not likely."

"What's the plan, then? Your dad get the time off to help you move, or...?"

"Yeah, Freddie has some kind of cello summer camp *thing* going on right before school starts, so Dad's going to fly in that week and help me drive my stuff out to Massachusetts while the kid's off learning to be the next Yo-Yo Ma or whatever." Lindy's grin belied her sarcasm, not that Hayden would have believed it anyway. Her friend adored her younger brother.

Hayden smiled and lifted her cup to take a sip, only to pause when motion by the door caught her eye. Inside the recessed entryway, a homeless man huddled against the cold. Tall and seeming way too thin even beneath layers of dirty coats, the man puffed warm air into his gloved fists and scanned the street like he was looking for someone.

"Where's Ray?" Hayden asked.

Lindy followed her gaze. "Huh. Not sure."

Hayden set the drink down and bent, checking beneath the counter before extracting a paper cup a moment later. With a quick motion, she popped the lid off her drink and poured out half of her hot chocolate. "Just a sec," she said to Lindy.

Weaving between the counter and a display of Mylar

balloons on the wall, she headed for the front entrance. The bell clanged when the door opened, and the guy glanced back. He bore a scruffy blond beard, but his eyes were a piercing blue. His layers of coats were ripped along the seams, and an odiferous cloud reeking of rotting garbage surrounded him as if he'd spent more than a few nights sleeping near a dumpster.

Or in it.

"Hey there." Hayden extended the cup, fighting to give no sign of how the smell made her want to gag. "Thought maybe you could use this?"

"Careful," Lindy warned from behind her, amusement in her voice. "She insists on putting about a tablespoon's worth of cinnamon and red pepper in that."

"It helps with the cold," Hayden protested.

The man chuckled as he reached out to take the cup. Between his gloves and his sleeve, a flash of skin showed, revealing the curled edge of a tattoo that looked like it might be some sort of snake.

"Is that military?" Hayden asked, nodding toward his wrist.

The guy tucked his exposed skin away from the cold and took a sip of the drink. "Yeah, something like that."

She nodded. "Ray—the guy who normally hangs out here? He was in Vietnam. Have you met him?"

"Mm, can't say I have." The guy wiped his mouth with the back of his gloved hand. "This is good, thank you."

"You're welcome. So, what's your name?"

The guy smiled. "You can call me Mitch."

"Hayden."

"Nice to meet you."

The phone rang inside the shop. Hayden cast a quick glance back at Lindy.

"Probably the Sanderson order again," Lindy said without looking away from Mitch. "Would you take it, Hay? She's yelled at me once already this week."

Hayden scoffed. Mrs. Sanderson had called nearly every day for a month, worrying over whether the flowers would be ready for her daughter's wedding. Normally, that would be annoying, but these days, Hayden could sort of understand the woman's anxiety. It was May. It was still snowing. It pretty much hadn't stopped since last August, and while their neighbors in the northern parts of Colorado were accustomed to winter hanging around, down here, in the southern part of the state...it was bizarre.

"Okay, well, take care of yourself out there," Hayden said to Mitch.

"Will do." The man glanced over as a cop car pulled around the corner. "That's probably my cue to get moving, anyway. Good luck with your phone call."

Hayden chuckled. "Thanks."

She let the door swing shut behind her while Mitch ambled down the sidewalk, clutching the hot chocolate in his hand. Lindy lingered by the entrance.

"You going to help me if she starts demanding a discount again?" Hayden called over her shoulder as she walked toward the counter.

Attention still on the wintry street outside, Lindy made a "you're on your own" gesture. "You're the one Johanna is giving the shop to when she retires. This is all you, my friend."

Hayden scoffed as she picked up the phone. "Thank you for calling Jo—yes, hello, Mrs. Sanderson." She threw Lindy a mock glare. "Yes, I know the wedding is—Johanna can still order the—No, we aren't trying to charge you extra, I promise. You—"

Fifteen minutes later, she hung up the phone.

"Well, that went better than usual," Lindy offered, smirking. Over the course of the past quarter hour, she'd sauntered up to the counter and begun idly organizing the floral shears into a row in front of her. "I think she likes you better than me."

"You're insufferable."

"It was your turn."

Hayden sputtered. "Oh, we're taking turns now?"

"Until that wedding is over, hell yes, we are."

"Mm-hmm, okay. I see how it is."

Lindy beamed her hundred-watt smile, the super-cheery one she ordinarily reserved for cranky customers.

Hayden shook her head, unable to hide a grin. "Fine." She took a breath. "You're probably right; she likes me better, anyway."

Lindy gave her a theatrical glower, which made Hayden's grin widen. "It was your argument in the first place," Hayden pointed out.

The bell above the entrance dinged, and she glanced over, a smile still on her face. "Welcome to Johanna's Flower...Shop."

Her mouth finished the habitual phrase, but her brain slid straight into a ditch at the sight of the six people walking into the store. A pair of women and four men, all seeming as if they ranged in age from late twenties to thir-ties. The women were opposites, one of them dressed in a sleek white coat with long pale hair, while the other was dark-haired and wore a scuffed-up leather jacket like she'd just gotten done with a bar fight. The men were tall and muscularly built, and one of them was so large he had to duck a bit to get through the doorway. Another appeared covered in tattoos, even up the sides of his neck and on his hands, while the third was leaner than the rest, with a sharp gaze that seemed to be making note of every pin and nail in the shop walls.

And as for the guy nearest to her…

Silver eyes. Hair black as midnight. She'd never seen him before in her life.

She'd seen him in her nightmares for as long as she could remember.

Trembling raced through her, every muscle screaming for her to run. The man continued onward, ignoring her and Lindy like he was on a mission. He wore a long dark wool coat that had to be designer, and his face had a sheer, sculpted look, as if the gods knew precisely what they'd wanted when they made him. And he was tall. Taller than Hayden, and she wasn't short. His pale eyes skimmed the nearby refrigerators while he walked, his every movement too calm, too smooth. Too *something* that wasn't human and never had been.

Just like all of them.

Everything about the six of them was wrong. Incredible…and wrong. The way they moved was too fluid. The way they studied the store was too sharp. Half of them stayed toward the front windows, their attention on scanning the shop and the street alike with a precision that reminded her of a military unit surveying potentially hostile territory, while the rest moved deeper into the store like they were checking for a trap. That they appeared like they could break her in half only added to the impression, though God knew she wasn't weak.

But then, she was alone. Or alone with only her human best friend beside her.

Facing a pack.

That was the only word for it. Every hair on her skin rose at the realization, and suddenly, she found herself wanting to growl. Retreat. Bare her teeth to fight, or maybe just run for the hills.

Alarm shot through her at the sensations, dampening them all beneath a rush of pure panic. She was human—or damn near close enough. She wasn't *like* that. She was a person, not an animal.

The smell of the silver-eyed guy twisted amid the floral bouquets on the air, and instantly, the urge to growl returned for a whole new reason. Her insides warmed. Her knees grew weak.

"Do you have any lilies?" he asked, studying the shop.

Hayden couldn't respond.

The guy glanced toward her, his expression friendly but distant, the way someone looked at a stranger. Because, of course, they were strangers. Total strangers.

Minus the fact he'd held a starring role in her nightmares for her entire life.

"Lilies?" he repeated, looking from her to Lindy as if wondering what was wrong with the mute shopkeeper in front of him.

"Um—" Hayden cleared her throat. Lilies…were a flower. Right. And they sold those here, where she worked as a regular human person who had nothing to hide. No problem. "Yeah, sure, they're just over—" She turned to point toward the refrigerators to her left and succeeded in knocking over the pen cup by the register. Ball-points and pencils scattered everywhere while she scrambled to grab them.

A muffled chuckle came from the dark-haired woman in the group. Hayden's face burned.

No chance they'd mistake her for anything but human now.

From the corner of her eye, she saw the silver-eyed guy cast a sharp look at the chuckling woman, and her laughter died immediately. His friendly expression returned when he smiled at Hayden.

"Lilies are in the back of the shop," Lindy offered into the awkward silence, walking over to the register to help with the mess. "Case farthest to the left."

Hayden ducked her gaze away while the guy nodded and headed where Lindy had directed him.

"You okay?" Lindy murmured to her.

"Yeah." Hayden nodded, certain her heart was pounding loud enough for the world to hear. She fastened her attention on stuffing the pens and pencils back into the cup, but she just knew Lindy was eyeing her skeptically at the response. It wasn't like Hayden to be clumsy.

But she couldn't help herself. Every fiber of her being was screaming to run or fight, and she couldn't do either.

Hayden's gaze slid over, cautious. None of them seemed to be paying much attention to her at all.

She made herself take a breath and locked her eyes back on the countertop. Really, though, why would they notice her? Just because this guy was impossible, just because everyone in this room was too, and just because if they *weren't* impossible, then they were the most dangerous things she'd ever laid eyes on…

Yeah, why should they show any sign of that?

She glanced around, wishing Lindy hadn't been so quick to put the floral shears away.

The refrigerator door closed, and she flinched. Carrying a bouquet of white calla lilies, the silver-eyed guy walked up to the register.

His scent came with him: earth and spice, musk and vanilla, with something weaving through it all that was unique to him. Her lips parted, tasting it in the air, and her tongue curled around the heady flavor. A shiver coursed through her skin, tingling along every nerve, chasing itself down into her bones.

Adrenaline shot after it like a lightning bolt. That tingling was familiar. It was the horrible urge to shift, except she sure as hell couldn't do that here, in the store, in front of half a dozen strangers and her entirely human best friend. Lindy didn't even know what Hayden was, and with luck, she never would. But the last thing Lindy needed was to discover werewolves existed by watching someone she'd known for six years lose control.

College graduate becomes dog-girl. News at eleven.

Clamping her lips shut against a whimper, Hayden dug her nails into her leg. They were too sharp. *Way* too sharp. She was losing this battle. And she shouldn't even have been standing so close to him, either. What if he could smell her too? What if—

"How…" He paused and cleared his throat. Hayden's eyes flicked up fast, finding his silver gaze locked on her, an unreadable expression on his face. Was that alarm? Maybe confusion?

Maybe heat?

He exhaled slowly, still watching her.

Definitely heat.

Her insides turned molten, a tangled mix of the need to shift and the need to reach for the total stranger and drag him closer. Her breasts tingled with desire, and the flesh between her legs throbbed. She wanted him. Needed him. Sweet God in heaven, she—

Scrambling after what little control she had left, she

retreated from the counter, and, in a desperate attempt to make the motion seem natural, she snagged a cellophane bag for the flowers from the roller hanging on the rear wall.

From the corner of her eye, she saw Lindy give her a questioning glance.

"How much?" the man asked tightly. Hayden's attention darted back to find him regarding the lilies intently, like they could answer his question.

"Um…" Math fled her brain as swiftly as if she were back in her economics final.

"Here." Lindy stepped forward and took the bouquet from him. "Let me just scan that tag for you, eh?" She ran the bar code beneath the scanner and then read off the total. "Do you need any kind of card with that?"

"No, thank you." His voice was as level as a wood plank, and he didn't so much as glance in Hayden's direction. "Just the flowers."

Lindy nodded and took his credit card. With quick motions, she rang up the order and then reached toward Hayden for the bag. Hayden handed it over and then swiped her sweaty palm surreptitiously on her jeans.

But her pulse was slowing. The need to shift wasn't as bad back here, where his scent was nearly drowned by a massive bouquet of gardenias on the rear counter. She felt like she could think again, and with the clarity came the reminder that there were five additional monsters in the store, all of whom had stopped moving entirely and now seemed to be watching her, Lindy, and the guy with equal parts curiosity and caution.

Fear sent more adrenaline prickling through her veins. God, they looked like a pack of wild animals beneath a veneer of humanity. She wondered if Lindy had noticed it.

Hayden exhaled, willing herself to calm down, stay in control, and not look like a threat to the impossible creatures in front of her. Because, dammit, she was better than this. She'd survived twenty-three years without anyone learning what she was, and she could damn well control this. Herself. She wouldn't give everything away to Lindy, and maybe, just maybe, she'd keep these people from doing anything horrific at the same time.

"Anything else we can help with?" Lindy asked the guy politely, but Hayden could hear the invitation for him to leave beneath the customer-service cheeriness in her tone.

The guy reclaimed the flowers and took a long step back from the counter. "Moorhill Cemetery. Do you know where that is from here?"

"Sure." Lindy beamed her hundred-watt smile at him. "Just take Oak Street down to King and turn left. It's about, what?" She glanced at Hayden. "Five miles on?"

Hayden managed a nod. Lindy turned the smile back on the guy.

"Great." He nodded. "Thanks."

"Have a nice day."

Hayden couldn't echo Lindy's statement and settled for whatever semblance of a smile she could muster. The guy nodded, seeming distracted, and walked toward the exit. The bell dinged when he pulled the door open, and the others followed him as he left the store.

Air rushed from Hayden's chest. Her hands were shaking. Her whole body, in point of fact.

And Lindy was watching her.

"You okay?" her friend asked, a wary and confused note in her voice. "You look kinda…freaked."

"Yeah," Hayden managed. "Just…" She settled for

something approaching part of the truth. "Whoa, hotness, right?"

Lindy nodded slowly, still studying her. "Total eye candy," she agreed noncommittally.

Hayden held onto her smile by sheer force of will. "I'll get some more flowers from the fridge in the back." Without waiting for a response, she fled toward the stockroom.

She drew another breath as the door swung shut behind her, leaving her alone in the dim space. A hanging light thinned the shadows of the concrete room, and the refrigerator chilled the atmosphere. But she couldn't smell him here. Only the dry scent of cardboard, the stale smell of concrete, and the crispness of flowers hung in the air.

For a long moment, she didn't move.

Her whole life, people like her had been the boogey-man. She knew they were out there, destroying innocent lives. Her parents knew it too. But through caution, smarts, and sheer dumb luck, her family had managed to avoid any of them finding her for over twenty years.

And then a pack wandered into the flower shop. More than that. A pack that included the guy she'd seen in her nightmares, even if she'd never met him before in her life.

She took a few steps forward, catching a hand on a nearby shelving unit to steady herself. He had to know what she was. That guy, when he caught wind of her scent...he had to. And he'd tell the others too. By now, they probably all knew, even if they couldn't know she'd never be like them.

A killer. A wild animal who attacked kids, transforming them into beasts too. Her human parents didn't know for sure if that was what happened to her—she'd been too little to remember it all when they adopted her—but it was what had killed her uncle when he and her mom were kids.

And no one else even believed they existed.

She swallowed hard, trying to focus, straining to hear behind her in case the bell over the door dinged again, signaling the monsters' return. She couldn't risk anyone finding out about her, but also, she couldn't let these bastards hurt anyone. Couldn't let them bite or maul some local child. She had to warn somebody, except she'd just look crazy. She'd be risking everything.

And in the end, she'd be revealed as a monster too.

2

CONNOR

CONNOR STRODE AWAY FROM THE QUAINT FLOWER SHOP, exercising every ounce of restraint he possessed to keep his fist from clenching down on the lilies. His skin shivered. His bones ached. And inside, his wolf yelped and clamored for him to turn around, for the gods' sakes, turn around.

But he hadn't survived this long—hadn't made sure his pack survived this long, either—by ever losing focus, even in the face of the impossible.

Gritting his teeth, he shoved his impulses down as hard as he could while his legs devoured the sidewalk, carrying him back toward the SUV they'd parked in one of the parallel parking spots around the corner. A free spot too, no meter in sight, in keeping with the small-town nature of this place. Locally owned shops with brightly colored, hand-painted signs lined either side of the street; a coffee shop here, a boutique there. The "downtown," such as it was, occupied a few square blocks, with quiet neighborhoods surrounding them and the college—otherwise known as the largest employer in this town—to the west.

Gods, he didn't think this thrice-damned village had changed in fifteen years. Hell, besides the addition of Wi-Fi, a retail district out by the state highway, and a few cell phone towers, it probably hadn't changed in a hundred. A picturesque college town situated among the mountains in southern Colorado, Mariposa was the epitome of picturesque. Decorative lampposts lined the streets and old-growth trees filled the neighborhoods. Every house seemed like it belonged on a postcard while, across the main thoroughfare, a cheerful banner invited everyone to the upcoming town picnic. Mariposa was a charming place for humans to raise their kids, to retire, and to live with the belief that they could truthfully say "nothing bad ever happens here."

To them, anyway. For fifteen years, no ulfhednar had set foot within a hundred miles of this town or its surrounding forests. His pack, their allies—hell, even their enemies—all stayed away. No wolf would dare risk coming back here.

And today, he'd found one working in a local flower shop.

He exhaled as he reached the SUV and tugged open the passenger-side door. The female was beautiful. Breathtaking, even. Tall and long-legged with waves of dark hair lashed up in a ponytail, and equally dark eyes that sent a jolt through him every time they met his own. For her to be in this town was insane. More than insane; it had to be a trap.

And everything in him wanted to go back and find out for sure.

"You okay?" Wes offered as he took the driver's seat,

mild amusement in his voice. Doors opened and shut behind him as the others joined them.

Connor didn't take his eyes off the road ahead. He had to calm down. Reacting like this…he wasn't a cub, smitten by his first sight of an attractive female, for the gods' sakes. "I'm fine."

"Pretty cute shopkeepers back there," Wes commented while his tattooed hand turned the key in the ignition. "You get close enough to smell which was ulfhednar?"

Inside his mind, Connor's wolf bared its fangs and snarled. He drew in a slow breath, ordering himself to get a grip—and *not* on her curves. Her skin. Her smell around him as he buried himself deep in—

He shifted on the seat, trying to ease the pressure of his trapped cock. Odin's fucking eye, he'd never been this aroused by the scent of a female in his life.

"The shorter one who rang you up was hot," Wes continued as if he couldn't read the tension rolling off Connor in waves.

Taking another breath, Connor noted with ironic relief that the only thing he could smell now was the stale SUV interior and the horrendous machinery exhaust clinging to the winter air. And it helped. For a moment there, he'd thought her scent had imprinted itself like a bolt right between his eyeballs, knocking him back as firmly as if he'd been punched.

Because, by all the *gods*…

He sucked down another breath of "spent too long in storage" air from the SUV. "Hot," he replied, his voice meticulously level as Wes pulled from the parking spot and started down the road. "And human."

His friend made a noise as if it didn't change a thing, which Connor didn't buy for a second. As the only bitten ulfhednar among the six of them, Connor knew Wes would sooner go hang out at a furrier's than he would lust after a human woman, if only because of his fear of doing to her what had been done to him as a child.

As utterly unfounded as that fear might be.

"So the other was the wolf, then," Kirsi chimed in. Connor looked back to find the dark-haired female giving him a wry glance before she turned to scan the town as if expecting hunters to materialize out of thin air.

"Or the owner," Tyson countered from the rear of the SUV as if counting off the options. "Or a customer who just came through. The woman was awfully clumsy for one of us."

Connor fought the urge to bare his teeth at the lean young male. Gods, he was behaving like a territorial moron. There was nothing between him and that female. There never *would* be anything between them, and not only because he had zero intention of becoming tangled up in something as distracting as sex, let alone—gods forbid—a relationship. His clan needed him focused. They counted on him, and in the future, when he took his father's place, they'd count on him even more. The stability and protection of their clan was his responsibility, and jeopardizing that because he'd let his guard down for a relationship...or because he'd lost one...

His stomach twisted with nausea, and he shoved the thoughts aside. No, he'd sworn off *that* years ago and had no intention of changing things now. The pack was his priority, now and always. Barring short trips at the behest of his father, he and the rest would be staying the hell out of this town, and thus away from her.

His wolf clawed at his mind, hating the notion.

"Perhaps she was simply startled by us," Luna offered

neutrally. From her seat next to Kirsi, the blond-haired female studied Connor, a piercingly perceptive look in her eerily pale eyes.

"Yeah, maybe," Kirsi allowed, her attention on staring down a pedestrian who had glanced toward the SUV. "No customer is leaving a scent like that over every inch of the place. A wolf definitely spends a *lot* of time there, and I'm betting it was her."

"I've been cataloguing every report our people bring in," Tyson argued with all the defensiveness of their resident tech genius and data guru. "Cross-referencing it with police scanners, reports from the Forest District, and any chatter on the web. There's no sign that another pack has tried to move in on our—"

"Is this really the most important topic at the moment?" Marrok offered from the rear of the vehicle, his deep voice a rumbling murmur. The large male rarely spoke, but when he did, he always got straight to the point.

"Well, it's more interesting than what's waiting when we come back here," Kirsi retorted.

Connor turned to face the road, feeling the silent agreement of the others behind him. What they were doing now, they did for him, but no one was looking forward to the *real* reason they had been sent to town today, never mind that it was their job within the larger pack of Thorsen wolves. If nothing else, debating whether the florist was ulfhednar served as a distraction.

From so many things.

The road rose as it twisted into the mountainous terrain north of town. Trees closed in on either side, and rocks and snow clustered beneath them. All around him, he could feel the tension ease from the others as they left human civilization behind, though none of them would be fully calm until they were back at the manor.

Or back in Alaska, where they belonged.

Connor shifted on the seat, the cellophane bag around the lilies crinkling as he moved. It hadn't been his call, coming here of all places. He never would have moved their clan back into the old manor outside Mariposa last week, nor packed up as if never to return to their compound north of Anchorage. When his father had insisted they go—because of the cold, the old man had claimed, like that fucking mattered during the past fifteen years *or* during the past one and a half, when his father sent Connor and his friends out to train for survival and defense in the barren wilderness—Connor had argued. For days and days, he'd argued, long past the point when even his position as the alpha's son would protect him from punishment for insubordination. If cold weather was truly such a problem, he'd said, then fine, they could move south. But returning to Mariposa, where humans or hunters or—gods forbid—the Order might find them?

The old bastard had lost his mind years ago, but he'd never done anything as insane as *this*.

Beneath the tires, the rumble of the road changed as Wes turned the SUV onto a gravel drive. Up ahead, a black iron gate stood open, its sides propped permanently wide by two stone pillars with wolves' heads atop them.

Subtle.

Connor looked away.

Wes steered the vehicle past the entrance and up the slope of the open hillside. Trees surrounded the snowy-white expanse, but at the clearing's heart, only stone grew in regimented lines of varying shapes and sizes, some spartan, some with flowers stuck in the permanent vases at their sides, the bouquets like splashes of color in a mono-chromatic world.

He remembered how green it had been last time he stood in this graveyard.

The SUV pulled to a stop, and in silence, the others climbed out. Drawing a slow breath, his hand tightening on the cellophane wrap, Connor braced himself and then did the same.

Cold wind swept past, taking advantage of the open space. He sniffed reflexively, checking the air, but only the scents of trees and nature came to him. Hunters were cautious, though, as well he knew, and the Order was too. He wouldn't relax until the six of them were back at the manor with thick walls and several million dollars' worth of security between them and the gun enthusiasts and wolf killers of the world.

In silence, the pack walked up the slope, past old graves with the lettering nearly worn away, toward the pinnacle of the hill where an ornate monolith stood, carvings of wolves chasing deer twisting up its granite sides. Four kinds of marble imported from Italy surrounded the base in concentric circles, while the Thorsen family name was engraved in large letters at head-height. Brilliant lights fixed in the ground would shine on the monument when the sun went down, denying even darkness the power to hide her grave. The whole display was ornate, decadent even. A testament to her memory and position in the clan, showcasing to everyone what riches, prestige, and power the family possessed.

She would've hated it. Quiet elegance had been her style, whereas this was clearly his father's work.

When Connor neared the top of the incline, the others melted back, fanning out in silence to take positions around the hillside, keeping watch so that, right now, he wouldn't have to.

He glanced toward them all, silently grateful, and Wes gave him a nod in return.

Gently, Connor unwrapped the lilies and placed them in the stone vase at the base of the obelisk. "Hello, Mother," he said softly. "Sorry, I haven't made it back..." He trailed off with a wry chuckle. He was bullshitting. She would've known it in a heartbeat.

His breath puffed out in the chilled air. For a long moment, he stared up at the spire piercing the gray sky. Crows flew overhead, cawing loudly in the stillness where, even to his ears, the noise of the city and the road were long gone. He'd thought, maybe, if he came here, he'd know what to say to her. But there were no words. Fifteen years later, and still...there were no words.

Maybe there never would be.

He'd killed her. It was his fault she lay here, beneath dirt and stone and cloudless sky. If he'd kept his focus that day, if he hadn't been so foolish, so insistent that she go on a run with him in the forest, only for him to become distracted by a damn deer at the one crucial moment when a hunter spotted her...

If he hadn't been a shame to his family name...

His father was right. Driven mad by grief, but right. There was no way to make up for what Connor had done. "Sorry" would never be enough.

His eyes closed, his face tightening as he wished for the millionth time that the ground would open up and swallow him. But it never did. The birds called and the wind blew and still...still the world continued.

With him. Without her.

Unfair as always.

He placed a hand to the cold stone. "Love you."

Exhaling sharply, he turned away and started back down the hillside. Behind him, the others fell in, their silent presence an undeserved comfort. They'd come together over the past twenty years, each of them finding their own way into this small pack-within-a-pack. They knew what happened, what he'd lost. They'd lost it too. Parents, friends, siblings, all taken by hunters or fate or worse. Despite the rest of the pack around them, in a way, the six of them were all each other had left.

The strays.

He glanced at his friends as they all reached the SUV. "Thank you," he said quietly.

They nodded. Luna gave him a small smile.

He paused, his hand on the door handle, torn between wanting to leave this sorrowful place and wishing he could delay the inevitable.

"We'll be quick," Wes said. The others murmured in agreement.

Connor sighed and nodded. "Let's get this over with."

The stretch of town his father owned was less well kept than the cute shops and coffeehouses at the heart of Mariposa. These old buildings had little to recommend them to tourists or locals compared to the brightly painted stores a few blocks away. The brick was decaying; the windows were dusty. Even the sidewalks were in worse repair, with the sections uneven and cracked like the earth wasn't as steady here.

Connor's eyes strayed toward downtown as Wes steered the SUV along the road. The female was there, just a few blocks away. The florist, impossible and too damn alluring. Being back in town made his wolf want to go in that direction right now, and gods, if that wasn't irritating.

But focus had never been its strong suit. Not on anything that mattered.

Scowling, he dragged his attention back to the matter at hand while, without a word, Wes pulled the SUV into a spot outlined by paint so faded, the markings had nearly disappeared. Reluctance weighed heavy on everyone in the vehicle. No one wanted to be here. To do this, to risk this. The strong-arm tactics were one thing, and his father's demands couldn't be denied, but humans were always a danger.

Any one of the trigger-happy bastards could pull a gun.

In silence, Connor pushed the door open. In the old myths, only a silver bullet would kill one of his kind. Ulfhednar in stories could withstand just about anything short of that one metal or perhaps losing their head. Reality was brutal, though, and didn't give a damn about fairy tales. And while his people might have been tough as hell, the mutilating force of a shotgun blast would kill just about anything.

As well he knew.

He let out a breath, trying to push the memories and fears aside. They'd be quick. Get the cash his father insisted they bring him and then leave. And if the human tried to argue or reached for anything besides his wallet, they'd take off his arms and maybe a leg for good measure.

Beneath his skin, his wolf stretched and growled.

Together, he and the others walked to the entrance. Like at the florist's, a small bell hung above the hardware shop's door, and it dinged when they came inside. The smell of steel and oil, plastic and dust assaulted his nose, taking up residence there like the store was a world unto itself, a self-contained bubble of scents that couldn't reach past the front door, where the wind and the winter would steal them away. Countless tools and supplies filled every nook and cranny of the shelving, with mismatched price tags arrayed above or below them in shades of yellow and green and blue. Lots of sale price tags too, bright red. The lights overhead attempted valiantly to beat back the shadows, but when his eyes flicked upward, he noted a number of the panels had dead bulbs, if not ones that were missing entirely.

Odd, considering what the store sold.

Luna and Tyson hung back, keeping an eye to the front windows and the door, while he and the rest walked deeper into the shop. The leanest built of the six of them, those two wouldn't look as threatening to the store owner, and *threat* was what they were after. With tattoos covering him, including on his neck and hands, Wes made the more conventionally minded humans balk, while Marrok's size and bulk had cowed even the angriest of drunkards back home in Alaska. Kirsi may not have been as tall or wide as them, but the way she moved—like death toying with ideas for your demise—made anyone but a sheer fool take pause.

Especially since she could make good on whatever method she chose.

Tugging his black coat around himself, Connor strode down the aisles toward the register. The six of them had been beyond the barest edges of civilization for the past year and a half, hunting in the snowy, barren wastes and learning to survive with nothing, all at his father's command. Connor suspected an air of more than typical wildness still clung to them, if the way humans tended to react to their presence was any indication.

Useful, that.

The shopkeeper was sorting inventory behind the long counter, while behind him, a display of power tools hung along the wall, interrupted only by an opening that looked like it led into the stock area of the store. As Connor cleared his throat, the large man looked up, startled, and then blanched at the sight of them, his throat bobbing in a gulp above the neckline of his red, monogrammed polo shirt.

Good. The faster they could get this over with, the better.

"Larry Dawes?" Connor asked shortly.

The big man shifted his weight, and Connor heard Kirsi take a tense breath behind him. If the guy went for a gun...

"Who, uh...Who's asking?" The shopkeeper glanced warily between the group of them. He was nearly as big as Marrok, but he didn't carry himself like a fighter. More like a man who had probably been muscular back in the day, maybe played sports or had recruiters wishing he would, though now most of that had gone to paunch with age.

"We're here on behalf of Tolvar Thorsen," Connor stated. "You owe him rent for this place. Three months of it, in fact. We're here to collect. Now."

Larry let out a breath, his eyes dropping to the countertop beneath his large palms. To his left, a phone started to ring, but the man made no move to answer it. "I know," he said as the ringing stopped. "I'm sorry. It's been a hard..." He frowned like he regretted the words. "Look, is there any way we could work something out? I—"

"No." Connor kept his voice flat. His father had been abundantly clear. He wanted the money, and he wanted it now. Never mind that Connor had seen the family accounts. The clan wasn't nearly as well off as he remembered from his childhood, sure. The old man had clearly been spending money faster than they could bring it in. But they also weren't destined for a poorhouse this side of the next millennium, especially now that Connor and his pack had come back from their involuntary exile and he planned on taking more of a role in managing things.

But the alpha's orders couldn't be disobeyed.

The shopkeeper shifted his weight again, grimacing as he moved. "I've tried to reach Mister Thorson to explain. None of his phone numbers have worked. If I could just talk to him? See if he—"

"You've had months to get things in order," Connor said, giving no sign of how he wanted to scowl. His father had so many numbers, he wasn't surprised whatever ones the old wolf provided Larry didn't work. "Give us the money now, or we'll have to—"

"Daddy?" A young girl's voice interrupted Connor's words. An odd sound followed from the rear of the shop, strangely rhythmic and rather like a cart being wheeled over dusty concrete. "Mister Miller is on the phone. He's having a problem with the table saw he ordered last..." Coming around the opening behind the registers, the girl trailed off at the sight of them all.

Connor held his face still, restraining any hint of his surprise. The girl couldn't be more than eight or nine. She wore a purple shirt with a cartoon llama on the front and floral-painted jeans, and she sat in a child-sized wheelchair.

One of her legs was missing. The other was in a cast from the knee down.

Holy shit.

"Annie, go on back." Larry didn't take his eyes off Connor and the others. "Tell Mister Miller I'll call him later, okay?"

"He's pretty cranky."

"Annie…" the man urged.

The girl stayed where she was, studying Connor and the others warily. "They don't look like customers."

"I said *go*." Larry's voice grew more forceful.

The girl looked between her father and Connor, and she frowned. Wheeling herself around, she returned to the back of the store, eyeing them all over her shoulder as she went. His jaw muscles jumping, Larry shifted his weight once more, positioning himself in front of the door as if to block the people before him from following the girl.

For a moment, the rhythmic noise of her wheelchair was the only sound.

"I can try to get you half," Larry started. "And if you give me a few more—"

"What happened?" Connor interrupted.

The man hesitated.

"Your daughter," Connor insisted, knowing he was being rude but too alarmed to care. "What happened?"

The guy's jaw worked around. "Car accident." He shifted his weight again, wincing.

"You're hurt too." It wasn't a question.

A slow breath left the man, and Connor could see the answer in the way Larry's jaw jutted out a bit, in the way he tried to make his already bulky form ever-so-slightly bigger.

Defensiveness. Aggression. Not bluster or shame. He was definitely wounded and afraid they'd know it. Afraid they'd overpower him and threaten his girl, too, probably.

Merciful gods.

"When?" Connor continued.

The man paused, clearly debating whether to answer.

At his back, Connor heard Marrok shift slightly. Larry tensed.

"Three months ago," the guy admitted. "Listen, I can get Mister Thorsen his money, I just need a little more—"

"The money went to her," Connor said on a hunch. "And your injuries too." He eyed the man again. "But mostly her. Didn't it?"

A heartbeat passed. Larry nodded.

"Didn't your insurance cover it?"

The man's face twitched with resentment. "Not enough."

Connor exhaled, glancing toward Wes, who met his eyes. After so many years, Connor could read the "*well, fuck*" on his friend's otherwise stoic face.

That pretty much summed it up, too.

"Was it your fault?" He turned back to Larry.

Now anger entered the man's expression. "Drunk driver in Denver. Ran a red light and t-boned our car at an intersection, pinning—" He cut off, and when he spoke again, fury thickened the man's voice. "Paramedics got her out. Kept her alive. Couldn't save both her legs, just the one. No, it wasn't my fault." The anger faltered, his eyes flicking down and then back again.

Connor would bet half his bank account the guy blamed himself anyway.

Looking away from Larry, he scanned the shop. The missing light bulbs, the sale signs on so many items. It made sense now. This man was trying to conserve every penny he had, and make back as many as he could too. And yet Connor and the others were supposed to force him to give up several grand, all because Tolvar Thorsen wanted even more money than he had already?

Screw that.

He turned back to Larry. "Here's how this is going to go. We're going to leave, and I'm going to make a phone call. Within the next twenty-four hours, a lawyer will come see you. He'll have a new lease agreement for you to sign." Connor stepped back, surveying the store again, a touch of theatrics in the motion. "Given the age of the building, the decline in value due to its condition, and the less-than-desirable location away from downtown..." He nodded thoughtfully. "I'd say you're overpaying for this place. Probably have been for some time, too. And that, well... hmm. That probably should have been addressed when last you signed a renewal lease. When was that, Mister Dawes?"

The man stared like Connor had grown another head. "Two years ago."

"Well, I think we should make an adjustment for that, don't you? Credit you for the difference between what the rent *should* have been and what you paid. That ought to eliminate the unpaid amount and cover future rent for... what do you say? Six months sound accurate?"

Blinking, the guy managed a nod. "Y-yeah, okay."

"Good. Then I'll make that call, the lawyer will come, and you're going to sign that new lease agreement right away, aren't you?"

The man nodded again, quicker. "Thank—"

"Take care of your daughter, Mister Dawes."

Connor turned and strode past Wes and the others.

"Your father won't be pleased," Marrok murmured when they reached the front of the shop.

Connor scoffed. That was the understatement of the

year. There'd be hell to pay with his father when he came back without the money, and the old wolf would probably have a coronary when Connor told him the rest. But he didn't care. He could buy the bastard out of the building if he had to.

He pushed open the door. "What else is new?"

3

HAYDEN

IN THE DARKNESS OF THE CAVE BENEATH THE EARTH, THE scarred man lay. Chains wrapped his limbs and torso, each link a sickening corruption of the entrails of his own child, gutted before him and turned to metal an untold number of centuries before. Above his head, an eagle stood watch, its talons dripping acid down to burn the man, making him scream and writhe.

The woman was gone, her succor taken from him for the few moments needed to empty the protective bowl she held above his head to catch the acid. She was the only one still loyal, the only one who'd stayed when the gods captured him and tied him for all eternity.

She was the only one who cared for him, and someday, even she would be gone. They all would be.

The scarred man didn't care anymore. Maybe he never had. His memory was long, but in the black abyss of acid and pain, so much had faded away.

Another drop fell from the eagle's talons, scorching a hot line across the scarred wreck of his face. He screamed with pain, *thrashing helplessly and unable to escape, just as he had for millennia.*

But this time, the leash of his bindings gave an inch more than ever before.

Trembling with residual agony, the man reached out and fumbled along the length of the chain, each link more familiar to him now than his own eternally scarring skin.

His questing fingers found it. A small loop of metal, ever so slightly stretched.

Footsteps came in the darkness, light and swift. The woman was returning, but it was not because of her that a new sensation fluttered to life in his chest. It was not for her that he felt an odd muscular spasm overtake his face, his throat, his chest.

But he remembered this expression. Remembered this feeling from so many millennia before, when he'd mocked the gods and made sport of their endless plans. Back then, he'd known this feeling well.

In the darkness of the cave beneath the earth, the scarred man began to laugh.

Gasping, Hayden lunged upright in a tangle of bedsheets and sweat. Her blankets snared her legs, her pillows felt like lumpy threats at her back. Laughter rang in her ears, a sound so terrifying, it made her want to run and hide because it promised more horror than even *she* could dream.

The blur of the dream faded. She was in her own room. The glow of the city street lamps streamed through a gap in her curtains, and her night vision picked out everything from among the shadows. Her furniture, familiar as always. Her backpack lay abandoned in the corner where, hopefully, she'd never need it again, and her clothes from the day were tossed on the back of her desk chair.

A woman stood at the foot of her bed.

Hayden's breath caught. An instant before, she'd been alone in the room, and now…

With large eyes like black pools, the woman regarded Hayden, her lips parting as though she was tasting the air. Despite the shadows, her figure glowed like she was made of moonlight. Her dark hair was long, and each strand stirred as if in a breeze while her pale dress glistened like sunlit snow.

It begins.

The woman's voice rang, the sound more inside Hayden's head than in her ears and echoing against her skull. Hayden winced, but the woman didn't react to the expression. Instead, she turned, walking away in measured steps with bare feet, never pausing as she approached the door.

And then passed right through it.

Hayden froze. She had to be dreaming. Sure, she'd never had this one. The end of the world, the screaming man, yeah. But this—

He'd never laughed before.

A shuddering breath left her chest. That meant nothing. None of this did.

Hayden looked around the room. Everything was the same as ever. Her bag, her clothes, even her alarm clock, glowing red in the darkness and ticking onward toward three a.m. Fumbling past her blankets and sheets, she pinched her leg as hard as she could, but even that didn't alter her surroundings.

But she had to be dreaming. She had to—

Hayden shoved her blankets aside and scrambled out

of bed. Rushing across the room, she yanked open her door.

The living room was empty. Her night vision picked out the furniture in threads of silver that hinted at shimmering colors. Lindy's door was closed, and beyond the pass-through to the kitchen, nothing moved.

She looked around, baffled. No one was here. Lindy wasn't screaming about someone in her room. And more than that...

A tiny breath escaped Hayden. She couldn't smell the woman. Not even a hint of her.

Which...was impossible.

Sniffing again like maybe she'd made a mistake, Hayden walked farther into the living room. Nothing changed. The air was still and carried only the scents of dinner from hours before, the strawberry tang of Lindy's shampoo and conditioner from when she'd passed through the room, and hints of coffee from earlier today.

There was no way someone could have no scent. Even the most fastidious people left a smell, albeit a soapy one.

Her heart began pounding harder. Weaving past the furniture quickly, she raced to the door and shoved on her shoes and then grabbed her coat. The hallway outside the apartment was empty, as was the staircase leading to the first floor. The lingering spice of someone's takeout dinner clung to the air, as did the body odor of the guy who lived near the front exit, but all of that was familiar, same as the gray utilitarian carpet and the scuffed walls. Cheap fixtures held lights to the ceiling, illuminating the length of the corridor in varying shades of aged, yellowing plastic. At this hour, everything was quiet with that breathless pause that came only when so many humans were asleep.

Her feet slowed as she came to the building entrance.

Winter air chilled her bare legs beneath her pajama shorts when she pushed open the door, and her skin pebbled against the cold. Shivers coursed through her, urging her to shift and let warm fur cover her. She exhaled, fighting the impulse, and her breath puffed out a cloud. Zipping up her coat, she paced slowly out onto the sidewalk that led from the enormous old house that had been chopped up into apartments decades before. The landlord had shoveled the walkway earlier in the day, but a new flurry of snow drifted down now, dusting the cement and glimmering in the streetlights. Higher drifts covered the yard, pristine and untouched. The evergreen trees near the building towered like giants, but around their base, the ground was undisturbed.

She turned a slow circle, but there was nothing. No trace, and yet nowhere the woman could have gone without leaving a single footprint.

Hayden hugged her coat to her chest. She wasn't losing her mind, and she didn't feel like she was dreaming. She'd seen the woman, *heard* her, and yet watched her walk through the bedroom door like—

The woman was right in front of her.

Hayden jumped, clamping her mouth shut on a shout, and her feet slipped on the fresh snow, making her scramble to stay upright.

With dark eyes, the woman watched. Up close, her skin glistened from within, as if moonlight shone through her form. Snow drifted down around her, twinkling like tiny stars as it came near.

Hayden's breath puffed out into the air. The woman didn't seem to be breathing at all.

Be ready. Her voice didn't ring as loudly inside

Hayden's mind this time, and her tone was sad, as if she feared Hayden wouldn't be prepared for something.

Hayden's mouth moved as she searched for a response. "Who—"

The woman vanished.

Flinching, Hayden stared at the space where she'd been. Between one eye blink and the next, the lady had vanished as if she was never there at all.

Shuddering breaths left Hayden as she warily glanced around, too startled to speak. But then, what good would that do? She had to be dreaming. This was too insane. Too surreal. There was no way this—

A rumbling sound broke the stillness. Startled, she turned, searching for the source of the noise.

The ground began to tremble, but there was nothing here. No cars, no trucks. No—

Beneath her feet, the earth started to shake harder. The rumbling grew louder and louder still, like a subway train was rolling through, just beneath the snow. Evergreen trees wavered back and forth, shedding their dusting of flakes, and car alarms began to blare in the night. From instinct and unsteadiness alike, Hayden dropped to all fours, bracing herself as the ground shook as though it would never stop.

And in her mind, for no reason at all, she suddenly swore she could hear the scarred man laughing.

4

CONNOR

RUBBING A HAND TO HIS BURNING EYES, CONNOR LOOKED away from the laptop screen and the glaring abyss of spreadsheets into which he'd fallen for…

He glanced to the clock and decided he was better off without that particular math.

Gods, his father's accounts were worse than he'd thought. The few ledgers Connor had previously seen were only the beginning. The deeper he dug into it—trying to offset the lost rent from Larry Dawes's hardware store, among other things—the more he found a tangled mess of account numbers for nothing or shell companies that existed nowhere. The family money had always come from a mixture of investments in just about everything from real estate to technology to gold, but over the past eighteen months Connor had been in exile, it had gone from a sprawling, self-sustaining empire to a rat's nest of sold properties and liquidated assets. He'd been up for hours at the mahogany desk in the sitting room outside his bedchamber, simply trying to make sense of what his father was doing, and at this rate, he'd be lucky if he got to sleep by dawn. Meanwhile, it'd probably be weeks before he could organize the chaos enough to protect the clan from the audit that would almost certainly *eventually* be—

The chandelier quivered, the crystals tinkling against one another.

He glanced up, confused. There weren't any floors higher than this one, and nothing on the roof should have—

The desk began to shake.

He pushed back from the mahogany table and rose to his feet. The floor beneath him trembled, the shivers growing stronger, while beyond the tall windows, the ground groaned like a giant in pain. From the shelves built into the sitting room walls, books and decorations tumbled to the carpet while the chandelier clattered overhead. Staggering, Connor braced himself on the wall, trying to keep his feet.

Shouts rose from deeper in the manor, and as quickly as he could, Connor rushed across the shaking floor. Ripping open the door, he leaned out to look down the length of the hall.

Wes yanked open his own door farther down the corridor. "What the hell?" he called to Connor, who shook his head, baffled. A dozen yards farther on, Marrok's door opened, and he stuck his head out, the large male looking ashen.

The shaking stilled. For a moment, no one moved, and then the sound of footsteps reached his ears. From around the corner at the end of the hall, Kirsi, Tyson, and Luna appeared.

"You okay?" Connor asked them all.

Nods answered him as they walked closer.

"I didn't think this part of the country got earth-quakes," Tyson said.

"Apparently, they do now," Luna replied evenly, scanning the ceiling and floor as if to make sure they were intact.

"Lucky us," Kirsi commented.

"I'm going to go check on my father," Connor said. "The rest of you—"

From deeper in the manor, cries rose.

"We can get that," Wes said. He glanced to the others, who nodded in agreement.

"I'll take the generators," Tyson added. "Make sure they're good to go, in case we lose power."

Connor thanked them and headed for the rotunda at the end of the hall. The massive circular space occupied the heart of the manor, with balconies on all sides overlooking the three-story drop. In vibrant colors, fresco paintings of wolves chased prey across the dome overhead while marble pillars supported the structure on all sides. During the day, the inlaid stone on the first floor glistened from sunlight that poured through windows at the edges of the dome. At night, golden lamps shone down.

He glanced to the columns and the display above, checking for damage, as he strode swiftly around the perimeter of the rotunda, heading for his father's rooms on the far side. His apartment, and those of his wolves, were all on one end of the space, while his father's sections of the house were on the other. Rooms for his father's people dotted the rest of the building, though the whole manor was large enough to house three times their total number, if not more. When his great-grandparents had started this building, they must have imagined so many more wolves living here, raising children, and roaming the expansive, walled-in preserve that formed their lands.

They'd be heartbroken to know how few of their kind remained.

As he neared the hall, he could hear his father shouting, his voice more angry than pained. Connor's feet slowed. The old wolf was speaking to someone, and it wasn't difficult to guess who.

Connor's teeth ground. Of *course* she was here.

Drawing a breath, he made himself keep going, though clearly, his father was fine. Currently shouting about a lack of time or some such thing, but fine. As the alpha's son, however, it was still Connor's responsibility to check and to get whatever orders the old wolf wanted to give. The alternative—leaving it to *her* to tell his wolves what his father wanted—was infinitely worse, considering Connor could just bet it was her doing that resulted in his pack being exiled to the far reaches of the Alaskan tundra for the better part of the last year and a half.

For "training." Right.

He closed his eyes briefly when he reached the door, bracing himself, and then knocked.

"Enter!" Tolvar shouted.

Connor took the brass handle and pushed the door open. "Is everything all right, Father?" he asked evenly.

Dressed in a maroon robe and standing barefoot at the doorway to his bedroom, Tolvar Thorsen still managed to radiate power and threat. His salt-and-pepper hair was cropped short, and his face barely showed a wrinkle for his age. Built like the granite and marble of the manor itself, he was unbowed by the years or by grief.

Or by anything.

With a clenched jaw, Tolvar eyed his son. "I heard shouting."

"Marrok and the others are checking on that now. Tyson is confirming the generators are ready as well, in case we lose power."

"Did I ask about the generators?"

Connor paused. "No, sir."

His father turned, pacing away, his clasped hands tapping against each other behind his back.

Connor's eyes darted to the other occupant of the room. Her hands folded delicately atop her lap and her legs crossed at the ankle, Ingrid sat in a stiff-backed armchair in the corner. A modest velvet dress, the color of blood, covered her slim form, and her white hair hung long. When she stood, the bone-straight strands would reach her waist. He'd never learned her age. The fine lines on her skin hinted at five or six decades, at the least, though he estimated more, given she hadn't seemed to age a day since arriving on their doorstep only a few months after his mother died. That she was a wolf, he knew, though he'd never learned from what previous clan. Within days of her arrival, she'd become his father's closest advisor, keeping his ear when so few others were ever heard or trusted. But that was all anyone could tell about their relationship, and all either of them would say. The gods alone knew what else she was to his father.

Besides poison.

With dark eyes, she met Connor's gaze. Her head bowed slightly as if in acknowledgment. He turned his attention back to the old wolf.

"I want a count of the wounded," Tolvar said. "Triage their conditions, but keep them here, do you understand? No one leaves for an ulfhednar hospital. There's not enough time." The alpha shook his head, his attention on the ground like a battle plan was laid out before him and his forces were losing badly.

"Time, Father?" Connor risked asking.

"Loki stirs, son."

Connor fought to keep any expression from his face. Loki. Of course. He should have guessed Ingrid would use that particular myth to explain the earthquake. Loki writhing in his chains.

Gods, he should have paid more attention in Religion and Mythology class growing up.

Tolvar looked away from the floor again. "The moment those damned humans open their stores in the morning, I want you and the rest of your lot to hit every grocer in Mariposa and the surrounding towns. Ingrid will give you the list. Take two of the SUVs. You'll need the room. But purchase only enough to keep the total under a hundred dollars at each location. I don't want anyone out there remembering a large purchase, do you hear me? We can't be having those humans hunting for us when the time comes."

Connor nodded—though internally, he scowled. "Yes, Father."

"You must be back here before sunset. Not a second later, or you'll spend the night out on the grounds. I've ordered Barnabas to lock the gates the moment the sun touches the horizon."

Slowly, Connor exhaled. After so long outside in Alaska, it wasn't much of a threat, but he knew the others were enjoying having soft beds again. "I understand."

"Go."

Connor gave a brief nod and turned to leave.

"You made a fortuitous choice today." Ingrid's quiet voice made him tense.

His jaw tightening, he glanced over at the female, saying nothing. Until he had the ledgers and the balances to prove to his father that letting Larry Dawes out of his current lease wouldn't cause any trouble, he'd just as soon keep what happened today quiet—"fortuitous" or not.

"Good to know," he offered neutrally, heading for the door.

"The flowers." Ingrid's lips rose in a small smile. "They have put us on the path we need."

Connor stared at her. Flowers? What the hell did the flowers he'd bought for his dead mother have to do with any—

Holy shit, was she talking about the florist?

Connor's skin crawled while, inside his mind, his wolf growled warily. Not waiting another moment, he strode out of the room, leaving the door to swing shut behind him.

How in the *hell* did Ingrid know about the florist?

He shoved the thought aside. Maybe she'd heard one of the others talking. Maybe she'd gone into town too and spotted them there. But however she'd done it, all it meant was that she was as nosy and disturbing as ever.

Nothing else to know here.

Gods, he hated that female.

He left the hall and descended the stairs. For nearly fifteen years, she'd trailed his father like a ghost, whispering in his ear like some latter-day Rasputin and filling Tolvar's head with her mythological fairy tales, "visions," and delusions.

And the alpha ate up every one.

That she claimed to be some kind of *seer* was bad

enough, never mind that anyone worth their fur knew the so-called seers had been wiped out by the Order years ago. That his father believed it was damn near intolerable. But supposed prophecies and whatever else Ingrid imagined were all that guided Tolvar these days. No matter what his father had been before Connor's mother died—strong, confident, fair, and above all else, *rational*—he'd now become nothing more than a paranoid monarch, tilting at the *shadows* of windmills when there were real threats in the world. But until the old wolf died or relinquished command, Tolvar was the leader of their clan. To the wolves, his word was law, and everyone knew it.

Just like they knew that, as long as he didn't royally fuck something up, Connor Thorsen, last of the main Thorsen line and heir apparent to their empire, would be Tolvar's successor.

But he wasn't *yet.*

Drawing a steadying breath, Connor slowed his steps as he reached the first floor. The elder wolves viewed him as the son of their alpha, *not* the alpha himself, as he was well aware. Barnabas, Cyrus, and all the rest accepted no order unless it came from his father, and treated Connor's friends as vaguely foreign pups, for all that Wes, Luna, and the rest ranged in age from upper twenties to their thirties and—if they were human—would have all moved away from the family a decade ago and only see each other online or on holidays.

Instead of being here, obeying the delusional wishes of a neurotic alpha whose allies would most likely view the six of them as juveniles until their fur went gray and their teeth fell out.

He ran a hand through his hair, pushing the irritation aside. Reality was what it was, and so, because they had their orders, he and the others would revisit Mariposa and a bunch of additional human towns besides, no matter how insane the trip might be. It wasn't like they had much choice. Disobeying Tolvar meant exile—in truth, this time, and possibly for good. So he'd gather his friends, and together, they'd go fucking *grocery shopping* because that's what the old wolf wanted.

And if nothing else, no matter what, he'd make sure he didn't run into that florist again.

5

HAYDEN

THE NEXT DAY, THE EARTHQUAKE WAS ALL ANYONE COULD talk about.

And with good reason.

"My God, girls." Johanna strode out of the stockroom, her attention on her cell phone screen. Her graying hair was frazzled from how she'd been anxiously running her hands through it the whole morning, and her normally cheerful face was wrinkled with worry. "The news says they're getting reports from outer *Mongolia* now! What does that bring it up to? Forty countries?"

"Forty-seven," Lindy said from behind the counter. With dark circles under her eyes that even makeup couldn't hide, her friend looked like she hadn't slept a wink last night after the earthquake woke everyone. Her hair was lashed back in a utilitarian ponytail, and from what Hayden could tell, she was on her third cup of coffee at least.

Johanna made a flabbergasted noise. "They think it was a seven-point-five in the Caspian Sea off the coast of Turkmenistan, but they're saying it might've been that high by Papua New Guinea too. The Faroe Islands are reporting an *eight* on the Richter scale!"

Gripping the broom tighter, Hayden returned her attention to sweeping up the broken glass from the vases that had fallen off the shelves in the night. The shop was still in good shape, all things considered. The vases were a near-total loss, and some of the flower buckets in various refrigerators had toppled over. But the electricity still worked, the windows were intact, and there weren't any cracks in the structure anywhere they could see. Most of the town had fared the same, though an old porch had collapsed on a house down the street from her parents and some rebar had apparently pushed up through a road near the high school, flattening several people's tires before the cops cordoned it off.

But compared to a lot of places, they were lucky. All over the world, word was coming in of earthquakes, some of them minor, some of them *very* not. Reports had been rolling in all morning via the news and social media. Pictures of collapsed villages, of bridges or roads destroyed. People across the globe were talking about the end of the world, about global warming, or calling the whole thing a conspiracy caused by whatever group they disliked the most. Johanna hadn't mentioned the death toll recently—a small mercy, considering it was too terrible to think about for long.

No one could explain the earthquake or how it'd swept the entire planet at the same time. Scientists seemed baffled. Politicians were already clamoring to spin it in their favor. There wasn't a super-volcano or an asteroid to blame it on. There hadn't been a nuclear bomb or science experiment gone wrong.

At least, not that anyone was talking about. Not yet.

"I read a few months ago that fracking can cause earthquakes," Johanna said, glancing between the two of them and her phone. "Do you think, maybe, that's what caused it?"

"Maybe," Lindy replied, but she didn't sound remotely convinced.

Hayden was silent. She hadn't seen anything strange all morning—nothing, in fact, since the woman in the white dress vanished right before the earthquake struck—but she still felt constantly on alert, like the lady might appear in the middle of the store at any moment and scare her half to death.

Or like the ground would start shaking again.

There hadn't been many aftershocks in their area. Only a handful, and the news—as relayed by Johanna—said they were lucky for that. Too much shaking might bring about a landslide or worse. No one knew what to expect after the entire planet shook.

The door rattled in its frame. Hayden looked over swiftly.

A dump truck drove by outside, and the rattling faded as it went.

She let out a breath, cursing quietly.

"Oh Lord, they're saying a subway collapsed in Australia," Johanna reported, shaking her head at her phone screen. "It sounds like a lot of people are trapped—"

Hayden set the broom aside. "Can I take a break?"

Johanna looked up from the cell, blinking. "Sure."

"Thank you."

Avoiding Johanna's and Lindy's eyes alike, Hayden turned and strode out of the store. The cold air hit her, stealing her breath, and briefly, she thought about going back for her coat, but that would just mean hearing about more death and destruction.

God knew she got enough of that with her nightmares.

Her legs chewed up the distance, and she hugged her arms to her middle, the cold air cutting straight through her woven sweater and the long-sleeved shirt she had underneath. Without a coat, her body kept trying to insist she shift, and it was hard not to listen. In another week or so, she wouldn't even have a choice. The three nights around the full moon weren't her favorite time in the world.

Her cell buzzed in her back pocket. With a grimace, she pulled the phone out and sighed when she saw the number.

"Hi, Dad," she said.

"Hey, honey. I just have a quick break between classes. I wanted to see how you were holding up?"

"I'm fine."

"Have you spoken to—"

"Mom's called twice already today."

"Ah, good." She could hear the chagrin in his voice. With her shifts as a nurse and his classes as a college professor, Ed's and Nell McIntyre's schedules rarely synced up. As a child, Hayden sometimes felt like the family messenger, conveying snippets of updates to them when they didn't even have time for phone calls, texts, and voicemails. "Well, honey, if you need anything—"

"I'll call," she assured him, smiling in spite of everything. "How are you doing?"

He made a hedging noise. "Well, we're all good here, but Old Ben didn't do so great. Looks like the repairs the college has been avoiding finally caught up with them."

"Oh, no."

"Yeah. The whole statue toppled right on its face."

Hayden laughed at the thought of the university's knight statue doing a face-plant.

"They cordoned off the football field," her father continued, amusement in his voice. "So none of the news outlets have caught the story yet, but you know they will."

"Oh, the chancellor will love that."

"Serves the cheap bastard right," her father said. "Oops, speaking of the lovely gentleman, I think that's him coming out of the Administration building now. I better get to class before he wants to stop and chat."

Hayden chuckled. "Thanks for calling, Dad."

"Take care, sweetheart. Love you."

"Love you too."

She hung up the phone, grinning down at the screen, and then tucked the cell away. Drawing a breath and letting it out slowly, she glanced around, feeling better than a few minutes before. Loads better, actually. The air felt clearer. The morning brighter, with the sun glinting off the snowdrifts shoveled to the edges of the sidewalk while the cold prickled like the touch of tiny crystals across her skin. The ordinarily dull-red bricks of the Mariposa Savings and Loan next to her seemed to glisten like gold-stone in the light. The man walking his little Pomeranian on the opposite side of the street made her smile, as did the young woman pushing a bright-pink stroller along the sidewalk up ahead. Shaking her head at herself and the suddenly blissful feeling alike, Hayden rounded the corner, figuring she'd circle the block before heading back, if only to enjoy the shimmering feel of the air and the—

Two black SUVs were parked outside DiAngelo's Grocery Store. The six people from yesterday—the *wolves* from yesterday—were busy carrying bags from the sliding glass doors of the exit and loading them into the back of the nearest vehicle.

Her feet stopped, and her breath did too. The silver-eyed guy with his long black coat was laughing at something the tattooed man said, and in spite of everything, her insides twisted hot and strange at the sight of his smile. It was beautiful. Handsome and made her want to smile too. Even if it wasn't directed at her, it warmed her all the same.

But she couldn't stay. Shouldn't even have stayed this long. They hadn't spotted her, though. The groceries occupied all their attention. Not taking her eyes off the people, she cautiously walked backward as she tried to retreat past the corner.

One of their bags ripped and cans clattered out into the street. The dark-haired woman called something sharp to the others, teasing clear in her body language and expression, and the blonde replied. Laughing, the brunette turned, glancing back and forth as she ventured into the street for the cans.

Hayden froze as the woman saw her. The others looked toward her too, and the silver-eyed guy's humor vanished from his face, turning to something much more intense and unreadable. It pinned her like a rabbit caught in a trap.

A red sports car surged over a rise in the road.

"Kirsi!" the blonde shouted.

The dark-haired woman didn't even have time to turn.

Bone crunched on plastic and glass. Like a rag doll, the woman crashed backward onto the hood of the sports car and tumbled over it. Blood splattered on the concrete and snow. Horror gripped Hayden as the woman's dead eyes stared at her, empty and yet accusing, never to move again.

Crystalline air bit Hayden's skin, and her body rocked, her right foot dropping suddenly as if the ground wasn't where it was supposed to be any longer.

And the woman was gone. The SUV too. Hayden was back with her cell phone in her hand, the screen blinking off as the call with her father ended, and she hadn't reached the corner yet.

Frozen, she barely breathed as her eyes crept up from her phone to scan the street around her. Everything was as it'd been only a few minutes ago. There was the man walking his dog on the opposite side of the road. And up ahead, the young woman pushing a pink stroller.

"What the hell?" Hayden whispered to herself.

With a shaking hand, she tucked the phone into her pocket. Trembling, she looked at the road behind her. Johanna's shop was there, just a few blocks back. She should just run to it. Get the hell off this street and…and wake up.

Again.

Her eyes slid to the corner. Except…

This was madness.

Like this whole day wasn't?

She walked forward, edging alongside the blessedly dull brick that housed the Mariposa Savings and Loan. Trembling, she peered around the building.

A shaking breath left her. The SUVs were parked in front of DiAngelo's. The silver-eyed guy and his friends were loading groceries into the back. The brunette was smiling, still alive, not broken on the road like a brutalized toy.

And then the bag ripped.

Hayden ran.

Alarm on her face, the brunette stopped as she saw Hayden barreling toward her. Shifting her weight, she seemed to brace herself as if preparing for an attack.

The red sports car flew over the rise.

"Kirsi!" the blonde cried.

Hayden lunged. The dark-haired woman faltered at her friend's shout, shifting ever so slightly off-balance for the second it took Hayden to slam into her, trying to knock her backward. The brunette stumbled.

But not far enough.

Pain like a red-white firecracker burst through Hayden's body as the car struck.

6

CONNOR

ONE MINUTE, THEY WERE LOADING CANNED GOODS NONE OF them wanted to eat.

The next, the florist was on the ground.

"Son of a bitch!" Kirsi cried, staring in horror at the female and the red car that hit her. The vehicle skidded, tapping the breaks for a heartbeat and then flooring it away.

Connor was moving instantly, abandoning the damned groceries and dropping to his knees on the concrete by the female's side. Her eyes were closed and a cut dripped blood down the side of her face. His fingers pressed to the side of her throat, checking for a pulse.

Oh, thank the gods, she was alive.

His hands were shaking.

He exhaled sharply and then dragged a steadying breath in. What was wrong with him? Crises didn't shake him up, and this—while, yes, bad—was a total stranger.

His wolf scrambled at the insides of his skull, not giving a damn about that logic. His muscles rippled and quivered while the beast fought to take control of his body. It wanted the blood of the one who'd hurt her, that blond-haired man he'd caught a glimpse of behind the wheel. It wanted to nuzzle her face, to nudge her and whine and nip at her until she woke up. Because she had to wake up. She *had* to.

"Anyone get a plate on that bastard?" Wes called.

Kirsi snarled. "Didn't have one."

"Is she alive?" Luna asked worriedly.

Connor made an inarticulate noise, managing a nod even as his mind reeled. No plate. Why the hell would the bastard have no plate on his car?

Rage surged through his body, making his skin tingle. His teeth lengthened; his breath came in ragged gasps. Muscles stretched in his back, his arms, his legs.

He'd kill that bastard.

"We have to go." Wes's voice seemed to come from far away. "The humans—"

A rough noise escaped Connor. He wasn't leaving her here.

But where could he take her?

Home. His wolf wouldn't accept anything less. But that was madness. He didn't even know this female. He couldn't risk the safety of the clan. Not to mention how his father would have his head for bringing a stranger there, let alone one who could belong to another pack.

And being near her was dangerous. Distracting on more levels than he could even—

A fist hit his jaw. His head snapped to the side and then back.

"Dammit, Connor!" Wes snarled.

Connor bared his teeth before his brain registered his friend and the urgent look on the male's face. Other details made themselves known in quick succession—specifically the footsteps running toward them and the shouts of voices he didn't recognize.

"*Humans,*" Wes hissed. "Get a grip, goddammit. You want these people taking her to a hospital?"

The warning caught his wolf's attention where nothing else could. She was in danger from these humans too, which meant it was time to go. A tremor coursed through Connor from head to toe, hot and tingling. The wolf receded to the back of his mind while his skin calmed and his muscles eased back into their human form. Everything in him wanted to beat the ever-loving shit out of something, but Wes was right. He couldn't lose control here, and they couldn't let the humans take her to one of their hospitals. They'd do scans, maybe blood work...

The doctors wouldn't know what they were looking at, but they'd sure as hell know she wasn't human.

He had to protect her from that.

"Oh my God!" an elderly woman cried. Dressed in a green apron with *Pam* embroidered on the right side, the gray-haired woman stood on the curb, gaping at them all. "Is that Hayden McIntyre? Mister DiAngelo! Ed and Nell's daughter is hurt! Call 9-1-1!"

"Fuck," Tyson muttered from where he stood nearby. "What now?"

Connor exhaled, ordering himself to focus. Ulfhednar were tough. They healed fast. And the car hadn't hit her full on, just struck a glancing blow. So maybe they could move her.

And take her where?

Cursing blurred through his mind. Humans and their hospitals or...home.

There wasn't a choice.

"Get her up," he ordered in a low voice. "Gently. Marrok, open the back of the SUV. Shove that crap aside. We'll lay her back there. Tyson, steady her head, just in case."

Tyson crouched quickly and did as he was told.

"What are you doing?" the elderly woman cried incredulously.

Connor glanced at her. "We'll get her help."

The woman apparently named Pam started forward as if to stop them. "You could hurt her worse, you idiots! She—"

Luna stepped in front of the woman, blocking her path. "We're professionals," she lied smoothly. "This woman needs to be taken now."

Pam sputtered, but Luna's silken tone was implacable. Ignoring them, Connor slid his hands beneath the female —*Hayden*, he corrected himself—as Wes did the same. Marrok hurried back from opening the rear SUV door. "Okay, one, two..."

They lifted her between them, Tyson holding her head and neck steady while Marrok took her legs. Kirsi hurried around to the passenger door, scrambling into the vehicle and then guiding them as they moved Hayden in.

In the distance, sirens rang.

"Go, go, go," Kirsi urged under her breath.

Connor jumped into the back and tugged the rear hatch shut while Marrok and Tyson ran for the doors of the other SUV. The goddamn groceries still fought him for space— bottled water, canned goods, and endless other shit like a prepper's wet dream—so he shoved them off the edge of the folded-down seats and let them topple into the footwell.

"You got her?" Wes called from the front.

"Yeah, move," Connor snapped back, holding Hayden as steady as he could.

His friends didn't waste another second. The vehicles peeled away from the curb and shot down the road, leaving Pam and the other human bystanders gawking in their wake.

7

HAYDEN

Beneath the waves, the primeval serpent stirred, silt slipping from scales the size of houses and rising in clouds amid the deep dark water. Tiny creatures that had never seen light darted away in terror, while old shipwrecks lost to the centuries crumbled like decaying bones.

Since the dawn of time, the creature had slept, buried beneath mud and gravel until, even if humans had found it, they would only have seen ridges and mountains running beneath the waters of the world.

It was unnoticed. Unknown. Lost to all except legend.

But no longer. Now, it was waking. Now, ancient forces called beyond the range of hearing, crying out for vengeance, for destruction.

For rebirth.

The creature stirred.

And when it rose, all the world would drown.

Hayden's eyes opened.

White like snow blurred in front of her eyes, resolving into diaphanous fabric. Four posts of dark, polished wood held the drapes suspended, while beneath her back, something soft and pillowy supported her. Something equally soft covered her, cool where it lay on her skin. Scents of lavender, wood polishing oil, and laundry detergent competed for precedence all around.

Her head ached like hell.

Memory played back. How she'd seen the woman get hit by that sports car...except she hadn't. She'd seen it before it actually happened.

And she'd tried to stop it.

Ragged breaths left her. If nothing else, she probably wasn't dead, if only because being dead probably didn't hurt this much. Whether that lady was okay was anyone's guess, though, and as for where she was now...

Wincing, she tried to sit up, only to have her body protest the motion with flares of pain. She could feel her own blood pounding in her veins, beating a rhythm against her skull, and she caught sight of eggshell-colored walls and the curved top of a large window draped in thick pale curtains before she collapsed back down into the soft embrace of whatever she was lying on.

"Careful."

The quiet voice was familiar. Her breath stopped.

To her right, something rustled and creaked. She rolled her head to the side to see the silver-eyed man pushing out of a wood-framed chair. His black coat was gone. He wore a white dress shirt now, the top button undone, with dark slacks. His black hair was disheveled like he'd been running his hands through it, and when he moved, the scent of him carried through the stirred air, making her pulse quicken. Warm spice and vanilla and something that she couldn't put into words but that seemed to shoot straight from her brain to the flesh between her legs.

Desire pooled inside her middle, tangling with apprehension in a way that left her paralyzed on the bed by more than just the way her body ached. As much as her rational mind wanted to move away, something dark twisted within her, hungry and practically salivating with the urge to nip and nuzzle him. With a suddenness like she'd woken up on the edge of starvation, her body craved to feel his weight atop her, pressing her into the bed, and his hands on her bare skin as he drove himself into—

He seemed to read something in her expression, or maybe just her tension, and he stopped. A trembling breath entered her lungs.

For a moment, he didn't speak. "How are you feeling?" he asked, a careful note in his voice.

She hesitated. *Ridiculously aroused* probably wasn't a good answer, for so many reasons. Wetting her lips, she opted for something else close to the truth. "Okay. Sore."

He nodded. "Understandable."

The seconds lengthened as his eyes never left her. Her insides quivered, her mind still torn between escaping him and letting him fuck her until she screamed.

Tearing her focus from him, she tried to take stock. She could feel her jeans still covering her legs. Her long-sleeved shirt remained. Presumably, her shoes were around here somewhere, which was more than good enough for getting away.

Taking a quick breath, she tried to push up from the bed, if only to avoid continuing to lay there, her body crying out to have him join her. Every muscle ached with the motion, and her palm slipped on the silken sheets.

He moved closer quickly, sliding a hand behind her

back and helping her sit up against the pillows. His face was only inches from hers, and his breath brushed her cheek while his strong arms supported her as if she weighed nothing.

Oh, sweet *God*...

Almost as fast as he'd reached for her, he retreated. She sat, motionless, her pulse pounding.

"Wh-who are you?" She fought to hold her voice steady.

He cleared his throat. "Of course. My apologies. I'm Connor Thorsen. Someone at the store said your name is Hayden McIntyre?"

Anxiety gnawed at the edges of how desperately she wanted to reach for him. If he knew her name, he could find out other things too.

Not good...

Time for a distraction. "The woman I pushed, is she—"

"Kirsi. She's fine."

A breath left Hayden, relieved in spite of herself. No matter what the brunette might have done in her past— attacked kids, ruined lives—Hayden couldn't stomach the idea she might've died, broken on the road like that.

"Did you recognize the driver or the car?" Connor continued.

Hayden shook her head. "Did they say what happened? Why they—"

"They didn't stop."

"Oh."

She fell silent, and other sounds crept in when he didn't fill the quiet. Faint voices past the door. Laughter too, all of it seeming far away. The spacious room was a mix of pale white walls and dark furniture, with understated opulence in the carved and polished wood. The bed around her was massive, much larger than her own, and the brief thought of sharing it with him flitted through her head again before she bashed it down.

"Where am I?" she managed.

"My father's house."

She swallowed hard. His father...who was probably like him. Like her.

How many of them were there?

"You're safe," he said, as if seeing her alarm.

She nodded, but it was all for show. That they knew she was like them...safe bet. But whether they knew anything else about her...about her family or friends...

Dear God. They could be hunting them down now, biting and clawing them, or whatever the hell they needed to do to turn them into...

She shuddered. "How long was I out?" she asked, trying to sound calm if nothing else.

He paused. "You've been unconscious for several hours. All day, actually."

She blinked, absorbing the words, and then immediately pushed the blankets aside, swinging her legs over the edge of the bed while her body protested with a chorus of aches. "Okay, well, thank you for, you know..." She didn't know how to finish the sentence. Sweet God, they could have found her family already. "But I—"

"I'm sorry."

She stopped moving, anxiety shooting through her. "Sorry for what?"

A grimace crossed his face. "My father ordered the gates sealed. No one in or out until we determine..." He winced slightly. "Our level of danger."

She stared at him. "Danger?"

"From you. Your clan. The one who tried to hit you

with a car." He hesitated, something oddly bitter flitting through his expression. "From anything. But he is the alpha of our clan, and I'm sure you know all that entails. The gates will stay locked until morning. Possibly longer, if…"

Eyeing him warily, she tried not to let on that she had no clue what he was talking about. "If…?"

His mouth tightened. "If your clan is a threat to us."

They were going to kill her family.

Her pulse raced. She couldn't stay, but if she told them she was alone here…maybe they'd simply kill her. If she pretended to have a huge "clan," whatever that was, then they might keep her as a hostage.

Best to say as little as possible and find out what information she could. Allay his suspicions and all that, and get him to leave the room. She never thought she'd be climbing down a rope of sheets to get out a window, but by God, if that's what it took to escape this place…

Done.

"Why are you in Mariposa?" she asked, a challenge in her tone.

He paused. "Why are you?"

Dammit. "I live here. What's your excuse?"

His eyes narrowed, more curiosity than anger in his expression. "No clan has come here for fifteen years." His gaze ran over her briefly, the curiosity fading into a tinge of threat. "At least, none that follow ulfhednar law."

Shit, shit, shit. Whatever that meant…shit. "You didn't answer my question. Why are you here?"

He was quiet for a moment. "My mother was murdered here. My father decided a few weeks ago that we needed to return."

Shit.

She swallowed hard, her bravado faltering in the face of that information. "So...you'll be leaving again soon, then?"

Please, God. Mostly. Except...

She exhaled, pushing down the odd whimpering feeling inside her at the thought of him going away.

"I don't know," Connor answered. "Maybe."

"You don't sound sure."

He paused. "It's up to my father." His tone made it sound obvious.

She faltered and then tried to play it off, nodding. "Right, of course."

Her eyes darted around the room, seeking inspiration. Something to make him leave, so she could get out of here and go home. On a dark wooden table near the door, she spotted her phone, and relief took the edge from her panic. But then, what if they could trace her calls? She couldn't just dial up her parents and lead the danger right to them.

Hayden swallowed hard. She'd get an Uber. Ditch the phone somewhere once the ride arrived, and ask the driver to take an indirect route, just in case. And sure, it'd suck to have to pay for a new cell, but that was nothing compared to this. She just needed to give him a reason to leave the room, and then she could—

"Who leads your clan?" Connor asked.

Her eyes snapped back to him. His brow twitched up.

She shook her head. "Oh, I don't think you'd recognize their—"

"Do you *have* a clan?"

God help her, what was the right answer? "Of course," she blustered. "But I don't see what business that is of—"

He made an incredulous noise. Her mouth clicked shut.

Never taking his eyes from her, he sank down onto the

stiff-backed chair again. "No ulfhednar makes a secret of their clan among our own kind. It's our identity. Our family. Our pack."

Hayden shuddered at the last word. A questioning look flickered over his face, as if he caught the reaction.

"Are you alone here?" he asked softly.

She kept her mouth clamped shut.

"For how long?" he continued, a hint of shock in his voice.

At her silence, he exhaled, sitting back in the chair like he was trying to wrap his head around what she wasn't saying.

Her eyes darted to her phone again. This wasn't going the way she hoped, but maybe she could still get him out of the room long enough to call 9-1-1.

Except that'd just be sentencing a bunch of strangers to die when the wolves tried to eat them.

Her stomach twisted with nausea. She had to leave—and *now*, before they could hurt anyone—but she was running out of ideas. "Look, I'm...I'm tired. Maybe, um—"

"Is that why you're so afraid of us?" He hesitated. "Of me?"

She trembled. "I'm not afraid of you."

A breath of a chuckle escaped him, disbelief clear on his face. "You are not doing a particularly good job of showing that, then."

"Maybe you're just *hoping* I'm scared of you."

He gave her an odd look. "Why would I hope that?"

She didn't respond.

His brow furrowed slightly. "You're in no danger from us."

Right.

The consternation on his face deepened at whatever he

saw in her expression. "I swear to you; my clan does not attack those on their own. We are not a threat to any who would be no threat to us."

A scoff left her before she could stop it and disgust twisted her face. "Because all the kids end up like you, anyway, right? If they don't die from being *mauled*, that is."

He stared at her.

She shifted uncomfortably on the bed, wishing she had more than a few feet between her and this guy who could turn into a rabid beast at any moment.

"Is that what happened to you?" he asked softly.

She kept her mouth closed. He didn't need to know she had no clue about her own history beyond being abandoned on the roadside. She knew what had happened to her uncle when he and her mom were kids. That was enough.

"Have you...been on your own ever since?" he asked gently.

At her silence, his gaze fell away. He seemed unsettled, but more shocked than angry.

Contempt twisted through her chest. What the hell was his problem? Did he think she should have been taken back to someplace like this as a child? That someone should have tried convincing her that being turned into a creature damn near a *monster* was, what? Good for her?

"Gods..." he whispered. He looked back up at her. "I'm so sorry."

His earnest expression was disturbing, like he really felt bad for her because she hadn't been brainwashed like he clearly had been.

Again, he seemed to read something on her face, as if, despite the fact she normally could keep her thoughts to herself, with him, she was some kind of open book.

And he didn't know quite what to make of what he was seeing. "You...believe we do that." His tone was mystified, as if he was feeling his way through the words. "Hurt children...to make them as we are."

She fought to keep her face from giving anything away.

A breath left him. "I'd like you to meet someone."

Connor rose to his feet. She tensed.

"Can you stand?" When she didn't move, he frowned. "I swear to you on my mother's grave, I mean you no harm. No one here will hurt you. You have my word."

She watched him warily. "And anyone else?"

Now he looked confused.

"People." She threw the word out like a challenge.

His confusion cleared. "Humans."

There was barely a question in the response, but a whole lot of tension.

She nodded once, tightly.

For a moment, he seemed to weigh his answer. "I can promise you we will only defend ourselves."

She didn't move. That could mean anything.

"Please," he sighed. "I...I hope this might help clear some things up, but I will need you to come with me. You'll be safe. I swear it."

She eyed him, and then the window, and then her phone on the table across the room. Odds were, he wasn't going to leave this alone. And she could push. Try to get him to leave the room. Or maybe make a run for it, though that probably was the lesser of any plans.

He wasn't taking his eyes off her. He looked all earnest and patient too, like he really thought this would convince her of something.

And it wouldn't. She knew it wouldn't. All she'd find out is that they were all exactly what she'd believed this entire time. Monsters. Liars too, now, considering he wanted to convince her they didn't attack kids when she was well aware that they did.

But then, if she went with him...she'd know for sure.

Swallowing against a mouth gone dry, she pushed to her feet. This wouldn't prove a thing about him, these people, or any of it. This would simply put to rest any niggling doubts, any late-night wonderings. It would show once and for all that she was right, that she'd always been right. That hiding what she was and not seeking out anything or anyone like her had *absolutely* been the best plan.

And then she'd leave this place...somehow.

"Fine. Show me."

8

CONNOR

No ulfhednar had ever looked at Connor like Hayden watched him now. She radiated a distrust so strong, she might as well have her hackles raised and teeth bared. Disgust was there too, broadcast in every twitch of her upper lip, but it wasn't for a presumed weakness or contempt of his clan. She thought him a monster; it was abundantly clear. He could almost guarantee she expected him to lie to her.

It was a far cry from the desire he'd smelled coming from her when she first woke in the guest room bed. In that perilous moment, his only thought had been to tumble her in the blankets then and there and let his wolf side breathe her in deep before ridding himself and her of all their pesky clothes.

But the gods knew he'd resisted—and that he would continue to do so.

Pulling open the door, he motioned for her to precede him into the hall. She shook her head immediately. "You first."

Without a word, he led the way, turning right at the door to head toward the heart of the building.

And kept an ear to the rustling of her jeans and the scents coming off her, in case she moved to attack.

Inside him, his wolf pushed at his skin, hating the fact she distrusted him. The wolf wanted to do something about it, though that something would almost *certainly* be ill-advised. She wouldn't be convinced by him shifting form in front of her.

But to be near her in his other form…

Connor bashed that thought down too. As strong as his senses were now, they'd increase tenfold when he didn't have his somewhat human physiology to contend with. He didn't need that distraction, not now, not ever. As it was, having her only a few feet away was damn near torture, with that delicious smell that was *her* and the warmth of her skin so close he could touch it…

He suppressed a furious groan. The moment he knew she wasn't going to bolt or scramble out of a window or what have you, he was going to get a cold shower and possibly bury his head in a freezer.

The guest rooms were primarily on the second floor, several turns of the corridor away from the rotunda and the center of the manor. Last he'd seen the others, they were in the southern game room on the first floor, though that was several hours ago. He'd spent much of the day keeping watch over Hayden. He knew it was foolish to have insisted upon being the one to do so—she was a stranger; any number of wolves could have checked up on her—but he hadn't wanted her to regain consciousness in an unexpected place alone, and his wolf wouldn't countenance the thought of anyone else taking care of her anyway.

Sometimes, that side of him was a fucking idiot.

Grimacing, he rounded the corner and kept going. If he'd had any sense at all, he would have fought off those ludicrous instincts and stayed away from her. There were any number of things—*important* things—he needed to attend to besides this.

But then, to be fair, Hayden waking up to someone else could have ended up in a disaster. Hell, it had been perilously close to disaster even with him, given what she thought of her own kind.

The thought chilled him as nothing else had thus far. What must she have been through? What must she have seen, to think all her own kind were like those rare, contemptible monstrosities who sought to add to the ulfhednar numbers through such horrific means?

And how had she survived on her own?

He took another turn of the hall. She'd done more than survive. She found a job in that town, working among the humans and living as one of them. And from how little she appeared to know about her own kind, it seemed she'd done that ever since becoming one of the ulfhednar.

As they reached the rotunda, he cast a brief glance back to her before he could stop himself. She didn't move like a wolf, he realized. She carried herself like a human. Their mannerisms, their body language. Every hint of ulfhednar musculature, flexibility, and agility was suppressed, making her gait more stiff than it should have been, with none of the naturally rolling, fluid motion of a creature accustomed to walking on four or two legs interchangeably. As they passed through the hall, he got the strangest impression that, while her nose twitched occasionally, her eyes seemed to lead her attention more than anything else. It was an unbelievably human behavior—born of creatures who primarily depended upon sight to give them information about the world—and disconcerting to witness in an ulfhednar, as if she'd spent so long hiding her stronger senses that maybe she didn't trust them as much as the sense whose strength was more comparable to the humans around her.

Could she truly have *never* encountered another one of her own kind?

At the sight of the three-story-high dome, though, she gave a tiny gasp, her mouth falling slightly open in shock. Blinking up at the paintings of wolves chasing prey across the ceiling, she stopped walking for a moment and then dropped her gaze to him.

The wonder in her expression disappeared as if she'd sealed it away behind a door.

His wolf whimpered, hating the sight.

Connor turned and made himself continue onward around the rotunda and the stairs to the first floor. To think she'd *become* one of his kind, rather than being born one like he and most of the others had been, was an assumption on his part. He realized that. But what other explanation could there be when she knew so little of the ulfhednar, and yet spoke of them attacking children?

If the wolf who assaulted her had not yet been put down…by the gods, they would be.

When he arrived at the first floor, his nose twitched, picking up the aroma of rich sauces and braised meats, and he altered his course to walk toward the southern dining room. The others would have abandoned any entertainment by now. Dinner took precedence, as well it should. They'd been surviving off whatever they could scrounge in the wilderness for far too long.

Behind him, Hayden's stomach rumbled quietly. He

quickened his pace. She'd been unconscious for most of the day. Of course she was hungry too.

The brown marble of the floor glistened under the inset lights on the ceiling, and columns of pale stone lined the hall. To the left, the library waited, sprawling past multiple doorways and filled with everything from soporific treatises on history and agriculture to best-selling romance novels. On the right, sittings rooms and offices occupied the space between other corridors that led deeper into the building. Paintings hung from the walls, endless scenes of landscapes and forests, wolves and prey, depicted in vibrant colors and collected over the past century from countless artists, some of whom went on to be world-renown and others who'd never been heard from again. When he glanced back, he could see Hayden from the corner of his eye, gazing around like she'd never seen anything like the manor in her life.

He hoped he was right about this.

The clatter of plates and metal utensils reached his ears as they neared the dining room. An oak table stretched the length of the long space, another sign his great-grandparents had intended this place to be filled by ulfhednar beyond the mere handful who lived here now. Twin chandeliers, bedecked in crystal, shone electric versions of candlelight down on the polished table. Marrok and Wes were at the far end, deep in discussion, while the others were helping carry dishes into the room.

Hayden hung back, eyeing all of them like they might suddenly turn rabid.

"Wes," Connor called. "May I borrow you for a moment?"

His friend glanced over and caught sight of Hayden.

Curiosity on his face, he said something brief to Marrok and then came toward them. "What's up?"

Connor gave a quick look to Hayden, and all his words dried up. How was he going to explain this in a way she would believe? She had no reason to trust any of them. The opposite, in fact, considering what she thought she knew about the ulfhednar.

Dammit, he hadn't thought this through sufficiently.

"This is Wes," he began to Hayden. "One of my closest friends. And also—" He braced himself. "—a wolf who was bitten as a child."

Wes tensed, and Connor winced a bit, wishing there had been a way to warn his friend of what he was about to ask of him. Meanwhile, Hayden's face tightened, her jaw muscles jumping, like this confirmed everything.

"Hayden believes," Connor pressed onward, "that this is how ulfhednar perpetuate ourselves. That we bite children to continue our species." He nodded toward the others in the dining room. "That *our* pack does that."

Wes stared at him, at Hayden, and then sputtered to Connor, *"What?"*

Connor grimaced. From the corner of his eye, he could see the others in the dining room glance over in alarm.

"Sorry." Wes cleared his throat. "Why in the world would you think that?" He addressed the question to Hayden.

Her mouth thinned, but her eyes darted between them like this wasn't quite the reaction she'd expected.

"None of these wolves were bitten," Wes continued. "There've only been—" He appeared to run a quick tally in his head. "—seven that any pack has even come across in the past thirty years."

"When we learn of an ulfhednar who is attacking humans to turn them," Connor added. "We stop them."

Hayden glanced between them again, and he could see the disbelief still struggling to maintain its foothold in her expression. She truly didn't react like them, he realized. Her face gave away so much.

"We *kill* them," Wes clarified.

Hayden blinked, her skin going a bit bloodless.

Wes gave Connor a skeptical look and then turned back to Hayden. "Any ulfhednar who'd do that to a person has to be put down. To intentionally destroy someone's life as they knew it, to rob them of family or friends, to go after *kids*..." He scoffed. "The sick fucks deserve it. The gods know the bastard who attacked me did."

Hayden was looking more uncertain by the second. "But..." She made a half-motion toward the others, who were now studiously minding their own business while rearranging the plates for dinner.

"We're born ulfhednar," Connor said. "As were our parents and theirs before them. We don't attack children."

She bit her lip.

"This pack took me in," Wes persisted. "Gave me a home when..." He grimaced. "Let's just say I had some pretty bad options. And the bastard who bit me, he'd gone after others too, except those kids didn't make it. So the pack put him down. Stopped him from ever hurting anyone again." Wes paused, looking a tad hesitant. "Is that what happened to you?"

Connor exhaled, quietly grateful his friend found a way to ask what he'd been wondering himself.

Hayden shifted her weight, seeming uncomfortable.

"It's okay," Wes urged.

She looked past them to the others in the dining room.

Marrok and Luna quietly discussed where to place the trays of food, while Tyson used a pitcher of water to top off all the glasses at the table and Kirsi needlessly rearranged the plates. No one so much as glanced at the doorway.

Wes met Connor's eyes over Hayden's head, curiosity in his expression. Connor's brow twitched up and down, a quick *I don't know anything either* gesture he knew his friend would understand.

"I'm not sure," Hayden said softly.

Connor's attention returned to her immediately.

"I, um..." Hayden fidgeted with the sleeve of her shirt.

"Any scars?" Wes asked gently.

"One."

Connor's wolf gave a low growl at the admission.

Hayden stopped herself from tugging at the sleeve of her shirt again. "But it's from a burn."

Wes hesitated. His friend was covered in old scars, Connor knew. Most of them souvenirs from the monster who'd changed him.

"I don't remember much," Hayden continued. "I..." She drew a shaky breath like someone preparing to dive underwater. "I was really young when...some people found me. About four years old...ish."

Oh, *gods*, Connor hoped she was born ulfhednar. He thought maybe she'd been in her early teens when she was bitten. Maybe even a bit older, given how similarly to a human she moved. But if someone had attacked a child *that* young...

Swallowing hard, he ordered himself to stay focused and not give any sign of the nausea churning in his stomach.

"And a pack found you?" Wes prompted, an impressive level of neutrality in his tone. Connor knew that must have taken effort.

Hayden went quiet again.

"I told you," Connor said. "We are no threat to those who would be no threat to us."

She looked back up at him, her dark eyes questioning now, as if begging him to please be trustworthy. In his chest, an unexpected feeling twisted. It mattered, he realized. It mattered to him in a way he couldn't even explain, whether she knew she was safe with him.

"What about humans?" she asked. "Are they...Do you hurt them?"

Connor hesitated, confused. "We aren't a threat, as I—"

"No, I-I got that. Just...in general, I mean. Like..." She exhaled, seeming frustrated that she couldn't figure out how to explain what she wanted to know.

"Did humans find you?" Connor asked.

Her flicker of tension was more than enough of a response. And on one level, it was obvious. Someone must have looked after her, especially if she'd been found that young. He'd simply never heard of humans reacting to the discovery of ulfhednar by *caring* for them.

He glanced at Wes. Quite the opposite, really.

"We won't hurt them," Wes assured her. "Right, Connor?"

He nodded. If somehow this was true, then of course the pack wouldn't harm whatever humans she'd met.

It was just highly difficult to believe it *was* true.

"Yes, absolutely," he managed.

Hayden fidgeted again. "My parents are human. They adopted me a few weeks after the cops found me, but before anybody really knew what I am. They protected me...from everyone."

Connor blinked, taken aback. Who in the gods' names were these people, that they took raising an ulfhednar pup in stride? "Does no one else know what you are?"

She hesitated and then shook her head.

Wes seemed equally flabbergasted. "And you've never met another one of your own kind, besides...?" He twitched his chin in a gesture that encompassed both himself and Connor.

Hayden shook her head again.

Connor met Wes's eyes briefly. "Well, in that case..." Connor motioned to the dining room, where the others were sitting down to the meal. "Perhaps it's time we changed that."

9

HAYDEN

HAYDEN FELT LIKE SHE WAS IN A DREAM—A FACT THAT, GIVEN how many things she saw in dreams, should have meant everything was familiar.

But she'd never *dared* imagine something like this.

"—so then Connor goes after the rabbit," the brunette named Kirsi told her. "And ends up face-planting into the snow *too*."

"In my defense," Connor countered. "That rabbit had more knowledge of the terrain than any of us did. I swear it led me across that hole in the ground on purpose."

"How is that a defense?" Kirsi protested.

"Okay, then," Connor chuckled. "How about the fact I was nine?"

Kirsi gave a derisive scoff, and the others laughed. Hayden buried a smile. Dinner had been cleared away some time before, and now the people around her leaned back in their chairs, relaxing and chatting with the ease of old friends.

Except they weren't people. They were wolves.

Like her.

Somewhere inside, she still expected them to suddenly reveal that this was all a lie. They were monsters. They feasted on children and bayed at the moon and were everything she'd dreaded meeting since the moment she learned how her uncle died. That they hadn't done so yet was only to get her to let down her guard, as a part of some trick known only to them.

Because if they were trustworthy…

She took a sip of water to cover her nervous glance around the table. They were nice, all six of them, from the badass Kirsi to the geeky Tyson. Friendly and funny and so comfortably welcoming, like they had guests all the time. Except she doubted that. She'd seen the way others passing by in the hall paused as if startled when they glanced into the dining room. She'd seen the way Connor went out to meet them and heard his voice when he assured them everything was fine, she was his guest, and, yes, his father was aware of her presence. The house was huge—palace-level huge—but there only seemed to be a handful of people in it.

An hour ago, she would have assumed this was a good thing. Fewer monsters in the world.

But now she felt unsure.

"Well, if I'm going to keep being the brunt of your jokes," Connor told Kirsi. "Then I'm going to need dessert. What do we think? Ice cream sundaes tonight?"

"Oh, gods," sighed the pale-haired wolf named Luna. "Yes, please, but, uh…" She grinned. "I'm going to request Marrok makes them this time, eh?"

"Second that," Wes chimed in.

"No one beats Marrok's culinary skills," Connor

explained to Hayden. "That male was reading recipe books before he could walk."

Marrok chuckled, though the large man looked a tad embarrassed.

"Chocolate syrup's in the pantry," Tyson added. "I grabbed some more at..." He seemed to rack his brain. "Well, *one* of the stores today."

A chorus of gratitude greeted the announcement, and Hayden found herself smiling again. From tonight's conversation, she gathered that the group had spent the past year and a half in the wilderness, though she wasn't quite sure why.

"Perfect." Connor pushed away from the table. "Hayden, you want a bowl?"

She almost started to say yes, but stopped herself. "Um, I...Thank you, but is there a way I could call my roommate? Maybe my family too? They've got to be worried sick."

Connor blinked. "Oh." He stepped aside as Marrok slipped past him on his way to the kitchen. "Yes, but..."

Hayden's heart sank.

"Your phone was damaged," Connor continued apologetically. "I asked Tyson to take a look at it, but when the car hit you and you fell, it..."

"It was smashed," Tyson filled in. "I suspect I can get your pictures and such off it, if you'd like, but it'll probably just be easier to buy a new phone than try to replace the screen and damaged components."

Hayden hesitated. "Thank you. Is there, uh, another phone or..."

Connor glanced at Tyson who nodded. The lean man stood. "I'll get you a secure line."

Hayden gave him a confused look.

"It's nothing," Tyson amended. "Just a sec." He strode out of the room quickly.

Her expression unchanged, Hayden rose to her feet while the others went to help Marrok with the ice cream.

Or so they all murmured as they left the room.

"Secure line?" Hayden asked Connor.

He grimaced. "One of my father's precautions against humans tracking us. It's fine."

She watched him as he followed Tyson out of the room, not sure she believed it was as "fine" as he made it seem.

A few minutes later, Tyson presented her with a cell phone. Still seeming uncomfortable, he hurried back to the dining room, leaving her with Connor in a small sitting room across from the massive library she'd noticed when she first came downstairs.

"So, um," she started to Connor. "I'm guessing you don't want me to tell anyone about you all or...wherever this place is."

"If you don't mind."

She bit her lip and then nodded. Clicking on the phone's screen, she hesitated a moment more before dialing Lindy's number. This wasn't exactly what she'd imagined an hour ago. Making this call with Connor right here. Not running for her life from wherever the hell she'd woken up.

Lindy's voice radiated caution when she answered the phone. "Hello?"

"Um...hey there."

"Oh my God, Hayden? What the...Where are you? Whose number is this?"

Hayden winced, guilt hitting her in a wave. Her friend sounded terrified—and of course she did. For all Hayden knew, people on the street had called her parents or the flower shop. It wasn't exactly a big city, after all. And Connor had even said someone recognized her after the car hit.

Small town gossip moved faster than the wind, which meant by now, everyone from her parents to her high-school janitor probably knew what had happened. Add into that the fact she'd vanished afterward—in the company of newcomers to town, no less—and God only knew what kind of theories were flying about.

She should have called sooner. Except, of course, things had been different an hour ago, which made that seem impossible.

Grimacing with discomfort, she glanced at Connor. "Hey. Yeah. Um..." She couldn't answer any of Lindy's questions without doing exactly what she'd told Connor she wouldn't: giving them away. "Sorry I, um...if I scared you." She winced, certain she was botching this already.

"Never mind that. Are you okay?"

"Yeah, I'm fine."

"What happened? Your mom and dad called Johanna's. Said some lady told them you'd been hit by a car?"

Hayden's mouth moved for a moment. "Yeah."

Lindy gasped. Closing her eyes briefly, Hayden pressed onward. "I'm fine, though. Really. It wasn't bad." She groaned silently. Like her friend was supposed to believe that. "Some people found me. They helped me. Gave me a phone. But I'm going to need to stay here for a bit. I mean, I'm okay; it's just, um..."

"Hayden, what the hell is going on?"

"I..." She racked her brain for an excuse. "I have a concussion. But I just need to rest. I'll be home as soon as it's safe to drive."

Lindy didn't respond, and the silence stretched, growing more awkward by the second.

Wincing, Hayden said, "I should probably go. Get sleep and all that."

"If you're that messed up, you sure you shouldn't just go to the hospital?" Lindy's tone was odd, but Hayden couldn't put her finger on why.

And it was a moot point anyhow. There was no way in hell she'd be going to a hospital full of humans who might figure out she wasn't one of them.

"Um...I'll think about it." Hayden glanced at Connor again. "Listen, I'll see you soon, okay?"

"Okay."

Hayden didn't know what else to say. Feeling awkward, she hung up the phone, only to stare at it for a moment. She needed to call her parents too. They were probably worried sick.

But as for how she'd explain absolutely anything without sending them to DEFCON One or doing exactly what Connor had asked her not to do...

Hayden glanced up to find him watching her. "So," he offered neutrally. "How'd it go?"

She shrugged.

"Thank you for not telling your friend where you were. Or about us. My pack, I mean. Or the manor." An uncomfortable expression flashed across his face.

Hayden nodded. "May I ask why the secrecy, though? I mean, where even *are* we—"

A man appeared at the doorway of the sitting room, and she cut off. Wearing a suit like a butler, with his gray hair close-cropped, the man regarded them both imperiously, one eyebrow arching as if in commentary of their presence here, together, or even on the earth itself. "Your father wishes to speak with you," he said with a pointed look to Connor. "Both of you. Now."

Connor grimaced. "Understood, Barnabas."

With a derisive twitch of his face, the man turned and walked away.

Hayden bit her lip briefly. "Are you in trouble?"

Connor sighed. "No more than usual." He glanced at Hayden, seeing the worry on her face. "It'll be fine. My father and I…Let's just say we haven't seen eye to eye for a long time. But whatever he wants to talk about, please know you're still my guest. The Thorsen pack continues to possess hospitality, even if some of us don't act like it. I will not let anything happen to you."

She swallowed nervously and nodded, trying to look reassured.

Connor led the way out of the hall and toward the enormous room with the domed ceiling three stories high. She eyed the marble pillars and the paintings above her again as they climbed the stairs. How had no one in town noticed this place? It seemed huge and describing it as a palace barely felt as if the term came close. It should have been a source of gossip for every busybody in Mariposa, and instead, she'd never heard a whisper of its existence.

Unless it wasn't anywhere *near* town.

Fear threatened to bubble up inside her all over again, and she forced herself to keep breathing as she continued after Connor. When they reached the third floor, he turned, heading for a hallway on the opposite side of the domed space. At the end of the long hallway, a pair of double doors waited, dark wood and glossy like they'd been polished enough to be glass. Pausing for a heartbeat, Connor seemed to brace himself before knocking.

"Enter!"

Hayden flinched at the harsh command from beyond the door.

Connor gave her a reassuring look. "Our guest, remember?" he whispered.

She nodded. He opened the door.

Even if she hadn't been told who they were meeting, she would have known the man in front of her was Connor's father. He looked like his son—light eyes, dark hair, albeit with the latter starting to go gray around the edges—but he was harder. Colder. Where Connor was chiseled marble, this man was rough and uncompromising granite. He looked as if the world could end around him and he would march onward with the insistence that any stragglers be left behind. She'd had a professor like him once, a cold, cruel man who didn't accept a single excuse for anything. Students could have been bleeding out on the floor in front of him, and the man would have merely docked their grades for making a mess.

She'd hated the professor. She didn't know what to make of the man in front of her now.

"Father," Connor said. "May I present Hayden McIntyre? Hayden, this is Tolvar Thorsen, alpha of the Thorsen pack."

Tolvar ignored her completely, regarding his son with all the judgment of a military tribunal preparing to hand down a sentence. "You were to keep her in the guest room."

"It is not our custom to starve our guests, Father," Connor replied evenly.

"Nor is it to give succor to those who would steal our resources! You have *no* idea the trouble you—" Tolvar cut off, throwing Hayden a furious look before returning his attention to his son, his voice becoming biting. "You will place the female back in the guest room and keep her locked in there until we determine the extent of the damage you've done."

"Father, she's not—"

"I have spoken!"

Tolvar's shout rang from the walls, and silence followed.

The faint sound of metal jingling broke the quiet. Hayden looked over to the corner to find a woman she hadn't noticed before. Slender, with silver hair that hung down to her waist, the woman wore a long-sleeve red dress embroidered with dark maroon threads. She looked like she belonged at a Renaissance fair, or maybe some New Age rendition of Woodstock. Silver jewelry shaped like crescent moons and stars glistened around her neck and wrists, and her eyes glinted with a laser-like interest that was locked entirely on Hayden.

"I see you found her," the woman said to Connor, an enigmatic smile curving her lips.

Connor threw an irritated look at the woman, as if he wanted to tell her to shut up.

The older woman didn't react. Rising to her feet, her jewelry tingling like tiny bells, she walked towards Hayden. "My name is Ingrid. It is a pleasure to meet you."

Hayden fought the urge to retreat. There was something about Ingrid. Something that reminded her of the ghostly figure she'd seen before the earthquake, even if they looked nothing alike. Didn't even sound alike, really.

But the…the *whatever* coming off her…

Hayden had never believed in "auras," never gave much credit to crystals or incense or chanting. But the woman in front of her seemed to charge the air with static and make the lights glow brighter as if they were getting more electricity than normal. Hayden's head filled with whispers as the woman watched her, like a dozen people were commenting on something, their words just beyond her ability to make them out.

Tolvar made an incredulous noise. "*This* is the one you've been waiting for?"

Ingrid smiled. Hayden's skin crawled.

The older man seemed taken aback, as if the woman's simple expression was answer enough. "Indeed." He cleared his throat. "In that case, very well. The female may stay and receive food as our guest...for now."

"What have you seen so far?" Ingrid asked Hayden as if Tolvar's statement hadn't happened.

Ice shot through Hayden's veins. "I-I'm sorry?"

Ingrid's smile broadened.

"What the hell is this?" Connor demanded of his father. "What is she talking about?"

Ingrid and Tolvar ignored him.

"Have you seen Loki in his chains, writhing in torment?" Ingrid cocked her head, studying Hayden as she spoke. "He deserves his punishment, you know. For the death of Baldur and the treachery that waits to unfold—"

"You *must* be joking," Connor interjected.

"Silence, boy," his father snapped.

"Father, she's talking about—"

"I know of what I speak." Ingrid's voice became every bit as imperious as Tolvar's had been. "She is a seer. The power of seidr surrounds this female like the air itself. Surely you have felt it?" She turned her laser gaze on Connor.

He was silent. Hayden trembled, wanting to retreat, but her body seemed frozen.

"Tell me," the woman said to Hayden. "Have you

heard the growls of the draugar, rising from their rest? Has Jormungand begun to stir in the watery depths? Ragnarok is coming, and none can stop its—"

Hayden's frantic signals finally reached her feet, and she backed toward the door. "I don't know what you're talking about. I don't—"

"I've seen you," the woman continued inexorably. "I've seen you standing in the ashes when the world falls down. Yours is the choice that could save us when the draugar rise and come for us all."

"Father, this is madness!" Connor protested as Hayden fumbled behind her for the door handle, finding only air.

Ingrid paced toward her. "You cannot hide from the destiny the Norns have set, young one. Ragnarok awaits! To hide from your truth will mean all shall perish and—"

Hayden's palm landed on the handle, and she didn't wait for anymore. Yanking the door open, she ran. The hall blurred around her, an ornate monstrosity of maroon carpets and marble pillars that might as well be a prison.

She had to get out of here. She should have known the other shoe would drop eventually, known somehow that *someone* here would be a monster. Connor wasn't. His friends probably weren't either.

But that woman...

"Hayden!"

Connor's shout rang through the hall behind her, but she didn't slow. Whipping around the corner, she raced toward the staircase.

He caught up to her anyway and grabbed her arm. "Hey!"

She yanked it away, breaking his grip.

"Listen," Connor said hurriedly. "Please. Ingrid's a fucking—"

"Who are you people?" Hayden cried. "*What* are you? What the hell is this place?"

Connor shook his head. "I don't—"

Beyond him, a flash of red caught her eye, and Hayden's breath stopped. The old woman emerged from the hall, making no move to hurry after them as she paused by the ornate banister that overlooked the drop to the first floor.

Hayden took off down the stairs.

"Did you see him before the earth shook?" Ingrid called.

"I don't know what the hell you're talking about!" Hayden shouted.

"I am talking about something you have the power to stop."

Hayden's feet slowed. She looked up again.

"Not all of it," Ingrid amended. "Not everything. But some. Enough to save...some." A hint of sorrow crossed her face. "I know what you've seen. I have seen it too, though I suspect not as much as you have. You possess a powerful gift, young one. A gift we sorely need in the coming days."

Hayden's hand trembled on the railing. "I don't know what you're talking about," she repeated, her voice shaking.

"Yes, you do."

"I just want to go home," Hayden said.

The sorrow returned to Ingrid's expression, stronger and tinged with so much pity it sent a spike of fear right through Hayden's chest. More than anything Ingrid could have said, more than any bizarre proclamation, the look made Hayden's knees go weak and brought tears to her eyes.

Ingrid looked as if she'd already seen the death of everyone Hayden ever loved.

"Of course you do," the woman sighed, her quiet words hanging beneath the vast dome.

Ingrid turned to Connor. "I will speak to your father and ask him to open the gates so she may return to her home." She returned her attention to Hayden. "Take what time you have, child. Treasure it."

Without another word, she walked away.

Hayden trembled. Her eyes slipped toward Connor, but she couldn't read the look on his face. "What..." She swallowed hard. "So..."

Connor pulled his eyes from the hallway. "I'll get the car."

10

CONNOR

PLENTY OF TIMES IN HIS LIFE, HIS FATHER HAD EMBARRASSED him, but never so much as he'd embarrassed Connor this night.

He glanced towards Hayden in the passenger seat of the SUV.

But he was at a loss for what he should say. Ingrid was a lunatic. She'd always *been* a lunatic, from the moment she appeared on their doorstep, a white-haired female with only a single handbag carrying all her worldly possessions. But while her ridiculous ravings were annoying, or even infuriating over time, they'd never filled anyone with the kind of fear he saw coming off Hayden in his father's apartment.

Connor's hands flexed on the SUV's steering wheel, a rage pounding through him so strong, his wolf wanted to take a bite of the dashboard. How *dare* Ingrid terrify Hayden that way? The female was his...*their* guest. The guest of the entire pack. And that old bitch had treated her to a full display of all the raving madness that had plagued the Thorsen clan since Connor's mother died.

And to what end? Simply to share her insane rantings about the end of the world? The great serpent Jormungand waiting beneath the waves. Loki trapped in a cave, chained by the entrails of his own child. Connor bit back a scoff. Those were fairy tales meant to scare young wolves, back before they learned that reality was full of enough terrifying things; no need to bring *magic* into it at all.

But Hayden didn't know that. Hayden lived in the real world, the rational world. The world of flower shops and grocery stores and little houses probably tucked away in some quaint neighborhood where the children played games in the street.

And apparently, Ingrid had been "waiting for her."

He clamped his teeth shut against a growl. Hayden would probably never want to see any of them again—and for that, he couldn't blame her. In her shoes, he'd certainly be running for the hills, determined to escape the lunatics. Never mind that the thought of never seeing her again didn't sit right with him. Never mind that it left the wolf inside him pacing frantically like a beast in a cage.

But whatever was wrong with the wolf inside him couldn't matter. It was just more evidence of how distracted he'd become. How much he needed to regain his focus: protecting the clan, even if that meant protecting it from his father's madness and Ingrid's lunacy.

Maybe that most of all.

No, chances were, this was the last time he was going to see her, and that would just have to be the way things were. After all, there wasn't a damn thing he could do about it. What was he supposed to say? Apologize to Hayden for the fact that his father's...*whatever* the hell she was, was mad as a fucking hatter and damn near useless besides? He couldn't explain that, not in any way she'd understand. He couldn't explain the years of frustration or the way legends guided his father more than logic ever could.

Gods, the male trusted myths the way witches trusted tea leaves.

Connor scowled. No, he had to let Hayden go. Back to the normal world and back to the humans, while he would just have to ignore the way the wolf inside him inexplicably wanted to howl in agony at the mere thought of it.

Or the way the rest of him had begun to worry about what they'd be leaving her to. When he thought she had a pack out here, that'd been one thing. But now? To leave her alone in a world with hunters and the Order and the gods knew what else...?

But it wasn't like he had a choice.

On a street sign, he caught sight of the name she'd given him, and he steered the SUV around the corner. Leaning his head closer to the windshield, he scanned the street for the address number. He wasn't familiar with this part of town any more than he was familiar with any other part of town. If not for her general directions and the GPS on his phone, he never would have found this place. And as for where she lived...

He searched for mailboxes to give him address numbers to go by, but they were few and far between among the old houses. But then, he didn't think she would live in a smaller house. She'd said something about an apartment. Yet, even from this distance and even with his eyesight, he was having trouble making out the numbers on the buildings—

"That one," Hayden said quietly, pointing. "The white Colonial on the left."

He nodded, torn by the desire to say something, anything.

Even if there wasn't any point.

Connor pulled the SUV up next to the curb and came to a stop. The wolf inside him, and his own damn sense, made him open his mouth when, really, he probably should've stayed silent. "I'm sorry."

He risked a glance over at her to find her regarding her folded hands in her lap. She looked drawn in on herself, but she wasn't making a move for the door handle.

"Whatever she said," he persisted. "It wasn't..." Damn him, this was already disintegrating into nonsense. "Ingrid has always been crazy. You don't need to—"

Hayden looked up at him, and he cut off. "You think she's crazy?"

His brow twitched down. "You don't?"

She returned her attention to her folded hands, where her fingers wrung against each other as if strangling the life out of each bone.

"I simply saw the way she scared you," he tried.

For a moment, she didn't say anything. "What was she talking about?" Hayden asked quietly. "Loki? Jormun...Jurmum...?"

"Jormungand." He felt as if he was betraying something by speaking the word, like he was buying into Ingrid's lunacy for even knowing the serpent's name.

"Jormungand." She repeated the term quietly, as if memorizing it. "What is that?"

Connor floundered, unsure where this was going. "Just an old myth."

"About?"

His mouth moved again. How could he tell her they were stories about the end of the world, ones his father bought into because he'd been torn up with grief about his mate's death? The tales Connor heard growing up made it sound like finding your mate was like finding the mirror of your soul, and sometimes, part of him even believed that. After all, he'd seen what happened to his father when his mother died. The old wolf might as well have died too—a fact that reminded Connor every day of the perils of ever letting himself be compromised the same way, given all the damage it had done to their clan. Moreover, how could he explain that his father had obviously needed *something* to give him a sense of stability with his mate gone, even if that something was totally irrational, and so the old wolf swallowed each one of Ingrid's lies.

Every street-corner preacher and babbling fool in history raved about the end of the world. And for all that he questioned his father's leadership at times and hated what the head of the Thorsen pack had become, Connor also rarely shared much about what his father believed, if only to protect the male.

Now Connor was supposed to share that with…with a stranger?

"Connor?" Hayden prompted, a worried note in her voice.

It wasn't just his father he was protecting, he admitted to himself. Even if he never saw Hayden again after this, he really didn't want her to leave thinking she'd narrowly escaped the asylum and all its ulfhednar inhabitants.

"It doesn't really matter," he said. "Ingrid tends to rely heavily on old stories as justification for—"

"You're not going to tell me?"

He froze at the hurt in her eyes.

"Th-there's nothing to tell," he stammered.

She took a breath, nodding, but he could see in her body language how she was pulling away from him and back inside herself. It was like the air was turning cold.

"But," he found himself saying. "I will, of course. If that's what you want. It's..." He searched for the right way to explain. "It's simply old myths, though. They don't pertain to anything."

"Old myths about what?" she pressed.

His mouth moved, and when he spoke, his voice sounded thin to his own ears. "The end of the world."

A shaky breath left her. She looked back down at her hands.

He gave a rough attempt at a chuckle. "See? It's nothing. I mean, if you want to collect some sandwich boards and ring bells saying the end is nigh, I'll join you, of course, but—"

"I might take you up on that," Hayden laughed weakly. "But, you know, only if you bring the bells."

She glanced up at him, an oddly pained sort of humor in her eyes. At a loss, Connor tried for a smile, and after a moment, she smiled as well.

To him, even that trace of her expression lit the vehicle like the sun.

"So," she continued. "Will you bring those the next time I see you, or...?"

The guarded hope in her eyes was like a dagger through his heart. He couldn't kill that. Couldn't watch it fade. But he shouldn't see her again. Being around her was...was...

Amazing.

But at his silence, she looked away, embarrassment filling her expression as she reached for the door handle.

"Yes."

Hayden looked back at his blurted response.

His mouth moved, trying to catch up with his racing thoughts. "I mean. No. I...I don't really own any sandwich boards."

She hesitated and let her hand fall from the door handle. Connor suddenly found himself breathing again.

"Well, that's too bad," she offered.

A chuckle left him. Her lip twitched.

But only for a moment.

"Connor, what else is in those stories?" she asked quietly.

Dammit. He should have said something to get them *off* this gods-be-damned topic.

She glanced over at him, her brow rising in question.

He scrubbed a hand through his hair. "They're myths. There are plenty of things in them, but...half of them are physically impossible and the rest are nonsense. And the myths about the end of the world—"

"Do they say when it's coming?"

He paused, confused. "Why would that—"

"Never mind. Sorry. I, um..." She glanced to her apartment building. "Maybe I should—"

"Hayden." He reached out, putting a hand to her arm, not pulling, not stopping her if she really wanted to leave.

But she paused all the same.

He could feel her tremble as she looked back toward him. Alarm crept through him. "What is it?" he prompted.

"You'll just think I'm crazy too," she said in a small voice.

Oh, gods. "No, I won't."

She didn't believe him. It was written in the sad, wry smile that crossed her face.

He stared at her, playing the conversation back to try to figure out why she would think he would believe that of her.

It was a short trip.

And the conclusion made no sense. Just because he thought those things of Ingrid didn't mean anything about Hayden. Why would she even suspect...

Unless there was more to what Ingrid said to her than he understood.

"Listen," he tried. "I...I don't like Ingrid. I think she's cruel and opportunistic, and she preys on people's weaknesses if she can find them. She's had her hooks in my father for fifteen years. But if there's something you..." He cleared his throat. "If I can help you somehow...?"

Hayden fidgeted.

"I-I'm not trying to pressure you," he amended. "You don't have to talk if you don't—"

"I have dreams." Hayden's words rushed out like she was throwing herself off a cliff. "About what Ingrid said. My..." She seemed to brace herself. "My whole life, I've had them. Almost every night. But...I've never told anyone, not since I was a little kid."

He hesitated, taken back. For her to tell him, then...

Connor slipped his hand down to hers. The trust she was showing him felt precious. Delicate. "What do you dream?" he asked gently.

"I see..." Hayden swallowed hard. "I see a man in a cave, chained up with metal made from...from the murder of his own kid."

Connor frowned. It sounded like she was dreaming old myths.

Hayden shifted on the seat, appearing uncomfortable, and he buried the expression.

"An eagle drips acid on his face, and he screams," she continued. "I dreamed that the night all those earthquakes happened. I see the world destroyed, and my home burned, and..." Her gaze flicked toward him, searching over his face for a moment in a peculiar way. "Other things."

He regarded her curiously as she looked away again. What did she mean by that?

"But when she said those things," Hayden continued. "I just..." She exhaled shortly. "How could she have known I dream that?"

Connor tightened his grip on her hand. He didn't know what to say. Ingrid got lucky? For all he knew, the female would have said that to anyone he brought to the manor.

Though why she'd mentioned the florist to him after he first met Hayden...

He shoved the thoughts down. He was being ridiculous. Whatever Hayden saw had to just be dreams, even if they were also the myths. And there had to be a rational explanation.

"When my mother was killed..." An old thorn of pain dug into him at the memory, and he pushed past it. "I dreamt so many horrible things. And perhaps, in your childhood you heard these stories, and whatever happened back then caused your mind to use that as a way of handling it."

"Yeah." She nodded, though he couldn't tell if she believed him. "Maybe."

Silence returned to the vehicle, and he didn't move to break it, watching as the digital clock on the dashboard ticked a minute away. He knew she'd be leaving soon, and there wasn't anything he could do about it. Nothing he even *should* do about it, since it wasn't like he would be staying in this town, regardless.

But his wolf was an idiot, and so was he.

"So…" Hayden began.

"Could I see you again?" he blurted.

She looked over at him. He didn't dare to breathe. He felt like a cub talking to a female for the first time, and his heart pounded loudly enough that he was certain she could hear because, the gods knew, he was being a fool.

But then, he wasn't going to be in town forever—which was a good thing, obviously—but he also wasn't leaving tonight. Or even tomorrow, most likely. And it was really rather foolish of him to just *avoid* her for weeks. That would be distracting too. Maybe even more than being around her. So it was logical, really, for them to spend time together, and since he knew it would end anyway, it wasn't like he would get too deeply involved.

He'd just be enjoying her company.

"I'd like that," she said quietly.

Inexplicable tension rushed from him, and he found himself grinning. "I would too."

A smile spread across her face and nearly took his breath away all over again. Gods, he loved the sight of that smile. It felt like sunlight on his skin.

"How about tomorrow?" he offered. "We could get coffee?"

She nodded. "That'd be great. Maybe around seven?"

"Seven, it is." He paused. "Though, I don't know any coffee shops around here."

"I'll take you to my favorite one."

Connor smiled. "Perfect."

11

HAYDEN

THE NEXT DAY, HAYDEN COULDN'T CONCENTRATE, NO MATTER how hard she tried. She flubbed ringing up an order of carnations for the Morrison twins. She forgot the store greeting when she answered the phone. If not for the fact that she *felt* fine, she would have been concerned she really did have a concussion.

"Are you sure you're okay to work, honey?" Johanna asked when Hayden hung up the phone. Walking over to the counter, the older woman set down a bundle of eucalyptus leaves and gave Hayden a worried look. "If you need to rest—"

"I'm good." Hayden managed a smile.

From the other side of the store, she could practically feel Lindy's skeptical gaze. When Hayden had come home the night before, her best friend hugged her like she'd thought Hayden died. But only moments afterward, Lindy became distracted—a reaction that only grew worse when Hayden told her of the date she had the following night.

She didn't understand it. But she also could barely concentrate on it.

Things hardly got better as the day went on. She survived the workday and got herself back to the apartment without breaking anything, but she still couldn't settle down. Thoughts rattled around in her head while she paced her bedroom, all of them bouncing back and forth between extremes like ping-pong balls. She couldn't wait to see Connor, really. The very sight of him was a turn-on, and to be spending time getting to know him too?

Incredible.

But she was *certain* she was making a huge mistake. Worse than that. She was kind of, sort of, almost betraying her family. After all, what would her parents think if they knew she was spending time with…with a wolf? What would they say if they knew she'd revealed what she was or told Connor even a shred of her history? Her whole life, they'd drilled into her that werewolves were a threat—predators at best, monsters who attacked children at worst. What her uncle went through…what her mother had seen…it was unspeakable. And while, sure, the wolves she met the day before had been surprisingly *not* monstrous, that didn't mean she should keep hanging out around them.

Or, when it came to Connor, maybe, possibly doing a hell of a lot more than "hanging out."

She turned away from her closet, her stomach churning. What had she been thinking, asking to see him again? She should call this off. Going anywhere with him *had* to be a mistake. It didn't matter that something inside her writhed with discontent at the thought of not seeing him again. That she felt an almost animal-like whine rising in her chest at the idea of staying away. If anything, that was more evidence he brought out something…*inhuman* in her and threatened her self-control.

Her family would be terrified for her if they realized all she was risking.

She rocked back and forth on her heels, her eyes straying to the pile of clothes on her bed, none of which seemed remotely appealing anymore. If she called him and canceled…that would be it. No more chance to learn about the wolves who lived only about twenty miles from town in a home inexplicably fit for kings. No more chance to learn *anything* about what she was. *Ulfhednar*, as he called it.

Hayden glanced at her laptop. She could just Google it. Maybe that would be enough. Sure, the few searches she'd done over the years, buried behind VPNs and private windows and whatever, hadn't turned up a damn thing besides fantasy stories and myths. But she had a word now.

She bit her lip. So then…she didn't need to do this. Didn't need to go out at all or see any of them ever again.

Including him.

Her eyes didn't leave her laptop while her fingers played with the hem of the latest sweater she'd tried on. Royal-blue chenille. Her favorite.

It'd be silly to keep wearing this if she just planned to cancel. And if she *did* cancel, she wouldn't need to feel like she was lying to her parents with every breath she—

The doorbell rang. She jumped a mile.

Maybe it wasn't him.

Running her fingers through her hair anxiously, she hurried to the door before Lindy could come out of her bedroom. Her stomach felt like it was full of bees. If it was Connor, she should probably just tell him to go away.

His smile stole her breath when she opened the front door.

"Hello," he said.

His voice sent shivers across her skin. He stood in the hall, his long black coat covering him, and the white collar of a button-down shirt peeking above the lapel. His clothes seemed to radiate money, and he looked out of place in the ramshackle hallway with its cheap fixtures and drab carpet that probably predated the internet.

"Hi." Her own voice sounded hoarse to her own ears.

He gave no sign of noticing. "You ready?"

Hayden's mouth moved. This was the moment, the one where she told the hot, incredible guy who'd sort of saved her life after she was hit by a car that, sorry, she needed to cancel after he'd come all this way.

"Yeah, I'm ready," her traitorous mouth said instead. Her arm reached over on autopilot, retrieving her coat from a hook on the wall. Shoving her phone, wallet, and keys into the oversized pockets, she stepped through the door and pulled it closed behind her.

"So," he said. "Where to?"

She took a breath, feeling like she'd run a marathon only in the past few moments. "Um—" She glanced toward the door again. Canceling now would be ridiculous.

It was only coffee.

"Right, um…" She smiled, turning back to him. "Pon-derRoasta. It's a café downtown."

"Sounds great."

He motioned for her to come with him, and, nervous-ness fluttering around in her stomach, she walked down the stairs and out the door. His SUV was parked by the curb, its black paint glistening under the street lamp, while snow fell all around them. She felt like they were in some kind of car commercial—the blissful, quiet type that marketed something to do with the holidays. Never mind that it was May. The vehicle was already warm when they climbed inside, and quietly, she directed him down the street.

"How long have you been in Mariposa?" Connor asked, his voice light like he was making polite conversation.

She cleared her throat. "Um, about ten years."

"You like it?"

Her shoulder twitched. "It's okay, I guess. When it's not freezing cold like this. There's normally a festival in the summer and—oh, turn in here." She pointed to the small building on the corner.

Connor steered the SUV around the turn and up into the tiny parking lot.

The cold air was crisp as they climbed from the vehicle. The coffee shop was situated in a converted bungalow, the walls painted bright teal and purple, and wind chimes hung from the eaves. Through the windows, golden light spilled out into the night, while inside, she could see a handful of people seated at the small round tables and several others waiting in line. Smells of coffee and chocolate, sugar and caramel wafted out onto the winter air when Connor pulled the wooden door open for her, and a thrill ran through Hayden as she walked in. For the first time in her life, someone else was probably picking up every single scent in the air, same as she was. It was such a small thing, she almost felt ridiculous.

But it didn't stop her from smiling.

Connor rubbed his hands together to warm them as

they got in line at the counter. "So," he said. "What do you recommend?"

"Well...I like the hot chocolate. But I tend to put a lot of pepper in it, so you might want to try the—"

"Sounds delicious."

Something inside her chest warmed.

The customers ahead of them moved to the waiting area for their drinks, and she stepped up to the register. She felt like her face was red as a stoplight while she placed her order, and her mouth probably looked absurd from all of the grinning, but she couldn't help herself.

A few minutes later, the drinks were ready, and the two of them found a table in the corner near the front window.

"So," she tried, her hands wrapped around her cup like it was a stabilizer. "What about you? Where are you from?"

Connor took a drink of his hot chocolate and then cleared his throat. "Lately, a small town north of Anchorage, Alaska. Not even much of a town, really."

"Like the..." She nodded in the general direction of his luxurious home.

"The manor, yes. But with some—" He glanced to the tables around them, but no one seemed to be listening. "—humans nearby," he finished quietly.

She absorbed the information. "Are there others, you know, like us there?"

"Some. Cousins, other packs, a few loners." He paused. "It's safer so far north. Hopefully, we'll be heading back that way soon."

Hayden looked down at her drink, unsure how to respond. "Your friends sounded like you all spent some time, um...camping? Was that fun?"

Connor scratched his cheek and then took another sip of his hot chocolate, and she couldn't help but feel like it was all an attempt to buy time. "We went because of my father," he finally said. "About a year and a half ago, he came to my friends and I and told us that we needed to leave. Survival training, he said. He didn't explain why. But, as a result, we spent eighteen months in the wilderness."

Silence fell between them when he finished. She glanced around, but no one else in the café was paying them any attention, and their words seem to have been lost underneath the hum of conversations, the clank of glasses, and the hiss-thump of the espresso machine. "That, um… seems like it would've been hard," she managed.

He shrugged. "We've lived outside before, though never for that long. It was difficult, but we had each other."

She shifted a little bit in the seat. "You guys are pretty close, then."

He nodded. "We've all known each other since we were c—children."

She wondered what word he'd been about to say.

"Most of my friends don't have any other family," Connor continued. "Things haven't been good for those like us for some time. That's part of why we prefer Alaska. Why, with most of our kind…" He drew a breath, and there was something pointed in his gaze when he continued. "You don't find many of us around here anymore."

She looked down, tightening her hands around the warmth of her drink. "What happened to their families?" Her voice felt small beneath the rush of the espresso machine and the murmur of pleasant conversations around her.

He was quiet for a moment. "It depends. Some groups

have become aware of our kind over the years, and... they've not taken it well." He grimaced. "They want to destroy us, in point of fact. And then there are those who simply seem to view *any* wolf as a threat. Hunters, ranchers. People like that."

She gulped down some hot chocolate and set her cup back down, her insides trembling with tension she didn't know how to address. No one knew what had happened to her family. For a long time, she hadn't even thought she had one—not a wolf one, anyway. But now—

His hand brushed her fingers where they clutched her drink. She tensed, looking up and meeting his eyes.

"Sorry," she managed. "Not exactly light conversation, is it?"

He shook his head. "It's okay."

"I just have so many questions," she said, her voice sounding a little desperate to her own ears.

He paused. "Do you remember anything?"

She swallowed hard, searching for the right words. "Not really. Some people found me at a rest stop off the highway, all alone. Just a little kid in a pink sweater with a burn on her arm and no idea of anything but her first name." Her eyes drifted to the other café patrons. "Pretty pathetic, right?"

He instantly made a disagreeing noise, and his fingers pulled hers from the cup.

She gripped his hand, still watching the café. "They never found any reports of fires or car accidents. Nobody came looking for me or called the cops or adoption agencies. There was just...nothing."

He was silent for a minute. "I'm sorry."

She shrugged. "It happens, right? That's what I figure. This kind of thing happens."

"Yeah, maybe."

Silence returned, and the sounds of the café felt far away. She took a breath. "God, listen to me. I'm really not good at this...you know, small-talk thing. I don't—" She cut off, frowning. Good Lord, did she want to just seem more pathetic by the moment?

"You don't what?"

"Go out like this much."

He chuckled. "Me, either."

Hayden glanced up at him and felt a smile tug her lips in spite of herself.

"But," he continued, "you live around here now. Family and all that?"

She nodded. "Been here for a while. Just graduated, actually. Or, you know, I will, once they get done with all paperwork and whatever."

"Congratulations."

"Thanks. So, did you go to college or...?" Awkwardness hit her, and she trailed off, concerned he might think she was judging him if he said no.

"Master's degree a few years ago," he replied. "Online MBA program through the University of Illinois, of all things."

"Illinois? From all the way in Alaska?"

He shrugged, grinning. "Before that, it was tutors hired by my father and whatever books I could scrounge from the library."

Hayden chuckled, recalling the library she'd seen. "Probably had your fair share of options there."

And probably explained why he sometimes spoke like someone from another century.

She kept the thought to herself, still smiling. She kind of liked it.

"True enough," he agreed.

"So why the MBA?"

"I concluded it was the best way to help the family business."

She waited, but nothing else came. "Which is...?"

He seemed slightly uncomfortable. "Little of this, little of that. My father has investments in a number of places. Or, he did. It's all rather up in the air right now."

She nodded, but things fell silent between them for a moment.

"So what's the plan now that you've graduated?" he asked as if pressing onward.

"Uh, well, my boss, Johanna, actually offered to let me take over the flower shop when she retires in a couple years."

His brow rose.

"It's pretty exciting for me," she admitted. "I love the shop. It's...well, you know. Easy to breathe in there. Calming. And I like the artistry with all the arrangements and everything, and a lot of the customers have been coming there so long, they're like family, so that's good too. But Johanna's offer is why I focused a lot on economics and business in college. Whatever I'd need to make sure the shop stays successful."

"Nice." He looked impressed.

She blushed. "But yeah, I mean, before that all happens, I'm going to take some time off. Travel a little bit with the money I've saved up, or..." Her shoulder rose and fell.

"Where to?"

"I don't know. Europe if I can afford it. Maybe Canada if I can't. We went up to Vancouver when I was a kid, but I haven't been back since."

"Ever thought about Alaska?" He gave her a little half smile that made her insides go all gooey.

She dropped her gaze back to her hot chocolate, her cheeks burning. "Alaska would be nice."

The conversation continued, meandering through favorite foods and movies—many of which she was shocked to find he hadn't seen—and on to local restaurants that she enjoyed. When next she looked up, a barista was stopping by their table to let them know the café was going to be closing in five minutes, and suddenly, she realized hours had gone by.

Laughing and holding refills of their hot chocolate, she and Connor returned to the SUV, the vehicle nearly alone in the dark parking lot. The streets were likewise empty, with all the shops and restaurants long since closed for the evening. As the snow drifted down, it was like they were the only two people left in the world, but in the warmth of the SUV, she felt as safe as if she were in her apartment.

Connor pulled the SUV to a stop in front of her building. "I had a good time tonight," he said, putting the vehicle in park.

She smiled. "I did too."

"Do you think—" He turned to face her in the seat. "—perhaps you'd like to do this again?" A hint of uncertainty touched his voice.

She hesitated. All her reasons for saying no felt like a distant clamor in her mind, and so the truth won out. "Very much."

His smile made something in her chest flutter like a bird, and she felt her cheeks warming in response. She should get out of the car, she knew. Go back inside. That was the safe thing, the smart thing. But something inside her seemed to be moving her body in spite of herself, practically begging her to reach out...just reach out...

Her hand crept over, touching his, the backs of her fingers straying along the backs of his own. The warmth of his skin made her heart quiver, and even the faint contact was electric.

Connor's other hand rose, gently brushing a strand of hair from her cheek. A question flickered through his expression, and in response, her fingers moved, taking up his wrist while her eyes never left his. She lifted his hand to her lips, breathing deeply to inhale his spicy scent. The effect was intoxicating, and she faltered, uncertain at the rush that coursed through her simply from smelling him. Trying to cover her reaction, she placed a light kiss on the inside of his wrist.

Desire darkened his silver eyes, and a thrill shot through her at the sight. Her heart pounded, all her uncertainty pushed to the background as he drew her toward him, and when his lips claimed hers, the contact sent pure heat rushing down between her legs.

She opened her lips to him, and his tongue plundered her mouth while he devoured her. The scent of him surrounded her like an aphrodisiac, and she couldn't have enough. It seemed to fill her, entering her lungs and imprinting on every cell in her body, setting fire to the pure need heating up inside her.

Her pulse flying, she broke from his lips, and on instinct, she leaned her head back and to the side, exposing her neck in a gut-deep gesture that somehow felt like equal parts submission and invitation, even if she couldn't explain why.

But at her motion, a hungry growl escaped Connor. The leather seat creaked as he shifted around in it, moving to be closer even as he drew her toward him. His teeth nipped at her neck, and she gasped, wet for him and desperate with desire. His hand slipped under her chenille sweater, only to pause, every muscle in his body tensing. "Is this—"

"Yes," she whispered. "God, yes. More, Connor. Please."

He didn't wait a moment longer. His hand slid up her side, pushing beneath her bra to embrace her breast. As he massaged her soft flesh, his mouth traced a hot line up the side of her throat, and she gasped in the darkness, clutching his coat. His fingers teased at her nipple, stoking the heat inside her. She wanted him on top of her. Inside her. Wanted these clothes away so he could take her right—

Headlights flashed across her eyes, blinding her for a heartbeat and jolting her back to reality. Connor turned, snarling with his teeth bared for an instant before he ducked his face away. Blinking fast, he withdrew his hand from her breast.

The car sped by without slowing, giving no sign the driver had even noticed them.

Hayden stared after it, shaking. What the hell was she doing? Having sex on the first date was fine for other people, but things weren't that simple for her. She'd been worried about simply *going out* with this guy, and now she was going to lose whatever shred of control she had left and sleep with him just like that?

God, she wanted to...right now.

"Sorry," Connor said, sounding breathless. "I shouldn't—"

"What?" She turned to him, alarmed.

He looked up at her, a new question on his face.

"You're not upset?"

She stared at him, at a loss for how to begin to explain. "No." Not at him. "I mean…" Her mouth moved. "No."

Connor nodded. "Then, uh…" He sat back in the driver's seat and raked a hand through his hair. "I don't suppose you'd want to, you know…do this again?"

God, yes.

She bashed the thought down. This was a bad plan. She should back out right this second, just like she'd been planning to do before he even showed up tonight.

Nothing inside her wanted to comply with that logic. "Um…"

"Get dinner, maybe?" he continued. "Or see one of those movies you talked about?"

Oh.

She bit her lip. That wasn't unreasonable, certainly? A movie. Dinner.

Sex in the backseat.

Hayden shifted on the leather, ordering herself to focus. She couldn't sleep with him. That was too much, too far, too goddamn dangerous. But movies and dinner would be fine. After all, those would basically take place totally in public, and she wasn't about to be an exhibitionist. So that would be entirely safe. And it wasn't as if she didn't have more questions about…well, everything in his world.

She could control herself.

"Yeah." She nodded. "That'd be great."

His smile was radiant. "What about tomorrow?"

Her head bobbed again. "Tomorrow."

"Perfect."

Silence fell between them, growing in awkwardness as the seconds slipped by.

"I, um…guess I should go," she said.

He made a neutral noise. She reached for the door handle, but Connor caught her other hand. She glanced back.

Never taking his eyes from hers, he lifted it and placed a kiss on the inside of her wrist, a gentle brush of his lips that nonetheless felt like it shot pure heat straight to her core. "Tomorrow, then."

God, this was going to be harder than she thought.

12

CONNOR

THE WOLF INSIDE CONNOR WHINED AS HE WATCHED HAYDEN walk back to her apartment building. Odin's eye, he wanted to go after her. Bring her to the manor. Hell, bring her to the rear of the SUV and thrust himself into her until she screamed as she came. His pulse was still flying from the feeling of her breast in his hand, her mouth on his own, and the sounds of desire she'd made at his touch. The smell of her arousal lingered in the air and made thinking damn near impossible. He wanted her. His wolf...gods, it demanded her now, no excuses or delays.

Mine...

He shuddered, clenching his hands on the steering wheel. She wasn't his. He barely knew her. They'd only met two days ago, and by all the gods, he needed to get himself under control if—

My mate.

"Fuck!" He wrenched his hands on the wheel and heard the steering column creak. She. Was. Not. His. Mate.

That was never going to happen—with her or anyone else.

At the door of her apartment building, Hayden paused, looking back at him. He tensed, wondering if she'd heard his shout, praying that she walked inside and didn't come back.

And that she would come back...right now...and get in the rear seat of the SUV because, by all the gods in all the realms, he needed to—

She gave a small wave and then disappeared into her apartment building.

He closed his eyes and fumbled blindly for the window control, rolling them all down so he could breathe without smelling her on the air. The bitter cold sapped the warmth from the vehicle immediately, but it cooled his blood and helped him focus as well.

Who needed a cold shower when winter encased the world?

He exhaled, opening his eyes again and ordering himself to focus. This had been a mistake. Going out with her, getting to know her, coming within a dozen *miles* of her...

His wolf whimpered, wanting to go after her that instant.

He snarled at it and put the SUV into gear. Pulling away from the curb sharply, he resisted the urge to floor the gas pedal as he took off down the empty road.

The town fell behind him, and dark forest roads took its place as he flew out of Mariposa at a speed just this side of reckless. But no one was out. No one stopped him. Even the police were probably asleep by now, and only the nocturnal forest creatures moved about in the world.

And him. Driving too fast. Because he had the hots for a female.

His teeth ground. That's all it was, really. Too long with no one available to him. Kirsi and Luna weren't options. They were like sisters to him, not potential bedmates. And as for the females he'd briefly dated in Alaska—before his father sent him off on his involuntary exile—they'd certainly been pleasant in their own ways and fun to share a bed with, but never once had his wolf reacted to them beyond mild interest. Meanwhile, none of the other wolves in their pack were even close to his age, and he didn't really see the whole "cougar" appeal.

So he was simply being irrational. Too long at sea, as it were. And so was his wolf.

Because it didn't believe a word of that.

He wrung his hands on the steering wheel. His options were limited. To stop seeing her was the obvious choice, though even *without* the wolf howling in his mind at the thought, he wasn't a fan of that. Cutting things off with her now would be hurtful, and something inside him shriveled at the idea of causing her pain. And, true, he'd have to leave eventually when the wolves returned to Alaska, but…that was a known factor. It wouldn't seem personal. It wouldn't hurt her.

Or him.

Much.

Connor drew a breath of the cold night air and steered the SUV onto the road to the manor. If he kept the fact he was leaving in mind, then seeing her again wouldn't necessarily be terrible. Yes, it had felt like a bad plan in the heat—gods help him—of the moment, but that was before he realized what was going on. She wasn't his mate. All those old, romanticized myths of wolves simply *knowing* their mates upon sight...that was bullshit. He didn't believe in fairy tales. And while, sure, she was a female to whom he was deeply attracted—and who seemed pretty damn attracted to him as well, thank the gods—he'd simply been too long without anyone in his bed, which left his wolf irrational and confused about what the hell it was feeling.

That was all.

So he could control this. He could make sure she knew he'd be leaving and that they would have to go their separate ways eventually, so that neither of them had any false expectations. They could enjoy each other's company, enjoy anything else that came of it too, and eventually part on good terms when it came time for this to be over.

All he had to do was keep his wolf side from taking command of his mouth or doing anything stupid.

He pulled up to the manor gate and flexed his hands on the steering wheel.

Simple.

His wolf wanted this to be anything but simple.

Somehow, Connor made it through the next week. He saw Hayden almost every evening, whether it was to go out to dinner or to watch a movie or simply to revisit that café. Since their first non-date or whatever that had been, he felt like they were dancing around each other, neither of them coming too close, as if she, too, wasn't certain she wanted to take that step in their...whatever this was.

He couldn't say relationship. They didn't have one, no matter what his wolf growled in the background of his mind.

But he liked Hayden. She was smart and beautiful and had a terrific sense of humor. He suspected he'd laughed more in the past week than he had in a decade. Somehow, she made him feel more comfortable among humans than he ever would have imagined possible, as if—with her there—the two of them *fit* in that alien world in a way that almost seemed...natural.

And, to his great surprise, he rather loved it.

Every day, he found himself distracted by thoughts of when he would see her next, of what activity they would be enjoying. The simple memory of her smile filled him with a warmth he could barely describe and would never have anticipated, as if her happy expressions were sunlight to a plant or a breeze on a summer's day. He found himself watching the clock, thinking of her, wondering how her day was going or whether she was thinking of him too. His thoughts often drifted to what she might enjoy doing next, or what he could do to make her laugh or grin.

And, of course, to what she would look like naked, her head thrown back in ecstasy, her luscious mouth moaning with pleasure, and her body convulsing with the orgasm he—

"Connor, you hearing me?"

He blinked, looking at Wes across the kitchen island. "What?"

The male chuckled. "I was saying, Tyson confirmed the security cameras in sector eighteen are working again, and Marrok and Kirsi will be out with your father's guards tonight on patrol. We're secure."

Connor nodded and took a gulp from the coffee mug in his hand. He could feel his friend's amused gaze on him. "Good," he said, not meeting Wes's eyes.

"When are you picking her up?"

Connor set down the cup. He hadn't told anyone his new obsession with the security of their border walls had anything to do with Hayden. He was fairly certain his visit to the small cabin on the western edge of their property today had gone unnoticed too. For that matter, there was no guarantee she'd want to change their plans tonight, regardless.

But Wes was no idiot, and Connor wasn't about to lie to his friend, anyway.

"Seven. When she gets off work."

Wes made a neutral sound, nodding. "Better get going, then. Sunset's only an hour or so after that."

Connor looked up sharply, and Wes's lips twitched in a smile. Without another word, the male walked out of the kitchen.

A breath left Connor. Gods, he was transparent.

He downed the rest of the coffee and then deposited the mug in the sink. Scrubbing a hand through his hair, he made a brief detour to the bathroom to brush the coffee smell from his breath, and then headed for the garage. The space was like a small warehouse filled with SUVs and sports cars and even a few vintage army trucks his father kept around. Ignoring all of it, he walked to his own vehicle and climbed inside, grateful to have avoided anyone else as he left.

Tonight would be fine.

He thumbed the garage door opener. True, he hadn't cleared this plan with Hayden, but...surprises were the spice of life, or whatever that human saying happened to be.

Worst case scenario, they went out to dinner a bit late.

He steered the SUV onto the road. Who was he kidding? He'd gathered she wasn't quite comfortable with all this. Worst case scenario, she never wanted to speak to him again.

Maybe he was making a mistake.

Doubt gnawed at him as he continued along the winding road toward Mariposa, accomplishing nothing except to make his stomach churn. Maybe he should have just brought flowers as a surprise instead.

Flowers for the female who worked in the flower shop. Genius.

He pulled to a stop in front of the store. He'd met Johanna a few days before and waved now as she spotted him through the windows. A kindly woman, as humans came, and clearly one who cared about her workers. Of Hayden's friend Lindy, he couldn't say much. She seemed friendly and polite in a detached sort of way, but he hadn't seen much of her. Even when he came to the apartment door to meet Hayden a few nights prior, she'd simply tossed him a smile before vanishing into her own room.

Hayden appeared at the flower shop door, waving over her shoulder to Johanna and Lindy before hurrying out to the SUV. He drew a breath as she climbed in. After a day in the shop, her scent was a complex mix of myriad blossoms, spice from her favorite drink, and an aroma he'd come to think of as simply *her*.

"Hey there," Hayden said as she pulled the door closed behind her. "You looking forward to Italian tonight?"

He braced himself. "Actually, I was wondering if I could change our plans a bit?"

She gave him a curious look.

"Surprise you," he continued. "If that's okay?"

At her silence, he resisted the urge to walk back the whole statement and agree that Italian sounded wonderful. It did, but—

"Okay," she agreed slowly.

He started breathing again. Giving her a smile, he put the SUV back in gear.

The town passed without him noticing it too closely while his thoughts spun about whether she would balk at what he was about to suggest. Over the past week, though, he'd become familiar with the streets and neighborhoods of Mariposa, until now he knew his way around without requiring GPS or other directions. The road leading away from town was likewise familiar: a winding ribbon of dark asphalt amid stark white snow and stalwart trees. When at last he reached the turnoff, he glanced over to see her eyeing the woods around them, tension lining her face.

Connor swallowed hard and pulled the SUV into the secluded parking lot. "Okay," he said as he put the vehicle into park near the edge of the woods. "If you want to turn around and go to dinner as we planned, that's fine. We can do that. But—" He drew a quick breath. "—the full moon is coming in only a few days. I can feel it, and I know you can too."

She shifted on the seat, looking uncomfortable.

"I know it's your business and none of mine," he pressed onward. "But...it worries me, you being out in the woods alone. And I thought that perhaps—"

Hayden shook her head. Hope drained from him.

"I don't," she said.

He hesitated, confused. "Don't...?"

She wetted her lips, and his wolf made a hungry noise inside his mind at the sight. He ordered it to silence, staying focused on her.

"I don't go outside," she said quietly.

"What?"

She shifted around on the leather seat again. "I go to

my parents' house. To the basement there. They have a cage—"

At his sudden intake of breath, she cut off.

"*Cage?*" He barely recognized his own voice. The growl carried through it, though, that he knew. The wolf inside of him wanted to find those people and rip their throats out. They *caged* this beautiful female in the basement of their home?

They were dead.

"It's not what you think," Hayden replied.

"*How?* How is it not—"

"I'm keeping them safe."

He stared at her, trying to process the words past his rage. "What?"

Hayden drew a breath as if steadying herself. "I used to just be down there when, you know, I needed to..." She looked uncomfortable, as if she was discussing relieving herself or something equally private. "But I didn't think that was safe enough. If something happens and I lose control, I could hurt them. So I had them do this to protect them...and anybody else."

"But..." He shook his head, still lost. "Why would you ever worry you might hurt someone like that?" A new thought came to him, chilling and horrible. "*Have* you done that?"

"No. Never."

He scrubbed a hand over his face. "Then why, in all the realms, would you think you would—"

Hayden made an irritated noise. "It's a long story. Mom and Dad weren't fans of it, but I insisted. Just in case."

Connor blinked at her, flabbergasted. Her idea. A *cage*...the epitome of everything their kind feared...was her idea. And for her whole life—

Shock coursed through him. "Wait. But that means you've never...Outside, you've never..."

"Only in the basement."

He couldn't begin to wrap his head around the thought. To *never* have run through the countryside or felt the wind in her fur or...

A breath left him. His plan had just gone from protecting her to something far more significant.

If she'd agree to it.

He inhaled slowly, trying to make himself calm down, and then he reached out, resting a hand on hers. "Would you like to?"

She looked up at him, and he could see the fear in her eyes. He knew she could still say no. That she could back out, change her mind, and insist they somehow go to dinner and pretend this conversation had never occurred. It was her life, not his, and if this was really too much, then—

"Yes," she whispered.

Elation filled him. He gripped her hand for a moment as he pushed the car door open. "Then we will. We can—"

"Wait."

He froze, his joy faltering. She looked like prey, suddenly indecisive about which way to run.

"I-I mean, is it safe here?" Hayden glanced around like hunters were going to burst from the trees. "I mean, we're in the open and—"

"We're on my family's land—or close to it. There's a wall about ten yards beyond that line of trees, and a gate onto our property too." He put both his hands over hers, willing reassurance into his voice. "There are cameras on the walls. They'll be watching for us, and watching to make sure nobody follows either. And the gate seals itself automatically. No one can get through it without permission." He smiled. "We'll be safe."

She drew a shaky breath, and then she nodded like someone agreeing to leap from a high dive. "Okay."

He climbed from the vehicle and glanced around. Marrok and Kirsi would be patrolling somewhere nearby, as would a number of his father's people, spurred on by the old wolf's paranoia if not Connor's need for utmost security tonight. Beyond the wall, there were monitors for everything from body heat to noise layered across the property, and enough high-definition cameras to track a mosquito in flight. Even on the road leading to this place, they'd secretly installed the devices, meaning no one could get within a mile of this parking lot without someone at the manor seeing.

Hayden would be safe.

He put a smile back on his face as he looked over at her. Standing on the opposite side of the SUV, she eyed the forest as if she'd never set foot outdoors in her life.

"So I just..." Her eyes twitched around. "I mean, we're going to...out here?"

"Would it help if I turned around?"

She nodded immediately. He bowed his head slightly and turned his back.

The faint rustle of fabric reached his ears, as did her shallow breaths. He swallowed, his cock hardening immediately.

A tingling sensation passed over his skin in a wave, carrying from behind him. He resisted the urge to glance back, waiting for her.

Gravel crunched softly to his right. A tiny whimper followed. He looked down, and his mouth dropped open slightly before he caught himself.

She was beautiful. Her fur was mostly gray, like dried wood, but carried hints of white like winter snow. She was slender, almost delicate.

And her eyes were liquid gold.

The wolf inside of him thrashed, demanding he lose this awkward human shape *right the fuck now*. He wanted to nuzzle her. Smell her with all of his strength. He wanted to chase her through the woods, breathe in the scent of her desire, and mount her because she was his. She had to be his.

Except…she wasn't.

Connor exhaled sharply, pushing the clamoring of his wolf away and ordering himself to concentrate. He could handle this. Shifting. Being around her. She deserved to experience running through the woods and living as her other self without him turning this into anything more. He and his wolf could do this.

For her.

Hayden made an anxious sound, regarding him with a trepidation like perhaps she'd picked up on the direction his thoughts had taken. But still, she didn't bolt. She only waited.

She trusted him, and the realization filled his chest like the dawn.

"Ready?" he asked her.

Her head bobbed in agreement.

Connor grinned.

13

HAYDEN

HAYDEN WATCHED CONNOR SMILE AND KNEW THAT, IF A WOLF could blush, she'd be as red as a cherry. There was such promise in the way he looked at her that it sent shivers coursing through her body.

Not to mention the heat she'd seen in his eyes.

Clearing his throat, Connor glanced around again and then moved to collect her clothes from where she'd left them on the hood of the vehicle. After bundling them into the backseat quickly, he moved to take off his coat.

She ducked her face away, her breath catching as— from the corner of her eye—she saw his white shirt join the black coat on the backseat of the SUV.

Her gaze crept back toward him.

Oh, holy hell, he was hot.

She turned away again, her fleeting glimpse of his well-toned torso emblazoned behind her eyes. But he hadn't watched her, so she probably shouldn't watch him either.

At least...she was pretty sure he hadn't.

The urge to look back a second time made her close her eyes, if only to hang onto her last shred of self-control. Yes, this incredibly sexy man was getting undressed *quite* literally in front of her, but that didn't mean she should gawk.

Surely, though, he would have moved away if he hadn't *wanted* her to gawk?

She kept her eyes closed, but that didn't stop her nose from catching his scent stronger than ever before. It made her body quiver and her insides heat like a furnace. But beyond that was more. Was *everything*. The breeze twisted past, heavy-laden with scents more potent than her human form had ever perceived…

A thud came as the car door shut, and then the sound of his bare feet on the gravel followed. She bit back the whimper that wanted to rise in her throat, even as she heard him rustling around near the SUV. He'd be naked if she opened her eyes; she just knew it. But then even those sounds fell silent, and suddenly a bizarre tingling sensation passed through the air around her.

Confused, she opened her eyes.

The black wolf in front of her stole her breath away. His eyes shone in the sunset, turning the rainbow colors of the ending day to countless tones of silver, and when he stepped toward her, his lips parted to reveal long white fangs.

Slowly, he paced around her. She didn't dare move, because even if she knew nothing of what to expect next, somehow, she knew that if she ran, he would chase her.

She just couldn't decide if that was a bad thing.

Shivers coursed through her, driven by anticipation as much as trepidation. Her whole life, when she shifted, she'd merely curled up and slept it off in the basement.

She'd never run. Never even gone outside, considering—at the time—it had seemed suicidal. But now, with him here...

If he chased her...if he *caught* her...then what?

The shivers grew stronger, and the wolf behind her made a huffing sound.

That was all it took.

She bolted for the woods. Connor made an eager noise behind her, and she could hear the gravel as his paws shoved through it, gaining purchase to tear after her. She raced past the tree line and bounded over fallen logs covered in snow. Scents filled the world, painting a map behind her eyes that unfolded at the speed of thought. This way, a rabbit. That way, a deer. Humans had passed by along the trail hours before, probably hiking near the wall —and there it was.

She slowed, staring up at the old stonework of the massive wall blocking her path. It had to be fifteen feet high at least, though it was hard to judge in wolf form. Iron spikes formed a fence along the top and small black cameras perched like tiny ravens at intervals up there. Several yards to her left, a gate that looked strong enough to withstand a battering ram was sealed shut, giving no hint of what lay beyond it.

Snow whispered beside her, a hiss of tiny flakes rustling, and she flinched, glancing over to find Connor there. He made a huffing sound again, different than the one before. Questioning, gentle, and somehow she just *knew* he was confirming she was still all right.

She hesitated, unsure not only of what to respond but even *how* to do it. She felt like part of her brain had become foreign, and the messages it sent made no sense. His movements were like language and part of her mind seemed able to translate it, telling her he was concerned, telling her—even as he paced in front of her, his steel-colored eyes tracking her—that he wasn't a threat.

He was worried about her.

She struggled not to whimper, worried too. What was this? This weird method of communication? She'd never experienced this, down in the basement when she'd shift form to be a wolf.

All alone.

Gently, Connor nuzzled and nipped at her, and on instinct, she butted her head against the side of his. A heartbeat after she moved, she hesitated, unsure what she'd just done. What had she told him in whatever language this seemed to be?

But he simply looked back at her, and, even if she couldn't understand a thing of what was happening, she could still read his eyes. Kind. Pleased. Reassuring to her, even, as if he was trying to tell her this was all right.

He turned and nudged her slightly before pacing toward the gate. Nervous, she trailed after him. Before the massive entrance, he paused, glancing toward the cameras tucked high up on either side.

A thunk came from within the door. Slowly, the gate swung open.

An open stretch of empty field waited beyond, a swath of untouched white snow surrounded by rolling hills and dense forest. The landscape rose, surreal in its beauty, toward mountains bathed by the sunset in myriad shades of gold and pink and purple.

Her breath left her, and something inside her instantly yearned to run. And this was his land, Connor had said. His family's territory, guarded by those he trusted. She could race across this beautiful expanse and never worry, because they'd be safe.

Safe...when she'd always been so afraid.

Connor paced a few steps ahead of her and then glanced back, eagerness radiating from him, and the language-that-was-not-language in her mind heard the invitation.

A soft whine escaped her, and she shifted her weight nervously. But she'd be okay. He'd promised.

And, after all, it was just for one night.

Hayden took a deep breath and raced with him across the snow.

Her white dress glistening as if it glowed from within, the woman stood over her. A breeze stirred the woman's long dark hair where it hung around her face like a curtain, though no breath of air touched Hayden's skin. With a shimmering hand, she reached down and gently cupped Hayden's cheek, her eyes filled with heartbroken sorrow.

"The end is coming," she whispered. "The dead will rise and the world will fall."

Hayden's eyes flew open, chills rushing over her skin, but the woman was gone. The sun beamed through a small window ahead of her, and the sound of chirping birds came from beyond the frosted glass. The scent of wood and wool hung on the air, and flecks of dust danced like crystals in the morning light. She was in a small room with an array of military-looking crates nearby and log walls on all sides, curled up on a low-lying bed beneath a pile of thick blankets.

And she was naked.

She froze, memory coming back. They'd run through the night until, at last, Connor brought her to a small cabin clinging to the shadows of the woods and at the edge of a snowy field that had shone silver-white in the moonlight. Nudging the door open, he'd led her inside, where they curled up beneath the blankets and away from the cold.

And some time in her sleep, as she had done every month for years, she shifted back to human form.

Except this time, she was miles from where she'd left her clothes.

And Connor's arm was curled over her side.

Scarcely daring to breathe, she glanced around quickly. They were alone in here. No strange woman watched them. No sounds but those of nature came from beyond the walls. And she was at a loss for what to do. She could shift back to wolf form, maybe. She'd never tried shifting so soon again after already having done it, and her body felt tired at the mere thought. But unless, somehow, there were clothes in those crates, what else was she—

Connor stirred behind her, and she felt his bare skin brush against hers. Heat spread through her core at the simple contact, and a tiny gasp escaped her.

He paused. "Sorry." His voice sounded choked. "I'll move. Just—"

Of its own accord, her hand grabbed his wrist, stopping him as he started to pull away.

What was she doing? She'd just had a dream with that bizarre woman again, who—for all she knew—could be lurking around somewhere nearby. Meanwhile, she was lying naked in an isolated cabin with a guy she'd only met a week before.

His arm eased back down against her, his palm flattening against her midsection. Her breath quivered. The heat of his body felt like a banked fire near her skin. His scent wrapped around her, thick with arousal. Desire pooled inside her, responding to him even as her mind raced.

"Is this okay?" he asked softly.

It had to be. She needed this more than she had words to say.

Hayden twitched her head in a small nod. "Yes." Her voice was a whisper, and carefully, she guided him lower along her body, knowing she couldn't have stopped herself if she tried. "Is this?"

He drew closer, and his soft answer stirred her hair, his breath warm in the cold cabin. "Yes."

His fingers slipped between her legs, and she inhaled sharply. Connor paused.

A protesting sound left her, and she pushed back against him, feeling his hard cock against her.

He made a hungry, desperate noise: part growl, part groan, and easily the hottest thing she'd ever heard. Quickly, he shifted around on the bed, pushing her hair aside with one hand. His lips found the back of her neck, kissing her, nipping at her, while the fingers of his other hand massaged tight little circles across her clit.

Her breathing sped up and her body rocked, torn between driving herself against his skillful fingers and grinding against his cock. Her leg moved, rising to give him access, and her nipples hardened with the desire to feel him thrusting inside her.

A gasp left him. His mouth traced a hot line along the

side of her throat, but he didn't move to penetrate her. Instead, his hand slipped deeper between her legs, his fingers pushing inside her and finding her g-spot, crooking against it and massaging her expertly. Short gasps escaped her as tingling heat built inside her and the cabin faded away. There were only his deft motions, his lips on her neck, and the hot scent of their bodies together. Only the thrum of pleasure coursing through her, radiating up from where he worked her body over and over and...

The orgasm took her, washing away the world. Her muscles clenched around his fingers, and she cried out, unable to contain herself while ecstasy rocketed through her, leaving her body quivering in its wake.

Panting, she sagged against him, her heart pounding. But Connor didn't stay still. His tongue flicked across the edge of her earlobe, surprising her with the desire it instantly awakened all over again. Shifting around behind her, he pulled away for a moment only to return, rolling her onto her back and then bracing himself above her.

She stared up at him, and her breasts tingled with anticipation at the dark desire in his eyes.

God, yes.

Her hand reached down, finding his hardness suspended above her, and her legs fell to either side, opening her to him. She couldn't stop herself. Yes, he was a wolf like her. Yes, that made him dangerous.

But she needed him inside her. She craved him filling her in a way that made her feel more animal than human.

Her mate.

The thought was a distraction. It wasn't anything she recognized. And it didn't matter.

She needed him now.

But at her touch, Connor's face tightened, and he pulled away slightly. Her brow furrowed with confusion.

Swiftly, he lowered himself and kissed her, hot and deep, before he drew away just as quickly. "I'm not done," he said.

A smile tugged at the corner of his mouth, and a heady promise filled his eyes. Without another word, he moved down her body and pushed her legs farther apart, lifting one to brace it on his shoulder.

Understanding hit her.

Oh, yes, please.

His tongue traced a line through the soft folds of her flesh and then slipped around her pleasure-swollen clit. She lurched at the contact, gasping with the intensity of the pleasure it woke in her, and she heard him chuckle even as he didn't move away. With one hand, he reached along the length of her torso and encircled her breast, massaging it while his mouth kept up its hot motions.

Her fingers fisted the surface of the bed beneath her in a desperate effort to keep still. Frantic gasps left her as every inch of her body seemed to come to life and every nerve attuned itself to his expert ministrations. She was wet from more than him, and if he'd entered her then, she felt like she'd die of ecstasy.

"God," she breathed. "Oh, God, Connor. *Connor...*"

He pinched her nipple, and the sudden jolt threw her over the edge. Crying out his name again, she thrust against him as the cabin and everything around her vanished in a wave of bliss.

Light kisses brought her back to earth, delicate and gentle on her breast, her chest, her neck. She opened her eyes, still breathing hard, and found the silver-toned satisfaction in his gaze.

Her hand slid between them, finding his cock again. "I need you in me," she whispered. "Now."

A growl heavy with desire left him, nothing human in the sound, but still Connor hesitated. Tension flashed across his face, as if he was struggling with himself.

Hayden's confusion returned, and then reality clicked. Oh God, what was she doing? It wasn't like they had a condom here, and good grief, how had she not thought of that sooner?

Her body wanted him. It didn't care.

But her brain did.

She wetted her lips, easing her hand from him. "I'm sorry. I—"

"—the hell I told you, Davey."

The low snarl carried from somewhere outside the cabin.

In an instant, Connor was on his feet. Striding quickly across the short extent of the cabin, he ducked to the side of the window before checking through it. His jaw muscles jumped, and he spun, moving swiftly to the window on the other side of the small space.

Hayden didn't dare breathe. No shouts rang out. Connor didn't duck away like he'd seen a threat. But he was also totally naked, his body nothing but carved muscle beneath smooth flesh like granite.

Alarm and arousal warred within her, and she swallowed hard against it all. He looked like a warrior, like some sinewed god of battles that shouldn't have existed in the modern age. Everything about him spoke of death waiting to strike, and his body radiated the lethal promise of a pure predator.

But no cries came from outside. No sounds at all, even to her sharp hearing.

Moving carefully, Hayden inched up from the blankets. The world was a winter wonderland beyond the frosty window, but a short distance away, she caught sight of two figures in white camouflage gear trekking through the drifts with rifles strapped to their backs.

Her breath caught. She recognized one of them. Mitch. The homeless guy from outside the flower shop a few days ago, the one she'd shared some of her hot chocolate with to help him stay warm in the cold.

Except he looked anything but homeless now.

What the hell?

Connor threw a quick look back at her small gasp. "Get *down*," he hissed.

She dropped back instantly, her thoughts spinning. Why would Mitch be here? And with a *gun?*

Crouching swiftly, Connor yanked open one of the crates along the wall and reached inside. "Put these on." He tossed her a bundle of clothing.

Hayden blinked, alarmed. Everything from a sweater to jeans and underwear were in her hands. A pair of boots followed, and then Connor set to tugging on his own clothes from the box.

Hurriedly, she followed suit.

Reaching back into the crate, Connor pulled out a walkie-talkie. Keeping his eyes on the people beyond the window, he clicked the device on. "Marrok? Marrok, come in."

A deep voice she recognized as the big guy, Marrok, replied. "Here."

"Hunters," Connor said. "Maybe worse. Armed. Out by the west cabin."

"Fuck. On our way."

Connor tucked the walkie-talkie into his back pocket.

"Get in the corner behind those boxes," he ordered, tossing the words at her without taking his attention from the people outside.

Hayden faltered. "But, if we appear human..."

Connor threw her a glance, and she trembled at the look in his eyes. Why the hell wouldn't it matter that they seemed human? Surely hunters wouldn't shoot *people*?

He certainly seemed to think they would.

She crouched and rushed to the tower of crates in the corner, tucking herself down between them and the wall. Turning to the window, Connor watched the hunters like he fully planned on ripping their throats out.

Hayden made herself keep breathing. When she'd worried her kind were a threat, this wasn't what she had in mind.

God, if those men started shooting...

These walls wouldn't stop them. Reality wasn't like the movies. Bullets shredded through so many things. And she and Connor were miles from the nearest hospital, and if one of them was wounded...

Seconds ticked past, and the loudest sound felt like the beating of her own heart. Even the birds had gone silent. And...wait, was that the sound of footsteps outside?

Oh God, that couldn't be good.

A rumble of tires broke the quiet, followed by the sound of slamming doors. Shouts rang out, and then gunfire followed. Connor ducked back, dropping below the windowsill as he retreated toward the corner where she hid. She tried to scoot over to make space for him, and he grabbed her arm, his attention on the windows and the door. Holding her still, he kept himself between her and the rest of the cabin, sheltering her with his own body.

She bit her lip, praying no bullets would hit him.

The gunfire stopped. Hayden held her breath, straining to hear anything from beyond the walls.

"Connor?" Marrok's voice carried from outside.

A gasp of relief left Hayden. Connor didn't move, keeping her behind him as he eyed the windows cautiously. "Clear?" he called.

"Clear."

Only then did Connor straighten, glancing back at her. "You okay?"

She nodded.

Shifting his grip from her arm to her hand, Connor led the way to the door. Marrok and Kirsi were waiting outside, along with a trio of others she didn't recognize.

But Mitch—or whatever his name was—and the other man were nowhere to be seen.

"Where the hell are they?" Connor demanded immediately.

"Bolted," Marrok said.

"Bastards took some shots at us," Kirsi elaborated. "They didn't seem interested in fighting, though. Just in slowing us down so they could get away." Her lips peeled back in a deadly expression that only had a passing resemblance to a smile. "But I caught their scent."

Connor nodded, and his jaw muscles jumped as he scanned the forest like he wanted to kill it.

Hayden shivered and turned away. She could only see the woods and endless snow around them, along with a mess of footprints disturbing the drifts. Hugging her middle, she rubbed her hands up and down her arms nervously.

"You two okay?" Kirsi asked.

Hayden moved her head in a nod, but she wasn't sure what to say. Self-consciousness gnawed at her because, even if by some miracle the people around her *didn't* know what the two of them had been doing in there, they still knew she'd shifted form last night. And after a lifetime of hiding that, to know everyone around her was aware of that felt...personal. Intimate in a wholly different way than what she'd been doing with Connor.

Though, God, what if they smelled that on her too?

Hugging her arms tighter to herself, she retreated a step, not meeting anyone's eyes.

"Back to the manor, then?" Kirsi asked.

From the corner of her eye, Hayden saw Connor glance her way.

Her stomach churned. Sure, the manor was probably safe...maybe even safer than her apartment, though the chances of Mitch following her or knowing about that place were probably slim to none. But Ingrid would be at the manor, with all her prying questions and her horrible myths and her claims that she'd been waiting for Hayden.

Shivers ran through her. "I'd rather go home." She didn't take her eyes from the snow.

Silence followed her words.

Connor cleared his throat. "We have security at the—"

Hayden looked up at him, and he fell quiet, reluctance on his face. But after a moment, he sighed.

"I want guards outside her place," he said to the others. "Kirsi, you can track them?"

The brunette nodded, shifting her weight like she was just waiting to be given the order to go before she'd race off.

"I'll go with Kirsi," Marrok said. "Backup."

Irritation flashed over the woman's face. "Better keep up."

The big man gave her a dark look. Hayden glanced between them, unsure what that was about.

"Then you'll follow us," Connor said to the other three, ignoring the exchange. Without waiting for a response, he turned to Hayden. "Stay close."

Only the intense look in his eyes made the statement come anywhere near a request. She nodded.

Still scanning the forest like the trees themselves might attack, Connor took her hand and led her into the woods.

14

CONNOR

ALL OF HIS WORK. ALL OF HIS EFFORT.

And those bastards had waltzed onto his family property like it was goddamn open season on wolves.

Worse, he'd recognized one of them.

Hayden's hand tightened on his, and from the corner of his eye, he could see her giving him a worried look. He pulled her closer. Right now, the fact he was telegraphing to every creature in a hundred yards how much he cared about Hayden's safety came far second on his list of concerns. The taller of the two men who'd stalked toward the very cabin where Connor had been fighting the urge to fuck Hayden until she howled was the same bastard who hit her with a damned car.

And now, that man and his buddy were out here somewhere. Hunting. In the Thorsen clan woods.

They were Order. They had to be. No one else was that persistent.

Or bloodthirsty.

His heart pounded. How had the bastards found them?

Had they been moved into Mariposa sometime in the past fifteen years? And if so, why? Werewolf hunters who came in *after* the ulfhednar left? It made no sense.

Neither did the fact they'd left Hayden alone. At least...until now.

He pulled her closer, scanning the trees in case anything moved. Even the Order shouldn't have been able to make it onto the property undetected. With all of Connor's preparations, with all the security Tyson had triple-checked...no. Not possible.

Except if one of those bastards hadn't slipped up and made enough noise to be heard, they could have just walked up and shot him and Hayden both.

Nausea churned in his stomach, the thought too terrible to contemplate. He'd been consumed by Hayden. By what he was doing and the delicious sounds and smell and taste of her. By the feel of her coming for him and the desperate need to be inside her. He hadn't spared a thought for their surroundings, trusting that—after all he and the others had done—they would be safe. No, the outside world could have fallen into the primordial abyss for all he'd been aware. It had been all he could do to resist the need to bury himself in her.

Because if he'd crossed that line...if he'd let himself fall that deeply and give in...

He drew a tight breath. She wasn't his mate. She was a beautiful, smart, funny, *amazing* female who deserved better than for him to sleep with her in a dirty cabin and then leave her life forever.

But if one of those humans had come upon them when he wasn't paying attention...

The wolf inside him wanted to howl in pain and terror.

At his side, Hayden made a small sound, and Connor

turned to her immediately. Worry in her eyes, she gave him a questioning look.

"You okay?" she whispered.

"Quiet," one of his father's people ordered in a low voice.

Connor bared his teeth before he could stop himself. The male jerked back in alarm.

Taking a breath, Connor fought to gain control of himself. "I'll be fine," he whispered to Hayden. "I just want to get you home safe."

She bit her lip. He couldn't tell if she believed him.

Holding her close, he continued through the woods, though he fought back a snarl at every little sound around them. The wintry forest was nearly silent—a pack of wolves, even in this form, would make any number of creatures hide—but the cold still caused branches to snap and leaves to slough away snow.

Every noise made him flinch. Each shift of the breeze made him worry the bastards had gotten downwind. More than anything, he wanted to rush Hayden back to the manor this instant. Yes, Ingrid was there. Yes, his father would be incensed.

But if it was that or Hayden's safety…

The stone wall that encircled their property came into view. His father's people motioned for Hayden and Connor to stay back while they approached the gate carefully.

He could feel Hayden's tension through the arm he had wrapped around her body. Gods, he wanted her out of here—and he wanted his *own* pack around them. He'd known the wolves with him now since he was a cub, but they were not Marrok, Kirsi, or the others.

Yet he understood Marrok's insistence on following

Kirsi. Things between those two hadn't been easy in recent years, though he'd never pried for details. But no matter what, Marrok would never leave her undefended.

His father's people leaned out of the gate, checking around warily before passing through the opening and motioning for Connor and Hayden to follow. The snow on the trail outside the gate remained undisturbed, with not even a sparrow's claw prints marring the white expanse. In silence, the group made their way past the trail and through the forest to the parking lot.

Connor's SUV stood where he'd left it, and no other vehicles waited in the lot. Out of caution, he'd parked near the tree line the night before, and he was grateful as hell for that bit of foresight now. Yes, he'd thought they'd be safe.

At least some part of him had been thinking about what would be needed in case he was wrong.

"Wheel well," he murmured to the male next to him, a gray-haired wolf named Cyrus who had guarded his playpen when Connor was a cub. "Front driver's side. The keys are there."

The male nodded. Watching the area carefully, Cyrus walked out onto the snowy expanse of the parking lot. Connor could hear his own heart beating in the silence, hear Hayden's short and nervous breaths beside him. At the vehicle, Cyrus paused, feeling with one hand for the keys inside the well while keeping his eyes on the forest all around.

A tree branch cracked.

Connor was moving before he finished registering the sound, shoving Hayden behind him while the wolves around them spun, scanning the woods, guns raised and ready.

No other noises followed.

Cautiously, Cyrus unlocked the vehicle and checked inside. He bent, confirming nothing was attached to the undercarriage either, before leaving the SUV.

"Vehicle looks clear," the man murmured, still watching the woods.

Connor nodded. Drawing a shallow breath, he made himself walk forward, keeping Hayden behind him as they approached the black vehicle.

A flurry of birds took to the air. He pulled Hayden around, pushing her toward the door while Cyrus tugged it open again. She climbed in quickly, scooting over to make room for him and giving him an entreating look to join her.

He paused, the hairs on his body rising. They were being watched.

"Inside. Now." Cyrus's voice was a growl as his eyes scanned the forest. The other two with them hurried around to the opposite side, one taking the driver's seat while the second hopped in next to Hayden.

Connor nodded and climbed in.

The passenger door slammed as Cyrus did as well. "Get us out of here," he ordered the driver.

The male didn't have to be told twice.

"Those men were out there," Hayden said quietly while the SUV rushed from the parking lot. "Weren't they?"

Connor's jaw clenched. He didn't want to worry her.

Bit late for that.

"Maybe," he said.

They drove back to town in silence, and when they finally reached Mariposa, he could feel how his father's people eyed him as he offered directions without needing to ask Hayden. He hadn't exactly told anyone where he'd been going this past week, beyond general information to his own friends who had clearly stayed silent on the matter.

His father would learn about it soon enough.

The SUV pulled to a stop in front of Hayden's apartment, and Cyrus and the others checked around carefully before allowing Connor or Hayden to climb outside.

"Stay here," he ordered the wolves. "Keep watch and signal if you see or hear anything."

They nodded and then headed towards the sides of the building to monitor the rest of the property. They'd do their job, he was sure of that. Even if his father had sent him into exile for specialized survival training, the old wolf's people were highly skilled.

He climbed the stairs ahead of Hayden, and every time he looked back, he caught a glimpse of the anxious look on her face. There was a chance—a slim chance, not that he cared—that they were wrong. Those were simply two idiot hunters wandering on protected land, one of whom happened to be the asshole who'd pulled a hit-and-run a week before. They weren't Order. They weren't anything. And they'd be caught soon enough.

But every wolf in the world knew the cost of being wrong.

He reached back when they came to the door. "Keys?"

She blinked at him and then handed him her key ring.

Carefully, he unlocked the door. The apartment was still, and as he eased inside, nothing moved. The curtains were drawn, sealing out the daylight and turning the place into a shadowy cave. He cursed himself quietly, wishing he'd taken one of the others' knives or guns. But as he moved carefully through the apartment, nothing jumped out at him. No gunshots rang out. Except for the distant sound of a neighbor's television and the occasional rush of traffic on the street, everything was still.

He turned back to Hayden, who was standing by the front door with wide eyes.

"What's going on, Connor?" Hayden asked in a small voice.

His chest ached. He didn't want to leave her, and he didn't know where to begin with explaining.

But he also couldn't remain here while those bastards were out there, waiting to find her again.

"Stay put, okay?" he said. "I'll call when—"

"You're leaving?"

Connor faltered. "You'll be safe here." Gods, she better be. "I'll leave Cyrus and the others outside to—"

"I recognized him."

Connor froze. "What?"

"One of the hunters. He said his name was Mitch, when I met him outside the flower—"

"He knows who you are?" Connor's blood pressure spiked.

Hayden nodded nervously. "Yeah. I mean, not..." She seemed to struggle for words. "He knows my name. But... he looked homeless, then. And smelled like he hadn't taken a bath in a month. I gave him some of my hot chocolate because he looked so cold and—"

Connor turned away, and she cut off. Oh gods, the bastard knew her name. Knew where she worked.

Where she'd been working this whole time...including the week since he hit her with a car.

Connor scrubbed a hand through his hair, trying to fit the pieces together in his mind. The Order wouldn't just

leave her alone. They would have tracked her down immediately.

Another wolf head for their walls.

He felt like he wanted to throw up.

"Connor?" Hayden sounded scared. "What is this?
Your friends came loaded for war, and you're all acting
like..." Her mouth moved as if failing to find the words,
and then she exhaled, giving up. "What's going on?"

Every half explanation he possessed dried up when he
met her worried eyes. "Have you heard of the Order?"

Her head shook slowly, her gaze not leaving him.

"They're a secret society. The Order of Nidhogg, so
named for some damn mythological serpent supposedly
gnawing at the roots of the World Tree. They're essentially
a doomsday cult, but they believe it's their mission to wipe
out 'werewolves.' Also known as us. The ulfhednar."

Her lips parted in a tiny gasp. "That's...when you said
they'd...they'd shoot us anyway..."

Connor nodded. "They train to spot our kind, and they
view it as a rite of passage to kill us." He paused. "We've
lost a lot of our people to them over the years."

Hayden pressed a hand to her mouth, turning away. His
eyes slid toward the curtains. He didn't know why they'd
been left closed, but he was grateful, if only because it gave
no hint to anyone outside that the two of them were in here.

"I need you to stay put," he said to her. "Just until we
can find these bastards. One of them already came after
you with his car—"

Hayden looked back sharply, alarm on her face.

"The taller one with blond hair," Connor elaborated.
"He was the one—"

"That's Mitch."

Internally, Connor cursed. So the man *had* come after her, almost immediately. And as for why he hadn't tracked her down since finding her at the florist...

Was it luck? Maybe Mitch hadn't realized who he—

"He wasn't trying to hit me, though."

Connor glanced back at her.

Hayden looked away, her hands wringing against each other in a nervous gesture he recognized from a week ago.

"How do you know?" he asked.

She bit her lip.

"Hayden?"

"I saw it." She wouldn't meet his eyes. "Before it happened."

Connor's eyebrows climbed.

"I walked around the corner and saw the car come over the hill." Her grip on her own hands tightened, turning her knuckles white. "It hit Kirsi." She took a shallow breath. "It killed her. And...and then I was back, and I hadn't reached the corner yet, and when I did, it was like what I'd seen a moment before, except none of it had happened yet."

She looked up at him, fear in her eyes, like maybe he would have an explanation.

Or at least not think her insane.

"That's why you ran into the street." His own voice sounded numb to his ears. He couldn't begin to understand how what she had just described was even possible.

But Hayden just nodded, watching him.

He exhaled, implications rolling over him. If what she said *was* true... "You risked your life to save hers."

Hayden gave a tiny shrug.

More than anything else, it made something inside him

melt. Nothing she said should have been possible—hell, it *wasn't* possible—but that also wasn't the point.

She believed it. And because of that, she'd thrown herself in front of a car to save his friend's life.

Connor walked over to her, taking her shaking hands. Her skin was like ice. "Thank you." He pulled her closer, wrapping his arms around her. She buried her head in his shoulder, holding him tightly.

He rested his head atop hers, his original worries returning like chattering birds in his mind. If that man hadn't been trying to hit Hayden specifically…If he hadn't come after her since meeting her at the flower shop…

Was it possible the Order didn't know she was ulfhednar?

Hayden didn't move like one of her kind. She didn't react like them either. Connor had noticed it when he first brought her back to the manor, and he hadn't even been watching for that the way someone of the Order would be.

Gods, they really might not know what Hayden was.

Until they'd seen her with Connor in the woods today, anyway.

His arms tightened around her. They might think she was a human he was targeting, though. Believing that was a gamble, to be sure, but the Order thought his kind were monsters.

Like Hayden had, when he first met her.

A chill stole over him, his thoughts slowing. She'd never explained why she believed that. Who had told her that or why. She'd only said she was adopted by humans.

And no one in the Order would *care* for a wolf.

Except she'd only been a cub…or, in human terms, a child. And even if empathy from a member of the Order was about as likely as a wolf tail on a human, maybe…

Maybe...

Hayden pulled back from him, and swiftly, he buried the disturbed expression on his face due to the dark direction his thoughts had taken. In the end, this changed nothing. Or, at least, almost nothing. It only meant she might be safer here than he'd anticipated. But he still had to find that bastard.

His pack was anything but safe.

"Stay put for me, okay?" He met her eyes insistently. "The others will still be here to watch the place, and I'll keep in touch. But I need to know you're okay."

"What about you?"

He brushed a strand of her hair away from her face. "I'll have the pack with me."

She took a breath, nodding like she was trying to let that be reassuring.

Bending slightly, he kissed her. "I'll call," he repeated when he drew away. "Just stay put for the day, if you can. Please."

She nodded again.

Trying to ignore the flash of regret that spiked through him as he released her, he headed for the door. If he had his way, he'd find the bastard within the hour and have whatever shreds of the Order were lurking around Mariposa rooted out by nightfall.

He just hoped to the gods that Hayden's parents weren't part of them.

15

HAYDEN

FIRST, THE WEREWOLVES WEREN'T MONSTERS.

Then, a secret society was hunting people like her.

And now, she was all alone in her apartment, waiting for the werewolves to save her from the secret society.

Her life had gone insane.

Hayden stood in the entryway, staring at the door as it closed after Connor. Her body felt numb, like somewhere between rushing away from the cabin and learning about "the Order," she'd lost all touch with the panic that should have been thundering through her.

But then, what good would it do?

She crossed to the door and flipped the dead bolt. Turning, her feet carried her to the windows on the opposite side of the living room, where she hesitated before carefully twitching aside the edge of the curtain and peeking through the gap at the bright, snowy day.

Connor stalked outside, moving fast. He paused when the gray-haired man who'd seemed in charge before—or in charge second to Connor, anyway—came up to him. They exchanged quick words, and Connor motioned to the building, something imperious in the motion. The man nodded. Without another word, Connor strode to the SUV, swung inside, and peeled away from the curb while the other man walked toward the building again, vanishing around the side beyond where Hayden could see.

A breath left her. So that was it. Now, she waited.

While everyone else went out and possibly risked their lives against a doomsday cult.

She turned away from the window, letting the curtain fall back into place. This was madness. Utter madness. She felt like, somehow, she'd swum out beyond sight of the shore and now she couldn't find her way back again.

For God's sake, prior to this, the weirdest thing she'd had to deal with was herself.

She rocked back and forth, chewing her lip. What was she supposed to do about it, though? Just stay up here in her apartment forever, hoping the people in this "Order" thing didn't come hunt her down?

Good grief, she felt like a cross between the Lady of Shalott and someone in the Witness Protection Program.

Striding back across the room, she retrieved her new cell phone from where she'd left the pile of clothes she wore the evening before. If nothing else, she could tell Lindy and Johanna to keep an eye out. Warn them that Mitch *clearly* wasn't to be trusted—to put it mildly.

Though, what could she actually tell them? Johanna was a Mama Bear. She'd demand answers from the guy if she thought he was threatening Hayden, and there was no way that would go well. And Lindy was her best friend. She'd be protective too.

Torn, Hayden thumbed on the screen as if maybe the phone would provide an answer.

Tension shot through her at the sight of a missed call from her dad.

Oh, God. What should she tell him? What *could* she tell him? He and her mother would be furious she'd risked so much, even if nothing had seemed all that risky at the time. They'd be terrified she was talking to the wolves, and if she told them there was a secret society of killers out there now too?

They'd probably start packing to leave town *today*.

She ran a hand through her hair. Maybe that was the right idea. Pack up, leave town, forget all about "ulfhednar" and the "Order of Nidhogg" and God knew what else. Start over somewhere else and pretend they'd never even *heard* of Mariposa, Colorado.

But then, maybe the wolves would take care of it.

She fidgeted with the phone, feeling sick from the fact she was, in reality, reassuring herself with the idea that the wolves might kill people. But maybe they wouldn't. Maybe they'd just scare the Order off.

Maybe the Easter Bunny would help them.

Exhaling sharply, she sank down onto the armchair, the phone still clutched in her hands. She couldn't tell her parents everything. Not yet. But perhaps she could still *hint* at it.

Or something.

After all, her dad would be worried if she didn't answer his call too.

Unlocking her phone quickly, she hit the call button. Her dad answered after only one ring.

"Hayden?"

"Hey, Dad. You called?"

He let out a breath. "Are you okay?"

Apprehension made the hairs on her arms rise. "Um, why do you ask?"

"You and I were supposed to go to breakfast this morning."

She blinked. "Right. Sorry. Um—"

"You sure you're all right? It's been hours, honey. You had me worried."

"Yeah."

No.

She scrubbed a hand over her eyes, trying to focus. "I'm sorry. I just..." Reality offered zero excuses. "Sorry."

"Okay..." He still sounded concerned.

Hayden took a steadying breath. "Listen, Dad, I..." She squeezed her eyes shut, willing herself to keep going. "Last night, I went out and—"

The front door lock clicked open, and she jumped a mile.

Lindy froze in the doorway, staring at her. "Hi."

Hayden started breathing again, her eyes darting to the wall clock. Good grief, it was half past noon. End of the morning shift.

"Hey," she managed, only to hesitate. No way she could have this conversation where Lindy might overhear. No way in hell.

And she couldn't leave the apartment, either. Witness Protection and all that.

"Hayden?" her father said on the other end of the line.

"Yeah." Dammit. "Look, um..." She got to her feet and headed for her room, giving Lindy a quick smile as she went. "I just wanted to say—" She shut the door. "Please be careful, okay? I...I heard there's a, um, serial killer in town, and I'm worried." She winced, hating the lie.

Her father was quiet for a moment. "I'll be careful. Your mom will too. You stay safe as well, okay, honey?"

"I will."

"Okay."

He knew that wasn't what she'd meant to say. She could hear it in his voice.

"I'll call you in a bit, all right, Dad?"

"Please do, sweetheart."

Pain moved through her chest. "Love you."

"Love you too."

Grimacing at herself, she hung up the phone. She'd figure out a way to let her parents know the entire truth. Eventually, anyway. And as it was, maybe her dad would think she meant she saw a wolf in town.

He and her mom would both be careful.

Taking a breath, she tried to push the apprehension from her face as she walked back out into the living room. Lindy was in the kitchen, getting a sandwich ready.

"Everything all right?" her friend asked. "You seemed…Well, jumpy as hell a second ago."

"Yeah. Fine." Hayden's eyes twitched toward the window, but she tugged her attention away again. "Work go okay at the shop this morning?"

Lindy set her food on a plate. "Oh, same old, same old. The Morrison twins were complaining about their corsages for prom, and Mrs. Sanderson called back for her daily bitch-fest about the wedding bouquets. She wants entirely new flowers now."

"You're kidding."

Lindy took a bite of the sandwich and shook her head. "Nuh-uh." She swallowed. "Johanna just about blew a gasket."

Hayden scoffed. She could imagine. It took a lot to get

the shopkeeper to raise her voice, let alone show real anger, but Mrs. Sanderson would try the patience of every angel in heaven.

"So…" Lindy prompted after swallowing another bite. "That hot guy coming around this evening?"

Hayden hesitated. "Um…yeah, probably. Maybe."

Lindy made a thoughtful noise. "Well, I can clear out if, you know, you want some privacy."

Awkwardly avoiding her friend's eyes, Hayden shook her head. "No, that's—"

An odd popping sound came from outside, faint like a firecracker far in the distance. She glanced toward the window sharply.

"What's wrong?" Lindy asked.

Hayden shook her head. "Nothing. Just thought I heard—"

The sound came again. The hairs on Hayden's arms prickled.

She headed for the window.

"Hayden?" Lindy called.

"It's nothing." She didn't look back to see if her friend believed her. She wasn't sure she believed it herself.

Carefully, she twitched aside the edge of the curtain. Everything seemed normal. There weren't any cars on the road, though in a residential neighborhood on a weekday, that wasn't saying much. She couldn't see anyone on the sidewalk or walking toward the building, and of the people Connor ordered to stay here, there wasn't any sign.

A splash of red paint showed on the crisp white snow by one of the evergreen trees.

Her brow furrowed. God, that looked like—

The curtain jerked closed in front of her. She flinched back to find Lindy pinning it shut with one arm, an expression on her friend's face unlike any she'd ever seen. It was ice but...

Deadly.

"What did you hear?" Lindy asked.

Hayden blinked, uncertain why it mattered. Because, surely, that hadn't been what she thought it was.

Maybe an art student had spilled some paint on the snow.

"What did you *hear?*" Lindy demanded.

"I don't—"

Lindy tweaked the curtain aside, her brown eyes sweeping the neighborhood swiftly and then pausing when they landed in the vicinity of the evergreen trees. "*Shit.*" Dropping the curtain, she grabbed Hayden's hand and then took off toward her own bedroom.

Hayden sputtered. "What are you—"

"Come on!"

Dragged by her arm, Hayden stumbled after her friend. Lindy raced through the door and across the room to tug open her closet. "Stay there," she ordered before dropping her grip and scrambling onto a rubber storage crate.

"Lindy, what's going—"

With a sharp shove, her friend pushed aside the small attic access hatch in the ceiling. A rope ladder fell through the opening, unrolling as it plummeted into the closet below.

Lindy hopped down from the storage crate. "Climb."

Hayden stared at her.

"Dammit, Hayden, climb! We're running out of time."

At a loss, she did as ordered. The ladder swung awkwardly with her weight for a moment before Lindy grabbed it and steadied the ropes. Above them, the attic was dark, and when Hayden's head passed through the opening, her nose tickled at the heavy layer of dust in the air. Wooden beams ran along the length of the space with thick layers of insulation between them. Overhead, the roof came to a pinnacle, more beams supporting it every few feet. To her left and right, small windows like portholes in a submarine let light in, while up ahead, a section of bricks hinted at what must have once been a chimney.

Hayden clambered up the final rungs of the ladder and pushed to her feet, careful to stay on the wooden beams and not put any weight on the wrapped layers of pink insulation on either side. Only a moment later, Lindy scrambled up too and turned immediately to pull the ropes up behind her. With swift motions, she unhooked the ladder and bundled it under her arm before pushing the access hatch panel back into place.

"This way." Lindy started across the attic, hurrying along one of the beams like a gymnast and heading for the opposite end from the fireplace chimney. "Hurry."

Blinking, Hayden glanced down at the hatch. She could push it aside. Jump down and run.

Except this was Lindy. Her best friend.

And that probably...*probably* hadn't been paint on the snow.

She trailed Lindy along the roof beam. The wall ahead was no different than any of the others all around them, barring the windows and the chimney. Just a plain stretch of unpainted drywall paneling, with manufacturer's marks in faded blue ink along the sides. But when Lindy came up to it, she reached out and dug her nails into the fissure between two panels, prying at them.

One of the panels swung open like a door.

"What is this?" Hayden asked, staring.

"Why do you think I wanted that bedroom? This apartment?" Lindy motioned for Hayden to go ahead of her. "Get inside."

Speechless, Hayden walked past her. The space beyond was no larger than a coat closet, lined by the same unpainted paneling as the rest of the attic and bearing a porthole window straight ahead. A few old hooks, rusted and dangling cobwebs, were bolted into the wall below the window, as if someone had intended to use this space as storage, but then gave up before finishing the job.

But she remembered what Lindy was talking about. How her friend had come back here twice after they'd first viewed the apartment. How Lindy had claimed to simply be picky about where she lived and had reinforced that by insisting on taking this specific room, too. At the time, Hayden had just thought it was a weird quirk born of how her friend spent her teenage years moving around a lot.

Now, though... "Lindy, what is going—"

"Quiet," Lindy hissed. She tugged the panel door closed behind her and then drew something from her pocket.

Hayden's eyes went wide as the switchblade flicked open in her friend's hand.

As if sensing her panic, Lindy glanced back and pressed a finger to her own lips in a shushing gesture. Her expression like stone, she nodded downward and pointed to the floor below them.

Hayden stared at her, confused. What the hell was—

A click came from the apartment below, faint and distant. The front door latch. She knew the sound. She'd heard it a hundred times. Soft noises followed: a small creak of a floorboard, a whisper like papers rustling against one another, a faint whine of a hinge on the bathroom door.

Someone was in the apartment.

Hayden barely dared to breathe. It couldn't be Connor. He would have called for her. And as for the people he'd left here…

The red splash on the white snow flashed through her mind. She shuddered, praying she was wrong.

Silence fell for a moment, and her eyes crept toward Lindy. Her friend's hand adjusted on the knife, and in the wintry sunlight through the window, the silver blade flashed.

A creak came from the direction of Hayden's bedroom —another floorboard—and then a squeaking rustle as the shower curtain in her bathroom was brushed aside.

Lindy drew a breath as if she was trying to stay calm.

Seconds crept past. Hayden strained to hear anything, but there was nothing. Was the intruder still in her room? Why weren't they leaving?

God, what were they looking at?

A floorboard squeaked in Lindy's room. Hayden's breath caught. The hinge of the closet door made a tiny whine.

Hayden glanced at her friend. The woman's knuckles were white around the handle of the knife.

A scratching sound carried through the attic. Wood on wood.

The access hatch.

Hayden swallowed hard. Her skin prickled with the urge to shift, and her instincts screamed to let out her fangs, her claws. Anything to stop whoever this was from hurting them both.

Though Lindy seemed unnervingly comfortable with that knife…

Rustling sounds carried through the attic. "Melinda...?" The man's voice was singsong, like an adult playing hide-and-seek with a child. "I know you're here."

Lindy's hair quivered as she trembled. Hayden didn't breathe. She recognized the voice.

Mitch.

"I thought that was you at the flower shop." Mitch's tone turned chiding. "Have you betrayed us, Melinda?"

Hayden's brow twitched down in confusion. Betrayed who? Her eyes flicked from her friend to the knife to the door.

Wait...

"We've been tracking this pack since one of our people spotted them outside Denver, but I didn't expect to find you here, working with one of them. Heh, *living* with one of them." The boards beneath Hayden's feet shivered slightly with Mitch's footsteps. "Did you know she had wolves around this whole building? Or that their pack leader is courting the bitch? Did you know we nearly caught them hiding out in the woods this morning, probably rutting like the animals they are?"

Hayden's skin crawled even as embarrassment flickered through her. God, the way he talked about her and Connor. And if he or his buddy hadn't made a noise out by the cabin, what might have happened?

Given the blood on the snow outside, she could guess, and it made her want to vomit.

"So why haven't you killed her already, Melinda? Did you make a bargain with that mangy cur? Do you think her kind will shelter you from what's coming? Or have you forgotten so much of your training that you couldn't even tell what she was?" Mitch chuckled, the sound like cold metal being drawn over flesh. "I'll admit she's clever. Even I didn't spot that one right away. But you? Surely Dal

Hegnar's prize pupil didn't let *that* get by her." He made a chiding sound. "What *would* your mother say?"

Lindy trembled hard, and her hand adjusted on the knife.

"Or is it your daddy's fault? Did he truly mislead you *this* badly? He's up north somewhere with your little brother now, isn't he? Minnesota, perhaps? Wisconsin?" Hayden could practically hear the smile in his voice. "All alone?"

Lindy flinched like she was fighting the urge to lunge past the panel door and stab the man.

"You know what's coming." Mitch's footsteps moved closer, scratching on the wood beams. "You've seen the signs, same as us. The gift will arrive any day now. The dead will rise and the world will fall."

Hayden froze. The woman in her dream had said the same thing. But how could this guy know—

"They *have* to die," Mitch continued. "You know this. It's the only way. Do you truly want to condemn your family to die with them?" His voice carried through the panel door as if he stood in the closet with them. "Let's gut the bitch together, Melinda. Offer her pelt as tribute and use her blood as atonement for your backsliding ways. You could still take your place at your mother's side." His footsteps stopped. "It's not too late to save yourself from his wrath."

Mitch fell silent. Hayden didn't dare breathe. The hush from the attic was so thick, she couldn't tell where the man was.

He could be aiming a gun at them right now.

Trembling wracked her, every cell in her body screaming to shift and run.

A small chiming sound came from beyond the door. Fabric rustled, and then Mitch let out a breath. *"Finally."*

The relish in his voice sent shivers racing over her skin.

"You had your chance, Melinda!" Mitch called, the words ringing from the attic walls. He waited a moment and then chuckled, his voice dropping to a murmur. "It's coming."

Quickly, his footsteps moved away. With a thud, he dropped into the closet below and then hurried out of the apartment at a pace just short of running.

Hayden looked at Lindy again. Her friend put a finger to her lips in a silencing gesture, a pleading expression on her face.

At a loss, Hayden didn't say a word.

With a deft motion, Lindy flicked the switchblade closed and shoved it into her pocket before drawing out her cell phone. Pressing her thumb to it quickly, she clicked on the screen and then tapped the icon for texting.

Even upside down, Hayden could read the swiftly typed message.

Call Houston.

Hayden gave her friend a confused look.

Lindy glanced up as if feeling the pressure of her attention. "Houston, we have a problem," she whispered. Tucking her phone away, she carefully crossed to the small attic window and hoisted herself up on one of the beams running along the wall. A breath escaped her. "He's leaving." Lindy paused. "*Really* fast."

She sank back down, her expression filled with unease.

Hayden stared at her. "Wh-who are you?"

"Your friend."

A choked sound left Hayden. "*And?*"

Lindy sighed. "And…I was raised by the Order of Nidhogg."

The attic was so silent, Hayden could hear the neighbor's television three floors down.

"*What?*" she blurted.

Lindy shrugged like she didn't know what to say. "I'm not your enemy. I—"

Hayden made a choked noise, gaping at her. How could she have not known this? How could she have not known her friend was…

What the hell *was* Lindy?

"I'm not like them," the woman said as if she could read the incredulity Hayden knew had to be on her own face.

Hayden's mouth moved, searching for an answer to that. "A-and all that stuff about your dad and your mom…?"

"It's complicated."

"So make it not complicated!" Hayden sank back against the wall, feeling like the world had become unsteady.

Lindy watched her for a moment. "All right." She took a breath. "I was raised to be an Allegiant, initiated by Dal Hegnar himself when I was eleven, but became unofficially Forsaken when I was a teenager. Mom's still in the fold. Dad isn't."

Hayden stared at her.

"Like I said." Lindy gave her a dry look. "Complicated."

Her mouth moving for a moment, Hayden floundered.

"What...what does that mean? Really?"

Shifting her weight, her friend grimaced.

"Please," Hayden begged, her voice shaking. "I-I've known you for years. You...What is this?"

Lindy glanced back up, a touch of guilt breaking past the hard exterior Hayden barely even recognized. "My parents joined a commune when I was two," she relented. "And, as far as I understand it, the place was all flowers and rainbows at first. Invested in sustainability and nature worship or whatever. 'Children of the Renewed Beginning,' they called themselves. Real health-nut, ecofriendly —" She chuckled, no humor in the sound. "—survive-the-downfall-of-civilization-type stuff. They just neglect to tell the newbies they want to *cause* that downfall first."

Hayden didn't know what to say.

"By the time I was a toddler, Mom had already been invited into the inner circle. Dad wasn't, not for a long time. He had no interest in secret 'clubs,' as he thought they were. He just wanted to garden. And me..." She scrubbed her hands on the sides of her jeans. "I was brought in early. Get 'em young, do it right, and you've got a soldier for life." She looked away uncomfortably. "When I was little, though, it was just games. Spot the Big Bad Wolf and all that. Then, later, it became self-defense stuff. Martial arts, guns, knives...whatever. And when I got old enough..."

"What did you do?" Hayden's voice was weak.

Lindy wouldn't meet her eyes. Her hand moved, unclasping the leather bracelet that covered her right wrist.

A tattoo in weirdly metallic, green-black ink wrapped the skin the leather had hidden, a snake circling around a knot shape that seemed eerily reminiscent of a dying tree.

"Allegiant rite of passage," Lindy said softly. "Among

other things. I don't think I killed anyone. A wolf, yes, but..." Her breath trembled. "I don't think it was...you know."

Hayden swallowed hard, her stomach churning.

Swiftly, Lindy looped the bracelet around her wrist again like she couldn't wait to have it back on.

"But—" Hayden stammered. "Why are you...I mean, you're here, and you didn't..." She looked around, trying to figure out a way to describe the past six years she'd known her friend, the past three they'd lived together here, the past *anything* that covered why Lindy was what she said and why Hayden was still alive. If anything Connor claimed was true—hell, if what *Lindy* was saying was true—that shouldn't have happened.

Hayden should be dead, and the thought left her shivering.

"Somewhere along the line, Dad started to become scared of what he saw happening to me. And to Freddie. My little brother was having nightmares, crying about ulfhednar coming to kill us all, and—"

Hayden's breath caught at the word.

Lindy glanced up, meeting her eyes briefly before looking down again. "*And...*" She gave a small cough. "Mom's answer was just to put a knife in his hand and tell him..." She grimaced.

"What?"

"'Shifter blood makes us powerful. We kill them so the world will die.'"

Hayden couldn't even blink.

"So when Dad finally overheard this," Lindy pressed on, speaking quickly. "He suddenly wanted to join the Order. It took a few months, but Mom got him in. She was so thrilled when he took his oath. Our whole family brought…" She cleared her throat. "Brought to apocalyptic salvation. But in reality, he had no intention of staying. He only wanted to hear all the secret teachings so he'd know everything he was up against in getting us free. He did everything they wanted, spouted every saying, engaged in every practice. Whatever it took until he could figure out how to get through to me and Freddie and find the cracks in all the crap we'd been taught our whole lives." Lindy rubbed a hand up and down her forearm. "He risked everything to get us out."

She took a breath. "When I was fifteen, he made his move. He filed for divorce from Mom, threatened lawyers and cops and claimed he'd been wearing a body camera for months. That his contacts had recordings of everything. But if the Order would let us go, he'd destroy the evidence. Never tell a soul. And by that point, I…I'd started to have lots of doubts, so I stood with him. Freddie did too. And —" She exhaled shakily. "—the Order agreed. After a fashion."

Hayden trembled. "What happened?"

Lindy looked up, meeting her eyes again. "They're why he doesn't have a left hand."

Holy God. Nausea joined her trembling. Her friend had always told her that was the result of a woodworking accident. "But…but you…" Hayden's eyes darted down, as if to encompass her friend's fully intact limbs.

"Mom intervened for us. Said my dad was dead to her, but Freddie and I were not. We'd be back, she claimed. We wouldn't truly become the Forsaken. She said we'd go out into the world, see what it was like, and then come…home. So they should leave us be." Lindy's face twitched with cold disgust. "After all, we'd need both hands for Ragnarok, right?"

"Ragna..." The ground seemed to rock beneath Hayden's feet.

"Yeah. The Order believes..." Lindy trailed off, discomfort on her face, and then she chuckled humorlessly. "God, you'd think it would be easier to say after all this time."

Hayden couldn't respond.

Lindy scrubbed her hands on her jeans again and drew a deep breath. "The Order of Nidhogg believes that, when the world ends, the old gods will return and unleash all kinds of horrors. Monsters from legends and that kind of thing. Total chaos. But they don't really care about that because...well, they believe they'll rule when all is said and done. That all kinds of great things will happen for them. So the destruction of the world is like their victory party." Her discomfited expression returned and she shifted her weight. "But the threat to that, in their minds—one of the threats, anyway—is the existence of the ulfhednar."

She looked up, meeting Hayden's eyes.

Hayden trembled.

"You really are hard to spot," Lindy said as if it were a compliment. "You don't move like them. Act like them. If I hadn't spent so much time with you over the years, I probably never would have caught on, so whoever taught you that, they...they did a good job."

Hayden stared at her. "All this time, you knew what I..." A short gasp escaped her. "My God, why didn't you say anything?"

"And risk what might happen?" Lindy sounded faintly incredulous.

"What might...?" She gaped at her friend, baffled, until suddenly, it clicked. "You thought I was going to *hurt* you?"

Lindy didn't answer.

"I..." Hayden choked on a gasp, her hand rising to press to her face before she caught herself and stopped her dusty fingers from touching her skin. "Lindy, that...that would've been..."

She couldn't even wrap her mind around it. So many years of hiding, of worrying what someone would think if they learned what she was, while this whole time—

"And your parents?" Lindy asked, interrupting her train of thought. "Or any of the others? Would *they* have understood? If they knew what I..." She scoffed and then shook her head like there was no chance in hell that would have gone well.

Hayden stared. Her parents? What would they have...

Oh.

Wow.

She swallowed hard. Risking herself was one thing. But if Lindy didn't know her parents were human...would that keep them safer?

How could it? The Order killed...The strange word stalled out in her brain.

Her kind.

But then, Lindy could have hurt her at any point over the past six years. She'd thought her parents were wolves all along and never hurt them either. And she'd saved Hayden's life just now.

"They're not like me."

Lindy's brow furrowed. "What?"

"I'm adopted. You know that. They're not—"

"I just thought different wolves adopted you."

Hayden shook her head.

Lindy looked baffled.

"I thought..." Hayden took a breath. "My whole life,

they were the only ones who knew what I was, and if I had known that you—"

"What about that guy, then? The...you know, hot one you were with last night?"

Hayden fidgeted uncomfortably before she could stop herself.

"You're blushing." Lindy's voice was dry.

Hayden ducked her face away. "I just met him that day at the flower shop last week. He and the others are actually the first people like me that I've ever seen."

She glanced back to see Lindy's brow rise. Hayden shrugged.

Her friend looked away. A moment crept by as car horns honked outside and someone's cell phone rang in the distance.

"I'm sorry," Lindy said. "I should have..." She sighed. "The Order drilled into me for my whole childhood never to tell anyone. They said that if a shifter found out what we are, we would die. Either by that one, or the next one, or whatever. And even if, after a while, I didn't really believe that about you, then...it just felt like if you'd wanted to tell me what you were, you would have, right?"

Hayden sputtered. "*How*? What was I supposed to say? 'Hi, by the way, I'm basically a werewolf'?"

"Versus what? 'Hi, I grew up with a doomsday cult who thought werewolves were the devil. By the way, please don't kill me'?"

They stared at each other for a moment, and then Lindy chuckled, and Hayden did too.

The humor lasted only a heartbeat.

"How many more of them are out there?" Hayden asked quietly.

Lindy's fingers played with the edge of her leather

bracelet. "I don't know."

Hayden watched her motion. "That why you never got it covered or removed?"

Her friend's lip twitched wryly. "What if the tattoo artist was one of them?" She dropped her hand from the bracelet. "They have people all over. A network they've built across the planet. Every day, I worry they'll find me, and even now, I sleep with a knife under my pillow. Mom and the rest, they haven't come after us, but...it's only a matter of time, really, until they figure out I'm not coming back. And the punishments for disloyalty are...extreme."

Shivering, Hayden glanced to the panel door. "You think he'll be back for us?"

"Probably." Lindy's voice was distant.

Hayden shivered. "We need to call Connor."

Lindy's head shook immediately. "No. No way. Ulfhednar know what to look for, and if they get a good look at this—" She lifted her bracelet-covered wrist. "—then they'll know I'm—"

"I'll protect you."

Lindy stared at her.

With an unsteady smile, Hayden tried for a reassuring look. "Like you protected me, right? But we need help and someplace safe to go. If Mitch knows about me, then..." Anxiety crawled through her as she thought about the man's stroll through their apartment. "He might start looking for my parents too. And I don't want you to lose a hand...or worse."

Her friend was silent.

"Please, Lindy. What else is there to do if he comes back?" She shivered. "*When* he comes back? Please, let me help you too."

After a moment, the woman gave a small nod. "Okay."

16

CONNOR

CONNOR DIDN'T MAKE IT A BLOCK FROM HAYDEN'S apartment before his father called.

Growling quietly to himself, he thumbed the control on the steering wheel. "Yes, Father?"

"Where the hell are you?" The shout rang from the SUV's speakers.

Connor braced himself. "Just had to run an errand. Has anyone seen a sign of the hunters from this morning?"

"Screw the hunters. Get back to the manor right now."

He blinked. *Screw the hunters?* What utter lunacy had consumed his father that he would—

"Do you hear me, cub?"

Connor cleared his throat. "I'm sorry, sir. You said I should—"

"Forget the damn hunters and get your ass back to the manor right now!"

"Father, I—"

A click cut him off as Tolvar hung up.

Connor's jaw worked around. This was madness. First

they moved here, down from the safety of Alaska and into the very territory that had seen Connor's mother killed. Then the old wolf sent them on bizarre shopping trips to everywhere from Mariposa's GetLots superstore to rural gas stations the size of a closet. And now, his father didn't care that hunters with rifles had been sauntering freely around his own property?

Not for the first time, the traitorous thought of what it would take to claim power while his father was still alive whispered in the back of Connor's mind. But, for the first time, he didn't bash it down. This was their people's safety at stake. How could Tolvar not care that hunters exactly like those who had killed his mate fifteen years ago were now roaming the property he had spent so much time and money making secure?

Was he insane?

Connor flexed his hands on the steering wheel. Ulfhednar weren't the military, for all that their training sometimes made him feel like they were. They were more like a monarchy, which meant there was precious little remedy for when a leader became unfit for his duty and yet wouldn't step aside.

Nothing that wasn't bloody, anyway.

His teeth ground. Fighting his father to the death or assassinating the old wolf certainly wasn't the answer. Wasn't even an *option*—and not only because no one had done it in centuries. The ulfhednar weren't animals, and Connor would be damned if he hurt his own family.

But if his father kept up like this, they might be screwed.

Indecision gnawed at him as he drove, and by the time he arrived at the manor, he was no closer to a plan of action than he had been to begin with. He couldn't risk his people. Couldn't risk Hayden.

Couldn't—or really, *wouldn't*—overthrow his father.

"He's in a mood and a half," Wes said the moment Connor walked in. The wolf gave a meaningful glance to the stairs leading to the third floor.

Connor sighed. "I'll take care of it."

"He had us pull back from checking the forest."

Connor turned to Wes, unable to hide his alarm.

"Even Barnabas looked surprised at that one," Wes continued, naming the oldest among Connor's father's trusted guards. "Your dad just said the hunters would no longer be our biggest issue soon enough."

Connor's alarm turned to incredulity. "And did he say what the hell *that* was supposed to mean?"

Wes gave him a flat look.

"Of course not." Connor let out a breath. "Dammit. Thanks for the warning." He headed for the stairs, taking them two at a time. If nothing else, he would have an answer for this.

No matter what.

The lack of shouting from his father's quarters seemed out of place, given how enraged the male had been only a short while before, but when Connor knocked, the bark of "Enter!" was the same as ever.

Connor stepped past the door, his eyes scanning the room automatically. His alarm grew.

Papers covered his father's desk and more filled a banker's box on the floor nearby. Through the doorway to the bedroom, Connor could see the wardrobe standing open with only empty hangers remaining inside. Tolvar's back was to him, his attention on sorting through the books on his shelves and placing them in a box at his side.

"You wanted me back at the manor, Father?" He kept his voice level.

Tolvar spun toward him, and Connor hesitated at the look in the old wolf's eyes. He seemed...anxious. Imperious, yes, but worried for the first time in years.

"Where the hell did you go?" his father demanded.

"I—"

"Never mind." Tolvar put a book into the box and then strode toward him, brushing past on his way to the door. "It's time I showed you. We have to be ready."

Connor glanced around, but Ingrid was nowhere to be seen. Somehow, that made him more nervous. The witch had something to do with this. He'd bet his savings on it.

He just had no idea what *this* was.

"Now!" his father yelled from the hallway.

Connor buried a grimace and went after him, jogging a bit to catch up to the old male who was striding through the halls at a pace just shy of running.

"What is going on, Father?" Connor called.

Tolvar didn't answer.

They reached the first floor, and Connor made a swift motion toward Wes to encourage him to follow. The wolf eyed him questioningly but did as he had been silently asked. They trailed his father down the hall and around a corner into a narrow corridor that led behind the conservatory. Tolvar moved quickly to a space on the hallway wall that looked no different than any other.

"The keypad is here." Tolvar pulled aside a square segment of the dark cherry-wood molding that ran at waist height along the wall. "The password is your mother's birthday."

The hairs on the back of Connor's neck rose. He'd

already known something was wrong, but this…this was really bad.

"Father, what's going on? Why is there a keypad in the—"

A thunk came from behind the plaster, and then a section of the wall swung outward like a door. The wall itself was thicker than Connor had expected. Almost two feet in width, with what looked like solid metal beneath the thin coating of plaster. Beyond the doorway, the metal continued along the walls, flanking a staircase that stretched down into darkness.

Tolvar reached through the opening and pressed his palm to a panel. Lights came on, illuminating the descent and revealing a stairway that led down for thirty feet.

Connor gave Wes an alarmed look, only to find the same expression on his friend's face.

"This way." Tolvar hurried down the stairs.

"What is this?" Wes murmured.

"I haven't the slightest idea."

Connor took a breath and followed his father down the steps. The metal clunked beneath his feet and the air was cool and dry. A quick glance behind him revealed a small green light perched above the door, while on the wall, the panel his father had used glowed electric blue with an outline of a hand.

He felt like he'd stepped squarely from reality into a science-fiction film. A large room lay at the base of the steps, with one hallway straight ahead leading farther into the complex and two more stretching away on either side. The walls were metal, and the ceiling was too, with inset lights glaring down on the stark floor. A table stood to the left, papers all over it and an array of flashlights standing in a line to one side, while monitors hung to his right, showing views of the property. Boxes were stacked along the walls, wood crates and cardboard alike, with markings on them for everything from MREs to toilet paper. More lights illuminated the corridors ahead and on either side, and the halls seemed to stretch for easily fifty yards before turning, more boxes lining their entire length.

He was standing in a prepper's fantasyland.

Connor turned to his father. "What the hell is this?" He couldn't restrain the incredulity in his voice, and he knew the alpha would bristle at the insubordination.

But his father didn't react at all. "Our protection," Tolvar said solemnly. "You needed to see this so you'd understand we have to be ready. The end is almost upon us. Now go back upstairs and pack what you'll need. I've had Barnabas and the others getting ready all morning, so they'll have some of your things already down here. But you'll need to go through and—"

"*What?*" Connor's protest rang from the walls.

A flash of his father's uncompromising personality showed through on his face.

Connor grimaced, trying to walk back the shout. "I am merely seeking to understand what this is about. Why are the others packing my things?"

"Not just your things. All of our things. We have to be ready."

"For *what?*" Connor said carefully, struggling to hold his voice level. "Father, what exactly is going on here?"

"The end, as I said."

When Connor stared at him, the old wolf turned away, running a hand through his gray-peppered hair. "There's no time to explain more. There's simply too much. After-ward, you'll understand."

"After what?"

Tolvar shook his head. "Go on." He motioned to the hallways. "Explore. But do it quickly. Then hurry upstairs and pack what you need. We're running out of time."

"Father—"

"*I will be obeyed!*"

Connor froze. The shout didn't startle him—after all these years, he was used to it. But the edge he heard in his father's voice sent ice racing through his veins.

Fear.

"Come on," Wes said quietly, nudging Connor with an elbow. "Let's, uh, do as he says."

His jaw muscles clenched, Connor followed his friend into the hallway directly ahead of them.

He felt like they were walking through a military bunker.

But then, that's what it was, wasn't it? A thrice-damned bunker right under the manor, and he'd never even known it was there. He glanced into the rooms on either side of the hall as he passed, seeing rows of beds in some, desks and workshops and an entire kitchen space in others. It was like a manor beneath the manor, but utilitarian and cold where the house above was warm.

"When the hell did he have time to do this?" Wes murmured.

Connor shook his head. "No idea. But he did it before we ever moved back here."

His friend nodded.

The complex seemed to stretch on forever, but eventually they found the other end in a bolted door that looked designed to withstand a battering ram from the gods themselves.

"Nothing getting through that," Wes commented, staring at the crossbars reinforcing the metal.

Connor didn't respond. He'd known his father was paranoid. That Tolvar was obsessed with myths and legends and anything Ingrid said. But he'd never suspected this.

Except now he knew where their money had gone. All of the drained accounts, all of the shuffled funds. The sheer scope of this place went a long way toward explaining the mysteries he'd seen in the ledgers last week.

Now he had his answer, and it was, in a word, insane.

"Don't suppose the IRS will let us use this as a tax write-off?" Wes commented as the two of them walked back down the hallway.

In spite of himself, Connor chuckled.

They continued on until they reached the original room where they had first entered the bunker. His father was still there, sorting through papers on the tables.

"Took you long enough," Tolvar snapped when they walked into the room. "Hurry and get upstairs. There isn't time."

"Time until what, Father?" Connor asked carefully.

"Too much to explain. Get upstairs and start packing."

Connor tossed a tired look at Wes. There was nothing for it. Going upstairs and packing would be ridiculous— just as ridiculous as buying all of the canned goods that clearly had been destined for this underground shelter. And his father wouldn't give it up. Connor knew him well enough for that. He would hound them until finally, Connor and his friends packed their bags and moved into the bunker.

And then what?

Connor sighed. At least they'd have beds. It was better than the eighteen months in the wilderness.

Though no one was going to be thrilled about the MREs.

He walked upstairs with Wes following behind him. Maybe his father would be satisfied with just one suitcase. And even if Tolvar wasn't, Connor didn't exactly have a house's worth of stuff. Moving to the basement wouldn't take long, as absurd as it was.

If only he didn't feel like he was entertaining a senile old wolf.

His cell buzzed when they reached the first floor. Drawing it out, he paused at the sight of Hayden's phone number. Why would she be calling? He hadn't heard anything from Cyrus or the others. Surely they'd alert him if something was wrong.

He tapped the button to answer the call and raised the phone to his ear. "Hey there," he said, welcoming the distraction if nothing else.

Hayden's response froze him to his core.

"When?" he demanded.

Wes stopped in his tracks, looking back as if startled by the tone of Connor's voice.

"Stay where you are," Connor said. "I'll be right there."

He waited only long enough to hear Hayden's agreement and then hung up.

"What happened?" Wes asked immediately.

"A hunter found her apartment." Connor dialed Cyrus's number.

He waited, seething, while the phone buzzed its electronic ring. Voicemail clicked on only long enough to inform him that there was no voicemail and then hung up.

Chills ran through him. He dialed the others quickly.

No answer. No voicemail.

Nothing.

Cursing blurred through his mind as his pulse raced. He shouldn't have left her. Shouldn't have fucked around in a thrice-damned bunker where—given the number of missed calls from her now popping up like dinging accusations on his phone—*clearly* there was no cell reception.

"I'll get the SUV," Wes said.

Connor looked up at his friend. The wolf's expression brooked no argument.

They ran for the garage.

17

HAYDEN

Standing in the center of her bedroom, Hayden wracked her brain. What the hell did someone pack when they were fleeing from a homicidal secret society? A few days' worth of clothes? A week? Would she even be able to come back for anything at all? She had a duffle bag of stuff beside her—sweaters, jeans, underwear, and a toothbrush —but what about anything else?

Her eyes landed on a collection of pictures on her dresser, images of her family and friends in cheap plastic frames. A pained feeling twanged in her chest. Grabbing a few from the dresser, she shoved them in her bag and then went to check the rest of the apartment again.

For the eleventy-billionth time.

Circling through the apartment, she felt lost. The living room didn't have much that actually belonged to them, given that the apartment had come furnished. It wasn't like she'd be leaving anything really important behind. The laundry room was pointless, and the dining room was too. In the kitchen, she took a steak knife from a drawer, holding it awkwardly with no idea how to bring it. She couldn't exactly tuck it in a pocket, and the back of her jeans wasn't an option either, considering that was just a quick way to stab herself in the ass. She settled for simply gripping it in her fist for the time being.

And she jumped every time a sound came from the hallway beyond the front door.

Over by the living room windows, Lindy sat on the arm of a chair, a bag already packed beside her and her attention locked on the neighborhood outside. When last Hayden checked, more snow had fallen, covering the blood by the evergreen tree. Mitch hadn't returned, but the wolves who were supposed to be guarding this place hadn't either. She tried to console herself with the idea that perhaps the wolves simply didn't know which apartment she lived in.

And ignore the fact that, one, Connor would have told them, and two, if they were looking for her, she suspected they'd pound on every door until they succeeded.

She wondered if anyone would find them.

She wondered if Mitch and his buddies had taken them instead.

Shifting her grip on the knife, she headed back to check her bedroom again, trying to keep breathing and hoping that, at any moment, the wolves whose names she didn't even know would pound on her apartment door.

Someone knocked.

She jumped, throwing a frantic look to the entrance, half expecting Mitch to come smashing through it.

"Connor was on his way up here," Lindy said as she rose from the chair. "I saw him outside."

Relief rushed through Hayden. She started for the door, only to have Lindy make a cautioning sound.

Hayden froze. "What?"

"He may have been intercepted." Lindy motioned for Hayden to stay back, the switchblade materializing in her hand as if from thin air. Pacing toward the door, Lindy moved as if she expected it to burst inward at any moment.

Stepping back again, Hayden floundered, fear beating a steady drumbeat inside her chest. This was insane. What kind of reality was she living in? But still...surely she would have heard if Mitch and the others had—

"Hayden?"

A gasp escaped her at the sound of Connor's voice. Lindy peered quickly through the peephole and then stepped back, throwing a quick nod to Hayden while the knife flicked closed and then disappeared into her pocket. Hayden rushed to the door.

Connor stood there, Wes behind him watching the hall-way. She resisted the urge to throw her arms around him, if only from relief that it was him and he was alive, but then, that probably wasn't a good idea.

The bad guys could show up at any moment.

"C-come in," she stammered, backing away instead.

"Are you all right?" Connor walked inside, scanning the apartment as if checking to make sure the Order wouldn't materialize from the drywall. Wes looked to Lindy, giving her a neutral nod. Lindy watched him like she expected him to go feral, but she twitched her head in the barest suggestion of a nod in return.

"They came to your apartment?" Connor asked.

Hayden cleared her throat, refocusing. "Um, yeah."

"How did they not find you?" Wes asked.

She could almost feel Lindy's tension ratchet up another notch. "We, um...we hid in the attic." Wes and Connor gave them both impressed looks. "Yeah, there's a...a hidden closet up there." Hayden shrugged, unable to hold their gaze for all that she wasn't technically lying.

It just felt like it.

"This must all seem pretty unsettling to you," Wes offered to Lindy, his tone utterly level.

The woman didn't take her eyes off him. "You have no idea."

Connor ignored the exchange. "You both shouldn't stay here. We can't find Cyrus and the others, but—"

"There was blood." Hayden's voice shook.

Connor glanced at her, and a chill crept through her. He knew they were dead. She was sure of it. He just wasn't saying it.

"Okay, well—" Connor glanced at Lindy. "Do you have anywhere you could—"

"I think he might know about my parents," Hayden interrupted.

Connor turned back to her, and Hayden couldn't quite read the look on his face.

"He was in the apartment," she persisted. "I heard him in my room, and I have pictures of them..." She swallowed hard. "If he could find me here or at the florist, then he could find them too. Can they come to the manor? Please? Lindy too. They—"

"Wait," Lindy protested. "I can go to a hotel. I don't need to—"

"He could come looking for you. If he thinks it'll lead him to..." Hayden's eyes twitched toward the wolves. "Us. You know he will."

Lindy was quiet.

"Please." Hayden gave Connor and Wes a beseeching look. "We only survived today because of luck, and my parents won't know what they're...what he..." She couldn't bring herself to finish.

"Did Mitch say anything about them?" Connor asked.

Indignation flared past her fear. Like that mattered? "No, but—"

"They might be better off staying put, then."

Hayden stared at Connor. "I'm not leaving my parents for the Order to find them."

Connor's eyes flashed between her and Lindy, questioning.

Hayden faltered. "I...it's okay. She knows. About us... now. Because I just told her." She fought back a wince at how badly she was flubbing this.

"You're taking it awfully well," Wes commented.

Lindy turned away quickly. "Listen, I'll get your parents, okay? And if the...*these people*—" She motioned toward Connor and Wes. "—don't want them back there, then we'll find somewhere else."

"I'm not leaving you to get killed by him!" Hayden protested. "Connor, what the hell? This is my family. My best friend. That guy broke into our home and—"

"Do your parents know about the Order?" Connor interrupted.

"What? Of..." Hayden sputtered. "Of course not."

She stared at him. His expression was entirely closed off.

Instinctively, she backed toward Lindy, putting herself between her friend and the wolves. "Why would you think they'd know about that?"

"I've just never heard of humans reacting so well to

learning about us." His eyes twitched to Lindy again, narrowing. "At least, outside of this town."

Lindy made a rough sound, that strange hardness Hayden barely recognized from her leaking back into her voice. "A guy just broke into our apartment and tried to kill us, and I...I'm in a room with..." She scoffed. "You have no *idea* how I'm feeling right now, pretty boy."

Connor's expression didn't even flicker, though Wes's eyebrows climbed.

Hayden looked between them all. "Connor, do you seriously think my parents are part of the *Order*?" She let every ounce of how absurd the words were fill her tone. "They've kept me safe for twenty years!"

At his silence, she blinked, struck speechless by incredulity.

"Maybe we should *both* go find your parents," Lindy stated coldly. "That creep said he was looking for these guys anyway."

Hayden exhaled roughly. Right. What other choice was there? She wasn't going to leave her family unprotected.

Or let Connor try to tear her apart from them.

"Yeah." God, what had she been thinking with him? If Connor believed that about her *parents*... "Thanks for coming, I guess."

She went to grab her stuff from the bedroom.

"Hayden," he called after her.

She didn't stop. Striding across the room, she snagged the duffle bag from the bed and then turned to head outside.

Connor was standing in the bedroom doorway. "Do your parents think the ulfhednar are monsters?"

She tightened her grip on her bag. "What?"

"Are they the ones who told you we hurt children?"

She scoffed. "We don't have time for—"

"The Order thinks we're monsters."

Hayden's eyes twitched to Lindy before she could stop herself. In the living room, her friend had backed toward her own bedroom, one hand in the pocket where Hayden knew she had a knife and her attention locked on Wes as if waiting for him to attack. Meanwhile, the other wolf was peering past the windows as if keeping watch, seemingly ignoring Lindy completely. "So?"

His hands moved in a shrug. "Then, surely, you see—"

A ragged noise escaped her. "No. No, I don't see—"

"I can't bring members of the Order into my home, Hayden. I can't let them anywhere *near* my people!"

This time, her eyes didn't budge from him.

He gulped down his anger. "If you know your parents aren't...that," he continued, his calm tone forced. "Then help me understand why."

Hayden exhaled roughly, flabbergasted. This was insane. She needed to go find her family, not take a trip down bloody memory lane.

But then, did she really think she and Lindy alone could protect her parents as well as a pack of wolves would?

Given how well she used that knife, Lindy probably could. But for herself, Hayden wasn't so sure.

"Please," Connor pressed.

"Mom's brother was bitten," she said, keeping her voice low. Lindy didn't need more fuel to think the wolves were monsters. "Back when they were both kids. Mauled by a wolf, everyone thought. And then, one night, he became one himself, right in front of her in the yard. And when all the adults heard her scream and grabbed their guns to protect her from the wolf they thought had returned to attack her too...It didn't end well." Her tone hardened. "But because they were scared, *not* because anybody was part of the Order."

Connor's gaze dropped thoughtfully. "And then, when your parents adopted you..."

"They didn't know what I was. But when they found out, Mom..." Discomfort rose in her. This was private. Precious.

And possibly the only way to convince him to help.

"Mom said her brother sent me. From heaven. To give her a chance to make things right."

Connor made a soft, rueful sound. He looked back up at her. "I'm sorry."

Hayden eyed him, distrustful.

"Your parents can come back to the manor. Your friend, too." He cast a half glance back toward the living room and then walked closer to her, reaching out and pulling one of her hands from its death grip on the bag. "I just want to keep you safe, okay? And suspicion is...a bit second nature, I'm afraid. At least where humans are concerned. But the thought of the Order coming anywhere *near* you..." His own expression of discomfort twisted his face.

She looked away, unable to meet his eyes.

"You've got great people around you," he continued. "And we'll keep them safe. But we need to get you where Mitch can't reach you, okay? Please?"

A breath escaped her. "Yeah, o—"

"What the fuck?" Wes's sharp curse broke the moment. Dropping her bag, Hayden hurried for the living room.

"What?" Connor called, a step ahead of her.

Wes stood by the window, his hands spread in a helpless gesture. "She's gone."

Hayden looked around fast. "Lindy?" She strode over to her friend's bedroom, and then peered into the closet and bathroom too.

Nothing. But her bag was still sitting beside the armchair.

"How the hell did she leave without you hearing her?" Connor demanded.

"Fuck if I know! I was checking outside, and I only took my eyes off her for a *second*." The man gestured again, clearly at a loss.

Hayden watched them both. Any second now, they'd accuse Lindy of being Order too, and this time, they'd be right. But until then...

She took out her cell.

Lindy picked up on the first ring. "I'm getting your parents."

Air left Hayden in a rush. "Why didn't you wait?"

Her friend was quiet. "Just tell me where to find you, okay?"

Hayden looked over to Connor and Wes, who were both watching her now. "We'll come meet you. It's not safe on your—"

"I'll be fine. Mitch doesn't give a shit about me. He's tracking you and the others, and if he sees you going to meet your parents, it'll only put you all in danger. So just tell me where to go."

Hayden ran a hand through her hair, torn. There was nothing for it.

Especially since Lindy had a point.

"Um...yeah, all right." She closed her eyes briefly. "Drive about twenty miles north on the state highway and then take Old Martell Road west." She continued on, giving the directions to the manor as best she remembered them. "Be careful, Lindy. Please."

"You too. Call you when we're on our way." She hung up.

"She getting them?" Wes asked.

Hayden nodded.

"We could follow," Connor offered. "Make sure they're—"

"No, it's…" A grimace twisted her face. "If Mitch is tracking me and I go there…" She shifted her shoulders uncomfortably. "She'll meet us. It's okay."

It had to be okay.

Struggling to push back the terror threatening to bring tears to her eyes, she looked around, feeling at a loss.

"Hey," Connor said gently. "Let's just grab your stuff, eh?"

"Yeah." Nodding with far more determination than she felt, Hayden hurried back to her room, willing herself to believe everyone would be safe and everything would be all right.

And not to remember the blood of the dead wolves, steadily being hidden beneath the snow only a few floors below.

The SUV sped along the state highway, the noise of the road barely penetrating the bubble of the vehicle's interior. In the backseat, Hayden turned her phone over and over in her hands, praying it would ring and terrified Mitch's voice would be the one on the other end when it did.

"Hey."

She flinched and glanced toward the seat beside her.

Connor gave her an insistent look. "They'll call. You'll see."

Swallowing hard, Hayden nodded. "Yeah. They—"

The phone chimed with her dad's ringtone.

"Hey, Dad, are you okay?" she answered, the words coming out in a rush.

"What in the world is going on, honey?" her father demanded. "Are *you* okay?"

A relieved breath escaped her. "Yeah, I'm all right."

"What's going on, Hayden? Lindy's here, saying we need to pack our bags and leave immediately?"

She pressed a hand to her eyes, still at a loss for how to explain this to them, and then cast a desperate glance to Connor and Wes.

"Whatever you want to tell them," Connor offered gently.

A constricted feeling seemed to loosen in her chest. He gave her a small smile. Up front, the radio clicked on, the sound low.

"Give you some privacy," Wes added.

The constricted feeling faded even more. "Um, yeah. Listen, Dad, there's...there's some people after me. Bad people. They—"

"Hayden." Her mother's voice cut her off, sounding farther away like she was on speakerphone. "Are these... certain *kinds* of people?"

"They're not wolves, Mom. They, um...they kill wolves. But..." She drew a relieved breath as the road turned ahead, revealing the gate that led onto the manor property. "If you'll please just go with Lindy, I have a safe place where—"

A click came from the phone. Her brow furrowing, she turned, glancing to the screen in confusion.

The call had dropped.

What the hell? Fear clamored in the back of her mind, throwing horrific scenarios at her. They were hurt. He'd found them.

Her hand shaking, she clicked the icon to dial them back, only for the cell to inform her it had no signal. Clicking the screen off and on again changed nothing. Neither did trying to call anyway, just in case the device was mistaken.

A shaky breath left her. This...this couldn't be Mitch. What could he have done, blown up the cell towers?

Maybe. Or maybe it was something about this property, instead.

"Um..." She looked around. A long cobblestone drive waited beyond the gate, sheltered by tall trees and winding up toward where she knew the manor lay. "Do you guys have something that stops calls here?"

"Huh?" Wes turned his head toward them, still keeping his eyes on the road.

"The call ended, and I don't have any signal."

Connor gave her a confused look. "Maybe it's a fluke. We shouldn't have anything that—"

A buzzing alert came from the radio, the sound faint due to how low Wes had turned the dial. Glancing back at them both, he raised the volume.

"—of the Emergency Alert System. Effective immediately, a shelter-in-place order has been issued for all counties in the listening area. Residents are instructed to shelter in place until further notice. Repeat. This is a—"

The broadcast suddenly cut off. With an alarmed expression, Wes reached over and clicked the button for another station.

Nothing. No sound. Just a hiss from speakers playing

only silence. The next station was the same, and the next after that.

Hayden trembled. What was this?

"Maybe the SUV's radio went out." Wes didn't sound like he believed the words.

"Yeah," Connor allowed. "Let's, uh, get inside."

Wes gunned the engine, sending the SUV surging along the last stretch of the driveway and around the bend into the courtyard of the manor.

Hayden climbed out fast, hauling her bag behind her. Warily, her eyes darted over the walled perimeter, the old-growth trees within its borders, and the enormous manor at the heart of it all. A three-story sprawl of dark stone, white pillars, and more windows than she could count, the place looked like a fortress built to stand for a thousand years.

And there wasn't a single chirping bird or rustling squirrel nearby.

Alarm spread through her in a rising crescendo of icy prickles. She couldn't hear anything. Not the crack of a frozen tree branch, not the whisper of sloughing snow. Even the wind seemed to have gone still, like a breathless hush had fallen over the world.

"Do you, um…" Her voice sounded tiny in the eerie silence. "Do you have a landline? Maybe I can—"

The woman in the white dress stepped from behind one of the trees. Like on the night she'd been standing in Hayden's bedroom, her feet were bare while her hair stirred as if in a strong breeze. Her angular face was solemn, her skin shimmering like it was covered in a layer of nearly translucent frost. She paced to the edge of the cobblestone courtyard, her body ramrod straight and her bearing like that of a queen.

"Go to the rooms underground." Her bell-like voice seemed to enter Hayden's head without the help of her ears. "Now."

"Hayden?" Connor called.

His voice came from far away. Hayden's hand rose, trembling as she pointed. "D-do you see the…"

He made a baffled sound. "See…?"

The door to the manor swung open, banging against the wall like a gunshot, and Hayden jumped. "Get inside!" Ingrid shouted. "Hurry!"

Instantly, the woman in the white dress stood only inches from Hayden's face, her dark eyes glistening like entire galaxies were drowning in their black depths. "Run."

The ground began to shake.

Wes caught himself on the SUV while Connor grabbed Hayden, the three of them struggling to keep their feet. The woman in the white dress vanished.

"Please!" Ingrid begged from the manor entry. "Get in here!"

The cobblestones of the driveway cracked, the earth beneath them rolling like a wave. A groan came from behind them.

"Holy shit!" Wes lunged away from the SUV as a tree came crashing down on the vehicle, smashing the roof and sending glass flying.

"Go!" Connor shouted.

Hayden gripped his arm as, together, they raced for the manor. The ground bucked, making them lurch around like drunks, and the sound like a freight train rumbling in the earth returned, familiar now from the earthquake a week before.

This time, it sounded like it was heading right for them.

Staggering up the two steps to the entrance, Hayden ran with Connor toward the door, her duffle bag jostling against her side as she struggled to hang onto it. Ingrid stumbled back, gripping the wall for balance as she tried to get out of their way.

"Down the hall to the bunker." Ingrid pointed. "Your father is there."

"Why the hell are we going underground in an earthquake?" Connor demanded.

Hayden turned, staring at him.

"Please!" Ingrid cried. "Your father—"

"Do it," Hayden gasped. "Underground. We have to—"

The building groaned around them. Outside, the earth cracked.

"Fuck!" Connor grabbed Hayden's arm and took off down the hall, Wes and Ingrid on their heels.

The tiles fractured beneath their feet while chunks of plaster rained down from above. Glass shattered and crashing sounds came from somewhere in the distance. Behind her, Hayden heard Ingrid speaking, her words garbled.

A cool sensation passed over Hayden's skin, radiating from behind her back. She threw a glance over her shoulder as they rounded a corner.

Alarm shot through her all over again. Ingrid's mouth moved with strange words, but her eyes were closed, and still the older woman was running.

But the ground didn't seem as unstable anymore.

"What the hell took you so long?"

Hayden turned back to see Connor's father standing by a doorway on the side of the hall.

"Get in here!" Tolvar shouted.

She ran with Connor toward the man, but her attention

was torn. Her eyes darted to the windows, to the trees, and the impossibly darkening sky outside. The earth still shook. Crashing sounds came from the forest outside.

And yet, even if the ground quivered beneath her, she didn't feel like she was running on a trampoline any longer.

"Downstairs, downstairs." Connor's father motioned rapidly. "We're running out of time."

A staircase lay beyond the doorway with metal walls on either side. Inset lights in the ceiling glared from the steel, making Hayden feel like she was fleeing toward the access hatch of a spaceship.

"The others—" Connor started.

"Everyone is down there already! Now go!"

Ingrid pushed past them, hurrying halfway down the staircase and then bracing herself against the wall, all the while continuing to chant.

Hayden balked in the doorway, throwing a look back at Connor. She knew what the woman in the white dress had said. She didn't have a clue what Ingrid was doing. But—

Brilliant light bloomed in the sky beyond the windows and the forest, turning the darkening clouds the color of orange soda before swiftly shifting to blood red. At the center of the ruined courtyard, the woman in the white dress stood with her eyes locked on Hayden, her hair whipping around her as if caught by a hurricane.

"Go!" Tolvar shouted.

Connor grabbed Hayden, pulling her through the doorway while Wes stumbled down the stairs ahead of them. With a ferocious cry, Tolvar yanked the door closed behind them all.

Ingrid chanted louder, her voice breathless, panicked, but never ceasing. In Hayden's mind, the words echoed, ringing against her skull. The cold feeling of the air strengthened, crackling as if with static electricity and making the hairs on her arms stand on end.

The rumbling grew louder. Beyond the door, crashing sounds drew closer.

All the lights went out.

18

CONNOR

Connor never imagined this was how he would die.

With one arm holding Hayden to him in the darkness, he braced himself against the wall and gripped the railing with his free hand, using all his strength to keep them both steady on the stairway as the earth groaned and growled like a wild beast around them. The metal door was thick, sealing out most of the sound from the manor beyond, but he could still feel the reverberation when things crashed down.

Maybe the whole building was falling.

Maybe they were being entombed in a metal-lined grave.

He clutched Hayden to his chest, burying his face in her hair and breathing in her scent. If this was the last experience he had on earth, maybe that was enough. Being here. Holding her. Imprinting her scent on his mind like a brand to carry into the next life and beyond, where maybe they would find one another, and maybe everything there would be okay. He could hear her whimpers of fear, feel her tears soaking his coat. Farther down the staircase, Ingrid was praying, her words a mixture of Icelandic and old Norse and the ancient language of the ulfhednar. Beyond that, though, there was nothing. Just the darkness and the groan of the earth and Hayden's trembling hands digging into his side.

But gradually, the shaking stopped.

He lifted his head slowly, looking around in the darkness. Even his sharp vision couldn't make out a thing, and after the constant noise, his ears rang at the sudden silence. Unsteadily, he straightened, his legs feeling strange and quivery, like he'd just gotten off a rocking boat.

"Everyone all right?" he called.

Scraping sounds came from the darkness, bringing to mind visions of his friends crushed beneath concrete and metal. But after a moment, wary calls of "yes" and "I'm okay" reached his ears from farther down the stairway.

"Nobody smells gas, right?" Tyson asked, a touch of nervousness in his voice.

"No," Luna said.

"Don't think so…" Kirsi added with trepidation.

Connor glanced down, feeling Hayden still shaking in his arms. "Are you okay?" he asked quietly.

"Yeah."

She sounded terrified.

He exhaled unsteadily. That made two—or more likely *all*—of them.

"Can you get the door open?" Wes called.

Connor nodded to himself. Right. Good thinking. In the darkness, he climbed the steps to the landing and felt along the metal door.

There was no handle.

Panic started a drumbeat at the back of his skull, and

he struggled to ignore it as he ran his hand up and down the smooth metal surface. Nothing. There couldn't just be *nothing*. How the hell—

"Father?" He struggled to hold his voice level, not wanting to panic the others. But he could feel the tension rise, adding to the reek of fear in the air. His friends weren't stupid; they knew him. They could probably feel his alarm the same way he felt theirs, threading between them all in an unspoken message, warning the pack of danger.

Gods, those ulfhednar traits weren't helpful now.

"Father, are you there?" he tried again.

Rustling sounds came from farther down the staircase. In the bunker room below, a light flared to life, making him wince in pain as his pupils rushed to adjust for the sudden glare. At the end of the staircase, he could see Wes still braced against the wall, Hayden's bag on the ground beside him where it had tumbled in all the shaking. With meticulous care, Ingrid descended toward the bunker, one hand on the railing to hold her steady.

Kirsi was at the base of the steps, and quickly, she lowered the beam of her flashlight to shine at the floor rather than in his eyes. "Need some help?"

"Yeah, can you bring that up here?"

She nodded and started up. Behind her, more flashlights clicked on, thinning the shadows. His father stood a short distance from the bottom of the steps, his head bowed as he spoke quietly to Ingrid. Around him, several of Tolvar's closest allies stood, surveying the walls as if making sure they hadn't cracked.

"Father," Connor repeated, fighting to keep his temper in check. "How do we open the door?"

"What?" Luna appeared at the edge of the stairway. "The door won't open?"

Connor could feel Hayden tense in his arms. She reached over, running her hand along the metal surface. "There's no handle." Terror threaded through her voice.

"What the hell do you mean there's no handle?" Tyson demanded.

Kirsi reached him, the beam of her flashlight revealing the smooth metal sheet set nearly seamlessly into its frame. Connor's fingers could barely gain purchase in the sliver of a gap around the door, and no other feature distinguished the surface.

Making himself keep breathing, he glanced to the wall, seeking the panel he'd seen when his father brought them down here before. Quickly, he pressed his palm to the black surface.

Nothing.

He shifted position, trying again. And again. And—

"Father," he called down, alarm breaking past his control and making him bite off the words. "How do we open the door?"

Tolvar turned his attention from Ingrid, regarding Connor. "The doors will open when the fires have passed." He resumed speaking to Ingrid quietly.

A breathless sound escaped Hayden. "Fires?"

Barnabas spoke up from Tolvar's side, his gray hair somehow miraculously without a single strand out of place and his bearing as stiff as if they still stood in the grand hall of the manor. "Surtr's fire has broken loose. The sensor above the door will turn green when it is safe to leave."

Shivers coursed through Connor at the nonsensical words. Surtr. Enormous fire monster from another realm.

Right. Of…of course.

He drew a slow breath, his body still trembling, and looked at the top of the door. There'd been a small round light there when he first came down to this place.

The thing was lifeless.

Chills spread through him. That didn't mean anything, the fact it looked as dead as a burnt-out bulb. The power was off; that was the problem.

"Do you see the light he's talking about, Connor?" Luna called.

"We need power."

"The generators should turn on soon," Barnabas assured him.

Connor glanced down, catching sight of Tyson at the base of the steps.

"On it," Tyson said immediately. "Which way?"

The older wolf regarded him for a moment and then pointed. Tyson hurried down the hall.

"So if the generators are down," Luna asked carefully. "Does that mean we don't have any air circulation in here?"

"Is there another way out?" Kirsi added. "Perhaps something with an actual door handle?"

"There are three exits," Barnabas said. "One leads to the garage; one leads into the forest. But none of them will open until the sensors are—"

"There's no backup?" Connor interjected.

Irritation at the interruption flitted across Barnabas's face. "We have made sure the generators are well protected from any interference or damage."

"Well, those aren't working right now," Connor said. "So I need a better answer. Father?"

Barnabas eyed him. "We have taken care of—"

"You've locked us in a metal box!" Connor exhaled sharply, looking away from the old, pain-in-the-ass wolf. "Father, answer me. Is there another way out of here?"

Tolvar placed a hand on Ingrid's arm, interrupting whatever she'd been whispering in his ear. "There is none."

Connor shuddered, rage pounding at his tight self-control like an electrical substation about to overload. On legs that were quivering with tension, he walked down the steps into the main room. He knew the smart move would be to hold his temper. The smart move would be to get as much information as he could.

But every muscle in his body screamed to pummel the face of the alpha who'd ruled their clan with an iron fist right up to the day he might have killed them all.

"How is this place still standing?" Marrok asked.

Connor's eyes snapped to his friend.

"Seidr," Tolvar replied calmly.

Connor's teeth ground. Magic. Right. Of fucking course.

"But you said there were fires?" Hayden asked, her voice shaking.

"Yes," his father said. "Everywhere."

A tiny, nervous sound came from Hayden, and Connor glanced back to see her clutching the corner of the stairway wall. "Okay," she managed. "But if there's a fire...will that...I mean, if we're locked in with it all around us..."

"The oxygen could be burning right now," Luna filled in. "Assuming the fires got into the manor."

"The bunker is airtight," his father said as though that was a good thing. "And the manor has the protection of seidr around it as well. We'll have sufficient air until the generators can take over circulating it, and Ingrid's power will protect us from—"

"*Enough!*"

Connor's shout rang from the metal walls. Tolvar's gaze slid to him, growing thunderous.

Shudders racked Connor. This was insubordination. Possibly worse.

And suddenly, he didn't give a shit anymore.

"What the hell is *wrong* with you?" he demanded. "You know, I put up with the mythology and the paranoia and the fact you moved us all down here when we could have been safe up in Alaska, but now you've fucking *killed us* if we can't get the hell out of—"

"That's enough!" Tolvar snapped.

"*No, it damn well isn't!*" He stared at his father, his harsh breaths coming like he'd run a hundred miles. "You delusional old *fool.*"

Tolvar made a furious noise. "Everything that is happening is exactly as I told you. That you were too enamored of your own opinions to see the truth is no concern of mine. I am acting to protect the clan, and I will not be challenged by a cub who won't open his eyes to what is real."

"What's 'real'?" Connor scoffed. "You want to tell me about what's *real*? I'm not the one who locked our people inside a metal tomb because he was scared of an earthquake!"

"I am saving all of our lives. Loki has returned and the Jotun are—"

"Loki doesn't *exist!*"

Connor turned away, raking his hands through his hair in an effort to keep from throttling the male.

His father made a derisive sound. "The moment those doors open, you will eat those words."

Connor shook his head, disgusted. There was no point to this. No point to any of it. The old wolf wouldn't be convinced, not until his son and all the pack suffocated in this metal tomb.

To hell with it.

"Barnabas," his father ordered. "Go help the cub with the generators. The rest of you, fan out and start making an inventory and organizing supplies. The fires will burn for at least a few days, possibly longer. We are going to need to—"

Connor didn't wait for more. Snagging a flashlight from the toppled collection on a nearby table, he strode off into the complex. His father was useless, but Connor was betting the supplies wouldn't be.

Somewhere in this doomsday mess, there would be a crowbar for the door.

19

HAYDEN

HAYDEN GRIPPED THE METAL WALL AND ORDERED HERSELF NOT
to freak out. They would find a way out of here. There
were *not* fires outside, no matter what Connor's father said
or what she'd seen in the sky in the moment before the
door slammed shut. She didn't know why there wasn't
any cell phone signal, nor what had happened with the
radio, but they were going to get out of here. They were
going to be fine.

And she would not freak out.

Her eyes tracked Connor as he stalked away,
murderous rage on his face. He'd find an exit. Or one of
the other wolves would. Or, hell, maybe she would. After
all, Lindy was coming to the manor, and her parents were
as well.

She glanced to the metal door, wondering if it was
worth it to start shouting for help. Maybe they should
wait. It would take Lindy and her parents time to get here,
after all. Assuming they knew where to look.

And assuming the wolves didn't run out of air before then.

Panic started to bubble up in her chest like a trapped scream. Pressing her lips together, she forced herself to turn away from the door and draw slow breaths through her nose, trying not to think about how each one consumed a bit more of the oxygen. But that was okay. They would be fine. Everything would work out just as soon as—

"You must begin your training for what is to come."

Hayden flinched. Ingrid stood right in front of her.

"What I have done will hold this place for a time," the woman said. "But I cannot sustain it forever. I am not as strong as I was in my youth."

"I-I don't know what you're talking about." Hayden tried to turn away. There were flashlights on the table nearby. She probably should get one.

"You knew to come underground," Ingrid said, following her. "You felt the seidr winding through this place in the moments before the fires began to burn. I saw your face when you looked at me. You—"

Brightness flared to life as all the overhead lights turned on. Hayden winced, ducking from the sudden, stinging glare. A hum came from the vents near the ceiling, and a whisper of air flowed into the room, thinning the smell of fear that had been clogging the space.

Sounds of relief rose from the wolves around her.

"I'll check the door," Kirsi said immediately. Marrok moved to follow her.

"Even if a lifetime of training cannot be replicated in days," Ingrid persisted as though the interruption hadn't happened. "You must focus on learning—"

Hayden headed for the stairs.

Above the door, a small round light shone brilliant red, while next to the frame, a panel glowed blue on the wall.

"How do we open this?" Kirsi called over her shoulder.

"As I told you," Connor's father said with regal patience. "The doors will remain sealed until the fires have gone."

Hayden trembled. There wouldn't be fires. They'd find a way out. They—

"Make a space!" Connor called.

She looked down the stairs to find him scaling the steps two at a time, a crowbar clutched in his fist. Marrok and Kirsi backed up quickly.

"If you damage the opening mechanism," his father called. "You will trap us all in here."

Disgust writhed through Connor's expression, but he didn't stop. Hefting the crowbar, he notched it into the small gap between the door and the frame.

"Where did you find that?" Hayden asked.

"Down the left hall," he said without taking his attention from the door. "Second door on the right."

Hayden nodded and hurried back down the steps. If nothing else, she could do this. Because they *would* find a way out of here—and sooner rather than later.

No matter what it took.

After three days, they gave up on the crowbars.

There were scratches all over the steel now and a dent from where Connor had thrown a crowbar at the metal in pure frustration. Wires dangled from the panel beside the door, testimony to Tyson's many fruitless attempts to bypass the encryption on the device without triggering the additional security precautions Connor's father assured them he'd put in place. The other two exits on the far side of the facility were much the same—dented, scratched, tangled with wires, and utterly unaffected by the wolves trying to escape their metal prison.

Well-stocked though it was.

There were two kitchens. Over a dozen storerooms with food and supplies. Seventeen private bedrooms and ten rooms like barracks with bunk beds arrayed in rows for an army of people to use. A gym full of equipment and weights was located to the south—or what they'd determined was south, based on the orientation of the staircase and the main room—with something that looked remarkably like a martial arts dojo nearby. There was a library, smaller than the one in the manor upstairs but stocked with hundreds of books nonetheless, and a computer hub full of desktops, laptops, tablets, and communications equipment.

The latter of which didn't seem to work at all.

She told herself it was just a glitch, the fact that her cell phone and every other method of reaching the outside world was nonfunctional. Or, more specifically, just a matter of being underground. Rather like her Intro to Chemistry class back in college, the one held in a subbasement with clanking pipes on the ceiling. Her cell had been as good as dead in that classroom, so maybe this was the same thing. And when the door opened, she'd find the cell signal had been restored and her parents had been worried sick.

As opposed to any other alternative.

The days fell into anxious monotony. Tyson worked day and night on any piece of tech he could find, barely sleeping or eating as he attempted to get outside communications operational. Kirsi trained relentlessly in the dojo, as if she could pummel the hours into submission. When she wasn't helping the others with whatever task they were currently doing, Luna could often be found in deep meditation in one corner or another, the twitches on her face hinting at her struggle to stay calm. Marrok proved to be just as good a chef as all of the wolves had claimed, and every day, he crafted meals and snacks that made life seem almost normal, if not for their surroundings. Along with some of Connor's father's wolves, Wes had taken to organizing their inventory and allocating supplies to every corner of the bunker. In case of collapse, he said. Didn't want anyone to starve if there was a cave-in.

Comforting a thought as *that* was.

But when the crowbars failed and the hacking attempts did too, she started to see less and less of Connor. At a distance, she'd spot him, his lean form striding fast through the halls to go check on something or other, or else crouched over rats' nests of circuitry with Tyson. But he never stopped. Never spoke to her. In the warren of the bunker, she hadn't even determined where he slept or if he did at all.

God knew she didn't.

The nightmares were relentless. Her home burning. The scarred man laughing as monsters strode over the world and crushed cities beneath their feet. A serpent larger than a mountain, surging up from the deep to throw tsunamis across the coasts and drown any who tried to flee. Lurching forms approaching through the shifting smoke and shadows, shrieking, howling. The sounds of ripping flesh and rattling bones carried with them as they came closer…closer…

Most nights, she woke up screaming.

She'd taken to sleeping in the rear corner of one of the barracks farthest from anyone else. The space was cavernous. Lonely. It reminded her of a horror movie she'd seen as a child. Most nights, she sat in the corner of a bunk, her arms wrapped around her knees as she trembled from the latest nightmares that left her unable to sleep.

But if nothing else, at least she knew she wouldn't wake the others.

During the daytime hours, she felt like a ghost, red-eyed by exhaustion, drifting here and there through plain metal halls that all looked identical. In a trance, she helped Wes sort boxes of supplies. Helped Marrok make meals or check on the water system that ran through this place. But none of it changed anything. None of it got them closer to an escape.

A few days in, Luna came to find her. She wanted to check on Hayden, she said, and to talk because word traveled fast with everyone trapped in a box, and she'd heard Hayden knew almost nothing about her own kind.

Or about what it really meant to be a wolf.

Awkward at first, their conversations soon became about every question Hayden had ever possessed. From how soon after shifting she could change form again—fairly quickly, though it caused tremendous stress to the system—to why the wolves seemed practically telepathic—their keen observation of body language was responsible for that, though between the six of them there was also something they called a "pack bond" that made them even more in sync—Luna explained more than Hayden had ever hoped to learn.

Including about her and Connor.

"So...wait." Hayden stared at the pale-haired woman where she sat across from her on one of the bunks at the back of the barracks. They'd been speaking for a little while, after dinner finished up several hours before. "*Can't get pregnant?*"

Luna shook her head. "Not unless you're in heat, no. STIs aren't really a factor either, owing to our physiological differences from pretty much everything else on the planet. We don't contract many of the same diseases as them."

Hayden blinked, absorbing the information. "Wow." Her brow furrowed suddenly, her thoughts flashing back to the cabin and Connor's reluctance to take things further when they'd been together. It had made sense at the time, when she assumed their bodies behaved more like a human's, but now...

"What?" Luna asked.

Hayden blinked, looking up again.

Luna gave her a pointed look. "Your face said—"

"Right. Um, just wondering about..." She shook her head. "Doesn't matter."

"Connor's really into you."

God, the wolves really could read every little glance and twitch of muscle. "Am I ever going to be this telepathic?"

Luna chuckled, blushing slightly. "Sorry. But honestly, he's..." She seemed to search for a word and then gave up. "It's nice to see."

Hayden hesitated. "I'm not, like, stepping on anyone's toes or something. Right?"

Luna's brow climbed. "You mean with us?"

Shrugging a shoulder, Hayden made a hedging noise. "You, Kirsi, the guys...?"

The blonde shook her head. "Not at all. Connor's like a brother to me and the males of our pack. And Kirsi..."

"What?"

"Let's just say Connor's not the one she wants." Luna gave Hayden a pointed look. "*Not* that she or he will ever talk about it, so you probably shouldn't ask. The gods know we don't anymore."

Hayden nodded, filing the information away.

"It's good to see Connor so…" Luna searched again. "Smitten."

Heat lit up Hayden's cheeks. "I don't—" She scoffed slightly. "I mean…he hasn't exactly been, um…"

Luna shrugged again, smiling. "We'll get out of here, and things…" She hesitated, a tension flickering through her expression as she dropped her gaze away. "Things'll be just…"

"We're going to be fine," Hayden assured her, ignoring the way her stomach twisted with doubt and her mind pelted her with images from her dreams. "Everyone will be."

The woman glanced up at her.

Hayden's stomach twisted worse at the look in Luna's eyes. "You don't think so?"

Luna hesitated and then folded her hands in her lap like she was drawing in on herself. "Of course we will."

Her smile looked odd. Sad but tense.

Nervousness prickled over Hayden's skin. "Do you know something I—"

Luna shook her head immediately. "No, no. I'm just… worried." Her tense, sad smile returned. "Like all of us. But I'm sure it's okay."

Hayden nodded. It would be. It *had* to be, her weird dreams and everything else aside.

There couldn't be another option.

"I've heard Ingrid talking, though," Luna started.

Hayden shifted position uncomfortably on the bunk. Ingrid had been following her for days, presumably to talk about magic and visions and all kinds of things. But Hayden had avoided the woman. Yes, she'd seen strange things before whatever the hell happened days before. Yes, she had horrible dreams. But Ingrid seemed to think it was the end of the world, and when she spoke to Hayden at the manor, she'd sounded like she believed everyone was going to die.

But they wouldn't. And as for the end of the world, this wasn't. Everyone and everything would be fine, and Hayden would be damned if she was going to listen to anyone who'd try to make her believe otherwise.

"She—" Luna cleared her throat delicately. "She says you can help. Us, I mean."

"I don't know what she's talking about." Shivers coursed through Hayden. "When we get back up there, everything is going to be okay. No one needs help, except to get out of here."

Luna nodded.

"Do you really believe that?" Ingrid's voice carried through the room.

Hayden tensed, biting back the urge to swear. From the door at the other end of the long room, Ingrid regarded her calmly and then paced toward her. Hayden shifted on the bunk, wanting to escape, but there was only one door and bolting around the woman and out of the room—while tempting—felt a bit ridiculous.

"I don't have anything to say to you," she told Ingrid.

"Then I ask that you listen."

"I'm not going to sit here and let you go on about—"

"Do you want your people to survive? Your family? Friends?"

Icy anger rolled through Hayden in a wave. "You don't know *anything* about—"

"But *you* know I am not lying to you about your dreams. You are running from this out of fear, but your dreams have shown you—"

"What the hell do you know about my dreams?"

Ingrid's lip twitched in a hint of a victorious smile. "You are a seer. You always have been. Just like your clan and your mother before you."

Hayden froze. Her eyes twitched to Luna. The woman blinked and otherwise didn't move a muscle while she watched them both warily.

"Luna," Ingrid said. "Would you please give us a moment?"

The blonde cast a quick glance to Hayden, who gave a wary nod. Luna hurried from the room.

"Where were you found?" Ingrid asked gently when Luna was gone.

Hayden trembled.

"I promise you by the power of seidr and all the gods, I mean you no harm." Ingrid reached out, clasping Hayden's hand. The old woman's skin was warm, but soft like rose petals. "My visions show truth, so please, just answer the question."

Hayden's mouth moved for a moment before she could find her voice. "A truck stop near Wolf Creek, Montana. The police said that—"

"Allow me to guess," Ingrid said. "Perhaps that you had been abandoned by a parent or accidentally left behind in their travels?"

Hayden's head twitched in a small nod.

"Indeed." Ingrid drew a breath and let it out in a slow sigh. Releasing Hayden's hands, she sank onto the spot on the other bunk that Luna had vacated. "About twenty years ago, a clan of wolves lived in Montana. They didn't have much. Trailers, a few houses, all in an unincorporated township far from humans, where they had resided peacefully for generations." Her eyes closed briefly. "Until the Order found them."

Quivers shook Hayden's chest.

"On their own, the Order should not have been able to hurt them. Those ulfhednar were seers, gifted in perceiving the future. Any threat should have been foretold and avoided long before. But the Order has tapped into dark powers over the centuries. Potent gifts from forces no mortal should dare engage, and they can use those gifts to hide from us. And so the Order surrounded them...and set fire to them inside their homes."

Hayden's hand crept over of its own volition, rubbing at the burn scar on her arm beneath her sweater.

"A few of the ulfhednar managed to escape the slaughter, but the Order continued to hunt them down. The last of the survivors—or so we all thought—was a female." Ingrid's face twitched with mild amusement. "A *woman*, as you would say." Her humor faded. "She died in the forest only nine miles from Wolf Creek. And she had a daughter, one we assumed had perished too. After all, the girl was barely four years old at the time."

Hayden's hand dug into the rough blanket beneath her. The world felt unsteady and blood rushed in her ears. "Wh...why didn't...The police should have known about—"

"The Order's reach is impressive. Or, perhaps better said, terrifying. Where the fires took place, their people covered it up, either by having their faithful in positions of power or through bribes or threats or worse. The police by

Wolf Creek undoubtedly never heard about the fire. But though the Order is powerful, they are not everywhere, and your mother made it over two hundred miles with you in tow before succumbing to her wounds." Ingrid's mouth curved into a sad smile. "I suspect her killers never looked for you both in Wolf Creek, because they never imagined she would have the strength to travel that far."

Tears stung Hayden's eyes. "Then how did you...I mean, the wolves. How did they, um, find..."

"It took the other clans time, but they located her body."

Hayden's hand rubbed up and down on her arm. "Were there any other survivors?"

Ingrid shook her head sadly. "None we've ever found."

"But did you know them? Do you know what her..." Tears choked Hayden's throat. "What her name was?"

"Fiadh," Ingrid said. "Fiadh Winters."

Hayden repeated the name, trembling.

"I met her once," Ingrid continued. "About ten years before she..." She sighed. "Before. Your mother was a beautiful woman. Very gifted. As were many of her clan." Ingrid paused. "As are you."

Instinctively, Hayden began to shake her head. "I'm not—"

"I've seen you," Ingrid persisted. "I've seen you standing when the walls come down and the draugar charge forth to kill the pack that must become your own. You are the one who can save them, Hayden. The one who *must* save them, or everyone will fall." The woman regarded her pointedly. "The question is...what have *you* seen?"

Hayden bit her lip. Telling Ingrid felt like a cliff. Like a point of no return. The woman would never leave her alone after this, not if Hayden told her the truth. But then, Ingrid would probably never leave her alone, regardless.

Her body ached. She was so tired…

A shaky breath entered her lungs. Dreams weren't reality, and everyone would be fine. Telling Ingrid about a bunch of nightmares wasn't going to change that.

No matter what the woman said after she heard them.

"Smoke," Hayden whispered. "And fire burning… everything. There's nothing left. Just debris around me and a picture that turns to ash and…" Her eyes flicked up to Ingrid. "Connor's there. I've seen him almost every night for my whole life, standing in the ruins. And more things. Creatures coming over the horizon. I can't see them clearly, but they shriek and howl and—"

"The draugar."

Hayden swallowed hard. "I saw a screaming man in a cave, chained up. For years, I saw him, always screaming. Always trapped. But when the earthquakes came—the first ones, about a week before we ended up down here?" She trembled. "He started laughing."

Ingrid closed her eyes, shaking her head.

"I see a monster under the waves, and I see fires burning everything over and over, but now…" She drew a trembling breath. "Now there's a woman, and she speaks to me. But she's not in my dreams, not always. Sometimes she's right in front of me, clear as day, but she can walk through walls like they don't even exist. Or like she doesn't." Hayden shifted with discomfort on the bunk. "She said the world will fall and the dead will rise. And she told me to come down here too."

Curiosity touched Ingrid's face. "This woman. What does she look like?"

"She's tall. Slender. She's got long hair and she wears a

white dress, and it all moves like there's a breeze even when there isn't one. Her eyes are black like the universe died in them but she can still see you, and when she speaks, I hear it in my head, but not with my ears."

"Fylgja," Ingrid said.

"What?"

"A part of myth, but one that—for a seer—can be quite real. An aspect of the self that can go ahead of you, behind you, and see what you cannot. These days, some might say she represents a connection to your higher self. The fylgja can take many forms—human, animal—and, in this case, a woman in a white dress."

"What does she want?"

"It would seem: to protect you. After all, you would wish to protect yourself, no?"

Hayden dropped her gaze away, her hand rubbing at her arm absently. Some of the things the woman…the *fylgja* had told her weren't protective, though. They'd sounded like warnings.

And they'd sounded terrible.

"Whatever comes," Ingrid said. "It is vital that you learn to use your gift—and to harness the power of seidr as well."

"Seidr," Hayden repeated. "You said that before. What is that?"

Ingrid tilted her head in an ambivalent gesture. "Seidr is, for lack of a better word, magic. But not rabbits from hats or waving about wands. It is—" She splayed her hands. "—partly your gift to see what is to come, and partly the ability to do something about it. There are spells for protection, for defense, for—" Ingrid gestured around her. "—holding up walls when the earth wants to tear them down. There are myriad uses of seidr, and those are what I would teach you…if you will allow me."

Hayden looked away. If telling Ingrid had been a cliff, then this felt like the fall. Trying to learn magic—even just *believing* in such a thing as magic—was like opening herself up to madness. Yes, she was someone who could change into a wolf, but she knew there had to be a scientific explanation for that. Yes, she'd had nightmarish dreams throughout her life, but dammit, she'd probably been traumatized as a child, watching her loved ones die in a fire.

Which explained a lot, really, now that she thought about it. Of course she saw her parents' picture destroyed in her dreams. Of course she saw monsters coming for her over the horizon. That was probably what it'd felt like to her, back when she was a child.

Though that didn't explain why she'd seen Connor.

"Let me at least show you what I know," Ingrid said, breaking into her thoughts. "Whether you choose to use or believe any of it, that is your decision." The older woman chuckled. "After all, what else are you going to do while we're down here?"

Hayden frowned. "The others could use my—"

"A few hours, that's all I ask. And later, if you wish to know more, then I will show you."

Her mouth tightening, Hayden regarded the woman. Ingrid wouldn't let up, Hayden suspected. Not given how persistent she'd already been over the past few days. So maybe it was better to just let her do what she wanted.

It wasn't like that meant agreeing to actually *believe* anything, after all.

"Fine." Hayden nodded. "Show me."

20

CONNOR

CONNOR WAS STARTING TO SUSPECT HE HATED HIS FATHER.

Days had passed. Maybe a week. He wasn't sure anymore, given that he'd barely slept while trying to get them out of this place. Time was the enemy. Too much of it meant they could run out of food or water or air. He couldn't risk sleeping through it and having even *more* go wrong. But no matter how hard he worked, or how much time passed, still…*still* the old wolf refused to put his palm on the damned door panel or provide them with a scrap of assistance toward getting out of here.

No, fuck it. Connor was *certain* he hated his father.

His smaller pack was doing everything they could to help everyone escape, though the gods knew Barnabas and the rest had provided no assistance at all. Tolvar had ordered his own wolves not to tell Connor or the others how to open the locks on their underground prison, although at least they'd volunteered information on where the hell the exits led. The thick metal door to the west opened a false wall in the garage. The one to the east emptied into a hidden door on the forest floor. *Where* in the forest, the older wolves wouldn't say. Only that it was "far enough."

Whatever the hell that meant.

So through days or weeks or endless eternity, Connor supervised. At least, that's what he told himself. Supervised and paced and circled repeatedly through the complex, assisting anyone who was working to get them out of here. He'd helped Tyson wire up one of the generators, hoping to short-circuit and open the door. They'd both nearly electrocuted themselves that day, and Connor could still feel a buzzing in his muscles—though that may have simply been adrenaline. With Wes, he'd tried to break open one of the air vents, but the damned things were so narrow that only a gopher could hope to get through. The three of them had torn apart several computers and wired Frankenstein versions of them back together, attempting to connect the damned things remotely to the manor cameras so they could figure out what the hell was going on out there, but so far, they'd had no luck.

And all the while, the lights above the doors stayed red and his father stayed tight-lipped, no matter what Connor did.

He couldn't believe he'd ever trusted the male. How had he missed the extent of his father's madness? Even when he'd first seen the bunker, he never imagined the old wolf would be willing to kill them all in here.

But if they could get the monitors working, if they could get a gods-damned *signal*, Tyson already had a plan for how to send word for help. It was rough and rudimentary and depended on whether the emergency personnel in the area happened to know Morse code and had a ham radio, but…it was something.

Something was all Connor had to hang onto right now.

He stalked down the hallway, his mind churning. Even if they couldn't get into the air vents themselves, running a wire through would—

Hayden's voice brought his thoughts up short, and his feet came to a halt. Her voice was low, her words unintelligible. She was inside one of the barracks, although what the hell she was doing in there was anyone's guess. Exploring, perhaps? Meeting someone privately, away from whatever room she'd found in this place?

The wolf inside him snarled at the thought.

Drawing a breath slowly in an effort to stay calm, he made himself take a step back. She wouldn't want to see him. And no matter how the wolf inside him growled and whined and paced...she still wasn't his.

After all of this, it was damn near guaranteed she never would be.

A familiar voice answered her, and the wolf inside him snarled all over again. Ingrid. What the hell was Ingrid doing, talking to Hayden so far from anyone else in the entire—

It *wasn't* his business.

Gritting his teeth, he forced himself to turn and walk back down the hall. Whether Hayden spoke with Ingrid was her decision. Regardless, he shouldn't be eavesdropping. It was bad enough that he almost came upon her in this tucked away corner of the bunker, now he wasn't giving her privacy either?

Gods, that would make everything even worse.

Connor rounded the corner, his muscles twitching with the urge to go find the gym and beat the shit out of a punching bag. He'd been avoiding her, and for all he knew, she'd noticed that. But he couldn't help himself.

What was he supposed to say? Sorry his father was a lunatic who'd locked them in a metal mousetrap and no one could say when they'd escape—or if they even would? Sorry she didn't know what had happened to her family, had no idea whether they were okay after that earthquake, and couldn't even make a phone call to find out?

It wasn't *only* his father's fault she was down here. Connor was the one who'd brought her to the manor that day. The gods knew she wouldn't be wrong to blame him too.

Not that he'd risked asking her.

Shame at his own cowardice twisted like a cold, leaden snake in his gut. The minute the doors opened, Hayden would be out of here, and well she should. This wasn't what he'd promised her—safety, security, a place to hide from the Order.

In an oversized coffin. What a joke.

She'd almost certainly never want to see him again. She probably regretted the day he ever walked into that flower shop.

The thought was almost too much to bear.

He headed for the front room, as they'd all taken to calling the first chamber inside the door below the manor. There was little chance she'd ever speak to him again, but he could still get her home. Wes should be by the door by now, working with Tyson on their latest plan to hack the palm reader. By now, they were willing to try just about anything, since it had occurred to them sometime prior that the mechanism for opening the door may have been damaged in the earthquake and, without their intervention, they might just be trapped down here forever.

So he'd help them, and he'd get Hayden out of here. And after that, things for the Thorsen pack were going to change. No more blindly following his father's orders. No more trusting that the wolf who had been such an icon to him as a child, who he'd practically *worshiped* growing up, possessed even a shred of his former wisdom or intelligence. Connor wasn't willing to overthrow the alpha in some bloodied battle to the death, but everything short of that?

If that's what it took to keep his people safe, fair game.

"Connor."

He tossed a glare over his shoulder. Barnabas stood in the middle of the hallway, his iron-pole bearing unbowed by time or the spike up his ass. With all the disdain of someone who'd probably changed Connor's diapers when he was a cub, the male regarded him coolly. "Your father will see you now."

Connor's eyebrow twitched up. Oh. Would he? Days of silence, of shut doors and non-answers, and *now* he would speak to his son?

"Do not keep him waiting." Barnabas turned and strode back down the hall.

Connor's wolf growled. Glancing up and down the corridor, he debated ignoring the order, if only because any "conversation" would probably prove fruitless.

Fruitless…but not without some merit. And regardless, he couldn't escape his father's demand forever. They were all locked together in a *box*, for fuck's sake.

Fine. He tugged down the sleeves of his sweater. The gods knew he had a few things to say to the old wolf too.

His father's study was located near the heart of the bunker, several storage rooms away from the computer hub. When Connor entered, Tolvar stood beside his oak desk, regarding his son like a school principal eyeing a recalcitrant student. Brown folders filled with paper were stacked neatly on a corner of the desk, while leather-bound books lined the shelves behind him. If not for the metal ceiling and walls, it would look like a small replica of his office upstairs.

Ridiculous.

"You wanted to speak to me?" Connor spat immediately.

His father's eyebrow twitched up. "I take it you are displeased with our accommodations down here. Let me assure you; the world above fares much worse."

"Well, I wouldn't know, Father, seeing as how we don't have any communications or cameras or *unlocked doors.*"

"That will change soon."

Connor's eyes narrowed. "You're going to let us out of here?"

"No need."

"What?"

His father drew a breath, folding his hands. "The doors will open in due time. Until then, I've arranged paperwork for you to review, which should detail the various protocols you may need to undertake to best represent our family's interests once we return to the world above. Barnabas has been instructed to aid you, of course, and I will accept your questions as well. You should review these matters quickly, however, as they are crucial parts of our family empire and—"

"*What?*" Connor gaped at the male, unable to restrain himself any longer. "Protocols? Paperwork? Are you fucking *kidding me?*"

The alpha stared at him.

"What the hell is this to you, Father? Some kind of game? You've locked us in a metal prison and—"

"I will have you listen to me."

"Or what? You'll kick me out? Send me out into the wilderness for a year and a half for *no* fucking reason? What *exactly* will you do?"

Tolvar's jaw worked around. "That was for your own good."

"No, it was because of *your* thrice-damned delusions and your obsession with the word of some old crone who parrots myths invented by people who probably thought the world was flat!"

"You will not—"

"No, you listen to me, Father." Connor stalked toward him. "I am *well* aware of what you think of me, and I have *tried* to make up for my mistakes. I have done, and will do, absolutely everything I can to protect this pack, no matter the cost, because *believe me,* I know the price of failure— and that's without you reminding me of it. But right now, protecting the pack means protecting them from you, so you'll excuse me if I don't have time for fucking *paperwork* while our wolves are trapped in this metal tomb!"

Seething, Connor turned and strode toward the door. This had been a mistake. Coming in here. Trying to talk to this mad old wolf when, in the time he'd wasted, he could have been helping—

"You did fail."

Rage froze Connor, and then his fingers curled into fists. His muscles quivering, he turned back to his father. "You—"

"And so did I."

Connor froze.

Tolvar drew a breath, regarding the desk before him. "You weren't entirely wrong about me. I blamed you after my mate died. I raged at you, at anyone. But mostly you. And you were a child."

Quivering radiated from Connor's core, and he couldn't tell whether it was rage, pain, or something so inherently made of both that it couldn't be parsed into such simple terms. His muscles shook, and when he spoke, his voice did too. "I tried...I tried to save her. When the first shot hit her, I tried—"

"I know."

"Then why didn't you *listen*! Why did you shame me in front of the entire pack, laying *all* of it down at my feet, as if I—"

"I was in pain. And so I failed you, and I failed her. I was not sufficiently prepared. I thought our defenses would be enough, that the measures I'd put in place would keep out even the most persistent of poachers." Tolvar pressed a palm to the folders on his desk. "And I was wrong. My lack of preparation cost everything, and if not for my failure, you and your mother would have simply had a pleasant day running through the forest, rather than..." He closed his eyes, his jaw muscles jumping.

A vice felt like it was gripping Connor's chest, making it hard to breathe.

"I am sorry, son." Tolvar looked up at him. "I am truly sorry."

Connor's brow twitched down. What the hell was happening? "Why...why are you saying this? What—"

"Because it needs to be said." A mirthless chuckle left Tolvar. "And because we are, as you say, in a metal box, and I do not know what we will find when we leave. Perhaps I am wrong. I suspect not. But since that day fifteen years ago, I have done all I can for you, and now you must be ready. Ready as you were not then, and more ready than you could ever *dream* you need to be. Everything I have asked of you has been to prepare you, and now…" He nodded to himself. "We both failed once. I trust you will not again."

Tolvar took his palm from the stack of folders and picked them up. "You will read these. Review them in detail and ask me any questions you have. Everything will become clear soon, and at that time, you will be ready. Do you understand?"

Not a bit.

Connor took the files the wolf extended to him. He couldn't even speak. For a decade and a half, he'd lived under the specter of his father's disgust and now…

"Come back when you finish reviewing the files," Tolvar said. "I trust that your business school training will help you understand what you read."

Connor's brow twitched down. That was the closest his father had come to a compliment in years.

"Go," Tolvar said. "You have much to attend to."

Connor hesitated, torn by the urge to speak and the fact he had no idea what to say. Without another word, his father turned away, clearly done with him.

At more of a loss than he could comprehend, Connor left the office.

Walking down the hall, Connor felt like he was in a daze. The old wolf had apologized.

Apologized.

He hadn't heard his father say sorry for so much as bumping someone in the hallway in…ever.

And the old wolf had apologized.

His eyes twitched down to the folders in his hand. He had no idea what to expect inside of them when he got back to his room. Account ledgers? A confession to selling all the family property to a drug kingpin? Nothing would surprise him anymore, given what had just happened in the—

"Oh!"

He collided with someone and stumbled back, barely keeping his grip on the folders. Hayden caught herself on the wall and stared up at him.

"I-I'm sorry," she said. "Ingrid asked me to grab some —" She cut off, seeming suddenly even more uncomfortable, as if aware of how mentioning Ingrid would probably go over with him.

He couldn't even find it in himself to care. "No, I'm sorry. I wasn't watching where I..."

Gods, she looked beautiful. He'd barely glimpsed her these past few days, and her scent made his wolf stretch and growl inside his skin. Exhaustion—a weight that he'd carried throughout all these days and nights of barely sleeping while he worked to get the doors open—seemed to fade to the background while his wolf pushed him to move closer to her.

Guilt reined him in before he could move a muscle. If not for him, she wouldn't be trapped down here. She'd be home and safe and probably wouldn't regret every damn minute she'd spent near him, seeing as how it ended her up—

Struggling to focus, he smashed the thoughts down hard. "Sorry. Didn't mean to almost run you over." He attempted a friendly smile.

Hayden hesitated.

He probably looked deranged, he realized, wiping the expression from his face.

"How are you doing?" she asked carefully.

"Fine." Renewed guilt hit him immediately. That was probably about the farthest thing from the truth, and he didn't want to lie to her. He just had no idea how to answer the question.

He cleared his throat to cover the pause. "You?"

She shrugged. "You know…"

Idiot. Of course, she wasn't okay.

Hayden tried for a smile, the result coming out strained. "I'll, uh, let you get back to…" Her eyes twitched down towards the folders in his hand.

"Right." His head nodded on autopilot. "I should let you get going too. It's getting late, and you probably want to get back to your room to sleep or…"

Connor trailed off, his thoughts short-circuiting. That wasn't what she'd said. She said working with Ingrid on something in the barrack, not heading to her bedroom to…to…

He drew another breath, inhaling her scent. Gods, she smelled incredible.

"Oh, uh, I'm not staying…" Hayden made an aborted gesture to the hall around her and then seemed to falter. "I mean, I just needed to grab a few things Ingrid asked me to get while she…" The uncomfortable look on her face deepened. "It's not important. Thanks."

With an awkward smile that bore more in common with a grimace, she tried to step past him. But his mind—slow, though it was—suddenly registered what she was *not* saying.

"Wait." An absurd thought dawned on him. "Where are you sleeping?"

She hesitated. "It's fine," she said. "I'm just going to grab—"

"Hayden?" he pressed.

She shrugged. "In the barracks."

"You...you've been..." He blinked. "*Alone?*"

At her hesitation, the wolf inside him was suddenly growling all over again, irrationally enraged by the thought she hadn't been. That some other male might have come near her. But that was just more idiocy. She wasn't his. And even if she *had* been his, which she wasn't, she still—

"Well, yeah." She shrugged.

"Why didn't you take one of the bedrooms?"

Hayden cleared her throat, looking distinctly uncomfortable. "I'm just going to go back and, um..." She started past him again.

"Did someone *tell* you, you had to sleep down there?" His wolf raised its hackles, snarling. If his father or *any* wolf in this bunker had told her she couldn't be near the pack...

"No, no," she assured him. "It's just—" She made an awkward gesture. "—you know, easier. I don't want to wake anybody."

His brow furrowed. "Wake anybody?" Memory slowly dawned over him. "Wait, are you still having nightmares?"

She gave a small, noncommittal shrug.

He wanted to kick himself. Of course she was. They'd been through hell, and they were trapped in a box, and her family was up there somewhere, probably terrified because they hadn't heard from her.

Odin's eye, *idiot* wasn't a good enough word for him.

"Come on." He shifted the folders in his grip and took her hand as he turned, heading for his room. Yes, this might look like he was planning something, but by the gods, that wasn't a sufficient reason to stop. He didn't sleep in that room anyway, beyond a quick nap whenever he couldn't go on any longer. There was no reason she needed to be down in some cold, empty barracks when she could—

"Where are we going?"

Not answering, he continued on, rounding the corner and then pushing open the door to his room. "You can sleep in here."

Hayden froze at the doorway, her nose twitching slightly. She could surely smell that this was his room. Smell that he had just invited her into his space—or, really, *insisted* she be here.

Her head shook. "I don't want to wake you if—"

"You won't. I'm not here often. But the walls are thick, so you don't need to worry about anybody hearing...you know. I just hate the thought of you being down there alone when..."

She could be in his bed.

Embarrassment curled inside his gut, and he scrubbed a hand over his burning eyes. Gods be damned, what was he doing?

Hayden looked at him, something tentative in her gaze. "How are you really, Connor?"

He set the files on the dresser next to the door, no idea how to answer her. "Once we get out of here, I'll be fine."

She nodded. "Did your father say anything about opening the door?"

A harsh scoff escaped him before he could stop it, and he could see the hope deflate in her eyes.

"No, but we have a plan," he amended quickly. She didn't need to hear his frustration. She needed to know they'd get out of here. "Tyson, Wes, and I intend to feed some cable through the air vents and get a signal out. The filters might be a problem. We know there have to be some up there, if my father thought there were fires and—"

Damn him, she didn't need to worry about that, either. There wouldn't be any fire, and everything would be okay, and he ought to shut up because—

"That's good," Hayden said weakly.

He should just go. He was only making things worse.

"So," she continued. "I'll grab a few hours' sleep, and then you can have the bed. Will that work? I don't want you to not get any rest."

"No, stay as long as you like. I was going to go help Wes and Tyson anyway, so you're more than welcome to stay here. In fact, I could take the barracks for a few nights or…something."

Hayden looked uncomfortable.

"Really." He reached over, taking her hand impulsively.

And then he froze, everything in his body suddenly hyper-focusing on the contact with her soft skin.

A shiver ran through him. He felt like it'd been a lifetime since their morning in the cabin together. Eons, maybe, since last he'd held her close. In all of a moment, his body ached, consumed by a need he couldn't figure out how to name.

Hayden blushed, a grateful smile crossing her face. "Thanks."

He couldn't make himself release her. After a heartbeat, her eyes slid down to their hands, and he fought off a wince. He was out of line. Dammit, he should let her go. Get back to work and do whatever he could to get those fucking doors open because that's the best way he could help—

Her thumb strayed across his skin and his breath

caught. The touch was gentle, but it felt as if it left tingles of light in its wake. Inside his mind, the litany of responsibilities descended into gibberish, rendered unimportant by the sensation of her hand in his.

And by the way she was stepping closer.

Her soft breath warmed the fabric of his shirt, the change so minute but vibrant to his heightened senses, and her scent surrounded him. Closing his eyes, he tried to resist it because, dammit, he needed to take care of her. Get her home safe and—

Gently, her fingers cupped his cheek, and his eyes flew open to find her watching him. "Is this okay?" she asked softly.

Connor swallowed, trying to find his voice. But what did he say? Gods, yes? That he wanted her on the bed right now because his body was aching and his cock was hard as granite and, by all the realms, he needed her?

He'd been fighting this for weeks, and in this moment, he couldn't even remember why.

"Yeah," he whispered. "It is."

His hand found her cheek and drew her to him, his lips claiming hers. Blindly reaching behind him, he swung the door shut and then returned to pull her closer, his hand raking up through her hair to keep her with him. Her taste felt like life pouring into him, washing away the bunker and the stress and the endless questions of whether they'd ever escape.

There was nowhere he'd rather be.

She made a tiny, desperate noise against his lips, her fingers digging into his shoulder blades and her body rocking against his. Desire burned through him, and he kissed down the side of her throat as she leaned her head to the side, giving him access to the delicate, vulnerable skin there. He could feel her pulse flying and smell the arousal coming from her, and the combination was intoxicating.

But this wasn't enough. He needed more. Needed her writhing with pleasure beneath him right the fuck now.

Moving fast, he lifted her, and immediately, her legs wrapped around him. Exhilaration thrilled through him to feel her there, pressing against his trapped cock, her lips still moving on his. The room was blessedly small, so it took only a moment to cross the distance to the bed and lower her onto the comforter.

He leaned back as her dark eyes looked up at him, her body laid out below him like an offering. "Gods, you're beautiful," he murmured.

She smiled, looking away like she was embarrassed. And that just wouldn't do.

Bending over her and bracing himself on the mattress, he kissed her again, nipping at her bottom lip while his free hand slid down between their bodies and slipped beneath the hem of her jeans.

"Hayden," he whispered into her ear. "You're the most beautiful thing I've ever seen."

His fingers moved between her legs, finding her wet and hot flesh there, and he captured her gasp with his mouth on her own. Massaging her gently, he relished the feeling of her rocking beneath him, her breaths coming short and desperate.

"Please." Her fingers tugged at the closure of his jeans. "Please, Connor. I need you in me."

Gods...the first time he'd heard her say that in the cabin, it had been damn near impossible to keep a shred of control. Now?

No fucking way.

He took his hand from between her legs and focused instead on removing the damn fabric keeping her from him. The button and zipper were the work of a moment. Tugging the denim and her underwear alike away from her, he slid his hands up her beautiful legs, making note of every faint gasp she gave. The backs of her knees were sensitive. That would be wonderful to explore later.

But he needed her now.

Continuing up her sides, he lifted her sweater away, drawing the bulky fabric over her head to reveal her beautiful skin. His eyes roamed over the swell of her breasts and the way her chest rose and fell as she watched him. He wanted to learn every inch of her, touch and lick and nip every part until she—

His gaze caught on the vicious scar of an old burn on her forearm, two inches wide and several more long. The scar was darker than all the skin around it, and rough like it'd struggled to heal. Instantly, Hayden moved to tuck it beneath her.

He put a hand to her arm. She froze.

Questions pressed at him, heavy with the need to know if anyone had dared hurt her or what they'd done. But that could come later. She was reaching for him now with her other hand, an uncertain look on her face as she tried to draw him back to her. "Connor?"

Gently, he drew her forearm up to his lips, watching her face as he moved. "May I?"

She didn't pull away, but he could see the confusion in her eyes.

He kissed along the length of her scar, never looking away from her. The confusion faded into something far more unreadable. Her lips parted and her hand reached out, brushing his face, her touch as gentle as his lips on her skin.

Swiftly, he returned to her, kissing her again. For a moment, she seemed taken back, and then she gripped his side, pulling him toward her with a ferocity that stoked the desire in him back up to an inferno. Her fingers moved to unfasten his jeans while he unhooked her bra, her warm skin so enticing. As the satin fabric fell away, he longed to take her breasts in his hands, but that would have to wait, if only for now. Swiftly, his jeans joined hers on the floor, and then he yanked his shirt over his head. Her lips parted as she watched him, and she moved back on the mattress as he climbed over her. Even beneath him, with his hands braced on either side of her body, the look in her eyes when they locked on him was all predator, no prey.

The wolf inside him pressed on his skin, urging him toward her, desperate to be in her. But in only a heartbeat, the sensation became more than that, more than the need to shift or the hunger to lay with this beautiful, intoxicating female. He could almost feel her wolf nuzzling against his own, fur on fur, invisible and yet present, as if they'd been waiting for each other all along.

His heart raced. Her legs fell open, giving him access as he lowered himself over her, and his cock slipped against her slick flesh.

"God, Connor..." she gasped.

Exhilaration thrilled through him. Gripping her hip with one hand, he entered her, hanging by a thread to his control to keep from thrusting into her with all his strength. But he didn't want to hurt her. Didn't want this to be even a tiny bit less pleasurable for her than it was for him.

And gods of the realms, this was the most incredible

thing he'd ever felt in his life. His body hadn't shifted, yet he could feel all her wolf with his, like the two of them were both that and human at the same time. She moaned beneath him, her fingers clutching at his ass as her hips rose, seeking more of him.

"Don't stop," she begged. "Please. Harder. God, please, harder."

His body responded before his mind could have a word, and with a thrust, he drove himself into her. She cried out, throwing her head back with a look of such ecstasy that it stole the breath from him. Her fingers clenched on him as his hand found her breast, massaging it as he drove himself into her, his human body and wolf as one in bringing pleasure to this amazing female.

Sweat built on their skin. With gritted teeth, he fought to restrain his orgasm, determined to give her every ounce of pleasure he could. The sensation of her wolf with his grew stronger, grew overwhelming, as if something within him was melding with something in her.

And that was good. Right, in a way he couldn't hope to describe. No one and nothing else in a thousand years would ever compete with the feeling he had, being with her now.

She was his. And more than anything, he was hers.

He gripped her ass, holding her to him as he thrust harder inside her. The room was gone. The whole world had disappeared. He could only feel her amazing body with his and the way her sweat-slicked skin moved beneath him, grinding against him, while the scent of sex filled his head.

Her muscles clenched around him, a cry leaving her as she came, and in only a moment, he lost his battle for control. A roar escaped him as the orgasm overtook him, and he clutched her to him while his cock pumped all he had into her.

His mate.

Breathing hard, he lay on her for a moment as his heart beat in his chest like a drum, and then he levered himself up on one elbow.

Her beautiful eyes found him, and her chest rose and fell quickly as she smiled. Reaching over to her, he brushed a strand of her sweat-soaked hair from her cheek, smiling in return, and then bringing her closer. Gently, he kissed her, tasting salt on her lips.

Breaking from her only long enough to retrieve a blanket from the back of the chair, he returned to her and spread the soft cotton over them both. Shifting around, he lay back on the pillows, and she nestled close, resting her head on his chest. A deep breath entered his lungs as he wrapped an arm around her, holding her to him, relishing the strange sensation that his wolf was still curled around hers, even as they lay here together in human form.

And that was fine. It felt incredible, and if he lived a hundred lifetimes, nothing would be more perfect.

21

HAYDEN

HAYDEN LAY IN THE BED, HER THOUGHTS LOST IN A DREAMY haze while Connor's bare chest rose and fell gently, his skin brushing her breast with every even breath. She felt... odd. Like something inside her was curled around something inside him and vice versa, contentedly dozing and sated in a way that was more than sexual.

Like something in her had been waiting for this, even if she never knew it existed. *Her mate.*

The thought seemed *right* somehow, even if the words felt alien. She couldn't explain it. This moment seemed precious, held in glass, like something she'd been searching for if only she could be lucky enough to find it.

And now she had. It was here. And so many questions she'd never thought she would ask were drifting through her mind, linked to it and special all on their own.

"Connor?" she whispered, wondering if he was even still awake.

"Mm?" He moved a little bit beneath her, and his hand rose to run along her hair.

Her eyes drifted shut contentedly. "What's it like? Being, you know, part of a pack?"

His hand paused for a moment. She waited, not breathing, worried she'd said the wrong thing.

"I don't know how to describe it," he offered, one shoulder rising slightly in a shrug. "The others and I... Some of us have been together for so long, I don't really remember life without them around me."

She nestled her cheek against his chest. "So, like friends, then?"

He was quiet for a second. "And more."

She hesitated. "How so?"

"They're part of me. They..." He shifted position a bit, putting an arm behind his head. "It's like family, but different too. When we're close, we know where each other are. We can feel each other there, like a unit." He chuckled softly. "My father tried to turn us into one, actually. Military style and all. Trained us since we were kids on...Gods, all kinds of things. Fighting, tracking, you name it. Said we'd need it someday."

He sighed. "But yeah. Like scent or hearing or any number of ulfhednar traits, it's stronger when we're in our other form." He twitched his head toward her. "I mean, you know."

She nodded thoughtfully. The world felt almost overwhelming to her senses when she shifted into a wolf.

"It helps us hunt," he said. "Keeps us safe. It's part of us."

Hayden lay against his chest. "So...was there, like, a ceremony or...?"

His hand returned, stroking her hair. "No. It just happens. Rather like humans, I would imagine. They don't have a ceremony marking the initiation of lifelong friendships or anything. They find their people, sooner or later, and they fit. It's like that with us, only—" He made a considering noise. "—more."

She wasn't sure what to say.

"You could fit here, too," Connor offered softly. "If you wanted…?"

Warmth swelled up in her chest, but it was overtaken almost immediately by a hot, prickling feeling—an unbidden, tangled mess of desperate elation and pain. The word *yes* hovered on her lips, and she wanted to say it. God help her, she wanted to say it so badly. She'd seen the connection between the others, even if she hadn't been able to describe it, and the feeling of being on the edges of that, of *knowing* something like that was right in front of her, but that she wasn't part of it, had been terrible.

But the truth pressed at her, sharp and wrong.

She swallowed hard. "My family is here," she whispered, hating the way she felt torn by the words. "My shop. My life. No matter what's out there—" A shiver ran through her and she pushed the fear down. "—I need to stay. And you…you're all going to leave."

Connor was silent. After an endless moment, his arms tightened around her, and his lips pressed to the top of her head. She nestled closer, tears burning in her eyes, and kissed his chest, wishing she could take everything back, never bring this up, and change the cold weight hanging in the air around her now.

He couldn't be her mate, whatever that really meant. Even if he was wonderful. Even if sex with him was more incredible than she'd ever dreamed—from the feeling of him inside her to the way he'd kissed that ragged, old scar she'd never really been sure how someone would react to seeing—they still couldn't be together. Not like that, and not when his dream was to return to Alaska, which would mean leaving everything and everyone else she loved, abandoning all her plans, with no clue if she would even come back again. She doubted the wolves wandered off from their packs willingly.

Not that she was part of the pack, either—and that thought, too, was painful.

Closing her eyes tightly, she lay beside him, pain and exhaustion weighing her down. She should probably just go. Head back to the bunker. Thank him for this and then leave because it was just too painful.

But he was warm, and safe, and nothing in her wanted this to end.

A knock came on the door. She drew a breath, opening her eyes with the sense that time had passed, though she couldn't tell how much. Connor stirred beside her, a tired noise escaping him.

She pushed up from the bed, uncertain what to do. Her eyes caught Connor's, and she could read the pain in his gaze.

Blinking fast, she looked away.

The knock came again.

"Just a moment," Connor called. His hand took her cheek, pulling her focus back to him. "We'll figure it out," he said softly.

She nodded, willing herself to believe.

A smile touched his face. Leaning closer, he kissed her, the gentle brush of his lips growing deeper in only a heartbeat. Her tongue tangled with his own as his hand moved to her side, bringing her closer to him and making that strange, animal-like sensation inside her stir and rub harder against whatever she could feel rising in him too. A hungry sound escaped him, and his fingers gripped her, pulling her back toward the bed, his body moving to draw her on top of him.

The knock came again.

Connor froze then groaned against her lips. Breaking from her, he shook his head, resignation and frustration mingling on his face. "They better have a *damn* good reason..."

Hayden chuckled in spite of herself.

He glanced back at her, smiling ruefully. "Later, yes?"

She nodded, hanging onto hope. They would make it work. Figure out something. This wouldn't be their last time together.

Maybe.

Connor shifted around in the bed, reaching for his clothes. Doing the same, Hayden picked up her outfit from the floor and chair nearby. Pulling everything on quickly, she couldn't help but cast quick glances back to him as he dressed, her body humming with arousal at the sight of his carved muscles.

He looked over his shoulder at her, and his mouth curved into a smile again.

She stifled a chuckle, grinning. He knew exactly what he was doing.

Tugging her shoes into place, she watched as he walked to the door, wondering if she should try to stay out of sight. But then, what did she have to be ashamed of? And anyway, it wasn't like the other wolves weren't aware of her interest in Connor and his in her.

Rising to her feet, she followed him across the room as he pulled open the door.

Wes blinked at the sight of them both and then seemed to refocus quickly. "Light changed."

Hayden's brain took a second to catch up and then her

mouth dropped open, exhilaration and relief running through her so strongly she couldn't speak.

"Which one?" Connor demanded.

"The one above the front room door. Went yellow instead of red, and your father says it'll be minutes, possibly, till it's green and we can get out of here."

Connor swore, relief and amazement in his tone. He grabbed Hayden's hand and hurried past Wes into the hall.

Hayden rushed after him. Tyson and the others were already in the front room, as was Tolvar. A moment later, she heard footsteps behind her, and she glanced over her shoulder to see Ingrid run into the room as well.

"How much longer?" Kirsi's voice was tense.

"Minutes, perhaps," Tolvar replied calmly while Barnabas and several of the older wolves came in from another hallway.

Carrying guns and air masks.

Hayden stared.

"What the hell are those for?" Connor demanded.

"Please take the weapons with which you are most comfortable," Tolvar said, rather than explain. "And everyone put on a mask. We must be prepared for what awaits."

Connor's friends cast him a wary look, but after a heartbeat, Kirsi stepped forward and took one of the semi-automatics and a mask from Barnabas.

"Come on," she said. "Sooner we do this, sooner we get the hell out of here."

The other wolves claimed weapons and masks. Connor eyed his father balefully, but he snagged one from the older wolves as well.

A click came from up the stairwell.

"Go," Tolvar ordered Barnabas.

The older wolf headed for the stairway, and the others followed.

Hayden stuck close to Connor as they climbed toward the door. Tolvar was overreacting. He had to be. What in the world did he expect to find up there? Grizzly bears? The older wolves were so grim, they looked like they were going to war.

Her mind pelted her with images from her nightmares. She swallowed hard, trying to ignore them.

At the top of the stairs, Barnabas paused, pressing a hand to the door, and Hayden heard Connor make a small, irritated sound beside her. Clearly, the older wolf had been able to unlock it too, not that he'd ever mentioned this to any of the people frantically trying to get the thing open for days on end. The metal door shifted in its setting, and the air pressure felt like it changed slightly.

Carefully, Barnabas pushed open the door.

Hayden's eyes closed briefly, her lungs instinctively drawing in a deep breath of the first fresh air she'd had in days.

But it smelled wrong.

Brow twitching down warily, she opened her eyes again. The others filed out ahead of her, and she heard Luna gasp when the woman stepped beyond the door. Climbing faster, Hayden scrambled up the steps, her heart starting to pound for the acrid stench on the air that was wrong. So wrong.

Her breath froze when she reached the top of the steps.

The manor still stood, though some windows had shattered. Charred bits of wood and leaves cluttered the hall beyond the door. Crystalline bits of fallen chandeliers glinted on the cracked tiles of the floor. The stench of smoke filled the corridor, making her eyes water and her nose burn.

But the world beyond the window left her body cold.

Nothing remained of the forest. Only matchsticks standing in clusters, blackened and thin, pointing like skeletal fingers toward a sky cast in shades of orange and gray and choked by clouds of smoke.

"Masks on," Tolvar said calmly.

Hayden's hands trembled as she pulled the mask over her head and situated it in position over her mouth and nose. The straps felt tight, tugging the plastic edges into her cheeks, and she could hear her breathing rasp as it exited the filter.

"Like Darth Vader, huh?" Wes commented to the others.

Behind the masks, she couldn't tell if anyone smiled.

"I'm going to check the computers and security systems upstairs," Tyson said. At Connor's nod, the lean man hurried away.

"This way." Tolvar's voice was muffled. With a motion for Barnabas to take the lead, he started down the hall toward the front door.

"There's no guarantee this came anywhere near Mariposa," Connor told her, his arm wrapping around her.

Her eyes locked on the windows, she nodded and followed the others. The front door scraped on the ground when Barnabas opened it, as if gravel and debris blocked its path, and her eyes stung worse with the breeze that came through the gap. The world was eerily silent as they left the manor, almost like the day of the earthquake when they'd all ended up in the bunker. Only the faint sound of branches scratching against each other in the breeze broke the quiet.

"What the *hell?*" Kirsi swore behind her mask, staring upward.

Hayden followed the brunette's gaze. Her knees wobbled beneath her.

Five broad lines were carved through the sky, varying in thickness with the center ones wider than the two on either side, but all large enough that if she held up her hand, even from this distance, they would be broader than her palm. The marks stretched from one horizon to the other, tapering at either end, and the area inside them was black like outer space, darker than an oblivion into which she'd fall and fall, freezing forever in endless nothing.

"What could have done that?" Luna asked in a small voice nearly lost behind the plastic muffling her.

"'And he will run throughout the realms,'" Ingrid said, her voice carrying through the mask, "'his lower jaw scraping the ground and his upper jaw against the heavens, consuming all in his path.'" Her eyes lingered on the tears through the sky. "Fenrir."

Hayden trembled, suddenly feeling small and exposed in the silent courtyard.

"That's not possible," Connor replied, but he didn't sound so sure anymore.

"And yet it is here," Tolvar said, striding past his son. "And you must be ready."

Hayden tore her eyes from the sky and looked at Connor.

He blinked, his eyes searching the ground as if not even seeing it. She reached out to him, and he gripped her hand tightly. Inside her, something stretched as if to rub against him—though whether to comfort him or herself, she wasn't sure.

"This..." Connor shook his head. "This can't..."

A shriek rose from the woods beyond the courtyard, and the sounds of scratching branches turned into a rattling wave, growing louder as it rushed towards them. A blurred shape lunged from the burnt-out bushes, all hands and teeth, flying at them with impossible speed.

The figure slammed into Tolvar. Hayden stumbled back as shouts rose and guns opened fire around her, but she couldn't take her eyes from the attacker.

Ripping hands. A face and body wracked by decay, with the skin hanging in tatters from dirty bone and withered muscle. Its clothes were caked in mud, and what remained of its hair stuck out in clumps from whatever flesh still clung to its skull. Already, it had sunk its teeth into Tolvar's neck. Its throat convulsed as if it was swallowing down his blood, while its body jerked and lurched under the hail of bullets.

Connor surged forward, firing fast with a semi-automatic. At the impacts, the creature ripped its face away from Tolvar's throat. Blood soaked its chin and its eyes were wild, cloudy with death. Unaffected by the bullets, it snarled at them like a predator facing prey.

A large gray wolf flew past her, slamming into the creature and knocking it off of Tolvar. With a whip of its head, the wolf tore its teeth through the monster's throat even as its claws ripped at the creature's chest as if frantic to kill the thing any way it could.

The monster shrieked, its body withering and decaying into dust.

"Grab my father!" Connor shouted.

Shrieks rose from the forest, wild and inhuman. Scuttling sounds followed in a wave, coming closer and closer.

Marrok and several others rushed forward, grabbing Tolvar.

Hayden trembled. The old man wasn't moving. His eyes were still open, and he wasn't moving.

"Fall back!" Wes shouted.

She looked toward the forest again. Out of the fog, figures like people were coming toward them. But they weren't human. Their bodies were decayed like the monster now turned to dust on the cobblestone courtyard. Some were moving upright. Others seemed to be on all fours, scuttling like crabs. Most had limbs hanging at odd angles, dangling from tendons or dragging behind them.

But their mouths were wide. Their cries rang through the dead forest.

And they were closing in fast.

"Run!" Connor cried.

The others bolted for the manor, though the wolf stayed, growling at the creatures barreling into the courtyard.

"Barnabas!" Connor shouted.

With a snarl that sounded a lot like a curse, the wolf tore after them. With his arm around Hayden, Connor raced up the steps, Barnabas leaping after them. They raced into the manor, Wes shoving the door shut behind them.

But it wouldn't be enough. Hayden glanced around quickly. The windows were shattered. The creatures could still get in.

"Get to the bunker!" Ingrid ordered.

"Tyson!" Connor called up the stairs. "Get your ass down here!"

Shrieks rose from farther in the manor.

"*Shit!*" Kirsi cried.

Tyson raced down the broad steps, laptops and other equipment clutched under his arms. "What's going—"

"Run, dammit!" Connor yelled at him.

They took off, tearing down the hall toward the entrance to the bunker. The shrieks grew louder and crashing sounds came from the corridor behind them. Frantic, Hayden threw a glance over her shoulder, seeing nothing.

The noise seemed to be closing in faster than they could run.

Kirsi slid around the corner and then swore, opening fire immediately. "They're heading for the bunker door! Go!" She took off running, continuing to fire.

On Connor's heels, Hayden rushed toward the bunker, Marrok ahead of them with Tolvar in his arms. The creatures stumbled and staggered, slowed by the onslaught of Kirsi's weapon, but still trying to reach the bunker first. Kirsi took up position by the door, shooting until her gun clicked empty, and then tossed the weapon into the bunker and grabbed for the handgun at her waist.

The creatures shrieked. Hayden swore she heard victory in the sound. The handgun wouldn't slow them.

Barnabas shot past, ripping at the creatures' legs with his teeth. Hands grabbed for him, clawing at his fur. Dust rose around him as he shredded hamstrings and calves and whatever arms came near.

But there were dozens of the creatures pouring in through the hallway.

"Go, go," Connor urged the others. "Barnabas, we're closing it!"

The wolf lunged from the cloud of dust, charging back toward them.

Hands caught his leg. He stumbled. A snarling creature lunged at his throat, its decaying mouth open wide.

A pale gray wolf leapt through the air and caught its

teeth on the creature's shoulder. Momentum carried the wolf around, hauling the monster back with it even as the creature turned to dust.

Barnabas scrambled up. He and the pale wolf bolted, sliding on the tile as they skittered around the turn and tore down into the bunker.

"Close it!" Connor shouted to Kirsi, pulling Hayden with him inside.

Kirsi grabbed the side of the door and hauled on it, trying to tug the handle-less slab closed.

Decayed and rotting hands snagged the edge of the metal. Kirsi cried out as they reached around the gap, their fingers tearing at her skin.

Luna charged past Hayden, an automatic rifle in her hands. Shoving Kirsi aside, she screamed and opened fire in the face of the creatures, the crack of the gunshots deafening as it echoed against the metal walls.

The monsters fell back.

"Shut the goddamn thing!" Luna shouted.

Kirsi grabbed the door and hauled it closed.

The light above the door clicked to red.

For a moment, no one moved. Hayden's ears rang from the gunshots, and her breathing came in short, frantic gasps. Faint thuds quivered through the metal.

But the door held.

Connor turned, hurrying down the stairs. "Get medical supplies!" he shouted at one of the older wolves. The woman nodded quickly and spun, racing down the hallway toward one of the storage rooms. "Marrok, tend to my father. If we need transfusions, there's equipment in west storage. The rest of you: is anyone else hurt?" As if in repeat of the question, Connor threw a worried glance at Hayden while she followed him down the steps.

She trembled, at a loss for how to respond. Every sound was muffled by the ringing in her ears, and her body was shaking as if she was cold. Her hand clenched and re-clenched on the gun she hadn't even remembered was in her grip, let alone figured out how to fire. Marrok and several of the older members of the pack were over in a corner, Tolvar presumably between them. The two people in wolf form paced. Huffs came from the larger wolf, fury clear in the sound. The other—Ingrid, she realized; the woman was the only other person no longer in human form—pawed briefly at the ground in unusual shapes that made the air tingle before she turned and jogged off down one of the hallways. Meanwhile, everyone else looked ready to open fire at the walls.

Shivers wracked Hayden harder. It had never occurred to her to be grateful for the thick metal on all sides.

"What the hell *was* that?" Kirsi demanded.

"Did you see where it came from?" Wes asked.

"It was in the damned *bushes!*" Luna cried, the gun still clutched in her hands. "I was looking right at them, and I didn't even see it was there until it—"

"Connor," Marrok interrupted, rising to his feet.

Releasing Hayden's hand, Connor hurried toward him. "My father, he—"

"I'm sorry," the larger man cut in, his deep voice quiet.

Connor stopped, and the air itself seemed to grow still inside the bunker. The others glanced at each other, horror in their eyes, while Marrok stepped aside, clearing a space for his friend.

Hayden stared as Connor walked forward, his movements unsteady. Tolvar lay on the ground, a bloody wound where his throat had been. His skin was ashen, his eyes unseeing. Barnabas lay down beside him, pain clear on his face even in wolf form. All around them, the others moved back, their expressions dumbstruck.

Gently, Marrok reached out, placing a hand to Tolvar's face and closing the old man's eyes.

The leader of the Thorsen pack was dead.

22

CONNOR

HE WAS GONE.

The words rang in Connor's head like a record player skipping, repeating over and over again and still never escaping utter insensibility. He was gone. His father, the rock of the Thorsen clan...

Was gone.

Immobile, he stared down at his father's body, unable to form another thought. The creature had torn through his father's neck, leaving nothing but blood and flesh that wasn't supposed to see the light of day. It was awful. Horrific.

And he was too numb to even feel like it was real.

One of his father's wolves appeared, a sheet folded in her arms. "Sir," she said softly, her voice nearly lost beneath how his ears still buzzed from all the gunfire. "May I...?"

He couldn't even move.

From the corner of his eye, he saw her glance away and

then nod. She bent, draping the sheet across his father's body, disguising it beneath white fabric like snow.

Connor felt like he was trembling. He couldn't really tell.

"It is the draugar." Ingrid's voice cut through the silence around him like a knife.

He turned, his body shaking harder. She'd shifted back, a white robe now around her. And to see her standing there, a new shudder coursed through his body, hard and radiating out like all his molecules would fly apart. The world blurred in front of him, turning red, turning dark.

Wes caught him as he lunged at the female, his friend snagging one arm across his chest to hold him back. But the wolf inside him still snarled and foamed at the mouth with rage. He'd kill her. That stupid bitch...

Ingrid stumbled back, her eyes wide. "Please, you must listen. The stories say—"

A wild growl cut the female off, and it took Connor a heartbeat to realize it came from him.

"*No.*" The word sounded barely human, but he didn't care. "No, you don't talk now. You don't open your *mouth*, do you hear me? You and your thrice-damned stories and myths. You don't speak again."

Ingrid kept her mouth shut, the first intelligent thing he'd ever seen her do.

Shaking, he turned, breaking Wes's grip as he paced from where his father lay. Rage was lengthening his finger-nails into claws. He could feel it, just like he could feel the sharpened teeth in his mouth and the way his bones wanted to change and shift. His neck popped as he twisted his head around, fighting the tightness of his own muscles and the fury pounding through him. He needed to think. Focus.

He couldn't. His father was dead.

"Connor." Hayden's voice quavered.

Agony speared his rage. She was worried; he could hear it. The wolf inside him trembled hard, torn in two by the need to rip apart anything in his path and the desire to comfort and be comforted by his mate.

Another shudder wracked Connor, renewed pain rising in him. *His mate.* He knew the thoughts that'd passed through his mind when he was with Hayden. He'd even heard stories about the feelings twisting through him now. It wasn't like the pack bond that existed between him and his friends—that preternatural sense of where each other was in the room. It was something else. Something more. Similar in the way a familiar backyard pond shared aspects with a deep dark pool in a cave, one where you couldn't see the bottom and had the sense it might go down forever with infinite mysteries inside.

But he'd been wrong. Or, really, she'd been right, and he'd been a fucking fool. She couldn't be that to him, not really. Not when the only thing that mattered was keeping this pack safe, and she needed to leave. Not when he couldn't even deal with the idea of her leaving right now or the foolish, pointless emotions pounding at him over it all.

Because he knew the fucking cost of distraction. Knew it down to his bones. He *couldn't* lose focus now. When he did, people he loved died.

His eyes slid toward his father, covered by a sheet and never to rise again.

Hayden's hand slid up his shoulder. A sharp breath entered his lungs, but nothing in him moved to attack. With anyone else, right at this moment, he wasn't sure he wouldn't have torn into them as soundly as the monster that just killed his father.

But this was Hayden. He'd sooner attack himself.

"Tyson." With effort, he tore his gaze from his father's body to find his friend still bearing laptops tucked under his arms. "The cameras. Did you get any of them to work?"

The male hesitated, and the wolf inside Connor wanted to howl.

"Not yet, but I'll see what I can do." Tyson nodded urgently, as if seeking some way to reassure him.

Connor nodded in return. "Do that."

Tyson hurried away.

"Luna." Connor looked to the female. "Stay here with Wes and Barnabas, keep an eye on the door. Kirsi, Marrok? Go check the other entrances, make sure they haven't been breached. You three—" He jerked his chin towards several of his father's wolves. "—shift and go help them. Apparently wolf form kills these fuckers. No one goes anywhere without one of us shifted from now on, got it?"

The others nodded, looking bloodless and ashen and so much more worried than even a moment before. If any of those things had gotten in the other doors…

He shoved the thought away. It wasn't the draugar. It *wouldn't* be the draugar. He knew the stories from his childhood, the myths about what would arise at the end of the world. He knew what he'd seen in the sky above the manor only moments before. But he couldn't believe…

His eyes strayed back towards his father, pain rocking him. It would all make sense, the old wolf had always said. It would all make sense, and Connor would see the reason for everything. And now…

He was still shaking, he realized. Or maybe it was the

room. Maybe the earthquakes had come back, ready this time to finally crush the metal box underground and take them all with it.

"Connor." Hayden took his hand, her soft skin warm and real. His eyes went to her, and he could see the questions there, even if she didn't say a word. Questions of worry for him, questions of what had become of the world.

Questions, when the answers were too horrible to even consider.

"I..." He didn't know what to say. Couldn't even think how to respond to any of this, except to protect the wolves around him. "I...I need to go help Tyson."

He turned to the others, his body still shaking as if it would never stop. "We preserve the body, and when we get the chance, we bury him. Now get ready."

Releasing Hayden's hand, he turned and strode out of the room.

23

HAYDEN

Hayden stared after Connor, something inside her whimpering at the pain she'd seen on his face and the coldness in her hand now that he'd let go. She wanted to go after him, to comfort him even if she didn't know how, but she had a feeling it wouldn't help anything.

The whole room could tell he was hanging on by a thread.

Drawing a steadying breath, she turned to Ingrid. "What the hell was that?"

"When the world ends, the dead will rise." Ingrid's voice was quiet.

A shudder ran through Hayden. "You're saying that thing...was *dead*?"

Ingrid sighed, laying the dark robe in her hands next to where Barnabas sat, still in wolf form. "It was a draug, one of the draugar and one of many things that will fill the world now. Even the realms themselves have been torn open, bleeding one into the other. The end has begun."

Hayden bit her lip, and Ingrid's eyes became sharp, a

questioning look flitting over her face. "Did the fylgja tell you of this?"

From the corner of her eye, Hayden could feel Wes and Luna looking at her in confusion, and it made her stomach churn. Even now, with monsters outside the door, she was a freak.

"What are you talking about?" Wes asked warily.

Hayden tried for a lie, but it wouldn't come. It felt wrong for more than just dishonesty.

Connor's father was dead, lying beneath a sheet only a few yards away.

But she couldn't make herself explain, either.

"If that thing was dead and it, um…" Her eyes twitched to Tolvar's body beneath the sheet, every zombie movie she'd seen in her life flashing through her mind. "Is Connor's dad going to, uh…"

Ingrid folded her hands in front of her. "The spells I have spoken over him will ensure he—" Pain flickered past her composed expression. "—remains as he is now."

"But…other people." Hayden shivered. "If those things bit them…"

"The draugar are not made by infection or disease, so a bite is not sufficient to transform someone. Legends say they rise after death due to the greed, envy, or discontent they experienced in life. But the ancients were so leery of the creatures that they even took special care in how they removed bodies from buildings for fear of causing a draug to return. Given what we're seeing now, it would be best to be cautious of any dead you encounter. They may well be able to rise."

Ingrid looked to the others. "You must all be ready. Everything you know of the world will have changed. You must be prepared."

"Prepared how?" Wes asked.

"Your training in the wilderness was only a start. Now, you will face a barren world with monsters you have only seen in your nightmares." Her eyes went to Hayden meaningfully before returning to the others. "Gather your resources and trust in your training. You will need them both."

"What...what if we just stayed down here?" Luna asked, a note in her voice like she couldn't believe what she was saying. "That's what Tolvar wanted, right? That's why he made this place?"

"Indeed," Ingrid agreed. "Staying down here is a possibility, though I doubt *all* of you would want to remain." She looked at Hayden again. "But knowledge of what you will face up there is also important. I can tell you of what I know, but I sincerely doubt that all of you would believe me." Her tone was pointed, and when she skimmed her eyes across the others, Hayden suddenly realized the woman had not missed the low opinion Connor and his friends had of her.

"I...I can't stay here," Hayden said into the silence. "My family is out there somewhere."

A tingle rushed through the air. "If they're alive," Barnabas commented, fastening the tie of the robe around his waist.

Hayden felt a snarl rise up in her throat, and she bit the sound back with effort. "They will be."

The older wolf looked away, clearly doubtful.

"We need to see what we're up against, if we can." Wes's voice was even.

Hayden nodded. He was right, she knew. They needed information first. But the drumbeat of panic in the back of her mind was overwhelming. She had to find her mom, dad, and Lindy, but she didn't have a clue how to do that. She knew very little about surveillance equipment. Nothing, in fact. She didn't know how to use a gun or fight with a knife or do basically *anything* that would keep her from being in the way of the wolves around her.

Hayden glanced toward Ingrid, who was bent over the sheet covering Tolvar's body and murmuring nearly inaudible words like some sort of prayer. Blood had started to seep through the white fabric, a slow stain from wounds drying up in death.

Shivers crept through her. Magic didn't exist. She knew what Ingrid had shown her: spells for protection, for attacking, for summoning the power of seidr. But whatever the old woman believed, that didn't make it real.

Right?

Hayden turned away. She had to get out of here.

"Wes?" Luna called. "You and Barnabas good to keep an eye on this door for a minute?"

The other wolf nodded.

Hayden's brow drew down warily when the blonde turned to her. "Okay," Luna said. "How about we hit the armory, grab some things, and then I show you how to use the weapons?"

A breath of relief rushed into Hayden's chest as gratitude bubbled up inside her. What Luna proposed was scary, but by God, it also meant doing *something*.

"Yeah." She nodded. "I'd like that."

24

CONNOR

"TRY NOW," TYSON CALLED FROM HIS POSITION BY A BANK OF monitors atop a table.

Crouched by the wall, Connor plugged the cord into the outlet. Across the room, screens flickered to life, showing black-and-white views of the destruction of the manor grounds.

"Thank the *gods*," his friend muttered, sinking into a desk chair. "I'd started to think the damned things were *designed* not to work." Tyson winced. "Sorry."

Connor shook his head, not responding. They'd been working for hours on rebooting the system with the equipment Tyson had brought down from the manor above. It seemed that, of all the things his father had prepared for, glitches with the camera system were out of his control.

The irony was painful. Maybe if they'd had cameras, they would have been better prepared.

Assuming Connor had believed what he saw.

He rose to his feet, shoving the thoughts away until

they were nothing but pointless smoke. It was easy, somehow. Ignoring it. He didn't want to think, so he didn't. He simply didn't. There were cameras now. Those would help protect them. And as for the rest...

His body felt hollow, like a gourd scraped empty of its insides. He had no plan anymore. There was only the next moment, the next thing in front of him to focus on.

And right now, that was checking the perimeter, getting Hayden home, and ignoring the sickened twist in his stomach at the thought of it all.

"How does it look out there?" he asked Tyson.

Frustration crossed his friend's face as he studied the screens. "It could be better. They're in the manor." He swore under his breath. "Forest looks overrun as well. But..." Eyes narrowing, he tapped a few keys and then nodded to himself. "The garage seems clear."

"Good enough." Without another word, he headed for the hall.

"Connor."

He glanced back at his friend.

Tyson hesitated, an uncomfortable and apologetic look flickering over his face.

Connor nodded. The other wolf did too.

Drawing a breath, Connor turned and strode out the door. The hallway was empty, and no one had come by in a while, ever since the others confirmed those creatures hadn't made it past the other two entrances into the bunker—a minor miracle, considering the forest door could have been easily breached.

Shivers crept over his skin, and he made himself keep moving. This time, the wolves would be ready.

Wes looked up from a table in the front room when

Connor strode out of the hall. Weaponry was arrayed before the wolf, from stacked boxes of bullets to various types of guns. Machetes and knives lay on another table nearby, along with holsters and sheaths and enough gear to take on an army.

His father had put so much effort into preparing for this.

Connor's stomach churned again, and he swallowed hard, forcing himself to stay on task. By the base of the stairs, Barnabas was honing the blade of a knife. The shink-shink noise of the metal sliding over stone was the only sound in the room.

Luna and Hayden were gone.

"They headed to the armory," Wes said, as if reading something on Connor's face. "They'll be back soon." He hesitated. "Luna was showing her some defensive techniques."

Connor paused, glancing back in the direction of the armory. He should have thought of that. All this time down here, and it never occurred to him Hayden might need—

"What's next?" Wes asked him.

Blinking, Connor turned his attention back to his friend. "Mariposa."

Wes hesitated and then gave a short nod. "I take it you all got the cameras working?"

"Garage looks clear."

"Good."

There was iron in the wolf's voice. A determination Connor felt, but hadn't expected to find among the others.

He needed to get Hayden back to her family. What was Wes after?

Footsteps came from the hall before he could ask. He looked over his shoulder to see Hayden and Luna carrying more guns between them, their winter coats already on.

Hayden hesitated at the sight of him. "Hey." She gave him a tentative smile as she followed Luna toward one of the tables.

He opened his mouth and couldn't think of a thing to reply to her. The world was an ash heap and so was any hope he'd held for things to be different. Whatever fantasies he'd had of making things work between them died the moment his father did. Now, his pack needed him. Hayden's family needed her. But to bring humans here...

His father would have howled at that. And didn't that matter? Upholding someone's plans, their vision—whatever the hell that had even been—was the thing people did when somebody died.

So shouldn't Connor? He'd failed his family despite every effort to the contrary, and now, both his parents lay dead. To turn his back on what his father would have insisted...

His chest ached like his insides were turning to lead, and his thoughts spiraled, cutting him as if they were made of razor blades. It wasn't right. To leave the humans would be to lose her. Yet in turning his back like a coward, he'd finally be doing what the old wolf would have asked, and wasn't that supposed to count for some—

"Connor?" Hayden walked toward him, and a sharp breath entered his lungs as he pulled away. She needed her family. That was all he knew. So he'd shut the rest away, and somehow, someday, it would all stop hurting.

And everything would make sense.

"Get ready," he told the others shortly, avoiding Hayden's gaze. "Barnabas, you and the others stay here. Keep Ingrid with you. Wes, Luna, I'll go grab Kirsi, Marrok, and Tyson. Meet us at the garage entrance in ten."

He turned, striding back toward the hall. "Let's get Hayden home."

25

HAYDEN

HAYDEN'S CHEST ACHED. THROUGHOUT ALL HER TIME learning with Luna, it hadn't stopped. Everything in her wanted to go after Connor and help him.

And she couldn't.

She wasn't even sure if he wanted her to.

In silence, she helped Luna and Wes gather what weapons they could carry. She could feel them watching her almost as much as they watched the hall down which Connor had disappeared, and she didn't know what to say to them. Before the door opened and everything went wrong, she'd imagined she would go back home. Check on her parents and Lindy. Come back and see the wolves after that. She thought maybe she could figure something out with Connor, some way to make things work between them in spite of all the obstacles in their path. But now?

She didn't know. Everything above the bunker felt ominous, like the next time the door opened, maybe some new horror would simply swallow them all whole. She could feel the tension in everyone around her, the quiet worry none of them were voicing. On every face was written the unspoken question of whether any of them should head back into the world above at all.

But she had to, and thanks to Connor, they were going with her. Once she found her family and Lindy, though, she had no clue what would happen. Would her parents come back here? Should they all go elsewhere? Surely the whole *world* wasn't like this.

Her thoughts flashed back to the impossible rips through the sky.

She shuddered. While she had no idea what that was or what those creatures actually were—supposed "draugar" notwithstanding—she was still going to find her family, and they would be safe. The wolves would as well. They'd get her parents and her friend and hightail it back here as fast as their vehicles could carry them.

Ever helpful, her mind served up images of her nightmares too.

Gritting her teeth, she bundled the rifles under her arm and followed Luna and Wes into the hall.

At the opposite end of the complex, Connor was waiting. A large wolf nearly the size of a small pony was with him, along with Tyson and Kirsi.

Hayden hesitated. That enormous wolf was Marrok. More than just concluding that by the process of elimination, somehow, she almost recognized him.

Kirsi snatched the rifle Hayden extended to her, irritation on her face. But she wasn't simply glaring at Hayden. Really, she seemed to be glaring anywhere *but* at the large wolf with gray-black fur.

Swallowing hard, Hayden continued offering the weapons around to the others, though the smell of their anxiety made her hands shake.

"Keep this," Luna told her when she came near, extending a handgun to Hayden. "Muzzle down, safety off, like we discussed. Keep your finger off the trigger until you're ready to fire. Remember, aim for the center of mass, not the head. It's an easier target, and it might slow them down long enough for Marrok to take them out."

Hayden nodded, gripping the gun and doing as Luna instructed.

Across the room, Kirsi made an angry noise. "You sure that door panel's going to work for you?" she demanded of Connor.

He nodded. "Barnabas had the master codes. I had Tyson reprogram it. When we get back, we'll add everyone's palm prints."

The others nodded, looking grim.

"Where are we headed in town?" Wes asked.

Hayden swallowed hard. "Seven-fourteen Maple Ridge Drive. The road's about three blocks east of downtown, past the grocery store where that car, um..."

"Right." Kirsi nodded, a hint of gratitude breaking through her hard expression.

Hayden managed a nervous nod in return.

"Masks on," Connor ordered, tugging his own into place as he headed up toward the door. "Let's go."

Marrok followed first, while the others came after, with Hayden at the back of the group. When Connor and the wolf reached the top, Marrok cast a quick glance back as if checking they were ready and then gave a quick nod.

Connor placed one hand just shy of touching the panel beside the door and then held up his other hand, three fingers raised. Drawing a breath, he ticked them down, counting.

Three...two...one...

He pressed his hand to the panel and then shoved open the door. Gun at the ready, he raced through with Marrok right behind him. The others charged up the stairs on their heels, and Hayden followed, bracing herself for any sound.

But nothing came. No screams from the wolves, no shrieks from the nightmarish creatures. Climbing the rest of the stairway quickly, she paused only long enough to shove the door closed behind her and then hurried out into the garage. Past the mask, she couldn't smell much of the smoke she knew had to be in the air, and the lack of her trusted sense frightened something deep inside her, as if one of her hands was tied behind her back in this new world full of monsters. A chill clung to the air around her despite the evidence of fires past the windows in the carriage-style doors, making her shiver in her thick winter coat.

The others jogged quickly across the length of the garage, rushing towards the SUVs, while Kirsi detoured to snag a ring of keys from hooks along the wall. Swiftly, the woman tossed the set through the air to Wes, who snatched them down effortlessly. Checking through the windows, he confirmed the vehicle was empty and then thumbed the key fob.

A clunk came from the doors as they unlocked. Hayden scrambled in. Marrok and Connor stayed outside until everyone else was in the vehicle, and then the two of them jumped in too, Connor slamming the door quickly behind them. Wes cranked the engine while the others rolled down the windows to make room for the guns, all the while moving with the efficiency and synchronicity of a military tactical squad.

Sitting in the middle of the backseat with Marrok on

her left and Connor on her right, Hayden clenched her hands around her gun and trembled.

"Ready?" Wes called over his shoulder, tension thick in his voice.

Connor nodded quickly. "Go."

Wes tapped the garage opener affixed to the sun visor above the driver's seat. The large doors creaked open, affording them all a slowly widening view of the burnt-out forests.

"Here goes nothing," Wes muttered.

He gunned the engine. The SUV charged forward.

The driveway was a mass of blackened ash and burnt logs, the latter crunching under the wheels while the former sent out clouds of grit into the air as they raced away from the manor, the garage door rolling automatically shut in their wake. Smoke choked the charred remains of the forest like acrid clouds.

Hayden gripped the gun in her hands, her palms sweaty. Her eyes skipped from one tree to the next, checking for monsters.

"There!" Luna cried from the front seat, pointing to the forest up ahead.

A shambling form charged the road from the right, shoving past the skeletal remains of the trees.

Connor didn't hesitate. Leaning out the window, he opened fire, and the figure stumbled, its leg going out beneath it and making it fall short of the road.

The SUV sped past, leaving the creature in a cloud of debris.

"Ten o'clock!" Wes called.

Kirsi opened fire. The creature staggered, slowed by the bullets.

On the SUV flew, racing for the highway through the

ash and charcoal ruins. Behind her mask, Hayden's breath felt hot on her face, and her pulse throbbed around the plastic biting into her cheeks. Eternity seemed to pass before the intersection for the state highway finally came into view, and the SUV careened around the turn onto the wider concrete.

"Holy shit..." Wes murmured, easing off the gas pedal at the sight before them.

Hayden clamped her lips shut against a whimper. A husk of a car sat on the road ahead, whatever color it had once possessed burned away down to the metal. Halfway out of the window, a blackened body hung as if the driver had tried to escape before the fire caught them and they burned alive.

"Just drive," Connor said, his voice tight.

Wes gave a tense nod and sped up again.

They flew onward, winding past more burnt-out vehicles. After a while, she stopped looking, locking her gaze instead on her hands gripping the gun. She could tell with every swerve of the SUV when they passed another vehicle, and she could hear the tiny gasps from the others when there had been people inside.

Time crept on, and gradually, the road leveled out, leaving the hillsides and flattening as it neared the town. In spite of herself, Hayden's eyes crept upward to the windshield.

A strangled whisper of shock escaped her.

The fires had reached Mariposa.

She felt a hand against her leg, and she jumped slightly. Glancing over, she saw Connor's fingers brushing her. With effort, she pried her grip from the gun and reached out, wrapping his hand in hers and clutching it hard.

Her beautiful town was in ruins.

The SUV rumbled down the hill toward Mariposa. Smoke still drifted up in idle wisps, rising as if to float out of the world through the blackened rips in the sky. Even from here, she could see that buildings had collapsed. Whole streets seemed crushed to rubble, their quaint structures reduced to anonymity by the destruction. Elsewhere, the shells of houses and businesses still stood, gutted by fire, painted black and brown by the smoke.

She'd only seen war zones in pictures, but this certainly looked like one.

The park outside the city was a swath of ash, its shade trees burned down to naked spires of charred wood. At its heart, a playground stood, its once cheerful jungle gyms now robbed of color, left as only burned poles and bubbled paint. The flower gardens planted by the local park district were gray streaks amid the destruction, still surrounded by decorative stones.

And bodies.

Trembling coursed through her, trapping a whimper inside her throat. Red and black from their burns, coated in ash by the destruction, the corpses lay where they had fallen, some by the playground, others by the empty pond, as if they'd fled for the now-evaporated water in an attempt to escape the flames.

Her breaths came short and fast, and her mouth moved as if to find words.

Or maybe just a scream.

As the wolves drove deeper into the town, more people lay dead on the sidewalks, while others were half-crushed beneath their own homes. In silence, Wes steered the SUV past them, weaving around the rubble and corpses alike. Clearly, some had fled toward the road, perhaps to stay away from the fires, though the flames had just caught up to them anyway.

Somehow.

"Why didn't they have anywhere to go?" Luna whispered, her voice small behind her mask.

Voiceless, Kirsi shook her head.

One of the bodies stirred.

Hayden's breath caught, an inarticulate sound leaving her, and she started for the window only to have Marrok growl in warning.

The body pushed up on one arm, reaching the other toward their SUV, and Hayden's mouth went dry. Empty eye sockets stared up at her above a dislocated jaw still trying to bite at the air.

"Holy fuck," Tyson breathed.

Accelerating, Wes turned the SUV toward downtown.

A whimper escaped Hayden. The street was a maze of cars with bodies inside, all of them burned. Some businesses still stood, their cheerful signs gone although the metal beams that supported them remained like accusatory fingers pointing at the wolves as the SUV drove by. On the doors and walls, bizarre symbols were painted in brown flaked paint—twisting, tangled things that made her skin crawl to look at them.

Though…maybe that wasn't paint.

A cold sort of horror poured through Hayden like ice water as the SUV continued onward, the sensation chilling her until everything felt numb and nothing felt real. The street was like a movie, distant, meaningless. Inside the tightly sealed SUV and behind her mask, she was unable to smell the destruction, unable to touch it. It was simply an image growing farther and farther away by the moment. With a detached calm, she found herself scanning the dead almost analytically, her mind filing away observations about which way they'd been facing or whether they'd been able to run. It didn't hurt as much that way, and with all their wounds, it wasn't like she could even recognize them.

And then...she did.

Recognition skewered her calm like a red-hot poker, making her gasp. It wasn't her parents. Wasn't Lindy either. But the bodies weren't burned as badly here, and she had the irrational thought that maybe the fire hadn't spent as much time on them. But she knew these people. There, the boy who'd checked her out at the grocery store each week, his face and his green apron only half burned. There, the barista from her favorite café, her legs and chest caught when stonework fell from one of the downtown buildings. Over there, the old man who sat outside the diner every morning, wishing people a good day. And there, Mrs. Sanderson, sprawled as if she'd been running. She'd never see those flowers at her daughter's wedding now.

Hayden's eyes darted, faster, faster, from body to body, each sight more horrible than the last. She knew them. She *knew* them from school and work and a thousand other places, and they were dead, all dead. What if her parents or Lindy or Johanna—

"Hayden?" Connor's voice seemed to come from far away, but it ripped her from her frantic search all the same. Whirling, she stared at him for a heartbeat, only to have her eyes go to the window beyond him, searching again.

His hand touched her cheek, drawing her around to face him. "Focus on me."

"But—"

"We're almost to your parents' house."

A strangled sound left her.

Connor met her eyes insistently. "Breathe. Please."

Her mouth moved, but she managed to draw in a short gasp of air.

"Good." His thumb stroked her cheek around the edge of her mask. "Take another breath. You've got this."

She swallowed hard and did as he asked. The spiraling feeling inside her head slowed. She felt the SUV turn, and she started to look toward the front again, but Connor's hand drew her face back toward him. "Stay with me. We're almost there."

Sucking down another breath, she trembled. Seconds crept by while Connor never took his eyes from her, searching her own as if to judge whether she was still hanging on. His hand was warm against her cheek, the contact solid and real and holding her steady in a way she couldn't define.

The SUV slowed.

Panic spiked through her. Connor threw a quick glance to the world beyond the vehicle, and she could see the tension flare across his face.

Oh, God...

Connor turned back to her. "Why don't you stay in the—"

She reached past Marrok to shove open the door before he could finish, practically barreling the wolf out of the way.

The cold air hit her like a fist, stinging her eyes with death and smoke. She faltered, but pressed onward, circling the SUV while the others climbed out.

Her parents' house wasn't gone, but only barely.

On shaky legs, she walked toward the remnants of the adorable bungalow she'd called home for years. Atop the small rise, a few walls remained: a side wall here, an interior wall there. The roof and upper floor were gone, as was the rear of the house. From her position on the road, she could see a straight line through to the next street beyond the backyard.

Silence hung over the world as thick as smoke, making even her breaths behind the mask seem loud.

She stepped up from the curb. Impossibly, the white picket fence her mother loved so much remained standing, the gate closed in front of the sidewalk as if everything was perfectly fine. But nothing else was. The rosebushes her father had planted when they first moved to the house years before were burnt to ash. Whatever snow had filled the yard had been melted by the heat, turning the ground to a frozen sludge.

With a trembling hand, she reached out to push the gate aside.

The wood crumbled when she touched it, and the hinges clattered to the ground, the sound jarringly loud in the eerie silence.

"Hayden, are you sure you want to—" Connor started.

Her feet scraped on the sidewalk, the sound muffled by the coating of ash and mud. Up the concrete steps, she climbed until she reached the place where the front door had been. Only half of its frame remained, gaping open at the destruction like a surrealistic painting of what could've been. Perhaps what should have been.

And what was gone.

She stepped into the house.

Everything was rubble, but suggestions of normalcy remained like a cruel joke. Remnants of her parents' unbelievably comfy sofa huddled to one side in a pile of blackened springs and ashen fabric. Charred lamps lay near collapsed end tables, burned nearly beyond recognition. Half of the stairway still stood, leading to nowhere, while the doorframe and wall of the kitchen were long since gone. The oven was destroyed, its sides turned copper and black by heat that had burned away its coating of eggshell-white paint. The refrigerator had toppled over nearby, charred too, its door gaping open with burned food inside. Chunks of drywall and wood from the floors above covered the ground all around her, obscuring whatever remained of the tile or carpet.

Except in one spot.

On numb legs, she walked across the room. By a gaping hole that had once been the staircase closet, a clear spot of carpet remained, several feet wide and sliced from the wreckage in a clean circle. Nothing was inside it, the absence jarring amid the debris caking the ground. The tan carpet looked as if it could have been vacuumed this morning.

She lifted a hand, reaching toward it. A faint tingle, barely stronger than the touch of misting rain, brushed her skin.

Shivering, she pulled her hand back.

A spot of vibrant color caught her eye at the edge of the circle. Pinned between two pieces of charred wood, her own smiling face beamed up at her from within the bubbled paper of a photograph. With trembling fingers, she reached down and picked up the picture. Her mom and dad smiled back at her, their arms proudly around the shoulders of her high-school self.

And then the photo crumbled to ash.

Cold spread through her. Oh, God. Why hadn't she realized?

This was her nightmare.

Her gaze crept up. This was it. The moment she'd seen all her life, every horrible piece of it surrounding her now. But it had never felt this real. Each time she'd seen this, she'd always known she would wake up, and now...

The words came, same as they had a thousand times. "I knew." Her voice felt raw, like it would be a scream if only she could breathe. "I—"

"I'm sorry," Connor said.

She whirled, gasping. His silver eyes met hers, sorrow filling his gaze, but it faltered at the alarm in her own. Reaching out quickly, she grabbed his hand, clinging to him in the desperate need for something solid. Something real, when this moment simply *couldn't* be.

"What is it?" he asked.

She shook her head. How could she explain what she didn't understand? This couldn't be happening. And yet...

Her eyes went to the horizon. She knew what came next. What *always* came next. Except now, she had a face to put with the oncoming horror. "We have to go."

Connor made a protesting sound. "We can search a while longer, just in case they—"

"No!" Trembles wracked her body. "We have to go. *Now.*"

She could feel the others watching her, and she knew how she must sound. Like Ingrid. Like a crazy person.

Shrieks rose in the distance.

"Oh, gods..." Luna stared at the horizon.

"Go!" Connor ordered.

He grabbed Hayden's arm, drawing her away from the destruction of her home as the wolves raced for the SUV.

26

CONNOR

FROM THE SEAT BESIDE HER IN THE SUV, CONNOR WATCHED Hayden, his wolf whimpering inside him. The wolf wanted to nuzzle her. Help her in any way it could.

And the man didn't know what to do.

They sped down the road, weaving around corpses and cars that he was sure she must recognize. The draugar hadn't shown up yet, but he'd heard them. They all had, shrieking and howling on the horizon. The monsters would be coming.

Because the monsters were real.

Old arguments tried to rise in his mind, dismissing the idea that the gods could've returned or that Ragnarok had come. It was madness. Nonsense. It was horror stories meant to keep cubs in line or provide a good chill around the campfire. It was *nothing*.

But then…how else did he explain the sky? How did he explain the fires or the destruction?

Or what had killed his father?

Connor squeezed Hayden's hand in spite of himself.

She may have lost her family too, just like he'd lost his father. He couldn't fathom it.

He felt responsible for it.

Gritting his teeth, he tried to push past the feeling. Nothing out here was safe, and not just because of the monsters they'd heard shrieking in the distance. Like downtown, a number of the houses here had symbols painted in dried blood on their walls, symbols that belonged to ulfhednar heritage but that the Order had stolen. For years, those bastards had been doing everything in their twisted power to turn emblems that once meant life or the sun or the names of the gods into signs defined by the Order—as if they could rewrite history and lay claim in the name of "purity" to something that was damn well never theirs to begin with.

Those bastards were out here somewhere. The gods knew why they'd turned the burned town into their own personal billboard, but it didn't matter.

The wolves needed to get out of here.

"Where would your parents go?" he asked Hayden.

Staring out the window, she flinched at the sound of his voice. Blinking, she turned toward him, her eyes unfocused. "What?"

"Where would they go? They weren't at the house, so where would they be?"

"I-I'm not sure. Dad might have...I mean, he...They didn't say where they were when I spoke to them on the phone before..."

"It's okay," Connor said when she trailed off. "Take a breath." She did. "Now try to think. Where would they be?"

Hayden's gaze skimmed around, and he wasn't even sure she was seeing the SUV. He *hoped* she wasn't seeing outside. They had entered a part of the town that looked like a park, and there were fewer bodies here.

But only by a degree.

"Dad might've gone to campus." Hayden seemed to be clinging to the words. "He's a professor. Mechanical engineering. Sometimes he goes in on Saturdays if he needs to get some grading done." Her hand rubbed at her forearm methodically where he knew she had a scar.

He set the gun on his lap and then placed his other hand on hers, stilling her motion. "And your mom?"

Hayden swallowed hard. "She works at the high school. She…" Her eyes squeezed shut as if in an effort to concentrate. "Some mornings she drives in early and drops off my dad, but, I mean, it was the weekend, and she probably wouldn't…" She took a ragged breath as if struggling not to cry. "She would have been at the…"

Connor gripped her hand as she trailed off again. There had to be some way to help her, but he had no clue. Surely her parents weren't hiding in a classroom somewhere. More likely, he'd only be taking her there to see their corpses. But meanwhile, those creatures were out here, and the longer she and his wolves stayed away from the manor, the more danger they would be in.

He exhaled, cursing silently. She wouldn't want to go back yet, for all that the only safe move was to return to the manor. Of course she'd want to check out every corner of the town, in case she could find them.

No matter how suicidal that might be.

She'd hate him, but he had to insist they head back. Because this was real, and because it wasn't safe. And because he didn't know what else to do.

"We need to return to the manor," he made himself say.

Hayden turned to him, horrified. "I...I'm not *leaving* them."

His mouth moved, but he couldn't force out the words he knew he needed to say. That the wolves were in danger too, and the odds her family was still alive were almost nonexistent.

Blinking like she was reeling inside, Hayden looked away from him. "Can we—" she started. "Could we go to the campus and just—"

"Holy shit!" Wes slammed on the brakes, lurching all of them forward.

Connor looked up. An army truck was barreling toward them, the thing tall and dark green and covered in back like a whole squad of armed humans could be hiding inside. Immediately, the vehicle pulled to a stop sideways on the street, blocking their path, and—just as he feared— soldiers jumped out, moving like a unit, some covering the street while the others pointed guns towards the SUV.

"Fuck." Wes cast a short glance back. "Any ideas?"

The wolf inside Connor growled. It had ideas, just no good ones.

If this was the Order...

"Stay put," he said. "If this goes badly, drive like hell."

Hayden made a protesting noise. "Connor—"

He didn't wait, pushing open the door. Keeping his hands in view and raised high, he stepped away from the vehicle. "What seems to be the problem?"

Besides everything, he added silently.

A soldier stalked towards him, gun at the ready. But the closer he got, the more alarm spread through Connor. The guy was a kid. They all were. Though they moved like a team, the oldest couldn't have been more than twenty years old, and most looked far younger.

"Who are you?" the soldier demanded.

Connor pulled his attention back to the boy in front of him. Gripping his gun tightly, the kid watched him as if daring Connor to attack, his young face determined beneath his camouflage-patterned helmet.

"We just got back to town," Connor said, making his voice as calm as he could. "We're trying to find my friend's family." He twitched his head toward the SUV.

The soldier looked at the vehicle and then back at him.

Breathing slowly, Connor did his best to appear nonthreatening. It was difficult. Humans with guns were a bad thing on a good day, and this was anything but. If the kids weren't Order, he highly doubted any of them would be up for anything else weird happening in their midst—at least, not without resorting to a "shoot first, ask questions later" response.

"Where are you coming in from?" The kid tossed the question out like a challenge.

He hesitated. "Farmhouse few miles out of town."

The boy seemed to evaluate the answer. "You got any description of the folks you're—"

A door opened and closed behind Connor. He threw a look back to see Hayden jogging towards him.

The kids with guns aimed all over again. Instantly, Connor put himself between them and Hayden, scrambling internally to keep his wolf from attacking out of pure instinct.

"What the hell?" he demanded of her.

She tossed him an angry glare. "Have you found anyone else?" she called to the soldiers.

"You need to stay in the SUV," Connor snapped.

Hayden didn't even glance at him this time. "Please. Have you found anyone else alive?"

The boy shifted his grip on his gun, and Connor's wolf snarled inside his mind.

But the kid didn't fire. "Yeah." He hesitated, a traumatized look flickering past his resolve. "Some."

Exhaling sharply, Hayden nodded. "Ed and Nell McIntyre. Have you found them?"

The kid hesitated, and Connor read everything horrible into the pause. He could tell by the way Hayden stopped breathing that she did too.

"You mean Professor McIntyre?" the kid asked.

"Yeah."

"He and his wife are back at base."

Hayden gave a whimpering gasp, pressing a hand to her mask like she was holding back a sob. Connor grabbed her arm, steadying her for fear her legs would go out beneath her.

"And Lindy?" she persisted. "Have you seen her?"

The kid winced slightly. "I don't know everyone's name, ma'am. I'm not sure."

Hayden nodded, looking nauseated.

Connor studied the boy. He didn't look like he was lying just to get them to trust him. But Connor's wolf side —hell, his human side too—wasn't about to leave Hayden with a bunch of gun-toting humans and just…what? Drive back to the manor?

Like hell. He skimmed his gaze across the kids, all of them so threatening with their guns and yet also looking like children playing dress-up.

"Who are you?" He tossed the question back at the boy.

The kid drew himself up as if hanging onto his military training for all he was worth. "Cadet First Sergeant Levi Doyle, Mariposa State University ROTC."

Connor eyed him. "You're all ROTC, then, I take it?"

Levi nodded firmly. "We're guarding the survivors under Major Rolston's command. Doing supply runs as well."

Slowly, Connor echoed the nod. "Mind showing me your wrists, Levi?"

The boy's brow furrowed, his expression more confused than defensive.

"Please," Connor added.

Glancing between them warily, Levi slung his weapon onto his shoulder and then tweaked back the edges of his jacket, revealing unmarked skin.

Connor glanced at the other soldiers and lifted an eyebrow.

"Why do you need to see our wrists?" one of the girls demanded.

Inside Connor, his wolf snarled.

"Just do it, Cadet," Levi called, not looking away from Connor or Hayden.

Her eyes narrowing, the girl did as commanded. Around her, the other soldiers did the same.

No tattoos. The girl had a few scars, and something inside Connor ached when he realized what those probably were. But there was nothing to indicate any of the kids were Order.

A breath left him. This didn't mean going anywhere with them was safe. It probably wasn't even smart. But he couldn't order the cadets to do a strip search, just in case they'd hidden their tattoos elsewhere. It was a miracle the young soldiers had done this much.

Besides, Hayden wouldn't return to the manor yet, and there was no way in hell he was leaving her alone with these people.

"Okay, then," he agreed. "Take us to the survivors."

27

HAYDEN

IN THE BACK OF THE SUV, HAYDEN TRIED TO KEEP FROM yelling for Wes to drive faster. She felt trapped, overcome with the urge to jump out and start running, if only that would help her move quicker through the nightmarish streets. Now that they had a destination, now that there was hope her parents were alive, everything was too slow. The SUV. The army truck ahead of them. Time itself. If she could've teleported across town, she would have.

And Lindy would be there. Johanna as well. Everyone would be okay.

Except for all the people who weren't.

She clenched her hands together to keep from reaching for the steering wheel. Every second meant the draugar could get to the people she loved first. She hadn't seen any more of the creatures since hearing them in the distance at her parents' house, but that didn't mean the monsters couldn't be waiting. Didn't mean they couldn't be there already.

Every second meant she might be too late.

The army truck turned onto the main road through the retail district on the edge of town, and the SUV followed. Unlike the downtown area, where there had once been quaint shops and old-world decor, the edge of Mariposa was a concrete wasteland of big-box stores and chain restaurants. The highway lay just beyond, linking Mariposa to the outside world and making it something of a commercial hub for all of the smaller towns in the area.

She could tell immediately that the damage wasn't as bad here. Maybe it was the lack of trees that had kept the flames from jumping, maybe the newer buildings had been more earthquake-resistant, but while some of the structures were burned to rubble, others were mostly intact, and the fire seemed to have extinguished itself at the boundary of the parking lots. A number of the grass swaths between them were charred, but here and there, a few trees still stood on their little islands in the middle of the lots. Likewise, cars near the center were more or less untouched, though bubbled paint covered those closer to the edges of the concrete expanses.

After so much death and destruction, all the colors looked surreal.

The army truck continued onward, and so the SUV did too, following roads that were cracked and uneven, evidence of the earthquake that had ripped through before the fire came. On the opposite end of the retail district, the army truck turned, heading toward the enormous warehouse-style superstore GetLots on the farthest edge of town.

"What the hell...?" Kirsi leaned forward in the seat.

Hayden blinked. Between them and the GetLots, there was a wall made out of everything imaginable. Buses. Cars. Shopping carts and scaffolding and other things she couldn't even name, all of them piled high in a barricade around the parking lot surrounding the store. Where the road met the barricade, a gate made out of what appeared to be the hoods of cars bolted together blocked off entry, and people stood over-top of it on a walkway, guns in hand. Lights like a construction crew would have on the highway stood along the barricades, pointed outward as well as inward, like they planned to light the world.

She swallowed hard, her eyes sliding to the horizon. Sunset was coming soon, and already the sky was deepening to the color of a blood orange. She could only imagine how dark it would be at night, since none of the lights in town probably worked anymore.

A shudder ran through her. Darkness or not, her parents would be okay. Lindy and Johanna and everyone else too. If nothing else, her people would be fine, and maybe they'd get out of here soon.

Though, really, there was only one place to go.

Her hands gripped and re-gripped each other. She'd been planning to take her family to the manor, back when the world made more sense and the only thing she'd feared was a crazy homeless man who believed he belonged to a secret society. Maybe that could still be the plan.

Though, maybe the Order was still out there.

Her thoughts flashed to the strange symbols she'd seen on the walls of the businesses and houses that were still standing, and she trembled.

The army truck pulled to a stop, and the SUV halted behind it. The cadet named Levi leaned out the passenger side window of the army truck and waved to the people atop the gate. They turned and called to someone else, and then the doors began to open.

Hayden tried not to gasp when they pulled past the gate.

Somewhere, someone had found tents, the kind she'd seen put up at marriage receptions to protect against the rain. Now, the white tarps were torn, but the tents still stood, with doctors and nurses moving underneath them.

Along with so many people laid out on the ground.

The army truck pulled to a stop in the middle of the parking lot, some distance away from the gate. The kids climbed out, and so Wes stopped, and all the wolves did the same.

Levi hesitated at the sight of Marrok jumping down from the SUV in wolf form, but he rallied admirably, refocusing on Hayden with only a few seconds delay. "Your parents and anyone else you're looking for will either be inside or..." His eyes twitched toward the tents. "You should check in at the customer service desk in there; they'll tell you where to go."

Hayden blinked. Customer service desk. Everything was feeling more surreal by the moment.

"What is this?" Connor asked, nodding toward the doctors and the people they were helping.

"Triage," Levi said. "Not everyone who survived is still standing." He cleared his throat, the brisk professionalism he seemed to be clinging to coming back over his face. "Now if you'll excuse me, we have supplies to unload."

Without another word, the kid turned and headed back toward the truck where the other soldiers were hefting a motley assortment of rubber bins from the back.

Hayden started for the door, and immediately, she heard the others move to follow her.

Gratitude pressed at her chest. No matter what else

happened beyond this moment, she was glad to have them with her right now.

The building was new, the GetLots having been built only a few months before. It'd been big news, earlier this year, with signs around town and memberships being sold on nearly every street corner. The paint still looked fresh on the cinder block walls outside, despite all of the destruction around them. Gray with bright red-and-blue stripes that were cheery and vaguely patriotic. When she walked closer, she could see the sliding doors had been propped open, their glass still bearing signs for hours of the store and advertisements for their pharmacy.

Behind the glass, though, a wall made of pallets of wood blockaded the entrance and obscured the view, and when she slipped past the gap between the doors, people with guns were waiting for her. More stood behind a barricade of carts to her right, the tangled wall blocking what used to be the access point where all the carts came in. A miasma of fear and sweat and unwashed bodies surrounded them, emanating from the store beyond the entryway.

"New arrivals?" an elderly woman with a rifle asked, eyeing her.

Hayden swallowed hard, trying not to breathe too deeply. Adrenaline already pounded through her, and the smell made it a thousand times worse. "Um, yeah." She managed a nod. "I'm looking for—"

"Hold on." Alarm filled the lady's voice, and she adjusted her grip on her gun, looking past Hayden. "What the hell kind of dog is that?"

"Mine," Connor said. "And he's not a dog."

"W-we got kids in—"

"Where we go, he goes."

The elderly woman started to shake her head, while the people behind her watched Marrok as if waiting for him to attack.

"Oh, he'll behave himself, ma'am," Kirsi said, an edge to her voice. "I promise."

Every line in Marrok's body seemed to tell Hayden how much the words were irritating him.

Kirsi's lip twitched, cold humor in the expression.

The elderly woman watched them a moment longer. "See that he does." She lowered her gun, looking back at Hayden. "You want to head for the table to your left, in the old customer service center. We got rosters there. If you're looking for someone, that's how you'll find out if they're here."

"Thank you," Hayden said.

The lady nodded firmly, still casting short glances to Marrok.

Drawing a breath, Hayden continued past her.

"Don't get pissy at me," Kirsi whispered pointedly. "*You* insisted on being the one to shift."

Marrok gave a terse growl.

The cloud of fear and sweat hit Hayden like a wall when she entered the store, but even as her body reeled, her mind did too. The store in front of her was surreal. From the ceiling to about halfway down the walls, it seemed like nearly a regular day. Signs for everything from housewares to car batteries to deli meats hung in bright colors, while ad slogans and sale signs proclaimed the best savings of the year. Square vents in the ceiling had been pushed open as if to let in air, and not all of the lights were on, leaving the place in dim twilight, but it still appeared shockingly normal.

But below, it looked anything but. Shelves and tables

had been shoved away from the center of the store to leave a vast open area for cots and sleeping bags. Metal pipes had been worked around and joined up into makeshift frames with sheets draped over them, creating separate spaces around the cots for some semblance of privacy. Voices rose from everywhere, their words bouncing from every surface and creating a din that was incomprehensible.

Her feet slowed. There were so many people, and yet when she thought about the entire town...this was all that was left?

She wanted to run into the crowd right now, yelling her parents' names. But she could see the tension on the faces of the wolves with her. There was easily a hundred people here. Maybe two hundred.

And some of the Order might be among them.

Biting her lip, she walked toward the desk, watching the crowd as she went. "Um, Ed and Nell McIntyre?" she said distractedly when she reached the counter. "Are they—"

"Hayden?"

She looked back sharply and her eyes went wide. "Johanna?"

The gray-haired woman gave a wordless cry. Dropping her pen and clipboard immediately, she rushed around the edge of the customer service desk and enveloped Hayden in a hug. "Oh my God, sweetie, I thought—Oh, never mind what I thought." She pushed Hayden back from her, holding her at arm's length. "Are you okay?"

"Yeah." Hayden blinked, taking in the dark bruise on Johanna's cheek and the way her gray hair was frazzled. "Are you?"

Johanna nodded, seeming on the verge of tears. "Even

better now. I…" Her brow shrugged over her watery eyes. "Mrs. Sanderson saved me, would you believe that? That crazy old bat. She just kept complaining, so I left the store and went to one of my greenhouses outside town to take pictures and *prove* to her she'd get her flowers and—" Johanna gave a tearfully ironic laugh. "—if I'd been at the shop, I would've…" Sniffling hard, she shook her head. "But enough about me! Where have you been, girl? Your parents have been worried sick!"

"Um—"

"Have they found you yet?" Johanna persisted. She whirled, releasing Hayden and hurrying back around the counter. Swiftly, she flicked through the papers attached to her clipboard. "Here they are. Their cots are in section C-17. That way." She pointed.

Hayden blinked. "Is Lindy there?"

"What? Oh." Johanna consulted her list again. "Yep. Right there with them."

A breath of relief left Hayden, and she cast a quick look to Connor and the others, most of whom smiled at her.

Connor's expression was entirely closed off.

"Uh—" Hayden faltered, turning back to Johanna. "Thank you."

The woman nodded encouragingly. "We'll catch up more soon, honey. Go find your mom and dad."

Hayden managed a smile for Johanna, nodding in return, and then she headed away from the desk.

What was wrong with Connor? For God's sake, she'd just found her family alive. Surely he should have been happy for her?

Her heart pounding, she pushed the thought aside. She'd figure out what was going on with him later. Now, she needed one thing, and that was to get through this crowd and find section C-17.

Wherever the hell that was.

She wove through the cots and sleeping bags, scanning for any kind of marker or sign. At first, there was nothing, and then a few people moved aside, and she caught sight of letters and numbers drawn in masking tape on the ground. Section E-5, it said. She veered left and kept going. Section D flew by and then, far back near the rear corner of the store, the beginning of C arrived. Tracking the marks on the floor, she continued in the direction in which the numbers ran. Her family had to be here somewhere. They had to—

Rounding a metal frame holding up a sheet, she caught sight of her mother several rows ahead and gasped.

"Mom!"

Nell looked up, and her mouth fell open. She seemed a little worse for wear with her graying hair pulled back in a messy bun and her clothes wrinkled and stained, but nothing slowed her down. Shoving away from the cot, she raced across the distance toward Hayden, pushing past several people on her way through the crowds. Ed leaned his head around the edge of a curtain, and then his eyes went wide. Quickly, he hurried after her.

"Oh my God!" Nell threw her arms around Hayden, making her stumble. "Where...*how*—"

Nell froze, her breath catching. Hayden pulled away slightly to find her mom staring past her to Connor and the others, alarm on her face.

Wariness spread through Hayden. "Um, yeah. Mom, Dad..." She glanced at the wolves. "This is Connor Thorsen, his friends, and, um—" How to explain Marrok? "Anyway, they—"

"Why are they *here?*" Nell demanded.

Hayden's wariness grew. "They helped me. I've been staying with them."

Nell shoved herself between Hayden and the others, jabbing a finger straight at Connor. "You're not biting *anyone* in this place, do you understand me?"

Shock made Hayden's mouth fall open. Oh, God, her mom knew. Lindy must have told her. But why would she—

Hayden's stomach sank. Why *wouldn't* she? Her friend couldn't have known Nell was scared of all other wolves. Hayden hadn't told her that.

"Mom," she tried, her eyes twitching to the crowd. Some people nearby were already staring, their faces cautious while they inched back from Connor and the rest. "They're friends. I swear."

Nell shook her head. "I'm not—"

"Mom, please. Don't make a scene. For me."

That brought her mother up short. For a moment, Nell was motionless, and then she dropped her hand to her side. "This isn't safe," she hissed to Hayden. "They shouldn't be here. *Look* at that one!" She jerked her chin at Marrok. "They're already—"

"*Please.*" Hayden's chest ached. She'd worried about this. Wondered how she was going to explain. But this was going off the rails faster than she could've imagined. They were standing in a crowd of humans who'd been through hell and looked antsy as it too. If these people found out *werewolves* not only existed, but that they were standing right here in the middle of them all?

Nausea twisted her stomach. "Let's go sit down, okay? My friends will—"

Nell clamped her mouth shut for a moment, glaring

between Hayden and Connor. "You all stay the hell away from my daughter, do you hear me?"

Connor didn't say a word. Without so much as a backward glance, he turned and walked away, the others following him.

Hayden faltered all over again. Wait, was that it? He dropped her off with her parents like she was some kid in grade school and just...left?

"What in the world were you doing with those *people*?" Nell whispered, snagging her arm.

Hayden exhaled, anger boiling up in her suddenly. "Surviving." She jerked out of her mother's grip. "And you did *not* have the right to treat them like that."

Nell blinked at her.

"Section C-17?" Hayden snapped expectantly. "Right over here?"

She started walking, not waiting for her parents to catch up. Her pulse throbbed in her throat and tears burned in her eyes, useless and asinine. After all this time of hoping and praying her family was okay, and after everything she'd seen today alone, this was just...too much. She hadn't expected a Norman Rockwell painting, but a cold shoulder from Connor and her mother nearly revealing werewolves to the world?

If she hadn't been in a crowd, she might have just screamed from the pent-up stress of it all.

Rounding the edge of the sheet-covered frame, she spotted Lindy sitting on one of the cots. At the sight of her, Lindy shoved to her feet. Rushing over, she threw her arms around Hayden.

"Oh, God." Lindy squeezed her so hard, Hayden could barely breathe. "I thought..." Her friend released her. "Are you okay?"

Hayden's mouth moved, wordless. She didn't know how to begin answering that. "You?"

Lindy seemed to search for words and failed. Still floundering, she released Hayden. "I'm alive. Better than it could be, right?" She glanced around, picking at her fingernails. "Are the, um...*others* here?"

A pained feeling rose in Hayden's chest all over again, and she glanced back to see her father talking in a low voice to her mother.

Beyond them, the wolves were nowhere to be seen.

Hayden shook her head. Even if Connor and the others were still in the building for the moment, they'd leave as soon as they could. Of that, she was fairly certain.

She just wondered if he'd even say goodbye before he went.

28

CONNOR

CONNOR WALKED AWAY, FEELING AS IF HIS WOLF WAS TEARING at his insides for him to go back and stay with Hayden. But his human side knew logic where his wolf side couldn't. Whether he stayed with her now or not, their situation was impossible—and it would end. She wanted to be with her family, and he...

Shivers crawled over his skin, and his eyes twitched to the crowd reeking of fear all around them. He had to get his wolves away from these humans.

Except that meant leaving Hayden among them, in a place where the Order might have gotten a foothold.

And there wasn't a damn thing he could do about it.

He bit back a snarl, walking faster. He'd seen the look on her mother's face. The rage, the repulsion—never mind her actual words. The woman had come perilously close to revealing all of them to the humans here, and given what she'd said, there was no chance in *hell* she'd go back to the manor with them—or that it'd be safe for his wolves to have her do so. And he couldn't ask Hayden to leave her family, which meant...

Nothing. He left. She stayed. Their time together was over.

A molten rock of pain throbbed in his chest while the wolf inside him thrashed and howled.

"What now?" Wes asked in a low voice, his eyes as much on the humans around them as Connor's were.

His teeth grinding, Connor didn't answer. Now, nothing. Now, he left. Now—

A little boy darted in front of him, playing a game of chase with his friends and paying no attention to the crowd around him. Connor slammed to a stop, his body shaking.

He couldn't risk his wolves. His father was dead, the world was a hellscape, and he couldn't risk his fucking wolves.

Wasn't Hayden one of them?

"Dammit," he muttered under his breath. Grinding his teeth, he veered toward the customer service station again. "Johanna?"

The older woman looked up, and she smiled when she saw him, only to falter at whatever expression was on his face. "Is everything okay?" She glanced down, seeming to catch sight of Marrok in wolf form for the first time. "Oh my."

"Can you tell me who's in charge here?" Connor demanded.

Johanna blinked. "Um, yes. Mostly." She glanced toward a door on the wall behind her. "Come with me?"

He wove around the desk and followed her, his friends behind him. Whatever happened, he damn well wasn't going to leave Hayden here until he learned every single way these humans planned to keep her safe. After all, maybe they knew something the ulfhednar didn't.

Even if he doubted that.

When they reached the door, half of his friends slowed, wordlessly taking up positions watching the crowd while Tyson and Wes followed him. Beyond the entrance, an office waited. A tinted window took up the wall to his right, affording him a muted view of the store outside. In the middle of the room, a scratched wooden desk stood with wrinkled maps of the city and state spread out across it. A folding table was shoved up against the back wall, atop of which was a motley assortment of radio equipment and microphones on stands. A middle-aged soldier in a military uniform stopped speaking to a tall gray-haired guy when Johanna opened the door, while the third man in the room didn't turn away from his focus on the old radios.

Johanna cleared her throat. "This is Doctor Reeves from Mariposa General and Major Rolston from the—"

"What's the meaning of this?" the major interrupted shortly, irritation on his face.

Connor stepped past Johanna. "We need to know everything about your security procedures here. What kind of defenses do you have? Have there been any attacks?"

Major Rolston blinked. "And just why the hell—"

"Mister Thorsen?"

Connor's eyes snapped over as the large man by the radios turned around. Alarm flashed through him, the world of a few weeks ago and today clashing against each other with surreal intensity. "Mister Dawes?"

"Well, I'll be damned." The hardware store owner pushed away from the table and crossed over to him, extending a hand. "You're—" He caught sight of the others beyond the doorway. "Hell, you're all alive!"

Warily, Connor took his hand. The man gripped it with both of his own and shook it hard.

"Good to see anybody these days, am I right?" Larry Dawes said.

Connor managed a nod. "Absolutely. Is your daughter—"

"Annie's here. She's okay. Little scared, but who of us isn't, yeah?" He shook his head. "We got lucky. Those damn fire tongues missed the store when they—"

"Fire tongues?" Connor interrupted, alarmed.

Larry's brow furrowed. "Didn't you all see the—"

"Excuse me," Major Rolston cut in. "Take a stroll down memory lane later. Just who the hell are you, and what business do you have interrupting us back here?"

Connor bit back a snarl.

"We want information," Wes said shortly.

"And we can help you," Tyson added.

Connor gave the lean wolf a guarded look. They hadn't discussed that.

Neither of his friends took their eyes from the major. Wes's expression was like stone and Tyson's was tense, as if he was urging the human to agree. Behind them, Johanna slipped from the room, closing the door behind her.

Major Rolston shook his head. "You want to help, go talk to the cadets outside and get a barricade assignment. We still have a chain of command here, not a free-for-all for whoever barges through the door."

"I'm not looking for a barricade assignment," Connor replied. "I want information about what you're doing here. What's your plan to protect these people, long term?"

The major gave them an incredulous look. "Do you have military experience? Survival training? Why the hell do you think I would just—"

"We're close enough," Connor cut in.

"Major," Larry said before the man could speak. "Let's just take a step back here, eh? I may not know their experience, but I can vouch for these folks. They're good people. They say they can help; I say we let them try."

The man eyed Larry for a moment. "Fine." He looked back to Connor. "You want to know what we've got? Fifteen ROTC cadets barely out of high school, a homeless Marine vet, five people with firearms training, and about thirty who shot a bow and arrow in PE class once. Thanks to a handful of construction workers and the mechanic who got their equipment working again, we built a barricade from whatever the hell we could find, but thus far, it hasn't been tested. We've got three shifts going around the clock and—"

"Wait." Connor held up a hand to stop him. "What do you mean, 'it hasn't been tested'?"

Major Rolston's jaw muscles clenched. "We've received reports of...*things* moving on the perimeter of town. We lost a convoy trying to go for help in Grand Junction, while another made it there but hasn't been able to get back since. They say anyone who comes up against these things dies. Nothing seems to kill the fuckers. Now, we're monitoring the situation as best we can, but thus far, whatever the hell is out there hasn't come in this direction."

"Which is good," Larry added.

"Which *means*," the major continued. "The longer this goes on, the more exhausted our people become, the fewer supplies we have, and the less likely it is we can repel an assault or find a way to reduce enemy numbers to the degree necessary to mount an escape."

Connor kept himself from scowling. So much for the humans knowing a way to deal with the draugar. "You have any idea who's drawing those symbols around town?"

He watched the humans closely for their reaction, but disgust was all he saw flash across the major's face, while the other two just appeared baffled.

"Vandals," Major Rolston scoffed coldly. "Sick ones, considering the damned things seem to be drawn in blood. Even in the fucking apocalypse, some jerk-off has to be out there trying to scare people."

Connor exhaled. The man could be lying, but he'd been catching glimpses of the guy's wrists since he set foot in here. No tattoos, and right now, the major seemed more ticked off than anything.

"And what's all this?" Connor twitched his head toward the equipment on the table nearby.

Larry shifted his weight. "Radios, mostly. AM, FM, shortwave, ham, you name it. I cobbled it all together from whatever I had in the shop, plus anything else we could find in town, but those zombies have made getting more equipment pretty damn difficult, given that we can't get out of town to scrounge more."

From the corner, Doctor Reeves scoffed. Connor glanced over, raising an eyebrow. The man had been so quiet this entire time, he might as well not have been in the room.

"Zombies." The man shook his head disgustedly.

"Well, what would you call them, then?" Larry demanded.

Grimacing, the doctor looked away.

"*Anyway,*" Larry continued. "The damned radios have been as good as dead for days. FM and AM went down before the earthquakes hit. We picked up shortwave transmissions for a bit, but now even those stopped about a day ago. We don't know if it's something to do with what went wrong in the sky, but we haven't been able to get anything for a while."

Connor exhaled, pushing down the trepidation that rose with Larry's words. "What were the transmissions saying?"

Larry winced. "Well, there was word of tsunamis, though with the earthquakes, I guess that's to be expected. It seems pretty bad out there, though. West Coast is flooded. East Coast as well. Some people sent word of creatures like what we've seen or…weirder. Bigger too. But after the fire tongues—"

"What does that mean?" Wes cut in.

His brow furrowing, Larry gave them all a quizzical look. "How the hell did you all miss that?"

"We were underground," Wes said.

"Trapped in a basement by the earthquake," Connor elaborated. "Took us a while to get out."

Larry nodded. "Yeah, well, guess you all were lucky, then. When the earthquake hit, there was this…shadow in the distance. Like an eclipse on the horizon but more defined, so people say. And when it passed, those black things were torn in the sky and all hell broke loose—pretty much literally."

"Fire fell out of some of them," the doctor said, his voice quiet. "Not all, though. Just some. Pouring like a goddamn waterfall, but moving like someone up there had a flamethrower. Miles and miles wide. Took out the town, the hospital. The forests burned for days."

Connor kept his breathing steady, his body rigid with the effort to keep from shivering. His father had said there were fires. Said the doors would open when they passed. And Barnabas had talked about Surtr, who was basically a fucking fire monster from another realm.

And if any of that was real, it meant the fires might come again.

"Missed some areas, though," the doctor continued in the same tone. "Here. A few neighborhoods on the edge of town. Couple spots in between like where Larry and his girl hid. Just luck of the draw. Fire spread, though. Burned most everything by the time it was done. But at least people could run from it." Doctor Reeves was silent for a moment. "If the smoke didn't get them."

"Air's pretty bad, as you can tell," Larry offered. "We keep hoping there'll be rain to clear out some of it, but—"

"Assuming that doesn't cause mudslides," Major Rolston pointed out.

Larry grimaced.

"Have you learned anything else?" Connor asked. "Any troops coming to help you all out, or…?"

The three men glanced at each other.

"If there's anyone left," Larry said. "We're pretty sure they've got their hands full."

"This is strictly need-to-know," Major Rolston added firmly. "Folks out there don't need to be starting a panic."

Connor nodded. Up until this morning, being around panicking humans had been about the worst thing he could imagine, given their propensity for shooting whatever frightened them.

Though, really, that was still pretty high on his worry list.

"What have you heard?" Tyson asked the men.

"Troops are scattered," Major Rolston said. "Flooding on the coast seems to have reached DC, and with most communications down...it's a mess."

Connor's brow twitched up. "Surely, even with DC gone, your military has procedures for gaining control of the situation?"

The major's eyes narrowed questioningly. Connor's brain caught up to his mouth. Shit. He'd said "your" military.

"Well, then there are the missing cities to consider," Larry said into the silence.

Connor looked at him sharply.

"*Missing?*" Wes repeated.

Larry shrugged. "That's how it sounds. The reports were garbled, but...yeah. Some survivors trying to make it to various cities sent word that when they got there, the towns were just *gone*. Not like destroyed gone. Gone-gone."

"Which ones?" Tyson asked, his voice tight. Connor glanced at him, curious.

"Atlanta, Wichita, Salt Lake. Bunch of smaller towns all over the place, and that's just the ones we've heard of. It's like they've been erased."

"You hear anything from Seattle?" Tyson pressed.

Connor's curiosity deepened. Who did his friend know in Seattle?

Larry shook his head. "No, but..." An apologetic look flickered across his face. "Most of the West Coast seems to have gone underwater, so..."

Tyson turned away.

"What about medical supplies?" Wes asked. "We saw the tents outside. What's the status on that?"

A wry expression crossed Doctor Reeves's face. "You all have medical training now too?"

Connor pulled his attention from Tyson. "Answer the question."

The doctor scoffed. "Just who the hell do you think—"

"We want to help you," Tyson cut in, turning back sharply. "And we don't want anyone else to die. But without a clear picture of what's going on..." He splayed his hands helplessly.

Doctor Reeves's jaw worked around, and his eyes went from the wolves to Major Rolston and back. "Supplies are getting low. The hospital got hit pretty bad. I had the day off, as did the folks working triage outside, so we were out of the line of fire—" His face twitched with cold irony. "—which means we're still alive." He worked his jaw around. "I've got a pediatric nurse, two orderlies, a gastroenterologist, and a guy who retired from family practice twenty years ago. Pharmacy here was helpful for supplies, but it's not going to last." Doctor Reeves grimaced. "We figure we've got enough for two days, maybe three."

Connor looked away, swearing internally, and his eyes landed on the tinted window. Beyond the customer service area, kids raced through the crowd, still playing games despite the destruction outside the building's walls. People sat on cots or milled around, seeming lost, while others appeared to be lining up toward the deli area. Perhaps dinner was coming soon.

But for how much longer? He'd seen the symbols on the walls in town, heard the draugar shrieking in the distance. The Order wouldn't be content to leave this place alone—if they weren't somewhere in here already. The soldier had no ink on his wrists, and the doctor had the sleeves of his maroon sweater shoved up to his elbows with nary a tattoo in sight. Back before the world went mad, he'd seen Larry's wrists at the hardware store, so unless the men were hiding their initiation marks elsewhere, he could hope that perhaps the room was free of the Order.

As for the rest of the people in this place…

He fought back a frown. How was he supposed to leave Hayden in this? These people had few supplies and fewer plans. And no matter what Tyson said, Connor had no idea how to help them all.

They were still human. Still frightened. And still so goddamn likely to hurt his kind if they ever learned the ulfhednar existed.

But leaving Hayden here *alone…*

"We told you what you wanted to know," Major Rolston snapped, interrupting his thoughts. "So what the hell can you all offer?"

From the corner of his eye, Connor saw Tyson look at him, silently questioning. Near the window, Wes watched the crowd, seemingly lost in thoughts of his own.

Connor's jaw clenched. What the hell had Tyson been thinking? Connor only wanted information enough to make sure Hayden would be safe, not to volunteer anything.

Though, admittedly, the humans probably wouldn't have told them jack shit if Tyson hadn't said that.

But what the hell was Connor supposed to say to this man? He couldn't reveal their identities. The guy seemed to be ready to shoot anything that threatened his *own* pack: these humans here in this store-turned-refugee-camp.

The best Connor could do was aim for something near the truth and hope the man accepted it.

He cleared his throat. "My friends and I spent the last

eighteen months in survival training in Alaska. Part of the —" He searched for a term. "—family business."

"Which is?" Major Rolston demanded, incredulous.

"Military contracts," Connor replied. "Among other things."

He kept his expression neutral. It wasn't quite a lie. In all the countless investments his father had made over the years, military contractors had certainly been on the list.

"We can take a look at your defenses," he continued. "See if there's anywhere they can be strengthened. My friend, Tyson, here is also skilled with technology. Maybe he can help you get those radios working again."

Tyson nodded immediately. "I saw some things outside that might help boost the signal."

Major Rolston didn't respond for a moment, watching them all. "Fair enough, but I want you all to see Cadet First Sergeant Doyle before you get started checking things over. Tell him I want you all assigned to patrol. Not—" He held up a hand when Connor opened his mouth to protest. "—because you're doing that, but because I want you all to have a perfectly legitimate reason to be checking out the defenses. People here are edgy enough, and those barricades are helping folks sleep at night. Last thing we need is them thinking they're not totally secure."

Connor's objections faded, a hint of respect rising in him for the man. "I can understand that."

Major Rolston echoed the motion firmly. "Then that'll be all."

The respect drowned under irritation at the dismissal in the man's voice. Gritting his teeth, Connor tamped down the urge to snap back because, if nothing else, arguing with a bull-headed human wasn't the most important thing at the moment.

Without a word, he turned and walked out of the room.

"How'd that go?" Kirsi asked shortly as the office door closed behind them. From their position near the exit from the customer service area several feet away, Luna and Marrok glanced back and then walked closer.

Wes scoffed. "We're on *barricade patrol*." Derision filled his voice.

Kirsi gave Connor an incredulous look. "Huh?"

"We're checking defenses," Connor explained, casting a questioning glance to his friend. What the hell had gotten into Wes?

"Why?" Kirsi asked.

Wes made a disgusted noise before Connor could answer. "The gods only know." He cast an angry look at Connor. "We need to be getting *out* of here. All these..." Wes lowered his voice. "All these humans. It's not safe— for us *or* them."

Understanding clicked. Connor stared at his friend. "You're not going to hurt anyone, Wes."

Fury crossed his friend's face. "You saw the way that lady looked at us. What she said. We're fucking *monsters* as far as she's concerned, and if these people find out—"

"They won't."

"And if we don't have a choice in that, because we're still *here*? We can't fucking kill those things in human form, and you know it."

Connor stared at Wes.

His friend's angry expression flickered, and Wes turned away, the struggle to rein in his temper clear on his face. "I'm sorry. I shouldn't have...I'm sorry."

Discomfort rolled through Connor. "Listen," he said to the others. "This isn't a dictatorship. Not anymore. If you all want to go—" He pressed onward over Tyson's objections. "—then go. But I can't leave just yet. I know what the risks are, but these people have no plan. And, yes, at the moment, I don't either, but—"

"Hayden's here," Luna said.

Connor looked over at her. The female smiled. A breath entered his lungs, relieved on some level that at least one member of his pack understood the dilemma.

"She won't come back with us," Kirsi cautioned. "And her parents..." She shook her head.

"I know," Connor said. "But leaving when these people are one attack away from annihilation is just—"

"We can't stay here, Connor!" Wes protested.

Tyson rounded on him. "And we can't abandon these people, either. If those draugar come for them, everyone here will be killed."

"What the hell do you propose, then?" Wes retorted. "Bring them back to the manor? That'll go great. You want to be the one to tell them what we—"

"No," Connor cut in. "We stay safe, but we stay separate. We check their defenses, like I told the major, and Tyson will get those radios working. There has to be a way to reach whoever survived beyond this town and get them to come here."

"Great," Wes commented. "More humans."

Connor restrained the urge to snarl at his friend in frustration. "More humans who might be able to defend this place so we can go back to the manor with our consciences clear."

Wes shook his head. "We should go back now. Use the equipment there to reach other survivors rather than hang around where—" His face twitched with discomfort. "—anything could happen."

"You're welcome to leave," Connor snapped at him.

Wes's jaw muscles jumped, fury in his eyes.

"It's too late to head back today," Luna interjected. "Sun will be setting in not too much longer and I, for one, don't want to get caught out in the dark with those things. Pretty sure you don't either, Wes."

The male looked away.

Connor exhaled, trying to rein his temper back under control. She was right. Being out in the dark with the draugar was madness.

Leaving Hayden felt like madness too.

His eyes skirted toward the section where her parents had been. He should stay away. He knew that. Seeing her again would only make it harder when he *did* have to go.

But he hadn't even gotten the chance to explain. To say goodbye.

Anything.

The wolf inside him paced and whined.

Drawing a breath, he shoved the feeling down. "Dinner, then," he said coldly, heading for the exit from the customer service area. "And we'll fucking figure the rest of it out in the morning."

29

HAYDEN

"But I don't understand," Nell said again, leaning in closer to where Hayden sat on the cot across from her. "If they were to bite someone here..."

Hayden held back a sigh. "They don't *do that*, Mom. Any of them. They—" She clamped her mouth shut as a young couple walked past, one man holding the other closely as he cried. "They're just like people. Mostly. They don't bite kids to make more of their kind."

"But this *Wes*, he—"

"Is an exception. And the one who did it..." She searched for a delicate way to describe capital punishment. "The other wolves made sure he never could again, and then they adopted Wes because he apparently had a rough situation back home. They're *not* monsters."

Her mom nodded, wringing her hands and looking thoughtful. Beside her on the cot, Ed watched them both, a worried expression on his face. He'd been easier to convince than Hayden's mother—only, she suspected, because he didn't have the horrific memories to go with it all—but he still seemed perturbed by something.

She hadn't had a chance to ask what. They'd spent the past hour talking in low voices, huddled together on the cots while Lindy sat nearby. Beyond hugging Hayden when she reached their little section of this makeshift refugee camp—and apologizing for letting slip to Hayden's parents that the others were wolves; she hadn't realized it was a secret—her friend had barely said three words.

"But these...people..." her mother tried again. "How can you be sure you can trust them *here,* with everyone around?"

Because she suspected she might love one of them.

Hayden pushed the thought down. It wasn't an answer, nor anything she wanted to get into with her parents, especially since it probably didn't matter anymore. Connor was going to leave, if he hadn't already. After all, she'd caught a glimpse of him across the room earlier, making a beeline for the door.

Which answered the question, really, of whether he'd even bother to say goodbye.

The hot lump of pain beneath her breastbone tried to rise in her throat again, and she struggled to push the feeling aside. Even if she damn well deserved better than the cold dismissal he gave her earlier, he'd also gotten her back to her family.

She couldn't quite hate him, given that.

"I trust them because they kept me alive," Hayden said to her mother. "And because they had plenty of opportunity to hurt people, and they never did."

Besides leaving her here, anyway, the only wolf in a crowd of humans...possibly forever.

Funny how that had never bothered her in the same way as it did now.

Tears wanted to rise in her eyes, and brutally, she shoved that feeling down with all the others.

Her mother glanced at her father.

"The one in charge of them seemed pretty ready to be away from us, though," Ed commented.

A cold scoff escaped Hayden before she could stop it. "Well, I'm sure he had his reasons, what with being shouted at like a wild animal and all."

"Hayden," Nell protested. "I only want to keep you safe. I don't—"

"Then *trust me*. I would never in a million *years* risk you or anyone if I didn't know the wol—" She caught herself, gritting her teeth briefly. "That they're safe."

Her parents were quiet. Dashing the tears from her eyes, Hayden looked away.

"Okay," her mother said softly.

Hayden glanced back. A little bit of the pain drained from her chest.

Somewhere near the deli, a bell rang and someone called that dinner would be coming in ten minutes. From the small, sheet-lined spaces around where Hayden and her family sat, people rose and headed for the far end of the room, where a line began to form.

"I saw the house," she said quietly.

Her father put an arm around her mother.

"There was a...a weird space? Over by the stairway closet?" Hayden watched them, waiting.

Nell wetted her lips. "You should probably ask Lindy about that."

Confused, Hayden looked at her friend. Picking at the

edge of the leather band on her wrist, Lindy wouldn't meet her eyes.

"How about we go get in line for dinner," Ed offered, "and the two of you can discuss that?"

Lindy glanced up, fear flashing across her face, but Ed simply nodded to her briefly and then took Nell's arm, bringing her with him as he headed for the line toward the deli.

Silence settled between them like a spectator waiting to see which of them would be the first to crack.

"What was that?" Hayden asked.

Lindy fidgeted with her wristband a moment more and then gripped the edge of the cot as if stopping herself from picking at the leather any longer. "Seidr."

Hayden blinked.

Lindy's eyes flashed up briefly. "You've heard of it?"

"Recently, yeah."

Her friend nodded. "That's what happened."

Hayden waited, but nothing more came. "So, I mean, could you do something like that again to protect people here or—"

"No." The answer was sharp, but after a moment, the tension lining Lindy's face faltered. "I..." She grimaced slightly. "It's not..." A breath left her. "It was hard enough holding it in place when the fire fell from the sky. I—"

"What?"

Lindy looked up at her again. "You missed that?"

Hayden floundered. "I..."

Memory flashed through her mind. Holy God, the light in the sky. That must have been...

"We were underground," she pressed onward. "A basement. Sort of."

Lindy's brow rose and fell. "Lucky."

Hayden shifted a bit on the cot.

"Your parents were near me," Lindy continued. "That's all that saved them. I had...*seconds*...when the fires started." A hoarse chuckle left her. "I didn't even know if it would work. I'd never really used it. Not like that, anyway, before the—" She cut off and then cleared her throat. "But it held. Even while the whole house burned, it..." Pain on her face, she trailed off.

"Thank you," Hayden said softly.

"I could hear them, you know?" Lindy's voice was choked. "Outside? People screaming. It didn't last long, not for the ones in the street, but from the houses...for the people *trapped* in the houses with flames just pouring right out of the sky..."

Hayden trembled, imagining it.

Lindy sniffled sharply. "I held the seidr around us as long as I could. And by the time I couldn't anymore, the fires had passed. Just shut off like somebody had turned off a faucet and all the flames just kind of died." She shifted her shoulders. "Nothing left to burn, I guess, so... we were safe." A harsh laugh left her. "I mean, we're probably all going to die of smoke inhalation but, you know, relatively speaking."

Her gallows humor died as Hayden took her hand.

Pain filled Lindy's eyes when she looked up again. "I never thought it'd actually happen," she said softly. "Ragnarok, all of it...It was just stories." Her eyes went to the line of people along one wall of the store, all of them waiting for food. "I wish it was just stories."

Hayden nodded. "Do the stories say anything else?"

Shrugging, Lindy pulled her gaze from the line. "Like what?"

"Like anything. Like what else might be out there or what happens next?"

Her friend looked to her askance like she couldn't understand the question. "Anything could be next. Hell, by all rights, we shouldn't even *be* here. Half the stuff described in the old myths about when Ragnarok kicks off should wipe out all life on earth, never mind all the stuff that comes later. Hati and Skoll eating the sun and the moon, the abyss Ginnungagap returning to swallow us all. Hell, anything could be out there now. Giants, elves, trolls…the gods themselves. I don't even know all the things that might have fallen through when Fenrir ripped through the realms."

"What?"

Lindy's brow twitched up. "The tears in the sky?"

A chill ran through Hayden. "Is that what happened?"

Her friend nodded. "Everything is falling apart, and it's going to spread. This…" A pained chuckle escaped Lindy like it was obvious. "This is the end of the world."

Lying on a cot hours later, Hayden couldn't close her eyes. The store was a cavernous abyss with only a few camping lanterns stationed throughout the space to break up the shadows. The underlying hum of the generators had fallen silent some time before—conserving both the machines and the gasoline the soldiers had scrounged to run them.

And now, there was only the sound of two hundred-odd sleeping humans and the scent of fear that hung around them like a permanent cloud.

Not that she could blame them for it.

Tugging her blanket up higher, she stared up at the

distant ceiling, her inhuman eyesight picking out the beams and rafters in a sheen of iridescent silver. Connor and the others had to be back at the manor by now, though she wondered if they would stay long. From their talks together, she knew he wanted to get back to Alaska. Maybe he and the others would head that way.

And God knew where she'd go.

She drew a breath, letting it out in a sigh. By over-hearing conversations around her all evening—consid-ering there was almost no privacy out here on the main store floor—she'd gathered that a number of theories were floating among the survivors, though the stories all felt as if they shared more in common with hope and rumor than anything solid. Colorado Springs was reportedly a safe haven. No, Colorado Springs was even worse than here. The military was on the move, bringing aid throughout the country. No, the military had been destroyed; no help was coming. Millions were dead. No, billions. Aid would be on its way. No, whole cities had gone missing.

Though, surely, that last rumor was wrong.

She wrapped her arms around herself, shivering. What-ever was happening, she knew they couldn't stay here. Dinner had been an amalgamation of whatever the survivors could put together from supplies in the store, and it had tasted surprisingly better than she expected, but she could see the tension on people's faces. The fear was almost palpable. Even a store like this wouldn't have enough food to feed everyone for weeks. Already, she'd overheard people commenting on smaller portions to their ration.

And when the food started to run out…

Anxiety drove her from beneath the blanket. Swinging her legs over the edge of the cot, she stared around in the darkness. She didn't know what to do. Walking back to the manor with her family in tow wouldn't be safe—and that was *if* Connor even let them in the door after how her mother had behaved. But Hayden didn't know how to hot-wire a car, and the internet wasn't there anymore to help her. She couldn't tell everyone here about the manor, if only because two hundred humans descending on the wolves' safe zone unannounced was bound to go badly.

Which left her with nothing.

She felt like she couldn't even breathe.

Pushing to her feet, she slipped by her parents and Lindy, asleep on the cots nearby. Soundlessly, she continued through the aisles. The few camping lanterns dotting the expanse of the store floor gave her plenty of light to make out the figures sleeping around her and the narrow walkways between them as she moved.

Even if she had no idea where she was going.

Scrubbing a hand over her face, she headed for the door. If nothing else, the smoky air outside would be an improvement over the fog of fear in this place. And who was to say that she couldn't help the people on guard duty anyway? Sure, she couldn't reveal *how* good her senses were, but she could probably find a way to explain if she did pick up on something.

It was better than staying in here, unable to sleep and getting more anxious by the minute.

Her nose caught a scent, and her body came to a stop before her mind could catch up.

Connor.

Baffled, she looked around. How could she still pick up Connor's scent in this place? The place was a choking cloud of unwashed bodies and fear, and hours had passed since he left for the—

"Hayden?"

She whirled.

Several yards away, he stood motionless, the blue-white glow of a camping lantern turning him into a study of light and shadow. The others were behind him, spread out through the aisle between the cots like they'd been on their way somewhere when she interrupted them.

She gaped at him. "What are you doing here?"

He seemed to falter for a moment. "We were on our way back from barricade duty."

"Barricade duty?" she repeated, looking between them all again in confusion. "I thought you were gone."

None of them responded, though even from this distance, she could see the displeasure on Wes's face and the way he kept looking back toward where she'd left her parents and Lindy asleep, as if wishing Hayden would return there.

Glancing over his shoulder to follow her gaze, Connor seemed to see his friend's expression too. He turned back, irritation flashing through his eyes. "No, but—"

One of the sleeping humans rolled over nearby, grumbling to themselves.

Connor's face tightened. He cast a quick look back to the others and motioned to them briefly before coming toward Hayden. Taking her arm, he twitched his chin ahead of him and then led her toward the automotive repair area not far from the front door of the store.

By the entrance, the guards didn't turn as the two of them slipped by, and in the near-abyss of the repair shop, even the nominal glow of the camping lanterns faded away. Only a hatch in the ceiling, open to let in air, allowed the distant glow of the lights on the barricades to penetrate the space. Her eyes strained to see by the meager illumination as she cautiously trailed Connor deeper into the shadows.

The reek of rubber stung her nose, though most of the tires had been taken away to add to the barricades outside. Broad bay doors that once would have opened to let in vehicles now were welded shut. A few damaged tire racks remained, shoved against the sealed doors, while whatever else had been bolted to the floors and walls had been ripped away, probably taken to support the barricades too. The ground was stained with oil that glinted in the darkness, and the air was cold, as if there was less insulation in the walls.

Though perhaps the relative warmth of the store owed more to the two hundred-odd humans sleeping in the same space than any kind of insulation.

Deep in the darkness, Connor released her. "Why are you up?" he asked in a whisper.

She shrugged, trying to bury the way her skin trembled at the sudden absence where his hand had touched. "I couldn't sleep." At his silence, discomfort pushed at her. "Listen, I'm sorry about my mother earlier."

Connor made a dismissive noise. "She's got her reasons, I know."

"Doesn't make it okay. I really am sorry. But I talked to her, and it won't..."

She caught herself, trailing off at the uselessness of the words. There wasn't any reason to say it wouldn't happen again. He would be leaving. She'd probably never see him after this, anyway.

But then, he should've been gone already.

"Why are you still here?" she asked.

He hesitated. "It got late."

"Oh."

Silence hung between them.

"So you're going back to the manor tomorrow, then?" she tried.

He scratched the side of his neck and looked away, the motion barely discernible in the darkness. "What are you going to do?" he asked rather than answer.

Uncomfortably, she glanced around. Even in the shadows where she could barely see his face, she still felt like she would be so transparent. She didn't want to seem pathetic, but what answer was there to give? "I'm, uh... still working on that."

"Do you have somewhere to go?"

She hesitated. Something in his voice struck her oddly, like he almost hoped she would say yes and confirm she had somewhere else to be, away from him.

Pain throbbed through her chest. Was that it? He wanted her to go? But why? He was the one who actually had somewhere safe to be, other than here.

The ache in her chest grew worse, like a hot ball of lead where her heart should have been. She cleared her throat and started towards the door. "I should get back—"

He caught her arm. "Hayden."

Her body stopped, shivering all over again. Everything in her felt like it was pushing toward him, like whatever part of her was a wolf was yearning to get closer to him. But she shouldn't be here. She should go back to section C-17 because, by God, he was going to leave anyway, so none of this would change anything.

It was difficult to make herself move. She could feel the warmth of his skin, a gentle and radiant heat only a few inches from her own. The soft pressure of his touch felt like a tether, linking her to this moment. He was so close, and in spite of every reason she had to walk away, she found

336

herself turning back towards him like gravity was pulling her in.

His grip trembled slightly, like maybe he was tense too.

"You're going to leave, Connor," she whispered. "What does it matter to you where I go?"

"Because I can't leave you."

Her eyes rose, finding his in the darkness. Gently, his hand brushed a strand of her hair back. In spite of herself, she leaned into the touch, resting against the hard skin of his palm.

"I need you to be safe," he said softly. "Here. Elsewhere. It doesn't matter. I...I need you safe." He shifted his weight, the tiny motion bringing him closer still. "I need you."

Her breath stilled. The warmth of him contrasted with the cold of the air behind her, like she stood at a precipice between one world and the next, and one small step would carry her over the edge.

"I need you, too," she whispered.

She drew nearer to him, desperation welling in her, and his lips crashed into hers. His hand raked through her hair, holding her to him as his mouth devoured hers and his tongue plundered her. Quickly, her hands slid beneath his sweater, craving to feel his skin, and he gave a short gasp at the contact.

But he didn't stop. His hands released her even as his lips struggled to stay with hers. With a swift motion he unfastened her jeans and pushed her clothing away before doing the same with his own.

Reaching down quickly, she grasped his cock. He was so hard already, and a bit of moisture clung to the tip of him. Her hand tightened on his solid shaft.

He groaned against her lips. Grabbing her ass, he

hefted her up from the ground, moving them back as he did. She gasped as her back hit the cinder block, the rough wall a shock of cold where it touched the skin below her sweater.

Desire pounded through her veins, every beat of her heart begging for what could come next.

With effortless shifter strength, he lifted her higher and then thrust into her.

A breathless noise escaped her. Wrapping her legs around him more tightly, she leaned her head back and dug her fingers into his shoulders, riding him as he drove himself into her frantically, desperately, as if claiming her.

As if he hungered for this every bit as much as she did.

Biting her lip, she squeezed her eyes shut, fighting to keep from making any sound. Anyone could hear them. Anyone could come back here.

But, God, the *feeling* of him…

His cock slammed deep into her, burying himself up to the hilt inside her, over and over, and it was all she could do not to scream from the pleasure of it. His hands clenched down on her ass, supporting her as she pushed her back against the wall and ground her hips into him, every part of her body desperate for all of him she could take.

A strange sensation rolled beneath her skin and then seemed to connect with him in fur and heat and fangs, as if whatever was in her was merging and tangling with the same thing inside him, every bit as a strong and wild as the night in the bunker.

Pure wolf.

His thrusting sped up, his breath coming in ragged gasps, and in a blinding rush, her orgasm overtook her. She could feel his cock pumping inside her as he came, and her legs clenched down on him, holding him to her as he poured himself out into her.

His head rested against her shoulder as his motions slowed. With her chest rising and falling in rapid breaths, she nuzzled her cheek to his hair, and his hands tightened on her in response.

"Gods," he whispered. "I love..."

He paused, and everything in her stopped. For a moment, he didn't move except to breathe, and then he looked up at her, resolve on his face.

"I love you," he said like he was taking a leap from a cliff of his own.

Her mouth moved. For all that she suspected—no, *knew* —what she felt for him, she hadn't really imagined she'd hear it from him too. Not after everything he'd been through. Not when she'd thought he was just going to leave. But now, something huge and warm and amazing swelled in her chest, stealing her voice because he...he'd just said...

"I love you too." Her words were a whisper.

His smile was like the sun.

Lowering her down, he kissed her, deep and gentle, taking his time. Her eyes closed, her body relishing the feeling of him.

The wolf she loved.

He smiled again when he finally pulled back from her. Bending down, he took her foot, helping her back into her jeans before pulling his own into place. His lips brushed hers again when he was done.

"Later was amazing," he whispered.

It took her a moment to place the words, and then she remembered what he'd said in the bunker. His request— his promise—that they'd have more time together, back when they'd been interrupted after their first time making love. A blush heated her face even as she grinned.

He took her chin, bringing her back toward him and kissing her again before taking her hand in his.

She followed him back into the rest of the store. As they passed the entrance, her eyes darted to the people there, but no one looked in their direction, giving her some hope the two of them had been quiet enough.

Though, maybe the humans were just being polite.

In silence, he led her back to the section where her parents and Lindy were sleeping, and none of them stirred when she and Connor arrived.

Turning, he lifted her hand to his lips and placed a small kiss inside her wrist. "Later," he whispered.

She wasn't going to stop smiling all night.

30

CONNOR

HE WAS IN LOVE.

Slipping back through the aisles, Connor found his wolves resting on their makeshift beds near the wall. All of them were as far from the humans as they could get and still be in this building, with Wes the farthest of them all. The male was still terrified he'd hurt a human, no matter how irrational the fear might be. Connor knew that, just as surely as he doubted his friends were truly asleep.

None of them could truly be comfortable in this place.

Curled on the floor beside Kirsi's bed of random pillows, Marrok proved him right immediately, looking up the moment Connor came near, his golden wolf eyes tracking him with a knowing expression. Connor ignored it. He knew he smelled of sex, of Hayden, but it wasn't like there was a shower around here to wash that off.

Even if he'd wanted to.

He lay back on the layers of bath towels that formed a hard bed for him and pulled the meager fleece blanket over himself. It was barely a place to rest and scarcely could be considered warm in this frigid world, but his body ran hotter than a human's, and he didn't want to rob the survivors of what comfort they could find, regardless.

The smell of her still clung to him, and he closed his eyes, breathing it in. The wolf inside him gave a sated grumble, contented by sex but still longing to curl around his mate. It would crave having her again after not too long.

And he was fine with that. How could he not be, when being with her felt right in a way he couldn't even define? The feeling of her permeated his world, softening the edges, bringing welcome comfort where, before, he'd never felt the need for any. And yes, the rest of the world was still a disaster and nothing was certain anymore, but he could still have peace in this one small moment where everything felt right for the first time in his life.

He had her. She had him. Whatever happened, he'd keep her and his wolves safe, whether it be from the draugar or the Order or the whole bloody pantheon of the gods.

Or the humans.

His eyes slipped toward the sleeping figures arrayed on their cots throughout the room. What the hell could he do for them? A couple hundred terrified souls, resting only a few yards from wolves they probably would have shot, back when their world seemed sane. He knew what his father would have done. Hell, Tolvar Thorsen hadn't even wanted humans to know about his *grocery* purchases in case they came looking for food or help. The alpha would have abandoned them all at the first opportunity.

But was that really what Connor wanted to do?

He looked back up at the distant ceiling. The loss of his father was barely hours old, and nothing about it felt real.

His mind still expected the old wolf to be there, waiting at the manor to yell at him when he returned. His gut still braced for orders he would have little choice but to follow. And his heart...

Once upon a time, he'd worshiped his father, and deep inside, that truth still ached. But the male had made mistakes, and Connor had as well, but maybe...maybe he didn't have to make his father's mistakes too.

Maybe Connor could simply do what he thought was right.

Trusting the humans with the secret of the ulfhednar and the manor was dangerous, though. It might save these people here, but it might also mean the death of everyone he loved. And if it came down to it, if it was the safety of the humans versus that of his pack, there couldn't be a question. That truth brought a stab of guilt, but it could never be a contest. He had to choose his wolves.

But would Hayden?

Cold spread through him, stilling his breath. She wasn't quite part of his pack, though the gods knew he wanted her to be, and she'd grown up with humans. If the moment came when the humans threatened the safety or the very lives of his wolves...

What would she do?

3 1

HAYDEN

IN THE BURNED FOREST, SHADOWS GATHERED, SHAMBLING AND *stumbling together amid growls and shrieks and moans. Limbs tangled by death, by decay, dragged in the ash and mud, leaving trails no sane person would ever follow.*

But then, he'd never had much interest in what the fallen world would consider sane.

At the border of the town called Butterfly, he waited, resting on a charred rock, a pocket watch in his hand—a gift from his father after his initiation. Green light and dark shadow twisted over and through his skin now; an aurora borealis of power and a tool for what was to come. His patience had been tested these past forty years. He'd wondered: would it be in his lifetime? Would he live to witness it, the Great Awakening, the moment when Chaos would finally be over and Order would begin? So many generations had lived and died, never seeing that long-sought day. Like them, he'd done his part, purged the world of as many shifters as he could, but still...he wondered and waited.

The shambling shadows drew closer. A smile lifted the edge of his lips, and he snapped the pocket watch shut. All his doubts were burned away the moment the realms fell, and now his reward was at hand, called to this place by the marks he'd painted in blood on buildings and doors. The time was upon them.

And all that was left of Mariposa would fall.

Hayden lurched awake, and for a moment, she couldn't place where she was. Shivers coursed through her body like she was encased in ice. Her eyes couldn't focus in the darkness. The smell of fear filled the air, making her want to shift and growl and bite. That had been Mitch in her dream. Mitch's thoughts and wishes and memories. He was out in the forest somewhere, just outside Mariposa.

And the draugar were coming.

The familiar scent of her family and friend threaded through the fear, orienting her, and the odd shapes around her resolved into sleeping humans. The darkness was quiet and still, filled only with the soft sounds of people breathing and the occasional whimper from someone having a nightmare.

Hayden glanced around, not sure what to do. A few days ago, she would have said a nightmare was just a nightmare, nothing more to it, but now, after she'd seen her parents' house...and with everything *else* that had happened...

Yelling that the draugar were coming would only incite panic, and possibly a stampede to nowhere, and then people might get crushed and die. Besides, for all she knew, that dream wasn't going to come true—*if* it even did —for weeks.

Her heart wouldn't stop pounding. At least she could tell Connor. Warn him or...

Or look like an idiot.

The fylgja stood at the foot of her cot.

Hayden froze. The woman stood, her hair stirring in an unfelt breeze, same as ever. Her dark eyes were deep like the bottomless fall of outer space, and her skin glistened like starlight. In the darkness, Hayden stared at her, trying to see what Ingrid had described. Was this really a part of herself? It didn't look like her.

The woman cocked her head to the side, regarding Hayden, and the light seemed to shift ever so slightly.

Hayden's breath caught. There it was, her own face. Staring back and yet...different. How had she never seen that before?

The fylgja's lips curved up at the edge, just for a heartbeat, such kindness and love in the expression that it stole Hayden's breath all over again.

"What..." Hayden whispered. "Why are you here?"

The woman's brow rose, a pointed look on her face. In silence, she turned her head toward the door.

And then vanished.

Adrenaline thrummed through Hayden as she climbed from the cot, scanning the area around her. God, what she wouldn't give for at least one window in this cinder block box of a building, if only to see outside and know whether it was already too late. Quickly, she slipped past her parents and Lindy, all of them sound asleep, and hurried down the aisle.

Dammit, where would he be? She hadn't seen where the wolves were sleeping when she found Connor earlier. Maybe they'd be outside again. Maybe they—

A strange feeling passed through her, like fur passing just at the tips of her fingers. Like the breath of a wolf on the nape of her neck, and she turned. What was this? Had she finally lost her mind, or was she still dreaming, and all of this...

Her nose caught a trace of Connor's scent. With a swift gasp, she rushed after it, threading through the cots by the patina of silver her eyesight cast on her surroundings. Her feet gained speed, carrying her at a jog past the customer service desk, the front door, and the auto repair shop too, the feeling of fur just beyond her skin and the warm huff of a wolf's breath growing stronger around her. Most of the humans seemed to have wanted to get as far from the front door as possible, with the majority of them gathered in the far back corners of the store. But not the wolves. The closer to the way out of here, the safer they probably felt.

She could understand that. Veering past the auto repair area, she hurried along the aisle, rushing through the darkness toward a collection of racks still bolted to the wall.

And there they were. Her feet slowed. Lying on the floor, they didn't even have cots, just piles of something. Towels, maybe? Why the hell hadn't they—

Marrok's head lifted, his eyes reflecting the meager light in an eerie sheen of blue, green, and gold. His head cocked to the side as if curious, and then he nudged the person lying next to him.

Kirsi jerked awake, a knife in her grip aiming toward Hayden. At the sight of her, the brunette's brow furrowed, her hand easing down. "What is it?"

Hayden hesitated, but the others immediately stirred at the sound of Kirsi's whisper. Looking up at her in confusion, they pushed their blankets aside while Connor climbed to his feet quickly, hurrying toward her.

"Is something wrong?" he asked.

Shaking her head, Hayden kept her voice low. "I don't know. Maybe."

Wes approached. "What's happened?"

She hesitated at the hard note in his voice. While she didn't know the guy well, he'd seemed fairly lighthearted and friendly.

Right now he sounded like he wanted to kill something.

"Um…" She put a hand on Connor's where he held her arm. "Can I just talk to—"

"You look like you've seen a ghost," Luna said softly, standing just beyond Wes.

Hayden grimaced, her eyes darting around. She knew what they thought of Ingrid. Knew she was going to sound nuts.

But the fylgja had been there every single time something bad happened, and if Hayden *was* seeing reality in these dreams…

"I just—" She winced. "I had a nightmare. Like the ones I've had for years, but…different this time."

Connor gave her a concerned look. "I'm sorry you had a—"

"I saw Mitch," Hayden pressed on. "But he didn't look…*human*…anymore. Not exactly. Something's happened to him. Changed him. But the draugar were coming to him, surrounding the town because of those symbols he drew on the walls." She trembled. "They were coming to attack."

The concern on Connor's face turned to compassion. "It makes sense you'd dream something like—"

"It wasn't just a nightmare." Hayden's words came out in a rush.

He paused.

She wetted her lips, willing her heart to stop thudding like a drum long enough for her to think straight. "I dream things. *Real* things…I think. I saw my parents' house, just like we found it. I dreamed that for *years* before it happened. And I—" Shivers ran through her as she looked up at him. This was it, the moment every good thing between them shattered because surely he'd think her a lunatic for what she was about to say.

But her family was at stake. Everyone was. And somehow, by some *miracle*, if this convinced him instead…

"I've seen you, Connor," she made herself say. "In my dreams all my life, standing there in the wreckage of my parents' house, over and over again. I saw you just how you looked in that moment, I heard the exact words you said, and—" Her words faltered. "—and I knew the draugar were coming. Just like I know they're coming now."

Connor stared at her, his brow slowly furrowing with confusion. He blinked once, twice, his gaze falling away from hers, and she couldn't read the expression on his face.

She looked to the others, finding similarly unreadable looks, and her body ached with resignation. Turning away, she cast a glance to the door. If she couldn't get the wolves to believe her—and why should they?—how was she supposed to get anyone else to, either?

Among the humans sleeping on the cots, a small voice whimpered. "Momma? Momma, where are you?"

A rustling followed. "Hush, sweetie," came a woman's voice. "Your momma can't be here now, but you need to sleep."

The ache in Hayden's body grew worse.

Connor released a breath in a rush. "When was this attack coming?" he asked quietly.

Hayden's eyes returned to him. At the guarded way he

was watching her, she trembled. "I don't know. Soon, I think."

He nodded and then turned to his friends, saying nothing.

Wes grimaced, looking away.

"We have to do something," Tyson said. "If there's even a *chance* she's right..."

"What do you suggest?" Kirsi countered. "We can't exactly tell these...*people* she just had a bad dream." She glanced at Hayden, wincing apologetically. "No offense."

Hayden shifted her weight awkwardly. "None taken."

"We don't have to tell them what she dreamed," Luna allowed. "We can just...keep an eye out."

Tyson nodded. "Listen and be ready if it happens."

Connor looked away.

"What?" Hayden asked him.

"And if this attack makes us reveal ourselves?" he asked the others quietly. "If they try to kill us?"

The wolves faltered.

"We don't hurt them," Wes replied softly. He wasn't even looking at the others. "No matter what. We run if we have to, but we don't—"

"No," Connor countered. "I won't risk any of you getting killed by this."

"I can't just leave these people," Hayden said.

Connor turned to her, and a chill ran through her at the look on his face, as if her words confirmed something terrible for him, though she couldn't figure out what it would be.

"Please," Hayden tried. "I know I must sound crazy, but I—"

"You all go." Connor twitched his head at the others. "Take the SUV and head back to the manor. I'll stay and—"

"Like hell," Wes interrupted, iron in his voice.

Connor glared at his friend.

"You said this wasn't a dictatorship anymore," Kirsi told him. "So fuck that. We're staying."

"There are *kids* here," Tyson added.

Wes nodded grudgingly. "We can't abandon them."

Connor turned away.

"Listen," Hayden said into the tense silence. "I'm just going to go outside and check, okay? I don't know when this is going to happen, but if it does—"

Connor muttered a curse, cutting her off. Stepping past her, he started for the door. "Come on."

She hurried after him toward the exit. The human guards gave them confused looks as they rushed past, the other wolves on their heels. Outside, the sky was a muddy shade of orange-pink from the dawn, and the air was thick with the smell of smoke, choking her and making her wish she hadn't left her mask beside her cot.

Scanning the barricade swiftly, Connor strode toward a collection of sheds on the right, near the base of the defense wall. "Anyone hear anything?" he snapped over his shoulder.

"Nope," Kirsi replied.

Hayden glanced toward the wall nervously. There'd been more daylight in her dream. Further into the morning, perhaps. But was it *this* morning? The fylgja had seemed to indicate those things were coming, but maybe—

"Major Rolston!" Connor called.

A gruff-looking man in a military uniform paused in the process of shutting one of the shed doors. Suspicion flashed over his face. "What do you all want?"

"Is there somewhere we can talk privately?" Connor asked.

The man eyed them all for a moment and then twitched his head toward the side of the shed. "What's going on?"

Connor glanced at the others and then followed the man there, reluctance on his face. "We...we have information. An attack is coming."

The major looked suspicious. "How do you know that?"

Connor grimaced, seeming to search for words.

Hayden looked away. The sky was getting brighter, though it was hard to say with all of smoke. The air was still terrible and made it hard to breathe.

The fylgja stood atop the gate.

Hayden's breath caught. The woman looked down at her and then pointed towards the world beyond the barricade. Hayden's body went cold.

"Connor..." She trembled. "It's now."

3 2

CONNOR

NO MATTER HOW MUCH OF A MESS THIS ALL WAS, IT DIDN'T change the way Connor's heart started pounding at the look on Hayden's face.

"What's now?" Major Rolston demanded. "What are you talking about?"

"Get up on the gate," Connor said to Wes. "See what you can—"

"Major?" the young soldier Levi called from atop the barricade. "Uh, you need to see this!"

Wariness prickled through Connor at the tight thread of fear in Levi's voice and the way the other people on the gate were moving, their body language screaming alarm.

The major looked between the wolves and the kid up above. "You come with me," he said to Connor. "Talk on the way."

Connor bit back a curse. They should have left. Should have gotten in the SUV and driven like hell for the manor and...

Dammit.

He strode after the man, ascending the stairway to the top of the gate rapidly. They'd studied this place in detail yesterday, examining every possible weakness they could think of, but there was precious little they could suggest to improve the defenses against an enemy that couldn't be killed by guns.

An enemy that was *here*.

Connor's blood went cold. The road stretched out ahead of him, lined by ash-covered parking lots, abandoned vehicles, and a motley collection of buildings. Meager light was brightening the sky, even as it struggled to thin the gray shadows still clinging to the world. Among the empty cars and husks of stores, the morning was eerily still, with the sense of something missing, something wrong, an energy that was absent and could only have been called "life."

But behind and between all the buildings, something was moving.

"Oh hell," Wes whispered beside him.

Lurching and stumbling, the figures staggered from the shadows, their shrieking cries carrying faintly on the weak breeze. He couldn't even be sure the humans had heard them yet, but the sight of the draugar alone sent fear scents spiking from all the people around him.

"Is *this* what you wanted to tell me?" Major Rolston demanded.

"Yeah," Connor replied grimly. He turned to Wes. "Check the other side of the parking—"

"Major!" A young soldier ran around the corner of the GetLots, her arm pointing wildly behind her. "Those things! They're coming up the road!"

"Shit." Major Rolston motioned to Levi. "Sound the alarm!"

The boy took off running down the steps on the other side of the gate.

"Weapons ready!" Major Rolston ordered his people before turning to Connor. "You. How the hell did you know they were coming?"

Connor glanced back to see Hayden ascending the steps behind him, her hand braced on the barricade wall like she was afraid the rickety stairs would go out beneath her. "That's not the important thing right now," he said to the major. "What matters is, you need to get these people—"

"*I'll* decide what's damn well important." Major Rolston stalked toward him. "And from where I'm standing, it's the half-dozen people who showed up, insisting on examining our defenses *right* before the biggest incursion of those creatures we've seen since this began. Now you explain yourself, and you do it this instant, or by God, I'll throw you off this barricade and shoot you dead before you hit the ground."

Connor shifted his weight, but didn't retreat, his body blocking Hayden from coming any farther up the stairs. "You don't want us as your enemy, Major. We—"

"Is that what you are, then?"

"No, we—"

"We're not human," Wes said.

Dread hit Connor like a two-by-four. Why the hell had he—

The major spun, going for his gun and swinging it toward Wes immediately.

Connor lunged, driving the man back as his shot cracked out into the tense silence. With a snarl, he slammed the major up against the barricade wall, sending the man's gun clattering away to the concrete beyond the barricade.

"Wes?" He threw a look at his friend. "You okay?"

The male nodded. His own gun was aimed at the nearest soldier, the kid frozen with his weapon half raised. "Fine."

Major Rolston struggled in his grip. "Open fi—"

Connor clamped a hand on the man's mouth and scanned the others swiftly. No one seemed hurt. But the humans on the gate and below it were all aiming their weapons at him, confusion and fear blatant on their faces. Maybe they hadn't heard Wes's words, but they clearly knew something was wrong.

Everything was wrong.

He glared at Wes. "Why the hell did you just—"

"What other answer is there to this?" his friend interrupted, resignation in his voice.

Connor bit back a growl even as his teeth lengthened and his muscles quivered. He could feel the major fighting him, shouting muffled orders to kill the wolves from behind Connor's palm. The shrieks of the draugar were closer now, and from the way the humans were glancing around nervously, he could tell they'd heard the cries. Those creatures were coming, and if the wolves were still in human form...

What other answer? Easy. Connor had made a bad call, that was the fucking answer. The pack never should have come here. Yes, there were children and, yes, there were innocents, but dammit, these gun-happy soldiers were about to prove right everything he'd ever—

A hand touched his shoulder. "Please." Hayden moved closer, her voice tense. "You're hurting him."

Connor looked back at the major. His skin bleeding around the claws that Connor's fingernails had become.

Hayden stepped past him, her hand moving to Connor's arm. "My friends want to help you," she said to Major Rolston. "They're the only ones who can stop those creatures."

The major's eyes went to her.

"They're not human." Her face tightened briefly, and her attention darted to the kid beyond Wes. The cadet's eyes were growing wider by the second. "*We're* not. But we know how to kill those monsters, and if you want these people to survive, you have to let us help you. Otherwise, everyone is going to die."

The major looked between them, a wary tinge of questioning entering his gaze.

"We're not your enemies, and right now you need friends," Hayden said. "We want to help you keep these people alive." Her hand slipped down to rest on Connor's and then paused. "But if you *dare* hurt my friends? If you *ever* point a gun at one of them again?" She leaned in closer to the major's face, her voice becoming a growl. "I will fucking kill you."

Connor's body went still. There wasn't a hint of doubt, a hint of falsehood in her voice. In his mind, he could almost see the wolf inside her, hackles raised and teeth bared at the bastard who had nearly harmed a member of the pack. And from the wolf inside him, he felt a surge of satisfaction that left him awestruck.

He'd been a fool to doubt her.

Hayden glanced at him, a determined light in her eyes that matched everything he felt for his pack. *Their* pack. His mate was standing right in front of him, staring down soldiers and the whole damn world to defend their wolves because it was necessary.

Because they mattered to her too.

Turning back to the major, she gently pulled at Connor's grip. Cautiously, he released the man, his muscles still trembling with readiness to rip out the guy's throat if he dared open his mouth to tell his people to fire.

Pinpoint cuts dripped blood from either side of the major's face, but he made no move to touch them. "What the hell *are* you?"

"You'll see," Hayden said. "But first, you tell your people not to fire at the wolves. Understood?"

Major Rolston studied them both. Carried on the breeze, the shrieks of the draugar were coming closer.

"Please, Major," Hayden urged.

"Don't fire!" the man shouted. "Go tell the others. There's…there'll be wolves coming. Don't fire at them!"

Below the barricade, the humans looked around in confusion.

"Do it!" Major Rolston ordered.

Still appearing baffled, two of the ROTC cadets nodded and took off running for the far side of the GetLots building.

Connor threw a glance at Hayden. "Get inside."

She turned to him in alarm. "What? No!"

"Your family is in there. If these things get past us…"

Hayden hesitated, and he could see the struggle on her face.

"Your human pack needs you too," Connor said, the words awkward but somehow feeling…right.

The battle in her eyes strengthened, but after a moment, she nodded. "You stay safe." The order in her voice was clear. "Come back to me." She cast a quick glance toward the rest of the pack below them. "All of you."

Before he could respond, she stepped in closer and kissed him hard. Breaking away quickly, she raced down the stairs and took off running across the lot.

His heart pounding, he watched her until she disappeared through the store entrance, and then his eyes slid to the major. "No guns."

The man nodded warily.

Gritting his teeth, Connor muttered a curse to himself and then shifted fast, his clothes ripping away, destroyed by the power reshaping his bones and muscles. Shouts rose from the humans below, and for a breathless moment, he waited for the sound of gunfire to annihilate any hope the humans could be trusted.

But none came.

As a wolf, he looked up at the major. The man's skin was bloodless, but he made no move to order the humans to open fire. Below the walkway, the rest of the pack looked around, watching the humans warily. Marrok's enormous form stood side-by-side with Kirsi, her fur the color of dark-stained wood, and her muscular shape seeming small only in comparison to him. Nearby, Tyson was a lean figure with brown fur while Luna was snowy white. On either side of them all, the humans retreated.

Connor returned his attention to the major, cocking his head in cold question.

"Don't shoot!" the man yelled, a slight waver to his voice.

Connor twitched his head at his wolves. Marrok and Kirsi raced off to the left while Luna and Tyson took the right. On the walkway with him, Wes nodded, the massive gray wolf staying put.

On the wind, the shrieks rose louder. Rattling noises joined them, and tearing sounds like tendons ripping and joints popping too. The air carried the scent of decay, of meat long since rotted by the sun. Beside Connor, the major turned toward the creatures while keeping one eye to the large wolves at his side.

Connor drew a slow breath, watching as the draugar sped up, staggering faster toward the barricade. This was it, then.

The monsters were coming.

33

HAYDEN

Hayden raced into the building, at a loss for what to do. How could she help the pack? No one was shooting at them yet, thankfully. But the draugar were only minutes away, and when they came, what was she supposed to do? Hide inside this place like a damsel in distress?

Not happening.

Skidding to a stop at the edge of the store floor, she scanned the crowd. She couldn't leave these people.

She damn well couldn't leave the wolves outside, either.

"What's going on?" a gray-haired woman called to her, pushing from the crowd.

"I heard a gunshot," a burly man supplied. "Are we under attack?"

Hayden faltered. Anything she said could incite a panic.

"We need you all to stay inside," came a young voice from behind her. She cast a glance over her shoulder to find one of the ROTC cadets behind her. The boy looked shaken, but he still fought to hold a professional expression on his face.

"Why?" the gray-haired woman demanded, starting toward him. "What's happening out there?"

Protests rose from the crowd surging after her, all of them clamoring for answers.

"Please!" The boy held up his hands as if that could keep everyone back. "You need to—"

"Hey!" A shout came from behind Hayden. She turned to see a big man coming from the office behind the customer service desk, and she recognized him. Larry Dawes, owner of her dad's favorite hardware store.

"Enough!" Larry bellowed. "Hear the kid out!"

The cadet seemed to steady himself. "We've got an attack coming. I need everyone who's trained on the barricades outside now. The rest, please stay in here. You'll be safer if you—"

Shouts of alarm rose, drowning out the cadet and Larry alike. In the crowd, she could see some people begin to cry, while others started grabbing whatever they could as if they were going to flee.

Even if there was nowhere to go. Nothing to do. No hope of escaping the monsters closing in on all—

"Hayden!" Lindy shoved through the crowd.

An idea struck her. Breathless, she ran to her friend. "Lindy, can you—" She looked around. "Wait, where are my mom and dad?"

Lindy nodded back toward the corner of the store. "Trying not to panic." Her friend held her arms clenched around her middle, a look on her face like maybe they weren't the only ones. Her eyes went to the store exit. "The Order is here, isn't it?"

Hayden hesitated. "The draugar."

"They'll be with them." Lindy looked sick.

Taking a sharp breath, Hayden tried to focus. "Okay, but can you do that...*thing*, like you did at my parents' house?"

Lindy turned back, her eyes wide with horror. "No."

"But—"

"No!"

Hayden stared at her.

"I-I *can't*. Please, I..." Lindy looked desperate. "Anyway, I couldn't hold a defense worth a damn around a place like this. It's *huge*."

Hayden turned away, raking a hand through her hair. There had to be a way to help these people.

"Could you?" Lindy asked.

She looked back at her friend. Lindy's brow rose, questioning.

Hayden faltered. "I..." The memory of Ingrid's words played through her head. And it was crazy. She barely knew anything about seidr. She'd had one minuscule afternoon talking with Ingrid about it all.

A smidgen of magical education wouldn't be enough to hold back the draugar she'd seen in the distance outside.

Let alone all the ones she'd seen in her dream.

"Hay, I can tell you what I know," Lindy begged. "And if there's even a *chance* you could..."

Her mouth moving wordlessly, Hayden looked away from Lindy only to have her eyes land on the crowd. People were crying. Children too, their parents or caretakers holding them close. Others were running for the door, whatever they could find for a weapon clutched in their hands. Knives. Baseball bats. Pipes taken from the walls.

The humans were going to fight. And if the wolves couldn't stop the draugar, everyone here was going to die.

Cold settled over Hayden. What other option was there?

She nodded. "I can try."

34

CONNOR

The draugar horde didn't stop until it was only a dozen yards from the gate.

And then every last one of them froze.

The reek of decay made Connor's stomach want to rise as he looked down at them. No shrieks rose from the mass. Not even a whisper or a rattle of bone. Like a wall of the dead, they stood in front of the makeshift defenses, their decaying mouths leering at the barricade.

Connor's eyes slid to Wes, and he found the same question in the wolf's body language that he knew had to be in his own. What the hell was this? The horde of the draugar stretched away on either side, encircling the human camp, and continued a hundred yards ahead of him, maybe more; a football-field length of hungry death waiting to strike.

Shudders ran through him. They looked scarcely different than the one that had killed his father. Gaping mouths. Sunken, rotted eyes. Tattered scraps of cloth that may once have been clothing flapping from their emaciated flesh and bones. Some were missing limbs. Others had rotted holes where their midsections should have been. And now, for once, none were moving. Not a gods-be-damned one.

"What the fuck?" Major Rolston whispered, his hands adjusting on the automatic rifle one of the cadets had supplied him.

A ripple started somewhere near the center of the horde, heading toward the barricade. As one, the mass of draugar parted, and from their midst, Mitch walked like a latter-day Moses flanked by a corpse-ridden Red Sea.

He looked nothing like he had before.

Shivers ran through Connor. An aura of green shifting light seemed to swirl over and through the man's skin. Darkness followed it, trailing along his arms, gathering in the hollows of his cheeks and around his temples until his head resembled a skull. His hands were like bone, his fingers long and knobby, and they moved as if stirring the smoky air. With pitch-black eyes that seemed to glow like pinprick stars were trapped in the dark sockets, he looked up at the soldiers and the wolves atop the barricade.

His lips pulled back in a smile, the expression like the rictus of a corpse.

"Oh, what fools you are." His voice was a rasp that carried over the wind and insinuated itself straight in Connor's ears. "Choosing to side with the corrupt and the contemptible. What pretty lies they must have told you, to make you trust in *wolves*."

"What business do you have here?" Major Rolston called down.

Mitch chuckled, the sound like bones scraping against one another. "I claim the world. What business do you have in it?"

Connor's teeth bared.

A grin on his eerie face, Mitch kept his dark eyes on the major as he splayed his bony hands, gesturing to the draugar on either side of him. "Do you have any inkling of what has come? Of the world you now find yourselves in? Like the serpent Nidhogg, we've chewed through Yggdrasil itself, tearing your reality down at its very roots. And now, our victory is at hand. The gods will die, and all the broken realms will finally collapse into the abyss. And then—" His fingers returned to their strange stirring motion. "—the Order shall rise."

One of the ROTC cadets on the barricade cast a wary look to the major. "What's he talking about, sir?"

"Keep your focus, soldier," Major Rolston snapped.

"Oh, yes, soldier." Mitch chuckled. "Do keep your focus."

With a roar too wild and deep for any human throat, Mitch jerked his hands upward. Green smoke shaped like chains thick enough to anchor battleships surged from the ground, rising high into the air over Mitch and the draugar. On the barricades, the soldiers shouted, firing frantically.

The bullets slammed into the air ahead of Mitch and ricocheted away like they'd hit solid metal. Around him, the draugar shuddered at the impacts but didn't fall.

"All your magnificent weapons!" Mitch cried, laughing, and then his voice dropped to a rasp as he smiled. "No better than swords and shields."

He threw his hands forward. The impossible chains lunged through the air, rushing toward the barricades. Smoke slammed into the wall piled high with debris, tangling through the defense, and with a jerk, Mitch threw his arms wide. The chains flew backward like they'd been pulled.

The barricade came with them.

Buses and shopping carts, cars and shelving alike erupted outward, scattering across the parking lot. The walkway pitched wildly as half the gate went with the collapse. Leaping wide of the crumbling defenses, Connor and Wes hit the concrete and scrambled out of the way while the humans shouted and the platform toppled.

"Major!" Levi shouted. The boy rushed for the ruins of the gate.

Draugar poured over the debris.

The humans opened fire.

Ducking low and praying the bullets didn't hit him, Connor skidded a tight turn across the concrete and raced after the kid. A draug snagged the cadet's arm, hauling Levi toward him with its mouth opened wide, its rotted teeth aiming for the boy's throat.

Connor jumped, slamming into the draug and the cadet alike. His fangs sank into the draug's arm, ripping at the decaying muscle and hauling the creature away from the boy. The flesh tasted like mold and dirt sodden with shit, and he gagged as the draug crumbled to dust around him.

Turning fast, his stomach roiling, he caught sight of Levi, still alive and scrambling back as more draugar charged toward them.

A spray of bullets erupted from beneath the rubble of the gate. The draugar staggered, their leg tendons shredded by the gunfire. Collapsing to their rotted hands and knees, the creatures still struggled to crawl toward the kid.

Connor leapt onto them, biting and tearing at their limbs. The draugar crumbled into dust.

"Major!" Levi cried. Reaching into the rubble, the cadet hauled on something there.

The major struggled out of the debris, bracing himself with his elbow while his hand clutched his weapon. Blood ran from a deep gash on his head, and his uniform was stained and torn. Supported by Levi, he clambered to his feet, his left arm hanging from the socket, dislocated.

Connor tore past them, ripping his teeth through a draug nearby. Turning fast atop the debris, he barked at Levi and then jerked his head toward the building.

"No!" Levi shouted. "I have to help—"

A chain of green smoke shot past them both, plowing into the crowd of people firing at the draugar. The humans screamed when it struck them, their bodies freezing mid-motion. Their skin turned ashen, crackling and crumbling as if being sapped of all life. Hair rained from their heads as their faces grew emaciated, cheeks sinking, teeth falling, and eyes rotting away. Like sounds stolen away by the wind, their screams withered into weak gasps as they collapsed to the concrete, their bones shattering into dust when they hit the ground.

"Retreat!" Major Rolston bellowed. "Retreat!"

Connor turned. Standing on top of a charred bus, Mitch laughed. "Yes! Run! Run for your pathetic lives!"

Mitch whipped his hand to the side.

The chains slashed across the parking lot. Humans threw themselves to the concrete, and the wolves did too as the smoke sliced past. Screams dwindling to gasps bore testimony to all those who couldn't move fast enough.

Snarling, Connor turned. He had only a moment while Mitch's attention was diverted, and no guarantee at all that his fangs would work where bullets had not.

All of them were going to die if someone didn't stop the man.

Connor charged.

Mitch's eyes snapped over to him instantly. A smile spread across his skull-like face. "Nice try, wolf."

He hurled the green smoke right at Connor.

35

HAYDEN

Shoving through the crowd, Hayden and Lindy raced back to her parents' cots at the far end of the store.

"We'll need some kind of oil," Lindy called over her shoulder. "Something to stabilize the symbols long enough for the seidr to take hold. A smaller defense wouldn't need it, but for something this—"

"What's going on?" Nell interrupted at the sight of them. "Someone said there were wolves attacking outside?"

"No, no." Hayden shook her head. "They're helping, but—" She threw a quick look to Lindy. "Please, we need oil."

Nell blinked at her.

"I'll get some," Ed said, taking off through the crowd.

"Hayden." Her mother looked between her husband and the two women in front of her, baffled. "What's going on?"

"The draugar are coming," Hayden said. "We don't have time to—"

"Here!" Ed rushed back, thrusting a bottle at them. "What do you need the oil for?"

Hayden hesitated, wondering how in the world to explain.

"We're doing it again," Lindy said. "Like at the house, only bigger."

Nell's brow furrowed. "But Hayden's not—"

"She can do it," Lindy interrupted, something hard in her voice.

Hayden glanced between her mother and friend, confused. "What—"

"Come on." Lindy twisted the cap from the bottle and shoved one of the cots aside with her foot. Crouching quickly, she began pouring the oil in patterns on the floor.

Still eyeing her parents warily, Hayden sank down beside her friend. The symbols were familiar. Similar to the ones on the buildings in town, drawn in blood, or like the few that Ingrid had shown her in the bunker.

"Focus," Lindy said, glancing up at her swiftly and then returning her attention to the symbols. "Focus on the earth beneath you, down through the dirt, through the rock, all the way to the magma churning at the heart of the world. Concentrate on it. Find the link."

Hayden's eyes darted to her in wary confusion.

"Everything is connected to Yggdrasil," Lindy said. "To the World Tree. Every world, every realm. Feel that connection. Draw on it."

Taking a short breath, Hayden tried to do as she said.

"Feel the air on your skin. The way it connects you to everything in this room. Focus on—"

She cut off as Hayden gasped.

"What is it?" Lindy asked. "What's wrong?"

Hayden stared, hope swelling inside her. "I think we've got help."

The fylgja walked toward them, the crowd parting around her without ever once seeming to notice she was there. Unblinking, the woman continued over to them, a small smile on her face.

"Where?" Lindy asked.

Hayden glanced at her friend. Appearing confused, Lindy looked around as if she couldn't see the fylgja at all. Circling around the symbols in oil, the woman crouched down at Hayden's side.

"Hay?" Lindy tried.

"It's all right."

Reaching out, the fylgja placed her hand atop Hayden's own. Her skin felt like a cool breeze on a winter day, and the weight of her hand was barely more than a feather.

Focus.

The fylgja's voice filled Hayden's head. Drawing a slow breath, Hayden looked back at the symbols. They were intricate in their own way. Old, too.

How did she know they were old?

Somewhere in the distance, she could hear Lindy asking her questions, worry in her friend's voice. Guilt tugged at the edges of her mind. She didn't want Lindy to be scared.

Everyone was so scared.

The oil shimmered like the light above it was shifting, a kaleidoscope of color passing across the glistening liquid. Cool air stirred around her in a sudden, gentle breeze.

All your will, all your desire, all your hope. Place it in your palm. Collect it there. Your power flows, growing stronger...stronger.

There wasn't going to be a way to hide after this. No

way to keep the world from knowing exactly how inhuman she was.

Focus the power.

Maybe there had never been.

Maybe if she tried, everyone would die.

Now.

Hayden placed her hand in the center of the symbols.

36

CONNOR

AN INDIGO WAVE OF LIGHT RUSHED PAST CONNOR, SLAMMING into the chain racing at him and shattering it like glass. On all sides, the draugar erupted into dust where they stood, their forms blasted away by the magic surging across the parking lot, past the fallen barricade, and out across the debris beyond.

Connor skidded to a shocked halt. That...that *felt* like Hayden. But that was impossible. He'd never even seen anything like the blast flying past him now.

How could it feel like his mate?

Snarling, Mitch staggered as the wave hit him, falling to his knees atop the charred bus. The sound of ripping metal, raw and shrieking, came from the bus roof as Mitch's hands dug into it, keeping him from toppling backward. But immediately, his head lifted up, the black pits of his eyes locking on Connor, rage contorting his death-mask face.

A roar left Mitch, loud enough to make the air shake.

Ducking low, Connor took off, charging toward the

man again. Whatever the hell that blast had been, by the gods, it'd slowed the bastard down.

Maybe it'd give him enough time...

He leapt through the air and landed hard on the debris. His paws scrambled on the wreckage, carrying him to the top of the bus. Mitch stumbled to his feet, his hands making swirling motions in the air as he had in the moments before he'd attacked the barricade.

Connor lunged.

Mitch swiped a hand toward him, green smoke tangling up from the earth below him at the motion, but Connor got there first. Slamming into Mitch, he sent the man tumbling from the top of the bus and down into the rubble, and the smoke scattered as he fell. Connor landed on him, his front paws pinning the man to the ground. Baring his teeth, he growled at Mitch, his muscles twitching with the urge to finish this.

A snarl came from behind Connor, but he didn't turn, satisfaction radiating through him. He knew that sound. Could feel his wolves moving around him like an extension of his own body, and knew it was the same for them. The pack circled Mitch, growling, rage in their voices. And deep in the dark pits of Mitch's eyes, Connor caught a flash of fear. Bullets wouldn't kill the man. They'd seen that in the countless attempts the soldiers had made to gun Mitch down.

But he suspected the pack could.

And he was willing to bet Mitch knew it.

"You think this ends anything?" the man spat at them. "Do you think you've *won?*" Contempt twisted his inhuman face. "There are thousands of us out there. *Tens* of thousands. We've hunted your kind to the edge of extinction, and now, there will never be enough of you to stop what is to come. You've *lost*, wolf. No matter what you do to me today, this war was over before it even began."

Near Connor's side, Marrok growled again. The enormous wolf jerked his head toward the soldiers, and Connor read the question in the motion. Did they turn him over to the humans? Let them lock the bastard up somewhere?

Connor pressed the man harder into the gritty concrete. They would need information, it was true. Whatever had happened in the world beyond Mariposa, it'd be better not going into everything blind. And clearly, the bastard liked to talk.

But there was whatever the hell Mitch had done to himself to consider, and whatever the hell he was capable of. Leaving him alive was a risk.

Everything was.

Keeping his eyes to Mitch, Connor twitched his head at Marrok. The wolf nodded and backed away before turning to run toward the humans.

"Oh, so you're the leader?" Mitch chuckled, grinning up at Connor. "The flea-bitten cur in charge of the mongrel pack." Disgust twisted his face. "Pathetic. Though, I'll admit, that was a pretty bit of seidr one of your kind unleashed here. Found a seer, have you?"

Tension rippled through Connor's body.

Mitch's grin grew wider. "Is it that bitch wolf you'd been courting? Is she the one? You won't save her. My brethren are coming. They'll trap your precious seer and skin that mangy mutt alive. Too bad you won't be alive to watch the bitch yelp and bleed and cry for you—"

Silver flashed at the corner of Connor's eye, and Wes barked a warning. Mitch stabbed his knife forward, aiming for Connor's jugular. Ducking fast, Connor lunged forward as the blade's edge passed above the back of his neck.

Blood filled his mouth as he ripped out Mitch's throat.

Eerie silence settled over the parking lot.

Slowly, Connor turned, blood dripping from his jaw and his teeth bared. Behind the pack, soldiers and civilians alike stared, their guns half-raised, their eyes locked on the wolves standing around Mitch's corpse. Uneasiness rippled through Connor's body. If the humans panicked, if they opened fire, the wolves couldn't stop them all.

And then the cheering started.

Thrusting their guns into the air, the humans shouted, their voices carrying all the abandon of people who most likely had thought they were going to die only moments before. Grinning, they surged forward, heading for the wolves.

Connor froze, and he could feel the wariness in the pack. But the humans didn't attack. Instead, they clapped the wolves on their sides, cheering them while one offered Connor a scrap of cloth as if to give him a place to wipe his face.

Awkwardly, he swiped off the blood, keeping one eye to his pack with no idea what to make of this.

"Well done!" Major Rolston limped toward them. "Very…" He chuckled roughly. "Very fucking well done!"

Connor watched the man warily.

"Now maybe one of you can explain what the hell that is?" The major jerked his chin toward something beyond Connor. "Assuming…Can you talk?"

Connor looked back.

The air at the edge of the parking lot shimmered blue-purple, the glow stretching up and over the store like the entire building and its surroundings were encased in a glistening soap bubble.

Alarm spread through him. Hayden. The blast had felt like Hayden and—

He took off for the store entrance. That was seidr. It had to be, and it felt like his mate. A blast that powerful could have fucking killed its creator, for all he knew.

Humans shouted in alarm as he tore into the store, and behind him, one of the soldiers yelled that the wolf was on their side. Connor slid to a stop on the gritty floor, searching frantically for a thread of her scent before racing off toward where she had been staying with her parents. Amid all the humans, any trace of her was nearly drowned, but maybe...maybe...

"Connor!"

Relief nearly took his feet from under him.

Hayden shoved through the crowd, dropping to her knees when she reached him and throwing her arms around his neck. He nuzzled his head against her side, breathing in the comforting scent of her before pulling back and looking her over worriedly. She seemed okay. Unharmed and happy and—

"I'm fine," she assured him. "Are you? Are the others? I..." She faltered, a strange look on her face. "I feel like I can...Oh my God, I can tell they're okay. I..."

Elation filled him. He nodded.

A breath left her.

"Hayden?"

Her mother's voice came from the crowd. Pushing past the other humans, Nell rushed out and then slammed to a stop at the sight of the two of them.

Questions flew over Nell's face.

Hayden tensed. Rising to her feet, she kept a hand to his side, and he could read the protectiveness in every line of her body. The claiming, and it thrilled something inside him. Because this was her pack, every bit as much as his. And she was his mate, just as she always had been.

If he had been human, he would have smiled from ear to ear.

37

HAYDEN

Support radiated up from Connor like a warmth passing through her hand on him, and Hayden relished it, letting it stabilize the fear she felt still fluttering somewhere inside. All around them, people stared. They hadn't stopped since the moment the seidr had left her, racing outward past the walls and out into the parking lot. Even now, she could feel it somewhere in the distance like a sphere all around her.

"Honey, what..." Her mother blinked, her mouth moving as if she couldn't find words. "What did you do?"

"I saw it," a nervous-looking man said, clutching a broom in his hand like it was a weapon. "That woman, she..."

A little boy pointed at her. "She did something, and that light rushed out and—"

The kid gasped, but Hayden didn't need to turn. She felt them pacing through the crowd, coming around her, and warm relief came with the awareness. She hadn't been losing her mind the night before. It was like a sixth sense; a feeling like where her palm ended, their fur began. They were a unit, and they were with her.

Her pack.

Keeping a hand to Connor's side, she drew a breath. "It's called seidr. It can protect us."

"But what is this?" the man gestured tightly to the wolves, as if afraid they would bite off his hand if he got too close. "What…what are these…?"

Hayden shivered, only to feel the support of the pack swell around her. "They're like me."

The crowd stared at her even more than before.

"We're called the ulfhednar, and we're not your enemies. Not if you aren't ours. Those things outside were the draugar, and if my friends are here, that means they're gone. We stopped them." Her fingers tightened on Connor's fur, praying her words were true. "And we can protect you."

Silence greeted her words for a moment, and then questions rose from all around her, the words tripping over one another, incomprehensible.

"Please!" She held up a hand, and the shouts fell away. "I'll explain everything I can. We all will. But…" A breathless chuckle left her. "First, my friends are going to need some clothes."

It took twenty minutes, but the humans managed to find clothes to fit the wolves in human form, though locating something tall enough for Marrok proved a challenge. The soldier in charge—Major Rolston, Connor told her—took the lead in reassuring the humans that the wolves really were on their side. He also threatened to toss to the draugar anyone who would, in his words, fucking touch one of their new best friends—though he readily acknowledged he couldn't explain the magic surrounding their compound.

Even Hayden barely could.

In human form and with the pack beside him, Connor invited those who wished to join them to return to the manor. The bunker had food, water, and walls the draugar couldn't hope to get through.

Assuming the protection spell around this place didn't simply stay intact too.

In the end, the humans agreed to go back with them—especially the ones with small children. As welcome as the defense around this place might be, the promise of the thick metal walls in the bunker won out over a magical soap bubble. Within minutes, the humans began packing up, taking what few possessions they had left and loading them into trucks and cars stolen from the surrounding parking lots.

Everyone seemed motivated to get out of this place before any draugar could come back.

"So, you're sure they won't mind us?" Nell asked her, stuffing a blanket into a small, green knapsack. "I mean, if they want their space, I understand that—"

Her mother cut off, blanching slightly. Hayden didn't turn, feeling Connor behind her.

"You're entirely welcome," Connor said to her. "As long as we're welcome with you."

A hint of a question floated in the statement.

Nell set the bag down. Crossing the small space, she reached out and took both of Connor's hands. "I'm sorry. I..." She took a deep breath. "I was wrong about you. All of you. Whatever monster hurt my brother…It wasn't like your wolves. Can you forgive me?"

Connor blinked. His hands adjusted on her mother's, holding them gently. "Of course."

Hayden's eyes stung.

Her mother smiled. Turning the expression on them both briefly, Nell said in a slightly choked voice, "I'll just finish up, then." Nodding to herself, she returned to the cot and picked up her bag, sniffling slightly.

Hayden hesitated. Should she go get her father? He was over with Lindy, helping the ROTC cadets pack one of the trucks they'd found. But then, she didn't want to leave her mother *crying*, for pity's sake.

"I'll just…" Connor nodded toward the front of the store.

Hayden echoed the motion. As he walked away, she crossed the small space, watching her mother with concern. "Mom?"

Nell sniffled sharply and made a questioning noise, not turning around.

"Are you okay?" Hayden asked.

Nell nodded quickly. "Yeah. Oh…" She smiled up at Hayden. "I'm more than okay."

"But—"

"I'm happy for you."

She faltered, staring at Nell, her mouth moving as she searched for words. "Happy?"

Nell's smile grew. "You were right. And you found your people, and they…they're good." She shook her head, blinking tears from her eyes. "I never wanted you to be alone, honey. I *hated* that you were alone." She shrugged helplessly. "I just always wanted you to be safe."

Hayden swallowed around the lump that had

suddenly found its way into her throat. Nell reached out, wrapping her arms around her, and Hayden hugged her back, careful as always not to let her strength hurt her mother.

Nell sniffled again, releasing her. "Now, you go on. I'll finish up here and meet you outside, okay?"

Smiling, Hayden nodded. "Yeah."

With a pat on Hayden's shoulder, Nell returned to packing.

Hayden swiped the tears from her eyes and headed for the door. People watched her as she passed, none of them coming too close, but that was okay. If her mother could change her mind about the ulfhednar and see that they weren't a threat…maybe everyone else could too.

Another half hour saw the trucks and cars loaded, and in a caravan behind the wolves in the SUV, they all left the GetLots behind. No draugar seemed to remain in the desolate town, nor did they rush from the woods when the line of vehicles drove past. She could feel the tension of the wolves, their worry for what they'd find when they reached the manor. The draugar had been in there when last they left it, and the wolves had already agreed with the soldiers to clear the place first before letting the civilians inside.

But no monsters rushed at them when the SUV came to a stop in the courtyard, and silence reigned while the wolves climbed from the vehicle. A breeze had kicked up in the past hour, driving the smoke away until the air seemed almost fresh, at least comparatively speaking.

Ingrid appeared at the front door of the manor, Barnabas at her side.

"They're gone," the man called. "All the scum, not six hours ago. Shuffled out of the house and the forest, heading for town, and we haven't seen one since." Alarm flashed across his face as the other vehicles pulled into the courtyard behind the SUV. "What the hell is this?"

"Peace," Connor replied. "Best as we can make it."

Speechless, the old wolf stared as the soldiers climbed from their truck, the major and cadets immediately looking to Connor.

"Security monitors are downstairs," Connor told them. "Bunker is through the main door and down the hall on your left. Tyson?"

The wolf nodded and headed for the door. At Major Rolston's command, several of the cadets hurried to join him while the rest moved to guard the perimeter. Kirsi, Marrok, and Wes accompanied them while Luna went to help the doctors with the wounded.

"You stopped them."

At the sound of Ingrid's voice, Hayden turned.

The older woman smiled at her. "I felt it, even all the way here. The seidr you unleashed was..." Ingrid chuckled. "Your mother would be proud."

Hayden glanced around and caught sight of Lindy disappearing into the manor. She'd hardly gotten a chance to speak to her friend in all the rush to leave the GetLots, but she wasn't sure if Lindy wanted her involvement mentioned.

Something inside Hayden suspected maybe not.

"I'm still not really sure what I did," she admitted.

"Would you like to learn? I've carved all manner of sigils and runes into the foundations of this place, but it still needs more protection than my power can provide. With your strength, it could be a formidable sanctuary from what is to come."

Hayden stared at her. "What's coming?"

Ingrid's smile faded, and her eyes moved across the wolves and humans all around them. "Many things. Some good. Some...not." She stepped closer, taking Hayden's hand. "But now, thanks to you, we have time."

Squeezing Hayden's hand briefly, Ingrid turned and walked back across the courtyard, pausing only long enough for several children to race ahead toward the manor door.

Hayden watched her go, unsure what to think. The whole world was different now, even from a day before. Humans and wolves working together. The bunker becoming all of their home—maybe the manor too, if they could repair it.

If seidr could protect it all.

She turned, her eyes running across the vehicles and the crowd. By an old delivery van, she spotted Connor. He was talking with the major, nodding and motioning to the grounds as he spoke. A warm feeling filled her chest at the sight of him. Maybe they really could do this, though. Whatever the world had become, here, in this place, maybe they really could survive it.

He caught sight of her watching him, and a smile flashed over his face before he returned to answer something the major had just asked. Major Rolston nodded at the response and then headed away.

Connor started toward her across the courtyard, and Hayden grinned, moving to join him.

"Mister Thorsen?" a young girl called.

Hayden slowed as Connor stopped, looking back. A little girl in a wheelchair was coming toward him. At the sight of her, he turned, crouching down in front of the child.

Curious, Hayden walked closer.

"You didn't tell Daddy or me you were a wolf," the little girl said solemnly.

Connor paused. "No, I didn't."

"Why?"

He cocked his head to the side, considering. "I was scared."

The girl blinked. "Of *us*?"

He nodded.

Immediately, the little girl reached out. Chuckling softly, Connor moved closer, allowing her to put her arms around him.

"You don't have to be scared," the girl said. "We're not going to hurt you."

Hayden pressed a hand to her mouth, her eyes stinging all over again as Connor hugged the little girl.

"Thank you," he said.

Still hugging the girl, he glanced toward Hayden and then twitched his head in a small gesture for her to come closer.

"Annie," he said, rising to his feet again. "I'd like you to meet Hayden."

The child looked up at her. "Is this your girlfriend?"

A smile pulled at the corner of his mouth. "Oh, she's much more." He put his arm around Hayden. "This is my mate." He leaned in close, speaking in a soft voice only she could hear. "Forever, if she'll have me."

Hayden grinned, kissing his cheek. "I'd like that."

38

LINDY

"This'll be fine, thanks." Setting her bag down on the bunk, Lindy gave Johanna a smile. "I'll let you know if I need anything."

Her expression remained until the moment the older woman was out of sight.

And then her smile faded into a wince of heartache.

Somewhere beyond that door, Hayden and the wolves were helping everyone get settled into their new home. She'd seen the way Hayden was with Connor, the way the two of them couldn't keep their eyes off each other, and God, she was happy for her friend. Hayden deserved this, and from the way Connor watched the woman, Lindy was pretty sure he'd treasure Hayden like the amazing person she was.

It was a beautiful thing to see her best friend find love and have a life, even after the whole world fell down.

At least one of them would.

Lindy's fingers played along the edge of her leather wristband. The bunker was growing louder as more people came down into the metal-lined halls. All kinds of strangers were getting started on their new life together, finally in a place they could all feel secure.

But they weren't safe.

Not as long as Lindy was here.

Pain welled up in her chest. She had no idea how to tell anyone. How could she begin to explain? On some level, it was a miracle she'd kept it a secret thus far, given what Hayden's parents saw that day at their house.

But even they didn't know the half of it. With luck, they never would. She wanted them to remember her the way she had been—happy, hopeful, someone who helped them —rather than as the nightmare she'd had no choice but to become.

Because as bad as the Order may have been today, it didn't even scratch the surface of the hell Lindy would be forced to wreak once this curse finally consumed her soul.

She drew out a scrap of paper and scribbled a quick note goodbye. This wasn't what she'd hoped for, back when she thought she'd gained the right to her own life. For a few short years, she'd been free to dream of college and a career and all of the future ahead of her.

But that time was over. Ragnarok had arrived, and the Order would be coming for her. And maybe no one here would understand—or maybe they'd hunt her down if they did—but for the safety of everyone, Lindy didn't have another option. The seidr filling the air in this place would drive her over the edge. She had to go before everyone she loved was destroyed with her.

She just hoped Hayden would forgive her someday.

Want to know what happens next for Lindy? Get Fated Curse: Book Two of the Shifters of Ragnarok Series!

Subscribers to my mailing list hear about all the new books. Join in today at skyemalone.com/mailinglist!

Did you love this book? Please leave a review! Visit your favorite book retailer, Goodreads, and Bookbub, and leave a review for how much you enjoyed Fated Sight!

Can Lindy find true love and escape the curse that awaits her? Mortal enemies are fated mates in Fated Curse: Book Two of the Shifters of Ragnarok!

GET THE INSIDE SCOOP!

Be the first to hear about all the new books when you join
Skye Malone's mailing list!

Go online today to skyemalone.com/mailinglist to join in!

ABOUT THE AUTHOR

Skye Malone writes action-packed fantasy and paranormal romance. A fan of magical books since childhood, they adore stories that pit ordinary characters against extraordinary odds and reveal the strength within. Abandoned buildings are their passion, along with old castles and deep dark parts of the forest where anything is possible. A graduate of the University of Illinois with a degree in English literature, Skye lives in the USA Midwest with a retired racing greyhound and a three-legged mutt.

[a] amazon.com/author/skyemalone

[BB] bookbub.com/authors/skye-malone

[f] facebook.com/authorskyemalone

[g] goodreads.com/skyemalone

[O] instagram.com/authorskyemalone

[twitter] twitter.com/Skye_Malone

CPSIA information can be obtained
at www.ICGtesting.com
Printed in the USA
BVHW071611250521
608091BV00005BA/74